KT-485-059

'Come on, you two,' Patsy broke in suddenly, and Thursday glanced up in surprise. She had almost forgotten the others were there. 'It'll be getting dark soon. It's not much fun cycling with no lights in the blackout.'

'Speak for yourself!' Elsie said, with a glance at Doug. 'I think it could be a *lot* of fun!' She gave Thursday a mischievous glance. 'And going by the way you two have got your heads together, I reckon you might think so, too.'

'Thursday looked sideways at Tony and blushed at the twinkling look in his eyes. Well, maybe it will be, at that, she thought, and gave another shiver of excitement. I never felt like this with Sidney, she thought, not even when he kissed me. I never felt anything much when he kissed me.

She wondered what it would be like if – *when* – Tony kissed her.

Lilian Harry's grandfather hailed from Devon and Lilian always longed to return to her roots, so moving from Hampshire to a small Dartmoor town in her early twenties was a dream come true. She quickly absorbed herself in local life, learning the fascinating folklore and history of the moors, joining the church bellringers and a country dance club, and meeting people who are still her friends today. Although she later moved north, living first in Herefordshire and then in the Lake District, she returned in the 1990s and now lives on the edge of the moor with her two ginger cats. She is still an active bellringer and member of the local drama group, and loves to walk on the moors. She has one son and one daughter. Her latest novel in hardback, *A Stranger in Burracombe*, is also available from Orion. Visit her website at www.lilianharry.co.uk.

By Lilian Harry

The Bells of Burracombe
Three Little Ships
A Farthing Will Do
Dance Little Lady
Under the Apple Tree
A Promise to Keep
A Girl Called Thursday
Tuppence to Spend
PS I Love You
Kiss the Girls Goodbye
Corner House Girls
Keep Smiling Through
Wives & Sweethearts
Love & Laughter
Moonlight & Lovesongs
The Girls They Left Behind
Goodbye Sweetheart

A Girl Called Thursday

LILIAN HARRY

An Orion paperback

First published in Great Britain in 2002
by Orion
This paperback edition published in 2003
by Orion Books Ltd,
Orion House, 5 Upper St Martin's Lane,
London WC2H 9EA

7 9 10 8 6

Reissued 2007

Copyright © Lilian Harry 2002

The right of Lilian Harry to be identified as the author
of this work has been asserted by her in accordance with
the Copyright, Designs and Patents Act 1988.

All rights reserved. No part of this publication may be
reproduced, stored in a retrieval system, or transmitted,
in any form or by any means, electronic, mechanical,
photocopying, recording or otherwise, without the prior
permission of the copyright owner.

All the characters in this book are fictitious,
and any resemblance to actual persons, living or dead,
is entirely coincidental.

A CIP catalogue record for this book is available
from the British Library.

ISBN-13 978-0-7528-4950-8

Printed and bound in Great Britain by Clays Ltd, St Ives plc

The Orion Publishing Group's policy is to use papers that
are natural, renewable and recyclable products and
made from wood grown in sustainable forests. The logging
and manufacturing processes are expected to conform to
the environmental regulations of the country of origin.

www.orionbooks.co.uk

To the Royal Naval Hospital, Haslar
and to all VADs, especially Helen Long
whose book *Change into Uniform*
inspired this story.

Chapter One

'Twenty-one today!
Twenty-one today!
She's got the key of the door,
Never been twenty-one before . . .'

The little house in Waterloo Street rocked to the sound of singing, and Thursday Tilford laughed, blushing at the attention. The song ended with cheers from the rest of the family, and Thursday's father gave her a smacking kiss, his moustache bristling against her cheek.

'There you are, love. There's your key.' He handed her a wooden key about a foot long, painted bright red. 'Made it myself.'

'Oh, *Dad*!' Thursday took it in her hands and almost collapsed under the weight. 'Am I supposed to carry this about in my bag?'

'Well, only if you want to.' He fished in his pocket and brought out another, an ordinary Yale this time. 'You can keep that for best if you like and use this for every day.'

Thursday grinned at him and slipped the Yale into her purse. 'And can I stay out after ten o'clock at night now?'

He rubbed his round, balding head and pursed his lips. 'Well, I don't know about that. Me and your mother will still worry about you, you know. That don't stop just because you're of age. Maybe we'll say eleven on Saturday nights to start with, eh?'

The rest of the family laughed. 'Go on, Walter, you

1

know young Thursday's been able to twist you round her little finger since she was a baby,' Thursday's grandfather called out from the front room. There wasn't space for everyone in either of the two downstairs rooms so they'd opened all the doors and spread between the two. 'Not like in my day. Girls knew what was what then. Knew they had to toe the line, or else.'

'Like our Flo, you mean,' Walter retorted, grinning. 'If I had a pound for every time I had to let her in on the quiet when she'd been out with Percy, so you wouldn't know what time it was—'

'All right, our Wal, no need to give away secrets,' his sister cut in. She touched her fair hair, newly waved for the occasion with a fashionable bang on her forehead – not that Auntie Flo needed much of an excuse to do herself up, Thursday thought with an inward giggle. That was a new jumper she had on too, pale blue in a lacy pattern, and she'd knitted one for Thursday's mum as well, only in pink, as well as Leslie's Fair Isle pullover. 'Stop your nattering and cut this birthday cake into slices. It's Thursday's day, she doesn't want to hear all about ancient history.'

The cake stood in place of honour on the sideboard, flanked by a pile of plates. It had been iced and decorated by Flo, who was clever at that sort of thing. The family had already admired it and sung 'Happy Birthday' as Thursday blew out the candles, and now they gathered round again as Walter picked up the big carving knife. Flo's two younger children, Leslie and Denise, stood by with a proprietorial air.

'I helped Mum make the icing,' Denise told Thursday. 'It took I don't know how many egg whites. And I made two of the roses on top – those two, see?'

'The ones with wobbly petals,' Leslie said, and she gave him a push. 'Well, they are. And I helped too, it wasn't just you. I helped beat up the icing.'

'Sounds like you were in a fight with it,' Walter

2

remarked. 'Move over now, let the dog see the rabbit.' He lifted the knife and poised it above the centre of the cake. Thursday's little mongrel dog, Patch, moved into the best position for catching crumbs and sat bright-eyed, his tail thumping the floor. 'I didn't mean *you*, you silly chump!'

'I'll have a bit with icing down the sides,' Thursday's younger sister Jenny said, her eyes fixed on the white sugar.

'You'll have what you're given, my girl,' her father told her. 'Your Auntie Flo made that for your sister, not you. And stop that shoving, young Steve, or I'll end up cutting slices of finger.'

'And the icing'll get blood all over it,' Steve told his sister ghoulishly. 'And if it does, that'll be your bit. And you know what you'll be then? You'll be a *cannibal!*'

Jenny made a face and squealed. 'Yeugh! That's a horrible thing to say! Tell him not to say things like that, Mum.'

Mary Tilford frowned at them, but it was a tolerant frown. Nothing was to be allowed to spoil this special day, Thursday thought affectionately. 'Don't start squabbling, now. Give your dad some elbow room.' She looked at her husband, cutting the cake, and at her elder daughter, tall and grown-up with her dark brown hair cut in a long wavy bob, wearing that new green frock she'd made specially for the occasion. You could catch quite a strong likeness in their expressions sometimes, even though in colouring Thursday was more like herself, and it was there now as they concentrated on the cake. She smiled, and then her face saddened.

'It's a beautiful cake, Flo, and it's been a lovely party,' Thursday heard her say quietly. 'But it's not the birthday I wanted for her, not really.'

'Nothing's the way we wanted it,' Flo said. 'Nobody wanted this war, for a start. Except for Hitler, of course, he's been wanting it all along only nobody could see it.'

Thursday handed them both a plate with a slice of cake

3

on it. 'Bet we won't see many more cakes like this for a while,' she said cheerfully. 'It's a good job we saved up all the fruit beforehand.' She sat down beside them and bit into her own slice.

Mary nodded. 'They say there'll be a lot of shortages from now on. You know they're talking about rationing. I reckon people will start hoarding all sorts of things.'

'They already have,' Thursday said through a mouthful of cake. 'My friend at work says her gran's got a cupboard full of tins. Ham, peas, baked beans, plums – she's got enough to keep her for six months, Annie says.' She bent and slipped a scrap of cake into Patch's waiting jaw.

'Well, she shouldn't have. It's taking food away from people who might need it. And that dog doesn't need it, either.'

'She thinks *she'll* need it,' Thursday pointed out. 'And Patch deserves a treat, same as anyone else.'

Jenny had managed to secure a piece of cake with icing down the side, and went into the front room to sit on the floor at her grandmother's feet to eat it, curling her legs under her. She always preferred the floor, and in any case with the whole family squashed into the small room there wasn't room to sit anywhere else. Her grandmother, Walter's mother, ate a few crumbs of her cake and then slipped her the rest. 'Can't be doing with all that fruit,' she whispered, 'and the icing makes me teeth ache.'

Jenny giggled. Granny had had false teeth since she was quite young and loved sweets, but Jenny was her favourite and could always rely on being given little extras. She went round to see her grandmother every Sunday morning after church, and passed on all the gossip from Waterloo Street as well as from the grocer's shop where she worked.

Steve had sat down beside his cousin Mike, who was in army uniform. He'd been in the Territorials before the war started, and joined up straight away, as a private. So far, all he'd done was basic training but already he was

4

behaving as if he were in the front line, and Steve was half envious, half thankful that as yet he hadn't been called up. It couldn't be long, though, if the war really did get started as they seemed to think it would.

'What sort of guns do they give you, Mike? D'you have your own special one?'

'Course you do. You've got to look after it, see – clean it and make sure it works properly. I wouldn't want to use another bloke's gun, just in case he hadn't bothered. Not that the sarge would let anyone get away with not bothering!' He made a face which conveyed to Steve exactly what the sergeant's reaction would be to 'not bothering'. 'It's Lee Enfields we've got. Rifles. But we're learning to handle mortars as well, and then there's machine guns and howitzers and stuff like that. There's a lot to learn. It's not just about pointing it at a Jerry and pulling the trigger. You've got to think about the weather – wind can make the bullets drift, see – and you can't always see what you're shooting at. That's where the observers come in, they go forward of the line and register the targets.' He stopped abruptly. 'I don't know as I should be telling you all this. We're not supposed to talk about what we do.'

'Go on, I'll be joining up myself before long,' Steve said, hoping his mother couldn't hear him in the other room, but Mike shook his head and refused to say any more.

Thursday heard, however, and she felt a sudden chill as Mike's words brought home to her the fact that there really was a war on and that young men like her cousin and brother could get killed – boys who had never even thought of joining the Forces, having to learn about guns and fighting, having to go to war. And girls too – not fighting, but helping in different ways, doing jobs they'd never even have dreamed of, so that the men could go away.

It was something she'd been thinking about more and

more just lately, and she knew that soon she was going to have to tell her family about her own decision.

Being twenty-one wasn't all fun and cake and keys of the door, she thought. You've got responsibilities as well. Responsibilities for your own life, and what you did with it.

Soberly, she collected the plates and took them out to the kitchen. There was already a large pile of crocks waiting to be washed up, and she rolled up her sleeves and turned on the tap. Her mother followed her and turned it off.

'Here, what are you doing? It's your birthday, you're supposed to be the guest of honour, not a skivvy.'

'And you did all the work getting everything ready,' Thursday told her. 'Anyway, you can't boss me about any more, not now I'm twenty-one.' She turned the tap on again and ferreted in the cupboard under the sink for the washing soda. 'You go and sit down and have another cup of tea with Auntie Flo. I bet it's the first time either of you's sat down all day.'

'Well, I won't say I'm not a bit tired,' Mary admitted. She regarded her daughter fondly. 'Mind you, I still can't believe I'm old enough to have a daughter of twenty-one.'

'Nor can I.' The enamel washing-up bowl was full now and Thursday turned off the tap again and swished the dishcloth into the water. 'You don't look much more than twenty-one yourself, Mum. Not a grey hair on your head.'

Mary looked into the scrap of mirror they kept over the sink. It was true that her hair was still the same rich brown, and even though she'd never bothered with her looks as much as her sister-in-law it suited her brushed smooth over the top and permed into neat curls at the side. She sighed. 'There'll be a few before this war's finished, I'm afraid. It's going to be a bad business, Thursday.'

'D'you really think so?' She thought of Mike, learning

6

about guns, and pushed the thought away. 'Nothing much has happened yet, and they say it'll be over by Christmas.'

'Christmas? That gives it five weeks!' Mary snorted. 'I lived through the last lot. They said that one'd be over by Christmas too, and it dragged on for four years. I can't see this one ending any quicker, and it'll be worse if we get the air raids they're talking about. They had a few of those last time, over on the east coast, but we'll all get a share this time.'

'Not here in Worcester, surely?' Thursday piled plates rapidly on the draining board.

'Why not? Why d'you think we've been dished out with all these gas masks and air-raid shelters?'

'Yes, but we're right in the middle of the country. The Air Force will get them long before they get this far.' She wasn't sure if she really believed it or just wanted to, but it was better than looking on the black side. 'They won't let the Germans bomb us, Mum.'

'Well, let's just hope you're right.' Mary picked up a tea towel and began to dry the plates. 'I tell you, our Thurs, the idea of air raids frightens me to death, it does really. I can't bear to think about them.'

Flo poked her head round the kitchen door. 'What are you two doing, skulking out here? *You* shouldn't be working anyway, it's your birthday. Leave that for now – we're listening to the wireless. The Queen's going to make a broadcast. Come in and hear it.'

Thursday couldn't remember ever hearing the Queen's voice before. The King had made a broadcast at Christmas, his voice stumbling a bit over the words – it was said that he had a dreadful stammer, as if he was very shy. It seemed odd to Thursday that a king should be shy, but then he'd never been meant to be one. It was supposed to have been his brother David, the Duke of Windsor now, who had fallen in love with an American divorcee and had had to give up the throne to marry her.

7

It sounded romantic, but Thursday could remember all the fuss and palaver there'd been at the time and she thought that by the time they'd got to the altar it couldn't have seemed romantic at all. They must have just wanted it all to be over so that they could go back to normal life – whatever that might be for kings who had just abdicated.

So Prince Albert, the Duke of York, had become King George the Sixth, and his wife Elizabeth was now Queen. And they were very popular, they and their two daughters, Princess Elizabeth – who would be Queen one day, unless another baby was born and turned out to be a boy – and her sister Margaret Rose.

Walter switched on the wireless. He had built it himself, carefully cutting out a fretwork pattern in front of the speaker, just like you saw in the shops, and it stood on a high shelf in one of the fireplace alcoves. It looked a bit like something off the instrument panel of an aeroplane, and when it was turned on needles quivered across little dials and it made little burbling and whistling noises before the crackling stopped and the announcer's voice came through. Walter had also fixed up a loudspeaker in the front room, and he turned this on for his parents and the boys and Jenny, who were still in there.

The Queen's broadcast was aimed at women. '*We, no less than men, have real and vital work to do,*' she said in her precise, cut-glass accent, and Thursday felt a tiny surge of excitement, which turned to disappointment at her next words. '*It is the worries and irritations of carrying on wartime life in ordinary homes which are often so hard to bear.*' How did she know that? How did she know what life was like in an ordinary home? Had she ever queued for groceries, or peeled potatoes? But Mary and Flo were nodding in agreement, and Thursday could see that they were touched by this reference to their own problems. '*The king and I know what it means to be parted from our children.*' That was true – the little Princesses were hundreds of miles away at Balmoral, in Scotland. '*All this has meant sacrifice and I would say to those who are feeling the strain: You are taking your part in keeping the Home Front, which will have dangers of its own, stable and strong.'*

'Don't it make you feel proud,' Mary whispered, and brushed a tear from her eye.

'She's a lovely speaker,' Flo agreed. 'And she really seems to know what it's like to be ordinary, doesn't she? As if she's done all the things we've done. You feel as if you could ask her in for a cup of tea and not have to worry about a speck of dust.'

The wireless programme continued, talking this time about women who had joined the Forces. Nearly fifty thousand had joined up so far, most in the ATS and the rest evenly divided between the WRNS, the WAAFs and the nursing services. There were so many wanting to join the WRNS that they'd actually stopped recruiting. You could still join the ATS, though, or the WAAFs.

'I can't remember what all these initials stand for,' Thursday's grandmother complained. 'ATS this and WAAF that. Which is which, for goodness' sake?'

'ATS stands for Auxiliary Territorial Service,' Jenny said importantly. 'That's the women's branch of the Army. And WAAF means Women's Auxiliary Air Force. And the Wrens are the Navy—'

'And JAT stands for Jabbers All the Time,' Steve butted in. 'That's why Mum and Dad called you Jennifer Ann. They knew what you were going to be like but the man said it had to be a proper name, so they chose Jenny because wrens chatter too.'

Jenny made a face at him. 'They wanted to call *you* Stupid. And Crackers for a middle name, but he said it had to be Charles.'

'Well, you can both thank your lucky stars you weren't called Sunday Morning and Boxing Day,' Thursday called out with a grin. 'Look what *I* got landed with – *Thursday*!'

Everyone laughed, but the older ones' faces soon sobered. 'It was meant to be a sign of hope,' Walter said.

'Born on the eleventh hour of the eleventh day of the eleventh month – they must have been signing the Armistice at the very moment you gave your first cry. We had to give you some sort of name to mark that, didn't we? That's why we called you Rosemary, for Remembrance, see – but we wanted something more as well so we had Thursday for a middle name.'

'That's right,' Mary agreed. 'And if you ever feel embarrassed about it, that's what you ought to remember. Mind you, we never really meant to call you by it. That was our Maudie. Being your godmother, she thought she had a right, see, and she always called you Thursday, right from the start, and then we all did. It seemed to suit you, somehow, and it seemed right – not much point in marking an important occasion if you hide it away, is there?' She paused and smiled. 'And *you* can thank your lucky stars, too, that you didn't get called something worse.'

'Why?' Thursday asked. 'What else did you think of?'

'November!' Mary said with a smile. 'That was what your dad wanted, to start with. I did put my foot down over that – but I was still half scared he'd do it, the day he went off to register you. I had to look at the birth certificate the minute he got back to make sure he hadn't.'

'Now, when have I ever gone against your wishes, Mary?' her husband asked, and everyone laughed again as she gave him the sort of look that suggested that he *always* went against her wishes. He laughed too and gave her a quick kiss. 'All right, we all know who's boss in this house!'

'Well, I'm glad you called me that,' Thursday said stoutly. 'I get a bit fed up having to explain it whenever I meet someone new, but I *am* proud of it, really, and I like having an unusual name. There's hundreds of Rosemarys about. Pity Auntie Maud's on duty at the hospital, I could have thanked her for making sure I didn't get stuck with it.'

'She said she'd look in tomorrow for a bit of cake, and to bring you your present,' Mary said. 'You can thank her then.'

'Oh, that's a pity,' Thursday said. 'I shan't see her, I'm going straight from work to meet Sidney at the Scala at six o'clock. We're going to have tea and see the new Joan Crawford picture. I'll see her next Sunday, we're going over to tea with her.'

Walter switched off the wireless and sat down beside his wife. They looked fondly at their family.

'Well, there it is,' Walter said after a few moments. 'The first of the brood grown up. I don't reckon we've done too bad a job, do you, gal?'

Mary shook her head. 'I don't reckon so, love, no. Mind you, we've still got to see how the other two turn out. There's still time for them to go off the rails.'

'Not too much,' Steve said, coming in to look for another piece of cake. 'It'll be my twenty-first next year.'

'And mine in five years,' Jenny said, picking up scraps of icing. 'Gosh, I wonder where we'll all be then. All sorts of things could happen in that time.' She broke off at the look on her mother's face. 'I don't mean *bad* things, Mum. The war'll be over in a few months, everyone says so. You've only got to listen to the news. Practically nothing's happened.' She pouted a little. 'I bet it'll all be finished and done with by the time *I* get old enough to join up.'

'Well, I just hope it will,' her mother said. 'I hope it'll be over before any of you has to join up.'

But everyone knew this really was a faint hope. Flo and Percy's eldest son Mike was already in the Army and Steve, at twenty, could well be called up soon. Women didn't have to enlist – at least, not yet – but a lot of them were volunteering. Thursday knew that her parents dreaded hearing that she had decided to go. Maybe this was the moment to tell them.

'We've got to do our bit, Mum,' she said gently after a

moment or two. 'We can't let other people do the fighting for us.'

'They won't let *women* fight!' Mary's voice was so sharp they all flinched. 'Even the Germans haven't come to that.'

'No, but we can do a lot of the jobs men do, so they can go. Anyway, I know what I want to do.' She looked around at them. 'I've decided to volunteer as a nurse.'

There was a surprised silence.

'A *nurse*?' Mary repeated at last. 'Like your Auntie Maud, you mean? Here in the Worcester Royal Infirmary?'

Thursday shook her head. 'No. I've been talking to the lady in charge of the First Aid Post. She says as I'm in the Red Cross and have done the first-aid course and everything, I can volunteer as a VAD—'

'Not *more* initials!' Ada Tilford protested from the front room, and Thursday smiled and moved over to the door so that she could talk into both rooms at once.

'It means Voluntary Aid Detachment, Gran. It's part of the Red Cross, and you can be either a mobile VAD – that means you can be moved – or—'

'I know what mobile means, thank you very much,' the old lady said tartly. 'It's all these initials I can't be doing with. There won't be any proper words left, at the rate we're going on. So what do these Voluntary – what was it? – these VADs do, then?'

Thursday grinned. 'Well, they're nurses. Not registered nurses, of course, like Auntie Maudie, they're not trained as much as them, but they work in the wards and help look after people. Mostly servicemen, I think. That's what it's all about, you see, it's to work in the Forces' hospitals.'

'So you wouldn't be working in Worcester, then?' Mary tried to keep the disappointment out of her voice. 'Or would you? There's Norton Barracks, they must have nurses there.'

'She said there's non-mobile ones as well,' her husband

reminded her. 'That'd mean you could live at home, wouldn't it?'

This was the moment Thursday hadn't been looking forward to. 'Well, I thought I'd volunteer to be a mobile one, actually. See a few other places while I'm at it.'

Mary stared at her. 'You mean you want to leave home?'

'It's not a question of *wanting* to, Mum. It's just – well, if I'm going to give up tailoring to do this, I might as well get some benefit out of it. Get a bit of experience, that sort of thing. See a bit more of the country, meet some different people.' She gazed appealingly at her mother. 'It's a chance, don't you see? I mean, what will I do if I stay here? Work at the tailor's until I get married, and then leave to be a housewife and have children. That's all, isn't it?'

'It's what I did, and it's always seemed all right to me,' Mary said.

Thursday sighed. 'I know, Mum, and I never meant there was anything *wrong* with it. It's just that nowadays – with this war and everything – well, it's different. I'd just like to take the chance, that's all. It's only while the war's on. It doesn't mean I'm going away for ever and you're never going to see me again.'

Mary sniffed. 'Seems to me you're just looking on the war as a chance to throw away everything you've got – your home life, your job, everything. And that's another thing. Tailoring. You've finished your apprenticeship and got a good trade at your fingertips. Why chuck all that away? You could stop where you are and help the war effort – they'll be turning over to making uniforms full time, if I know anything about it. Why waste all that training and start learning something else?'

'Well, if you want the truth,' Thursday said, beginning to feel exasperated, 'I'm getting fed up with tailoring. I was never all that keen in the first place. It was you got me into it, just because I was all right at sewing at school.'

'And what's wrong with that?' Walter demanded. 'That's what mothers and fathers do, isn't it, see that their children are set up in a decent job? Your Uncle Percy did it for Mike here, and I did it for Steve down at the porcelain factory, and we'd have got young Jenny into a hairdresser's only the premium was too much and she said she didn't mind going into the grocery shop.'

He was starting to sound really angry and Thursday wished she had never started this. The rest of the family was silent, and Jenny looked almost ready to cry. The party's spoilt now, Thursday thought miserably, and it's all my fault. I should have waited till tomorrow, only I'm going to the pictures with Sidney then, and I thought with everyone here together it would be better . . .

'So what's wrong with tailoring all of a sudden?' her mother demanded. 'I haven't heard you complain before, and you do plenty of sewing at home – made that frock you're wearing and that new blouse you had on yesterday, and—'

'*Nothing's* wrong with it, Mum, and I really do appreciate all you did, getting me the apprenticeship and everything. It's just that everything's different now. Girls have got a bit more chance to do something interesting before they settle down.'

'*Interesting*!' Walter exclaimed. 'Since when have we had a right to expect to do *interesting* jobs? Earning a living's what we've got to do, my girl, and if it's interesting as well, we can think ourselves lucky, but we don't chop and change just because we're a bit fed up. There's been a Depression, if you remember – people thought themselves lucky to have a job at all, never mind being *interested*.'

'But wouldn't you rather have a job you were really interested in?' Thursday asked. 'Wouldn't you rather be doing something you enjoyed? I mean, you never seem to think anything could be any better. You think everything's got to go on being the same as it's ever been. Like that time the union wanted you to go on strike—'

'We won't start talking politics,' Walter broke in, his face reddening with anger. 'You know what I think about strikes and unions. They might have done a good job at one time, but now it's all greed, that's all, and if you ask me it was the General Strike started the rot in this country. And if I hear any of you talking about going on strike, *ever*, well—'

'All right, Walter,' Mary said quickly.' No need to get aeriated. Nobody's talking about going on strike. I don't know how we ever got on to the subject.' She turned back to Thursday. 'And that's another thing. You talk about girls settling down. What do you think Sidney's going to say about this?'

'Sidney?' Thursday echoed. 'What's it got to do with Sidney?'

'Well, he's your chap, isn't he? I thought you'd probably be getting engaged now you've turned twenty-one. What's he got to say about you swanning off to goodness knows where? Or haven't you consulted him either?'

'No, I haven't, as a matter of fact. And I don't know what made you think we're getting engaged. I'm not thinking of marrying Sidney, and what's more I don't think he wants to marry me. He hasn't asked me, anyway.'

'Well, that's a relief,' Steve observed. 'We don't want a wet like that in the family.'

'But you've been going out together for the past eighteen months!' Mary cried. 'Surely you must have some sort of understanding.'

Thursday stared at her. It had never even occurred to her that her mother had begun to see Sidney as a future son-in-law. She glanced quickly around at the rest of the family, feeling embarrassed and annoyed. Honestly, if she'd thought all this would be dragged out she wouldn't have said a word about volunteering. How had they got around to Sidney anyway? He was nothing to do with the family. She hadn't even asked him to her party. To tell the truth, she'd only ever gone out with Sidney in the first place because she'd felt a bit sorry for him. She'd never meant it to become a regular thing, but somehow it hadn't been possible to give him the push without hurting his feelings, and he didn't deserve that. He wasn't such a bad chap, after all.

'Yes, we have got an understanding,' she said curtly. 'We like going dancing and we like going to the pictures and maybe for a walk of a Sunday afternoon, and that's it. It's just a couple of evenings a week, Mum. We're not talking about spending the next fifty years together.' She thought of Sidney in fifty years' time, balding like her father only thin and stringy instead of round and smiling – not that Dad was smiling much now! No, that wasn't what she wanted.

Mary stared at her again and shook her head. 'I don't know about you young girls, I'm sure. It was different in my day. When a young man and a girl had been going out together for six months or so, and he'd been coming round for Sunday tea once a month, it was as good as a ring on her finger. It was *understood*.'

'Well, it's not now. Not by me, anyway. And in any case, Sidney won't be around much longer, he's got his papers. He's going into the Army.'

'Oh, Thursday! And you never said.'

'Well, why should I? I'm saying now. And you don't need to look like that, Mum. I'm not breaking my heart. Look – Sidney and me are friends, that's all. Neither of us has found anyone we really like so we've just sort of drifted into the habit of knocking about together a bit, just to have someone to go the pictures with and that, and that's all there is to it. But we don't want to drift into anything more.'

'Sounds sensible,' Flo remarked. 'I've known a few girls drift into marriage and then wish the tide had turned a different way. You wouldn't want your Thursday to end up with the wrong chap, would you, Mary?'

'No, but I'm not so sure Sidney is the wrong chap,' Mary said. 'I've always thought he was a really nice boy. Polite and considerate. Got a good job. And they get on well together. What more could you want?'

'You got on all right with that Stan Gibson, if I remember right,' Walter remarked, 'but you never married him.'

'That was different,' his wife said, blushing. 'There was never the feeling between me and Stan Gibson that there was between us, and well you know it, and I'm sure I don't know why you have to bring his name into this—'

'But that's just what I mean, Mum,' Thursday broke in before her parents could embark on a well-worn argument. 'There isn't the feeling between me and Sidney either. We're just friends. To tell you the truth, I'll miss Patchie more than I'll miss Sid.' She ruffled the mongrel's ears and he gave a little whimper of pleasure and leant his head against her knee.

Walter grinned at her. He seemed to have recovered his temper a bit – maybe he hadn't been as keen as his wife to have Sidney in the family. 'I think she's got you there, Mary. Anyway, none of that's important now. What we've got to think about is what our Thursday's decided to do, and what we've got to remember is that she's of age to do it. So tell us a bit more about this nursing, Thurs. Where d'you think you'll get sent?'

'I don't know,' Thursday said, relieved to have got back to the subject. 'I don't know all that much about it, but I thought I'd go down to the office tomorrow and get the details. I don't suppose it'll happen all at once anyway.' She looked at her mother. 'You don't really mind, do you, Mum? I'll still be coming home whenever I can, and I'll write every week.'

Mary sighed. 'Well, you know we've never wanted to stand in your light, your father and me. It's for you to decide, 'specially now you're of age. It's just – well, I've been dreading you telling me you were joining up. I knew you'd probably do it some time, but – well, it's not what I wanted for you. I wanted to see you settled in a nice little house, not too far away, with your own man and your own family. It's the proper life for a woman.'

'It'll come, Mum,' Thursday said gently. 'It'll come for me, same as it did for you. But it's got to be the right man, hasn't it? And the war's made everything different. Nothing's the same any more.'

'No,' her mother said sadly, 'and sometimes I wonder if it'll ever be the same again.'

Chapter Two

Flo and Percy left soon after that to walk home. The streets were dark, with no lighting because of the blackout, but there was a glimmer of light from the sky and they knew their way well enough. They walked in silence, arm in arm, for a few minutes, then Flo said with a sigh, 'Mary was proper upset about Thursday coming out with all that about nursing, wasn't she? I can't say I'm surprised, either. It's all come so sudden.'

'It's throwing up the tailoring she doesn't like,' Percy said. 'All those years learning the trade and then she chucks it all away. I don't blame Mary for being upset over that.'

'Yes, but it's the idea of Thursday going away she really doesn't like. You don't know who they'll be mixing with, do you? I mean, they might think they're grown up at twenty-one but they're still girls really. And Mary really was beginning to hope she and Sidney would settle down together. He's a decent, sensible young man.'

'Well, maybe she'll have a talk with Maudie about it. She did say she's coming round tomorrow. A word with her own sister might help her to see it differently, 'specially as Maudie's a nurse herself. I dare say that's where Thursday got the idea from in the first place.'

Mike, Leslie and Denise were walking in front, as they'd done ever since they were children. 'You three run on ahead,' their mother would tell them, and off they'd scamper, hopping along the pavement trying to avoid the cracks or pretending they were cowboys and indians. They didn't play those games any more but, like their parents, were talking about Thursday and her sudden announcement.

'I thought Auntie Mary was going to hit the roof,' Denise said with a giggle. 'I've never seen her so cross.'

'It was a surprise to her, that's all,' Mike observed. 'She probably thought Thursday would stay safely at home, making army uniforms and getting married to Sid the Sprat. At least she seems to have a bit more sense than that!'

'I don't know why she goes about with him in the first place,' Denise said. 'He thinks he's God's gift to women, and really he's nothing but a twerp. I wouldn't walk down the street with him. Here, look out, Les, you nearly pushed me into that lamppost.'

'Sorry, didn't see it. I wonder where she'll get sent. Anyway, it livened up the party, it was getting a bit boring, what with the Queen on the wireless and everything.' Leslie shoved his hands deep into his pockets. 'Me, I'm going to join the Air Force as soon as I'm old enough, but you needn't tell Mum and Dad that.'

'The *Air*—' Denise began, and then squeaked as her brother pushed her again. 'You mean you want to be a pilot?'

'Yes, why not? I can drive a car, it can't be any more difficult than that.'

'They'll never let you. You've got to have qualifications.'

'Like what? Don't you think they'll be training blokes to fly? Like they're training Mike here to use a gun? I tell you what, they'll be crying out for pilots, and I'm going to be one. But you mind you don't say anything, see, our Dizzy. I'll see about it myself, same as Thursday has, and then tell 'em, otherwise it'll just mean a lot of arguments.'

Mike had been striding along beside them, not speaking. Now he glanced over his shoulder and, seeing that their parents were still deep in conversation a few yards behind, spoke quietly.

'There'll be nothing to argue about soon. Once this phoney war's over and the real one starts, everyone'll get called up one way or another. We'll all get sent somewhere, and it won't always be somewhere we like, but we're going to have to put up with it. If you'll take my advice, you'll get your oar in first, Les, and put in for the RAF as soon as you can, if that's what you want to do.'

'I wouldn't mind being in the Air Force, too,' Denise said dreamily. 'WAAFs, that's what they're called, and the uniform's ever so smart. I wonder if they'll let girls fly?'

'Well, that's something you're never likely to find out,' Mike told her brutally. 'I don't reckon the war's going to be over by Christmas, like some people think, nor by next Christmas neither. But it'll be over before *you* get old enough to do anything about it, our Denise. You're only fourteen, still a kid, so don't go getting any daft ideas in your head about helping to win the war.'

Denise scowled at him, but her scowl was wasted in the darkness. She scuffed her toe along the pavement and kicked a small stone. It rattled away ahead of them.

'You boys,' she said mutinously, 'you think it's all for your benefit. Well, I think Thursday's right. Women are going to help win this war, and you won't be able to do it without us. And I bet there'll be something I *can* do before it's all finished. You see if there isn't.'

To Thursday's surprise, she found that Sidney did mind her going away, after all.

'You never said anything about volunteering,' he grumbled when they met the next evening for their regular visit to the Scala Cinema. They were sitting in the little red plush tearoom, having a pot of tea and a round of toast before going in. 'You never said a word.'

'I didn't really make up my mind till yesterday. Then I woke up and thought, I'm twenty-one. I can do as I like! And I knew that was what I wanted to do.'

'You could still have said.' His mouth was pushed out

petulantly, like a little boy's. Sometimes Thursday found this rather endearing, but today it irritated her. She looked at him in the Fair Isle pullover she'd knitted him last Christmas, under Auntie Flo's instruction, and the brown tweed jacket he seemed to wear every time they went out. His fair hair was combed smooth and he was clean and had had a shave, but he still looked more as if he'd *tried* to look right than actually succeeded.

She stirred her tea, even though she'd given up taking sugar because it was soon going to be rationed, and then frowned as a splash landed on her sleeve. 'Oh, botheration! It's the jumper Auntie Flo knitted me, too.' She found a hanky and dabbed at the stain, answered him as she did so. 'I didn't think you'd be that interested. You're going away yourself soon, after all.'

'That's different. I'm going into the Army.'

'I don't see why it's different. I'm going to be a nurse. You might be glad to find a few nurses around the place when you're at the Front.'

'Oh, so now you've decided I'm going to be wounded, have you? Well, thanks for nothing!' He was definitely sulking now and Thursday felt her irritation grow.

'Don't be stupid. I haven't decided anything. But it stands to reason some people are going to be wounded, and they'll need nurses. It *is* a war, Sidney.'

'They won't have girls like you at the Front anyway,' he said. 'They'll have proper Army nurses there. These VAD people, they're just dogsbodies. They're not properly trained, you know that, don't you?'

'I know they can do a lot to help,' she said quietly. 'They can make things easier for the trained nurses – take some of the donkey-work off their hands.' She met his eyes. 'I don't mind being a dogsbody, Sidney, I just want to help. I don't need to spend years going through a training course to do that, and I don't want to. I want to help *now*. And it's nothing to do with you.'

He stared at her. His face flushed and she wondered

22

suddenly just how much she really did like him. After all, what did they do together? They came here to the Scala once a week or else went to the Odeon, depending what film was on, and they went dancing on Saturday nights. Sometimes he came round for tea on Sunday and sometimes she went to his house and sat at the table with his mum and dad and ate beetroot sandwiches and soggy fruit cake or a heavy sponge. Occasionally they'd get the train to Great Malvern and go for a walk on the hills, perhaps climbing the Beacon for tea in the little café at the top, or they might go to the little market town of Ledbury and visit Thursday's Aunt Maudie. But they didn't really have much in common, she thought. They didn't talk much, except about the films or the dancing. As she'd told her mother, they just went out together from habit.

I ought to have broken it off with him ages ago, she thought. I bet I could have had a dozen boyfriends in the time I've been going out with Sidney. We don't even kiss, except for a goodnight peck on the cheek. I've been wasting my time.

'What do you mean?' Sidney demanded. 'What d'you mean, it's nothing to do with me? What sort of a way's that for a girl to talk to her chap?'

'You're not my chap. Not in that way.'

'Well, what way d'you call it, then? We've been going steady long enough. I thought just lately we'd started to – well, you know – get really fond of one another.'

Thursday sighed. She'd been aware of a feeling of relief when Sidney had told her he'd got his papers. It solved the problem of how to break away from him. And then, feeling a little guilty, she'd set out to be extra nice to him for the last few weeks he was at home. Now it looked as if that had been a mistake and he'd got the wrong idea.

'I am fond of you, Sid,' she said. 'But just as a friend – the way we've always been. It's never been any more than that, you know it hasn't.'

'Oh, I know that, do I?' he said. 'And how would you

23

know what I know or don't know? You don't seem to know that you ought to have talked it over with me before you went off and volunteered.'

'Well, I don't see why I should have,' she retorted. 'It's my life, isn't it? You don't own me, Sidney.'

'Maybe not. But I was going to suggest we got engaged, wasn't I? You'd know that, of course, seeing as you know so much about me already.'

Thursday stared at him. Her mouth felt suddenly dry. She licked her lips and then said huskily, 'Get engaged? What are you talking about?'

'Well, what do you think I'm talking about? Getting engaged, that's what. Proposing to you. What else d'you think I meant?'

Thursday took a deep, shaky breath and cast about for something to say. 'I never thought – I had no idea – you never even *hinted*—'

'Just like you never hinted you were volunteering to go off as a nurse.' Sidney hesitated, then said, 'Look, Thursday, I didn't mean it to be like this. I meant to ask you properly – go down on one knee and all that – but with you springing this on me – well, I just blurted it out. But I'll do it properly, if that's what you want. And we'll go and choose a ring together at Samuels.' He brushed his fair hair out of his eyes and gazed at her appealingly, his round face more than ever like a little boy's. 'Only I'd rather not do it here, if you don't mind.'

'I don't want you to do it anywhere,' Thursday said, her voice wobbling a little. She had a dreadful feeling she was going to either laugh or cry. 'I don't want you to do it at all. I don't want to get engaged, Sidney.'

'Don't be silly,' he said, his babyish look vanishing behind a scowl. 'Every girl wants to get engaged.'

'Yes, but to the right man.' Am I going to have this conversation every day? she wondered wildly. 'It's not like that between us, Sidney. We're just friends. You know that.'

'There you go again, telling me what I know! Shall I tell you what I *thought* I knew, Thursday? I thought I knew it meant something, us going out together all this time. I thought I knew you were fond of me, like I am of you. I thought I knew you'd miss me when I went away, that you'd want to belong to me. I thought I knew you'd want a ring on your finger. Obviously,' he concluded bitterly, 'I was wrong. I should have asked *you* what I knew in the first place. You could have told me that I didn't know what I thought I knew, and – oh, hell and damnation,' he swore, and several people glanced round from other tables. 'I don't even know what I'm saying any more, let alone what I'm *thinking*.'

Thursday bit her lip. If I laugh at him he'll hit me, she thought, and I'll end up crying anyway. And I don't really want to laugh. It's not funny. It's not funny at all.

'Oh, Sidney,' she said miserably, 'I'm really sorry. I didn't know you were feeling like that, honestly. I really thought we were just friends, going out together because – well, because we didn't have anyone else to go out with, I suppose. At least, that's what it was in the beginning. And then it turned into—' She was going to say 'a habit' but Sidney interrupted her.

'It turned into something more. That's what I felt, too, Thursday. I *knew* you felt it, too!' His scowl disappeared and he beamed at her. 'You see? It's all right – I know I sprang it on you, and I didn't mean to, but it's all right really, isn't it? We'll get engaged and you can forget this nursing thing. Forget about being mobile, or whatever you call it, anyway. I wouldn't mind you doing it here in Worcester. But—'

'*No!*' Once again, Thursday saw people glancing round at them. She lowered her voice. 'No, Sidney. I don't want to get engaged to you. And I'm definitely not going to give up the idea of being a VAD.' She looked at his stricken face and felt a stab of remorse, even though she knew she'd never given him any cause to think she was in love with him. 'I'm sorry if you got the wrong idea,' she said quietly. 'I never meant you to.'

There was a silence. Sidney fiddled with his toast and crumbled it into tiny pieces. He picked up his teaspoon and twisted it between his fingers. Then he looked up at her and shrugged.

'Well, I suppose that's it, then. Call it a day, shall we?'

'Oh, Sidney.' Thursday looked at him sorrowfully. 'We don't have to do that, do we? We can still be friends.'

'Don't see much point, do you?' He glanced at his watch. 'D'you want to see this picture, or don't you? It's nearly time for the start. Or don't you even want to sit next to me any more in case I get the wrong idea?'

'You've bought the tickets now—'

'Oh, don't worry about that,' he said bitterly. 'What's a little thing like a couple of one-and-sixpennies when your life's just been ruined? I can't say I feel much like sitting through it, anyway. It's only that soppy romantic thing you wanted to see.' He glanced at his watch again. 'In fact, if I get a move on I reckon I've just got time to get round to the Odeon and see the Roy Rogers. You can have the rest of the toast. Oh, and I brought you this for your birthday.' He dragged a small package from his pocket. 'Sorry it's not very much, but somehow I thought I might be buying you a ring. Dunno where I got a daft idea like that.'

'Sidney—' Thursday began, but he was already on his feet. She saw him go over to the waitress and pay the bill, and then he was on his way to the glass door. '*Sidney* . . .'

He turned and gave her a curt nod. 'It's OK, Thursday. I get the picture. Sorry I won't be seeing you home, but I dare say you can find your way, even in the blackout. Or you could always find some other poor sucker to take you around and pay for you.'

He vanished through the door and Thursday sank back into her seat, her face burning. He's made me feel like a common little gold-digger, she thought, half humiliated, half furious. But what could I do? He always insisted on paying. Men always do, and why shouldn't they? They get far more pay than girls. But it doesn't mean they own us. It doesn't mean we've been bought.

She wondered if Sidney had really wanted her to marry him, or even to be engaged. Or was it just because he was going away and wanted to feel he had a girl at home, tied to him? And because he didn't want some other man taking her out?

You're better off without him, she told herself. He'd no right to behave like that, ordering you about, telling you what you could and couldn't do. And just think what it would have been like to be married to him! You're well out of it.

All the same, she felt unexpectedly lost and miserable, sitting there by herself playing with a slice of cold toast. A few minutes ago, she'd been a girl with a regular boyfriend, a boyfriend who was a bit dull and stodgy, to be sure, but a boyfriend all the same. Someone to go around with, someone to share things with.

Now she was on her own, and it felt as if something was missing – yet at the same time she was conscious of a thread of relief. Not to have to listen to Sidney going on about his job in the bank any more. Not to have to listen to his braying laugh as he told one of his tedious jokes. Time to herself. Time, perhaps, to find another boyfriend – a proper one this time.

People were getting up and leaving. Thursday glanced at the clock on the wall and saw that the film was due to start in another ten minutes. Sidney had dropped the tickets on the table as he stormed out. There didn't seem to be much point in wasting them. Not both of them, anyway.

Thursday picked one up and followed the other customers out of the little restaurant and into the main part of the cinema. It was Joan Crawford in *Ice Follies* and her pictures were always lovely – so romantic. She felt she could do with a bit of romance.

She forgot all about Sidney's present. It lay on the table beside the plate of half-finished toast and the teapot, and the waitress found it when she came to clear the table. It was kept in the office in case someone claimed it, but nobody ever did and in the end the waitress opened it and found a little brooch in the shape of a letter T.

Her name was Anne, so it wasn't any good to her. She took it home and gave it to her mother.

Once the film was over, Thursday walked home through the darkened streets alone. There was enough moonlight to show her the way and as she crossed the bridge to St John's she paused to look at its silver path on the river. The tower of the cathedral was reflected beneath her, like a shimmering fairy palace. It seemed impossible that war was being waged only a few hundred miles away, and even more impossible that it might penetrate this peaceful place.

A duck landed on the water with a clattering of wings, and the reflection shattered. Thursday shivered. It was almost like a premonition – a vision of what might happen, in reality, to the great tower that had for so long dominated the city. She stared at the broken shards of moonlit water and experienced a moment of strange clarity. A broken city, she thought. A city bombed from the sky; devastated ruins. It could happen. Here in peaceful Worcester – it really could happen. She felt suddenly chilled to the bone, and understood her mother's fear.

But I was right to volunteer, she thought, staring at the black and silver water. I was *right*. We all have to do our bit – every one of us. In whatever way we can.

She had been to the Red Cross office during her break from the tailor's workshop at lunchtime that day. There had been a queue of people – young women like

Thursday, older women who wouldn't be able to join the Services but wanted to do something to help, and even a few men who were probably over forty and therefore also too old for active service, or not physically fit enough.

'We need as many young women as we can get, but at present we're only taking those over twenty-one,' the woman behind the desk told Thursday when she reached the head of the queue. 'How old are you?'

'I was twenty-one yesterday. I've brought my birth certificate.'

The Red Cross officer looked at it and her eyebrows went up a little. 'Thursday? Is that really your name?'

'It was because of the Armistice. My father was in the Army, and he and Mum got married when he was on convalescent leave with gunshot wounds. I was born at eleven o'clock in the morning on 11th November 1918, and they felt they had to commemorate it somehow. They made it my middle name, but I've always been called by it – nobody ever calls me Rosemary.'

'Well, you certainly shouldn't get mistaken for anyone else.' The Red Cross officer wrote it down and then handed Thursday a sheaf of forms. 'There are rather a lot of them, I'm afraid. D'you want to take them home or fill them in here? You can use that table in the corner where the other girls are sitting.'

Thursday squeezed on to the end of the table and began to look at the questions. They seemed to want to know an awful lot about you, she thought. She caught the eye of another girl who was obviously thinking the same, and they made a face at each other.

'I feel as if I'm writing my autobiography. Why ever do they want to know all this?'

'In case we get killed, I suppose,' the other girl said. 'Some Red Cross people go right to the Front, don't they. It's almost like being in the Army.'

'They won't send us to the front line, though. That's just the men, surely.'

'Well, they've probably only got the one set of forms.' The girl wrote for a while and Thursday began to fill in her own papers. 'Where d'you live?'

'St John's. What about you?'

'Powick. Are you going to be a mobile or stay at home?'

'Mobile, I hope. I want to see a bit of the world!'

'I'd like to do that, too,' the girl said wistfully. 'But my mother's not very strong and she doesn't want me to go away. I expect I'll stay here in Worcester.'

'You might be in Powick Hospital itself,' Thursday suggested, and the girl made another face.

'I hope not. I'm not too keen on being in a mental hospital. But they say it might be used for medical cases as well, so that wouldn't be so bad. Anyway, the main thing is to do something to help, isn't it.' The girl finished the last form and signed it with a flourish. 'There! That's done. And I'd better scram. I didn't tell my boss where I was going and she'll go mad if I'm late back.'

Thursday finished her forms, too, and handed them in. Then she hurried out into the street and walked quickly back to the tailor's shop.

It would be nice not have to do sewing for a living, she thought. Thursday didn't mind sewing, she'd always been good with her hands and she liked the feeling of satisfaction that came from seeing someone wear a garment she had made. But it was often fiddly work, and could be very frustrating. She'd seen the senior tailor throw a jacket right across the room in fury when he'd spent all afternoon trying to set a sleeve and it still hadn't come right. And men's suits were such dull things to sew, in their dreary greys and blacks and browns – not like pretty skirts and dresses.

I suppose I ought to have volunteered to make service uniforms, she thought, but the mere idea of sewing thick, rough khaki or naval serge made her shudder. No, she was ready for a change, and the idea of working with people, helping in a way to sew their bodies together, was much more interesting and attractive than toiling away in the hidden back room of a tailor's shop. And all afternoon, as she worked on yet another men's suit, she imagined what it would be like to be bustling about a ward full of wounded servicemen, cheering them up, helping them to recover to go back to war again.

The water had settled again now, the reflection of the cathedral once again still and serene. But it was getting cold, just standing here leaning over the bridge, and Thursday straightened up and strode briskly to the other side. Walking through the streets of St John's, she wondered where she was likely to be sent. Somewhere in this country, probably, although there wasn't much happening yet – but there'd be plenty to do if the raids they kept talking about really did happen.

She thought of the vision she'd had on the bridge, the ruined cities, the devastation, and knew that there might be a great many injuries to deal with. They'd need all the nurses they could get, and since there wasn't time to train enough new ones, the VAD nurses would be needed to take on many of the less skilled tasks. But we'll be able to learn to do the others, too, she thought, and felt a tremor of excitement. Why had she never thought of being a nurse before? Why had she allowed her parents to find her the apprenticeship in the tailor's shop and condemn her to the drudgery of the needle and thick grey flannel?

I wonder if I'd have enjoyed working in the porcelain factory any better? she thought. That was where both her father and brother worked, and she'd begged to be allowed to get a job there when she'd left school, imagining herself making some of the beautiful figurines or the famous decorated plates and dishes of Worcester porcelain. But Walter had told her that only really artistic people got that kind of work, and she was more likely to find herself mixing slip or heaving china out of the kiln.

'It's hard work and it won't set you up for life like

tailoring will,' he'd said, and that had been that. There was no more argument.

He was probably right. Her apprenticeship was over and she had a skill literally at her fingertips and a trade behind her. She could even set up on her own if she wanted to, making suits and dresses. That was what her parents had wanted for her, something that would stand her in good stead for the rest of her life.

I might even have married Sidney if we'd gone on much longer, she thought. Suppose all this hadn't happened and he really had proposed. I might have said yes, just because everyone expected me to, just because Mum liked him. I might have married him and lived a dull, ordinary life making clothes for the neighbours, and never known any different.

But now everything had changed. And as Thursday fitted her new Yale key into the lock and opened the front door, she knew that her life had turned in a new direction.

Patch rushed to greet her, and she didn't give another thought to Sidney.

On the following Sunday, Thursday caught the train and went to Ledbury. Auntie Maudie hadn't been able to come to the birthday party because she was a nurse at the little cottage hospital, and she'd invited Thursday and Sidney to tea to make up for it. She looked at Thursday in surprise when she turned up on the doorstep alone, and set her hands on her plump hips, regarding her with bright brown eyes.

'Where's that young man of yours, then?'

'He isn't my young man any more,' Thursday said, stepping over the threshold. 'Not that he ever was, really. We were just friends, Auntie.' She bent her head to kiss her aunt's cheek, feeling as always like a giant beside her.

'Is that so? Your mother was expecting an engagement.'

'Well, there isn't going to be one.' She followed her aunt along the narrow passage to the back room, fending off the attentions of the little white Jack Russell which bounded eagerly to meet her and pausing to stroke the ears of the stately white Persian cat which was sitting on the back of the armchair. 'All *right*, Nipper, you don't have to lick me to death. I'm pleased to see you, too. And how about you, Snowy? How many mice have you caught this week?'

The house was at Homend, one of a row on the opposite side of the road to the hospital, so it was nice and handy for Auntie Maudie to get to work. The front room, its window almost obscured by an enormous aspidistra in a pot, was kept for 'best' but the back room, with one wall taken up by Auntie Maudie's piano, was a cheerfully untidy muddle of newspapers, sheets of music and skeins of khaki wool. In her spare time, Maudie knitted balaclava helmets and socks for the Army.

Her aunt moved the latest piece of knitting from the battered armchair. 'Sit down here, love, and I'll make us a cup of tea. How did the party go? I was sorry I couldn't get over to it, but you know I was on duty.'

'I know. We were sorry you weren't there, Auntie. It was a smashing party. Dad gave me the biggest key you've ever seen, bright red it was, and made out of wood.' Thursday waited while her aunt went out to the scullery and filled the kettle. 'But there's something else I've got to tell you. I've got a bit of news.' She bent to fondle the little dog's ears as he pawed with enthusiasm at her skirt.

'News?' Maudie came back into the cluttered little room. 'What's that, then, if it's not an engagement?'

'I'm going to be a nurse.' Thursday felt a grin spread over her face. 'Like you. Well, not quite like you. I'm not doing the full training or anything like that. I'm going to be a VAD.'

'A VAD?' Maudie's round face broke into a smile. 'That's grand! I've always thought you'd make a good little nurse. Are you going to be mobile?'

Thursday nodded. It was a relief to be able to talk to

someone who understood and approved of what she was doing. 'I thought it was a good chance to see a few more places.'

Maudie pursed her lips and raised her eyebrows approvingly. 'You might as well get what you can out of it. So what have you done so far? And what does your mother think about it? Oh . . .' Her eyes sharpened. 'Is this why young Sidney's not with you? Took umbrage, did he?'

Thursday grinned. 'You could say that. Acted as if he owned me, and we weren't even engaged! And then he said he wanted us to *get* engaged. Just so that I wouldn't go out with anyone else while he was away.'

'Cheek!' her aunt said warmly. 'They're all the same, these men, they just want a table to put their feet under whenever they choose to come home. Not that my Bill was like that. He was good as gold, and looked forward to the day when he'd be able to leave the Army and stop home for good. It was just a shame he never got to the end of his time. But I hope you're not too upset about Sidney, Thursday.'

'I'm not upset at all. I don't know why I went out with him for so long, to tell you the truth.' The kettle began to whistle and Maudie went out to the scullery to make the tea. 'I never realised how much he got on my nerves,' Thursday went on, raising her voice a little. 'It's like putting down a heavy bag of shopping, finishing with him. Not that Mum sees it that way,' she added ruefully. 'She thinks I've passed up the chance of a lifetime.'

'Rubbish!' Maudie called, rattling cups in their saucers as she set the old wooden tray. 'That's just my sister, always did think marriage was the only life for a woman. Well, mine was good while it lasted, I won't say it wasn't, and I miss Bill every day, but I can't say I haven't enjoyed being on my own as well. A nice, interesting job like nursing, looking after other people, and a couple of animals to come home to, and nobody to make a mess of your kitchen – well, there's a lot to be said for it! And so long as neither of you's broken-hearted over it.'

'Broken-hearted!' Thursday said with a giggle. 'He went straight off to see a Roy Rogers picture!'

'That's men for you,' Maudie said with a smile. 'Anyway, there's plenty more fish in the sea and you're young yet. So come on, tell me about this VAD business.'

Thursday settled into the armchair, reaching behind her to stroke Snowy's head again and letting Nipper climb on to her lap where he sat gazing adoringly into her face. 'Well, I've been and enrolled. I filled in a lot of forms and they're going to let me know if they'll take me. I'll have to do some training first, and that might be in Worcester. And then – well, they'll send me somewhere else. I have to be attached to one of the services as well, so I've applied for the Navy.'

'You're bound to go away, then. There's not much sea around here!' Maudie poured the tea. 'Well, anything you want to know, just ask me. I may have only been in a little cottage hospital but I've done plenty of nursing. And now I've got a present for you.'

Thursday stopped in the act of spreading a thin layer of margarine on a slice of bread. Rationing hadn't started yet but was expected soon, and meanwhile things like butter were becoming hard to obtain. Nobody liked the taste of margarine much, but there was a pot of home-made blackberry and apple jam on the tray as well. Auntie Maudie's blackberry and apple jam was famous in the family.

'But you've already given me my birthday present.' She had found it on the table when she came in from the pictures the evening after her birthday – a tiny box containing a pair of pearl earrings. She was wearing them now and she touched her ears to show Auntie Maud that she appreciated the gift. 'They're lovely, and I forgot to say thank you when I came in – I'm ever so sorry.'

'That's all right, love. I saw you had them on. But this

isn't a birthday present. It's – it's more of a good-luck present, I suppose.' Maud jumped to her feet and bustled out of the room. 'You just stop there a minute, and don't give that dog too much bread and jam – he'll be fat as a pig at this rate.'

Thursday heard her footsteps running up the stairs. She spread another slice of bread and jam and bit into it, wondering what her aunt was up to now. Although she and Thursday's mother were sisters, they weren't really anything like each other. Mary was quiet and domesticated, her whole life revolving around her husband and family, whereas Maudie was as bright and lively as a wren, always on the go. She worked hard at the little hospital but she was just as busy in her off-duty times – going to church on Sundays, country dancing twice a week, and now organising the townsfolk into helping the war effort by knitting balaclavas or socks for the Forces. She also kept her little garden as neat as a pin, and everyone knew her and Nipper when she took him out for his walks.

'Here,' she said, running downstairs again. 'I want you to have this.'

She handed Thursday a small box. It was a bit like the one the earrings had been in, but it was longer, as if it contained a necklace. Thursday put down her slice of bread and wiped her fingers on her hanky. Then she opened it and gave a little gasp of surprise.

'Oh, Auntie Maudie! It's lovely.'

'My Bill gave it to me,' Maudie said quietly. 'When he went away in the Great War. I'd just started nursing then, you see, and he wanted me to have something they'd let me wear on the ward. It went all through with me and now I'd like it to go with you.'

Thursday stared at the little silver watch that lay in the box. It was on a slender chain, with a pin on the other end. She lifted it out, gazing at the clear face.

'It's upside down, see,' her aunt showed her. 'You pin it on your dress and then you can see it when you look down. You can use it when you're taking a patient's pulse, anything that needs timing. It still keeps perfect time.'

'But you can't give me this!' Thursday protested. 'Not if Uncle Bill gave it to you. You must want to keep it. Anyway, don't you use it yourself?'

'Not now. I've got another one I wear at the hospital. And I really want you to have it, Thursday.' She hesitated for a moment, then said quietly, 'If Bill had come home from the war we'd have had our own family. But it wasn't to be, and when our Mary asked me to be your godmother I thought of you as the nearest I'd ever have to my own daughter, and so I've always done. And if I'd had a little girl, she'd have had that watch, so I want you to have it. And since you're going to be a nurse, like me . . .' She stopped, and Thursday saw that her eyes were full of tears. She leant over quickly and gave her aunt a kiss on her round little cheek.

'I'll wear it all the time. It's lovely. Thank you.' She handed the watch to her aunt. 'Pin it on for me now, will you?'

Maudie did so and they both gazed at it, resting on Thursday's breast. The silver glowed faintly in the firelight and the glass gleamed. Maudie nodded a little.

'It looks very nice. And I'll be happy to think of it on a ward again – a wartime ward, I mean. Looking after soldiers and sailors. I'll be happy thinking of you wearing it.'

Thursday got up and went round the little table to her aunt. She bent to put her arms around the plump little body and give her a gentle kiss.

'I'll think of you whenever I pin it on,' she said softly. 'You and Uncle Bill.' She had never known her uncle, he had died the year before she was born. But his photograph stood on the mantelpiece, a smiling young soldier with fair hair just showing beneath his army cap, next to the photograph of the wedding with Maudie a plump and smiling young girl with bright eyes and dark curls.

37

Thursday looked at the pictures now and felt a lump in her throat. It was such a shame they'd never had more than a scrap of married life, such a shame that they'd never had a family. You could see in the picture how happy they would have been, and what lovely parents they would have made.

Maudie followed her eyes. 'I still feel he's with me, you know,' she said softly. 'I touch his photo every morning and I say goodnight to him when I go to bed. We've never really been parted.'

Thursday thought of Sidney and her impatience with him. It would never have been like that for us, she thought. If we had got married, we'd have been like a lot of other people I know, bickering and squabbling and just rubbing along together because there's nothing else you can do. But we wouldn't have felt like Auntie Maudie feels about Uncle Bill.

Maudie nodded at her. 'I can see what you're thinking, love, and you're right. You've got to wait for the right man before you give your own life over to him. And there will be one for you, I'm sure of that – only it was never poor young Sidney, decent young fellow that he is.'

Thursday smiled a little tearfully. 'I suppose there'll be a right girl for him, too. He's had a lucky escape, same as I have!'

'You're telling me!' her aunt laughed. 'It'll take a strong man to cope with you, our Thursday! Anyway, tell me about the family, I didn't have much time for a proper gossip when I called in the other evening, I had to catch the train home. How's your Auntie Flo? I bet she's worried about her Mike, isn't she? He must be going away soon.'

'Well, yes, except that there doesn't seem to be much happening yet, does there? People are saying it's just a phoney war and won't come to anything after all, and others are saying we're going to be bombed to bits. It's hard to know who's right.'

'It takes time to get a war going, I suppose. But I reckon these air raids are going to come all the same. Hitler's probably just waiting till the winter's over. And he wants to win the war at sea before he starts using the aeroplanes.'

Thursday nodded. 'Dad says that too. He says there's no sense in flattening the country if he's going to invade us, and he's got to get rid of the Navy first so he can bring the troops over by sea. Then he'll start bombing the military airfields, and harbours like Portsmouth, and the important cities like London.'

'Well, whatever they're going to do there's not a lot we can do about it,' Maudie said. 'Tell me a bit more about your birthday. What presents did you have? I know your mum and dad were giving you that nice brooch, she showed it to me when they bought it. What else did you get? Oh—' she leant forward eagerly '—and what's the latest talk? What about that Mrs Hoskins up the road, has she really gone off with her fancy man or did her hubby send him packing? The last I heard, she'd been seen with a suitcase, getting on a number eight bus.'

They settled back in theirs chairs for a good gossip, while Nipper bustled round the rug clearing up all the crumbs he could find, and Snowy rose majestically from her perch and clambered down on to Thursday's lap where she curled into a white, foamy ball and purred herself to sleep.

At last it was time to go. Thursday kissed her aunt and touched the little watch still pinned to her blouse. It felt like a talisman, she thought, a lucky token to carry with her wherever she went. It had, as Maudie had said, already gone through one war. Now it would go through another.

'I'll take the greatest care of it,' she promised as she slipped into her coat.

'That's right,' her aunt agreed, and touched the watch's face with her fingertip as if bidding it goodbye. 'And when all this is over you can bring it back to me again. Just so that I know it's taken care of you, like it took care of me. You'll keep each other safe.'

Thursday slipped out of the door and walked quickly up the street towards the railway station. She could feel the watch, just touching her breast, as she stepped along. It was older than she was, she thought, and had already been through a world war. Now it was going to serve again.

Somehow, it felt like a promise.

Chapter Three

Jenny worked in a grocer's shop, one of a row of small shops not far from Waterloo Street. She'd been there since she left school at fourteen, and enjoyed weighing out the biscuits which were kept in glass-topped bins in front of the counter, and slicing ham or bacon on the big circular slicer. She liked putting sugar into thick blue paper bags and wrapping sweets into paper cones for children. And she liked chatting to the customers and getting all the gossip.

'Mrs Hoskins has definitely gone off with that bloke from Evesham,' she said at home, as the family sat round the tea-table the day after Thursday's visit to Auntie Maud. 'I heard it in the shop. Old Mrs Gabbage says Mr Hoskins is going after them with an airgun.' She giggled. 'Wonder where he'll aim it!'

Her mother gave her a reproving look. 'Jenny! That's enough of that sort of talk. And I don't think you ought to be gossiping about Mrs Hoskins anyway. She's had a lot to put up with from her hubby. He always was a bit ready with his fists.'

'All the same, he is her husband,' Walter said. 'He's got his rights.'

'It's enough to put you off marriage, hearing about men like him,' Thursday observed, helping herself to the Marmite. 'I don't blame Mrs Hoskins for running off.'

Walter stared at her. 'Don't blame her? She made her vows, didn't she? "Love, honour and obey", that's what the service says. "Till death us do part." Not just till some fancy man comes along and takes her eye.'

'Well, I don't remember anything in the marriage service to say a man can knock his wife about,' Thursday said. 'I wouldn't stand for it, I can tell you.'

'Well, I can't say I agree with him doing that,' Walter allowed. 'All the same, the marriage vow's a serious promise, and who's to say *why* he hit her – if he really did, it's only talk, mind. If he'd found out she was carrying on behind his back—'

'Well, I don't think we need talk about it at the tea table,' Mary interrupted. 'What else have you been doing today, Jenny, apart from gossip?'

'We've been getting all sorts of forms about rationing,' Jenny said gloomily. 'They say the books'll be out soon. Then you'll only be able to have a tiny bit of meat each week and about an ounce of butter and a couple of tablespoonsful of sugar. It's going to be murder weighing it all out.'

Mary stared at her. 'We'll get more than that, surely. That's starvation rations.'

'Well, I don't know the exact amounts, but it really isn't much, Mum. And people are starting to hoard. You can tell they are. They come and get as much as they can from us and then they go round all the other shops to get more. We've stopped serving people we don't know. It's not fair on the regulars.'

'Are you allowed to do that?' Thursday asked. 'Refuse to serve them?'

'We just tell them we haven't got what they want, and keep it under the counter. Some of them get a bit nasty, but what can they do? It's illegal to hoard, and it's not fair.'

'So that's what you're doing, Mum,' Steve told his mother. 'Hoarding. *I've* seen that bag of sultanas and raisins you've got at the back of the cupboard.'

'It's only a pound or so,' Mary protested, colouring a little. 'I've been saving them for the Christmas cake, that's all. And I'd have made it by now if it hadn't been for

Thursday's birthday. You couldn't have called it hoarding then. Could you?' she added, a shade anxiously.

The family laughed at her. 'See, you're looking guilty already!' Steve grinned, but Thursday nudged him.

'Don't, you're upsetting her. It's all right, Mum. It's not hoarding, just a pound of dried fruit, and like you say, it would have been a cake by now. Anyway, what were you doing, our Steve, ferreting about in Mum's cupboards? I bet *you* weren't thinking of doing a bit of baking.'

It was Steve's turn to colour, remembering the days when he used to come home from school and, if the house was empty, steal raisins from his mother's store. He'd been caught one day when she'd come downstairs unexpectedly and found him with his hand in the jar, and he'd never been allowed to forget it.

Jenny finished her tea and pushed back her chair. 'I'm going to the pictures. *The Wizard of Oz* is on at the Scala. I might be a bit late in, Dad.'

'Oh, might you? It wouldn't occur to you to ask permission, I suppose?' Walter tried to inject a stern note into his voice.

She gave him a cheeky look. 'You wouldn't want me to miss the end of the picture, would you? I'll come straight home after – you needn't worry that I'm lurking in doorways with a boy!'

'You'd better not be, either. And just who are you going with?' Mary asked as Jenny pulled open the door to the scullery.

'Jean. Got to go now, we're meeting in ten minutes.' Jenny gave her face a sketchy wash at the kitchen sink and then whisked upstairs. They heard her light footsteps skittering above and then she bounced back down the stairs and through the back room on her way to the front door, keeping her face averted as she passed the table. Walter reached out to detain her but she was gone, calling a brightly casual goodbye as she went. Steve winked and Thursday looked at the table, hiding her grin.

Walter and Mary looked at each other.

'That girl's put lipstick on,' Walter said. 'She tried to hide it, but I saw. Bright red. You'll have to do something about her, Mary.'

Mary sighed. 'I've tried, but what can I do? She'd only put it on outside. She's nearly seventeen, Walter, they all wear a bit of make-up at that age.'

'Well, I don't like it. Making herself look cheap.'

'It's only a bit of lipstick,' Thursday said. 'And it's not a really bright one.'

'Yes, come on, Dad,' Steve said. 'There's no harm in it. The blokes don't like a girl who doesn't make something of herself.'

'That's just it! She's not old enough to be thinking of things like that. Boys, and make-up and all that. She's still a child.'

'She's old enough to get married,' Thursday pointed out. 'Sixteen. I was going round with that Billy Stratton when I was sixteen.'

'You never told me about that,' Walter said. 'I'd have put my foot down if I'd known. And she can't get married, not without my consent, not for another four years and more. It's this twenty-first of Thursday's,' he said to his wife. 'It's given her ideas. And it's this war, too. Girls not much older than her talking about joining up. And that's another thing,' he went on in a grumbling tone. 'You've unsettled her with this talk of being a mobile nurse. You could just stop on at the tailor's, they're making uniforms now and there's plenty for you to do there and it's useful war work. But, no, you've got to go off and volunteer to be a nurse, and not even satisfied with the local hospital. Seems to be you're all just itching to get away from home, the lot of you. I mean, why? What have we done wrong that you're so keen to leave us?'

'It's not that, Dad. You know it isn't. I just want to do something different, as well as useful. I've never really liked being at the tailor's, you know that. And I *want* to be

44

a nurse. I was talking to Auntie Maudie about it yesterday, she was telling me lots of things, and *she* thinks it's a good idea for me to go.'

'It's not the nursing I object to so much. It's this wanting to go away. As if your home's not good enough for you any more.'

'Calm down, Dad,' Steve said. 'It's nothing to do with that. It's just a chance, isn't it? A chance to see something different.' He paused, then said, 'I'm thinking of volunteering myself, as a matter of fact.'

His parents stared at him.

'Volunteering? You?' his mother said at last. 'Oh, *Steve*.'

Walter leaned forward and put his elbows on the table. Jenny and Thursday were forgotten. His voice was serious.

'Are you sure about this, son? You don't have to do it, you know. They're not calling up your age group, and maybe they won't. You want to give it some thought. Once you're in, you won't be able to come out again, you realise that?'

'I know, Dad. But Thursday is right, what she says – we can't sit round and do nothing. We've all got to do our bit. You heard what they said on the six o'clock news – there might not be much going on at home yet, but there's plenty happening at sea, with these new magnetic mines Mr Chamberlain was talking about, and ships being sunk all over the place. They're going to need men, and I don't want to wait to be called up. I'd rather go now.'

'Not into the Navy!' Mary protested. 'I can't bear to think of you at sea, Steve. You know how I feel about boats.'

He grinned at her. 'It's all right, Mum, I won't volunteer for the Navy. That'd be pretty daft, when we live practically in the middle of the country. Anyway, we've got our own regiment in Worcester. It'll be the

Army for me. Or maybe the Air Force, I wouldn't mind learning to fly a Spitfire.'

'You want to think about it, all the same,' Walter said. 'It's not pretty, war isn't. I saw the last lot, remember. I still got the scars of bullets in my shoulder. I saw men die and it's not what it's cracked up to be. Death or glory, they said, but there's not much glory about it, I can tell you that.'

'Walter . . .' Mary said in a trembling voice, and he glanced at her.

'There's things it's not right to talk about in front of your mother. But you need to think about them, all the same. Let's go down to the Red Lion a bit later on, have a bit of a talk. I won't stop you doing what you feel's right, but I don't want you to do anything in a hurry, all right?'

'All right, Dad.' Steve was startled. He'd expected argument, he'd expected tears from his mother, but he hadn't expected this reaction from his father. Taking him to the pub. Treating him like – well, like one of his mates. Especially after the way he'd gone on about Jenny and her bit of lipstick.

'I was just going to make a cup of tea,' Mary said a little plaintively, and once again Walter glanced at her.

'You put the kettle on, love. There's no hurry for me and Steve. And let's listen to the wireless for a bit. It's Arthur Askey and Richard Murdoch, isn't it? That'll give us something to take our minds off things a bit.'

Mary went out into the little kitchen, and Thursday followed her. She put her arms around her mother and held her tightly.

'I'm sorry about all that, Mum. I didn't want to start that argument again. 'Specially with Steve saying what he did.'

Mary looked at her. Her lips were trembling.

'I thought we'd have you all at home for a bit longer, or at least close by. Now it seems as if the whole family's breaking up. It's such a lot to take in, all at once.'

'I know, Mum. I know. But we've got to do what we think's right, haven't we? You and Dad have always brought us up to do that.'

Mary sighed and nodded. 'Yes, we have. I suppose we just didn't think of all this. After the last war, well, we just didn't ever think it could happen again, did we?'

'Perhaps it won't,' Thursday said, but without much hope. 'Perhaps it really will just turn out to be a phoney war, and all be over soon. And then we can all go back to being the way we were.'

But she knew they never could. Already, the world had been changed, and their lives with it. None of them would ever be able to go back to quite the way they were.

'I've never talked much about the Great War as they called it,' Walter said to Steve as they sat over a pint of beer each at the Red Lion. 'None of us what was in it wanted to talk about it once we were home again. We were too bloody glad to *be* home, and we just wanted to put it all behind us. But now . . .' He sighed and rubbed a hand across his face. 'Now it seems as if we ought to have said more. Maybe it would have stopped this new lot.'

'I don't see how it could have done,' Steve said. 'Hitler would have been Hitler no matter what you'd told us. It wouldn't have stopped him going into Czechoslovakia or Poland, and that's what we're fighting for, isn't it? And to stop him taking over the rest of us, too – France and England, and all the other countries in Europe.'

'I suppose so. Well, yes, you're right, it wouldn't have stopped him. But maybe we'd have stepped in a bit sooner. Or done something different . . .' Walter rubbed his face again. 'I dunno. And it's not what I brought you down here for neither. Talking about what we ought to have done isn't going to change things now. But I don't want you going into the Army, or anything else, without knowing what's in front of you.'

Steve lifted his tankard to his lips and waited. Coming

out for a drink wasn't something he and his dad did all that much. Walter preferred to come to the Red Lion on Friday nights for a pint or two with his own mates, while Steve generally spent his time playing football or billiards. In fact, now he came to think about it, he couldn't ever remember them coming down on their own, specially.

Walter didn't seem to be in any hurry to start speaking. His brow was creased and his lower lip curled over the upper, as if he was pondering how to begin. He took a sip of his own beer and cleared his throat.

'Like I said, it wasn't pretty. It was a cruel war. Well, war's always cruel, stands to reason, but this one – well, it seemed worse than anything you'd ever heard of. Young boys, hardly trained enough to know how to hold a gun, hardly *big* enough to hold a gun, some of 'em, sent over the top when the generals knew full well they'd be mown down like grass in haymaking. It was always the same, see. The enemy were there and as soon as they saw a movement, they'd shoot. So if you sent enough soldiers, they'd just go on shooting till they ran out of ammo. Then the proper fighting could begin.' He looked at his son with eyes that seemed to see another time, another place. 'Cannon fodder, that's what they were called afterwards, and that's just what they were. Sent to use up the enemy's ammo. Piles of bodies, And not all of 'em properly dead, neither. But you couldn't stop to do nothing. You had to climb over 'em or kick 'em out of the way.' His voice was as dry as sandpaper. 'It was sheer bloody murder.'

Steve could not speak. It was only what he'd already known, in a dim sort of way, but the picture his father's words conjured before his eyes was much more graphic, more shocking, than the vague knowledge he'd had before. He saw young men of his own age – younger – climbing the banks that had been thrown up by the digging of the trenches, facing a hail of bullets, falling back on those who were waiting behind . . . What was it like to have the body of a screaming, bleeding friend fall on top of you as you were yourself being urged to go over the same murderous bank?

'And it wasn't just the killing,' his father went on. 'It was the trenches themselves. Up to our knees in mud, we were, and the rain just bloody never stopped coming down. Came down like stair-rods, it did. And the cold – it got right through to your bones. You were never dry, never warm. Your feet rotted in your socks but you never took 'em off so you didn't see . . . And there was nowhere to bury the bodies, and no time. They just lay there, stinking, at your feet, till they was part of the mud and filth and stench of it all . . . And the *rats*.' He shuddered. 'The only ones with plenty to eat, *they* were. The only ones who could take it.'

He stopped. His voice was trembling. Steve stared at him, transfixed. He wanted to reach out, to touch his father, but he hadn't done that since he was a little boy and still kissing his dad goodnight. He could barely even remember it. He felt sick; sick and helpless.

That's what Armistice Day's all about, he thought. And the Remembrance Day service, and all those poppies. That's why they called our Thursday 'Thursday'.

'There was heroes in every trench,' Walter said. 'You had to be a bloody hero to stick it. And there was those that went mad, too, mad with terror and pain. You couldn't blame them, could you. You couldn't blame 'em – youngsters of sixteen and seventeen, some of 'em, no older'n our Jenny, lied about their age to go and serve, thinking it was all going to be glorious and they'd come back with medals – it was what they was *told*, see? And if you didn't go, if you didn't volunteer and didn't have no uniform to wear, people stared at you in the street and shouted after you, and girls give you white feathers to show you were a coward. And then, when they found out what it was really like – well, some of 'em bore up OK, but some of 'em just went to pieces. *And I don't blame 'em*,' he said, fixing Steve with an accusing stare. 'I don't blame 'em at all. They was just boys, that's all, bits of boys. They didn't deserve ... what happened to them.'

There was a moment of silence. Then Steve asked huskily, his mouth dry, 'What was it? What did happen to them?'

'They were executed,' Walter said baldly. 'Shot at dawn, by their own mates. That's the ones who weren't shot by their own commanding officers straight away, without bothering to set up a firing squad. Cowards, they called 'em, cowards and deserters.'

The pub had been a noisy place a few moments ago. Now, it was as if everyone had stopped talking at once, as if the laughter and shouting had ceased. For a moment Steve felt as if he were there with his father, seeing what his father saw: a wavering line of dirty, dishevelled soldiers, some of them younger than himself, just boys, being marched on to a bleak patch of muddy ground in the cold and colourless dawn. There was no sound of birdsong in the lowering sky, no sign of life on the harsh landscape, only grey hopelessness and miserable fear in the blind-folded faces. He saw them stop and stand in line, turning sightlessly to face the guns, guns held by men they knew, men who had been their friends and comrades. He heard the bark of the command, the harsh crack of the rifles. And then it was over. The bodies lay fallen in their own blood, their own brains spattered around them. The bodies of boys who had volunteered, who had lied about their age to go and serve their country, but who had found the horror too much to bear.

'It don't matter whether you're a volunteer or a pressed man,' Walter said at last. 'You follow the same rules. They took children and treated 'em as men. And it'll be the same this time, Steve.' He came back from the past and looked his son in the eye. 'I don't want to stand in your light, son, I never have. Your mother and me, we've tried to bring you up to know right from wrong and we've tried to teach you to know your own minds. You've got to do whatever you think is right. But you ought to know what it can be like. What it *will* be like. It wouldn't be right for me to let you go off not knowing.'

'No, Dad.' Steve fiddled with his glass. 'But it's different this time. If Hitler invades – or if there's air raids, and there are *going* to be – we're all going to have to fight. It's not going to be a matter of going to France or Belgium or Germany. It's going to be here – in Worcester. None of us are going to be safe.' He looked up at his father. 'We've got to stop that happening, Dad. We can't let him march all over us like he's marched over those other countries. We can't have him putting us into ghettos like he has the Jews. This is *England*. We haven't been invaded since – since William the Conqueror. And I'm damned if I'm going to let it happen again – not if there's anything I can do to help prevent it.' He met Walter's eyes again. 'I'm glad you told me those things, Dad. I think it's right that you did. We *ought* to know what you and the others went through in that war. But we can't let them stop us now. We've got to go and fight. I just hope I'll be one of the ones that *can* take it. But if not, well, at least I'll have tried.'

There was a long silence. Steve looked at his father and went to fetch another two pints of beer. He brought a whisky too, and set it on the table.

'Drink that, Dad. It'll make you feel a bit better.'

Walter nodded. He drank the whisky and coughed a little, grinning weakly. 'Not used to it! I'm sorry if I was a bit – you know—' He looked embarrassed and Steve spoke quickly.

'It's all right. And thanks for telling me.'

'You won't say anything to your mother? Only I've never really said all that much – didn't want to upset her. And now – I wouldn't want her worrying any more than she's got to, see. It's bad enough for her as it is. It's bad enough for everyone.'

'Yes.' Steve looked at him. Mum won't know these

things, he thought, but Dad will. Dad's going to be torturing himself day and night, thinking of the last war and imagining me and Thursday and even Jenny in this one. And so will all the other men who went through those things before.

'I won't say anything,' he said. 'And I'll think about it before I volunteer – I promise you that. But I'm going to have to go some time, Dad. You know that, don't you?'

'Yes.' Walter sighed and lifted his tankard. 'I know. And all I can do is wish you luck. Good luck, Steve – and God go with you.'

Chapter Four

Thursday's papers came through just before Christmas.

The envelope was on the mantelpiece when she came in from work that evening and she opened it standing in front of the fire, still in her coat. It was cold and foggy outside and the damp still hung around her, droplets sparkling on the brown woollen gloves Auntie Flo had knitted and on the hair that peeped out all around her beret. She dropped the gloves on the fender to dry and tore the envelope open with her thumb.

'When have you got to go, then?' Mary asked. She'd been on tenterhooks all day, seeing the envelope sticking out from behind the clock where she'd put it that morning. How she'd had the strength not to open it herself, she didn't know, and now she was hovering anxiously by the tea table, picking up plates and putting them down again, moving the pepper pot, fiddling with the cloth. 'It's not too soon, is it?'

'January,' Thursday said. 'Early January. They don't say where I've got to go, there'll be some more papers coming about that, but I've got the Wrens. I mean, that's what I'll be attached to, so it'll be a naval hospital.'

She stared at the paper, feeling a tremor of excitement. It was coming true, it was really happening. She was going to be a nurse, a VAD, and work somewhere near the sea with Wrens and sailors. It was a whole new world opening up before her. She felt a twinge of nervousness somewhere in the excitement and looked at her mother, biting her lip and grinning all at once.

'Well, at least you've got Christmas with the family,'

Mary said, trying to hide her disappointment. She had resigned herself to the fact that her two elder children would be leaving home but had clung to the hope that Thursday would be kept nearer to her home. Why the girl had to volunteer for the Navy, she had no idea, not when she could surely have done the same sort of nursing here in Worcester, or at Norton Barracks. It was as if she *wanted* to get away from them all. It's hurtful, Mary had said to her sister when Maudie had come over one afternoon last week, but Maudie had shaken her head and said girls were different nowadays, more independent, and this war had unsettled them all. They didn't seem to think they were doing anything unless they were sent away somewhere. 'And you don't need to worry about your Thursday,' she'd said. 'She's got a good head on her shoulders, and she'll be subject to hospital discipline, as well as Service rules.'

'We'd better make the most of it,' Mary said now. 'Christmas, I mean. It might be the last one we have all together. For a while, I mean,' she added hastily, turning away.

Since the night when Walter had taken Steve to the pub, Steve had said no more about volunteering, but that didn't mean he'd forgotten the idea. Mary never knew what it was Walter and Steve had talked about that night in the pub, only that Walter had come back looking grey and drawn, and had had bad dreams for a week afterwards. It had brought back all the nightmares he'd been through in the Great War, things he'd never talked to her about and which she'd had to find out from hearing him cry out in the night. I don't want my Steve to go through things like that, she thought. But there didn't seem to be anything she could do to stop it. As Steve had said himself, if he didn't volunteer he'd get called up and then he might not have any choice at all in what he did.

Thursday looked at her mother. She knew Mary was upset about her going away, and now that it was really happening she felt a twinge of guilt and sympathy. She went to Mary and put her arm around her shoulders.

'Don't worry, Mum. I'll be all right. And I won't forget you and Dad, and everyone at home. I'll write to you as often as I can.'

Mary tried to smile. 'I know, love, and I know you won't do anything silly. It's just – it's just that I'm going to *miss* you so much! And Steve as well, when he goes. The house will seem so empty.'

'Well, I'd probably have gone soon anyway, if I'd got married,' Thursday said, but Mary shook her head.

'That's different. You'd have been living nearby, and you'd have had the sort of life I expected for you. The sort of life I could *understand*. This going off to a hospital somewhere hundreds of miles away, living with strangers and working with sailors – well, I can't sort of picture it. That's what's upsetting.'

'I'll tell you all about it,' Thursday promised. 'I'll write so many letters, you'll get fed up reading them. I'll tell you all about the other girls and the doctors and patients, and what it's like by the sea, and everything. I'll even draw pictures if you like!'

Mary laughed and brushed her hand across her eyes. 'They'll tell me a lot, I'm sure! You were never much good as an artist, our Thurs. I remember those pictures you used to bring home from school, we had our work cut out puzzling out what they were supposed to be.'

'Well, it isn't till after Christmas anyway,' Thursday said, folding the letter back into its envelope. She shrugged off her coat. 'So like you say, we'd better think about making it a good one. Is there a cup of tea in the pot? It's freezing outside.'

Making Christmas a good one seemed especially important this year, when things were so uncertain. The war news was grim. The Russians had bombed Helsinki and there was fighting on the Western Front. The King himself had visited the soldiers along the Maginot Line.

The war at sea had already brought losses, and in the South Atlantic there had been a huge sea battle which had culminated in the capture and scuttling of the *Graf Spee*, the German pocket battleship which had caused so much trouble for the merchant navy.

Yet the British Isles remained untouched and there was still an uneasy feeling that the war hadn't properly started. Barrage balloons drifted like flying whales above the cities, although there was no sign of an air invasion; Canadian and Australian troops arrived in their thousands by sea and air, and still Hitler seemed to be keeping his distance.

'He's waiting for the spring,' Walter said as the family gathered round the supper table that evening, listening to the six o'clock news. 'It's going to be a bad winter, if you look at the holly. He'll sit tight till the weather's better and then all hell will be let loose.'

'It seems so dark these days,' Mary said, bringing a large pan of stew to the table and starting to ladle it on to the plates. 'I had the lights on and the blackout up by half-past three this afternoon. What with the Government stopping British Summer Time at the end of November, you only get a few hours' daylight these days.'

'Well, there wouldn't have been any more daylight even if they hadn't,' Steve pointed out. 'Still, it's murder on the roads. I think it's daft, not letting cars have any lights. You can't tell when they're coming, 'specially when it's foggy like tonight.'

Jenny nodded. 'There was a man nearly got run over outside the shop this afternoon. He fell on the kerb and someone brought him in for a cup of water. He looked ever so shaken up.'

'At this rate,' Steve said, 'there'll be more people killed on the roads than in the fighting. Hitler won't have to bother sending any planes! I wouldn't mind another dumpling, if there's any spare, Mum.'

'You just wait till everyone's been served,' his mother told him. 'Anyway, I made two each so there won't be any

56

left over. I'm afraid there's not a lot of meat in it, but it's got the flavour and it's full of your father's vegetables.'

'Lots of carrots, anyway,' Steve remarked. 'They're telling us to eat plenty of them to help us to see in the dark. We should have eyes like cats' soon!'

'Good job I've got the allotment,' Walter said. 'And the carrots did well this year. Can't do much about the cod-liver oil they want us to take as well, though.'

'*I'm* not swallowing the horrible stuff,' Jenny declared. 'I had enough of it when I was a baby.'

'You had cod-liver oil and malt, and you liked it,' Mary reminded her. 'I'll get one of those big jars from Boots and we'll all have a spoonful after tea every day. What with all these shortages and rationing just about to start, it won't do any of us any harm.'

'How long does it take to work?' Thursday wondered. 'And how many carrots do you need to eat? Someone told me if you ate too many you turned orange.'

'That's how they help people see in the dark,' Steve said. 'They don't do anything to your eyes, they just make us all bright orange so we can see each other more easily. Anyway, if you're going to be a nurse you ought to know that sort of thing.'

'Well, I soon will if we get a lot of orange sailors coming into the hospital,' Thursday said with a giggle. 'Is Auntie Maudie coming for Christmas Day, Mum?'

'Yes, unless they want her to be on duty. But they do try to get everyone home for Christmas at the cottage hospital. And your Auntie Flo and Uncle Percy will be round, too, of course, and Granny and Grandad. The usual houseful.' Mary looked pleased, then sighed. 'Goodness knows how long it'll be before we get another chance to have everyone together.'

'Better start making paperchains,' Jenny said to her brother. 'The ones we made last year got all screwed up and torn when we took them down, remember? I wonder if we'll be able to get any coloured paper.'

Coloured paper was another thing that proved difficult to find in the shops, but they managed to track down enough to make a few strings of paperchains, the coloured strips glued together in neat loops, and they supplemented them with strips made from newspaper coloured with paints from Steve's old paintbox. The effect was cheery enough, and Walter got out the fairy lights that were stored carefully from year to year, and the glass baubles that hung on the little tree.

'It looks good, doesn't it?' Thursday said, surveying their work as they finished decorating on Christmas Eve. 'Really bright and pretty. And it'll look even better when Dad's underpants are taken off the fender.'

'Oh, you!' Mary exclaimed, snatching them up. 'I'm sure I never left them there. Anyway, there'll be no more washing done till after Boxing Day, so that's that. Now, breakfast will be at eight o'clock so that I can get the turkey in the oven – we were lucky to get it, Mr Huggins only had just enough for his regulars – and I want us all to go to church together for the eleven o'clock service. Your auntie and uncle will come round in time for a sherry before dinner, and they're bringing Gran and Grandad with them. We'll have dinner at two.'

'And we'll all turn to and help with the veg,' Maudie said. She had arrived at teatime and caught the bus from the railway station, staggering in laden with parcels, and would stay until the trains started to run again on Boxing Day. Nipper was with her, and had quickly started a game of chase with Patch, until both dogs were banished to the garden, but the white Persian had been left at home in Ledbury with a neighbour popping in to feed her. 'There's a huge pile of sprouts to be done, and plenty of carrots.'

'And a good big pudding,' Mary added. 'Flo and me put all our dried fruit together. Make the most of it – if this rationing's what they say it's going to be we'll not see another one like it for the duration.'

The dinner was indeed as good as any pre-war Christmas dinner had been, and the family crowded round the table, exclaiming over the crackers Flo had brought and putting on flimsy paper hats and reading out silly jokes and riddles. 'When is a door not a door?' 'When it's ajar.' 'When is a sailor not a sailor?' 'When he's aboard.' 'Why shouldn't you put a clock at the top of the stairs?' 'Because it will run down.' Each joke was greeted with groans of derision, and Leslie complained that he'd heard them all before.

'That's because you've *told* them all before,' his sister Denise said, poking him with her elbow. 'Now we know where you got them from – Christmas crackers.'

The only member of the family missing was Mike, who had now been posted to a camp in Northamptonshire and couldn't get leave, and after dinner Walter poured a small glass of port for all the adults and proposed a toast.

'To absent friends,' he said, lifting his glass. 'To Mike and all the other brave lads who can't be at home at Christmas.'

'To absent friends,' they all echoed, and there was a moment's silence as Mary and Flo bit their lips and gazed at their tablemats. Thursday glanced at her mother, knowing she was thinking of herself and Steve who would both be going away soon. Steve still hadn't volunteered, but he would soon, she knew – probably as soon as Christmas was over. And she herself would be gone in less than a fortnight.

Dinner over, they cleared the table and gathered round the wireless to hear the King's speech. He was speaking not only to his country but to his Empire, thanking them for coming to Britain's aid. '*The Mother Country can never be sufficiently grateful to you,*' he said in his mild, hesitant voice. '*We are all members of the great family of nations which is prepared to sacrifice everything that freedom of spirit may be saved.*' The women had tears in their eyes when he finished, and Walter and Percy cleared their throats.

'Say what you like,' Mary said, as if someone was likely to argue with her, 'he's making a good king. He might be a bit quiet and shy, but to my mind that's better than that brother of his. And he's got a lovely wife and two dear little girls.'

'Princess Elizabeth will be Queen one day,' Jenny remarked. 'I wonder what it feels like, knowing you'll be Queen and eating off gold plates.'

The boys made faces at each other. They weren't interested in royalty and gold plates. Walter switched off the wireless and Leslie produced the Monopoly set he'd been given for Christmas, and they settled down to a game.

'I'd love to go to London,' Jenny sighed, landing her flat iron on Mayfair. 'See all those posh places. Oxford Street – Selfridges – Buckingham Palace. Can't we have a trip up there some time, Mum? It's easy on the train.'

Walter looked at her in exasperation. 'Don't be daft, girl. There's a war on, haven't you heard? London's one of the places they'll bomb first. There'll be no trips to London nor anywhere else until this lot's finished.'

'And you can pay me fifty pounds rent,' Steve told her. 'Mayfair's one of the poshest places of all, and *I own it*!'

The family laughed at Jenny's expression and Thursday felt a sense of relief. For a moment, her father's remark had brought the war vividly back to her mind. She looked round at her family, their faces laughing and happy, and wondered where she, Steve and Leslie would be this time next year, and what they would be doing.

Her eye caught her mother's and she knew by the expression on Mary's face that she was wondering the same thing.

On New Year's Day, there was a royal proclamation that made all men aged between twenty and twenty-seven liable for service in the armed forces.

'That's it,' Steve said. 'I'm going down the recruiting office first thing in the morning.'

'You don't have to,' his mother said, without much hope. 'They're calling up chaps twenty-three and over first.'

'And the rest of us by the end of the year. I can't sit around and wait, Mum. I don't want people calling me a coward. I ought to have done it before.'

Mary sighed and said no more. She knew he couldn't be stopped now. It was only a matter of months anyway.

Thursday was already packing. She was off next day, and her destination was a naval hospital on the south coast, near Portsmouth. 'Right beside the sea,' she said delightedly as she dragged her suitcase down the stairs the following morning. 'Just think, I've never even seen the sea and now I'll be living right beside it! I'll be able to go swimming.'

'You'll have to break the ice first,' Steve commented. Snow had started to fall a day or two after Christmas and it was bitterly cold. The roads were at a standstill and trains were being held up by snowdrifts. Flo and Percy had had a flood when their pipes froze, and people were running out of coal because the trains couldn't get through, and when they did it was almost impossible for the horses to haul the coal trucks through the icy streets.

'Well, I won't be swimming in this weather, dope!' Thursday told him. 'In the summer, I meant.' She looked out of the window at the whirling flakes. 'I don't know what time the train's going to come. The timetables are all over the place. I'll probably catch last Wednesday's 10.45!'

'You don't think you ought to wait a bit? Till the weather eases off a bit?'

'Mum, I've been called up! It's the same as in the Services. I've got to go. It's not a Sunday-school outing.'

They can't wait to get away, neither of them, Mary thought sadly. They think it's a big adventure. And all Thursday is going to be doing is scrubbing floors and wiping people's bottoms, whatever she might think. Wasting all that apprenticeship at the tailor's which would have stood her in such good stead. And it's not as if she couldn't have done war work there, she could have been making uniforms. And as for Steve – she tried to close her mind against what might happen to Steve.

'There'll be only you at home soon,' she told Jenny when Thursday had gone upstairs to fetch a family photograph to squeeze into her suitcase. 'Thank goodness you're too young to get any ideas about going away.'

'I wish I could,' Jenny said. 'I wish I could join the Wrens or the WAAFs. It's not fair, having to stay at home while everyone else gets all the fun.'

'There's not much fun about war,' Mary said sadly. 'Not for mothers, anyway.'

Thursday came downstairs again, with Patch at her heels. She pulled on her tweed coat and blue beret, and then bent and ruffled the dog's ears and laid her face against his rough head. 'Oh, Patchie, I'm going to miss you so much. I wish I could take you with me.'

And that puts us in our place, Mary thought wryly. Never mind her mother and father, or her brother and sister. It's that blessed dog she's going to miss! But as Thursday hugged her to say goodbye, she caught the glint of tears in her eyes and knew that, now that the moment had come, it was as hard for Thursday as it was for herself. For all her brave talk, the girl was shaking with nerves.

'Are you sure you don't want me to come to the station with you?' she asked, but Thursday shook her head.

'It's best to say goodbye here, Mum. I'll only make a fool of myself otherwise.' She held her mother tightly, feeling suddenly like a little girl again, and wishing desperately that she need not go. 'Goodbye, Mum,' she whispered. 'I'll write as soon as I arrive. And – and look after yourself, won't you? Write and let me know everything that happens.'

'I will.' They held each other for a moment longer and then Mary pushed her gently away. 'And whatever I've said about all this – about not wanting you to go and all that – just remember that me and your dad are proud of you. Really proud of you.' She took a deep, shivering breath. 'Go on, now. Go on.'

Thursday went out into the frozen street. She looked up at the morning sky, grey and heavy with yet more snow. She gave her mother one last look, and then turned away, hefting her suitcase to cross the road to the corner.

I don't know why I'm doing this, she thought suddenly. I didn't have to. I could have done what she wanted, and stayed on at the tailor's.

But she knew that she could not have done that. Her eagerness to be doing something special, to see new worlds and different people, to be of real use, would never have allowed to her to take the easy path. This was something she must do, and as she turned the corner and looked back to lift her arm in a last wave, she felt again that tremor of excitement, and knew that what she was doing was the right thing, the only thing.

Squaring her shoulders, she lifted her suitcase a little higher and began to walk into her own new world.

Chapter Five

'Just our luck,' the soldier next to Thursday said gloomily, 'to get caught in a flipping blizzard.'

The train had stopped yet again, out in the middle of nowhere. Thursday, who was next to the window, rubbed the glass with her glove and peered out but there was nothing to be seen but whirling snow, a wasteland of white stretching away for miles. She wondered what time it was and thought about eating the sandwiches Mum had packed for her lunch.

'Could be in the middle of flipping Siberia,' the soldier said. 'In fact, I wouldn't be surprised if we were. The driver hasn't got a flipping clue. I bet he's lost.'

'How can you get lost, driving a train? You have to go where the tracks go.'

'There's tracks go all over the place. If the points are frozen and the signalman can't change them, the train'll just go wherever the track went last time they were changed. We could be in Scotland by now.'

'We could be nearly in London,' Thursday said tartly. She was getting a bit tired of the soldier's gloom. 'We could be nearly there.'

The silence that met this optimistic remark was heavy with doubt. The rest of the passengers who were crammed into the crowded compartment sighed and stared ruefully out of the windows or glanced at each other and muttered resignedly about the weather and delays. It was bitterly cold in the carriage and everyone was wrapped in heavy coats, with thick woollen gloves and scarves. When Thursday had first got on, she'd been going to take off her tweed coat and woollen gloves, but it was so cold she'd kept them on, and now it seemed even colder. There were several soldiers, another girl about Thursday's age, a man with a beard and a couple of middle-aged women festooned with shopping bags. Most of the soldiers were smoking.

Thursday peered out again, hoping to see a sign of habitation somewhere, but there was not so much as a church spire to be seen through the scattering flakes, only a white blanket thrown over empty fields with a blurred huddle of ermine-coated trees in the distance. Maybe he's right, she thought, and we've somehow reached Siberia. Or Scotland. Maybe we're not even on the tracks any more.

The train, which had stopped a quarter of an hour ago with a heavy sigh that seemed to echo the soldier's gloom, gave a sudden shudder and the engine let out a shriek. Everyone looked up hopefully, but after a moment of shaking and rattling, the train subsided once more and the passengers sighed in unison.

'I'm going to see what's up,' the soldier said with sudden decision. He got up and pushed across Thursday to open the door. 'I'm not stopping here to flipping well freeze to death.'

'Don't be daft,' one of the other soldiers said. 'You'll freeze all the quicker out there, and if the blinking train starts again you'll be left behind out in the middle of nowhere.'

'It'd be more sense if we all got out,' he retorted. 'We're buried in a flipping snowdrift, that's what it is, and if we all went and gave a hand clearing it, we'd be able to get moving.' He got the door open and a blast of bitter air and snowflakes swept into the compartment, blowing away the smoke. 'I can see the engine,' he reported, leaning out perilously. 'There's blokes shovelling. Come on.'

He dropped into the snow, landing waist-deep, and began floundering along the track towards the engine. The other soldiers glanced at each other and then got up, muttering that they might as well do something as sit here, and one by one they dropped out of the carriage and followed their comrade. The bearded man and the middle-aged women stayed where they were. Thursday glanced at the other girl.

'I'd go too, if I was wearing trousers.'

'So would I.' The other girl was small and wrapped in a navy overcoat, with dark curly hair peeping out from a scarlet beret. 'But I'd probably disappear completely, it's so deep.'

The snow had been falling ever since they had left Worcester, whipped into a blizzard by a howling wind. There had already been a week of snowstorms, and the roads were almost impassable everywhere. Nobody knew how long the severe weather was likely to last.

'I don't see why they can't let us have weather forecasts,' one of the middle-aged women grumbled. 'The Germans must know what it's like. They're probably getting it too, even worse.'

'Wouldn't make any difference if we did,' her friend said caustically. 'They're never right anyway.'

The bearded man said nothing. The dark-haired girl looked at Thursday and grinned.

'Where are you going? I'm going to train as a nurse. Red Cross VAD.'

'So am I!' Thursday looked at her in delight. 'Maybe we're going to the same place.'

They looked at each other with sudden caution. Everyone had seen the posters warning people not to talk about the war in public places. WALLS HAVE EARS, they declaimed, and there was even a picture of a railway carriage just like this one, showing two people talking with a spy hiding in the luggage rack above them. Thursday glanced involuntarily upwards, and then they both looked at the bearded man who was staring out of the opposite window.

'It'll be good if we are,' the dark-haired girl said, and mouthed the word 'Portsmouth' at Thursday. Thursday nodded and mouthed back 'Haslar', and the dark girl nodded too, her brown eyes sparkling.

Thursday knew nothing about Haslar, other than that it was a naval hospital and that it was not in Portsmouth itself, but in Gosport, the town on the other side of the harbour. The train journey was a long one, with three changes before she would arrive at Portsmouth, where she would be met by a pinnace – whatever that was – to take her across the harbour. She smiled at the other girl, relieved to have company. Perhaps she would know what a pinnace was.

'I suppose we might as well eat our sandwiches,' she said, getting out the greaseproof paper bag. The other girl did the same and they munched companionably for a few minutes. 'What's your name? I'm Thursday Tilford.'

'Thursday?' the other girl said, opening her brown eyes wide. 'You mean like the day?'

'Yes.' Once again, Thursday explained the reason for her name. 'I've got so used to it, it doesn't seem out of the way to me, but everybody else thinks it's queer, of course. I suppose I could tell people to call me Rosemary, since no one's going to know any different, but I'd never remember to answer to it.'

'Oh, no, don't do that! It's nice. I wish I had an unusual name. Mine's Patricia but everyone calls me Patsy. Patsy Martin. I'm from Evesham.'

Thursday nodded. They must have been on the same train from Worcester but in different compartments, coming together only after the second change in their tortuous journey across the Cotswolds. She'd seen Patsy on the platform then.

One of the middle-aged women shifted the bags on her knees and said, 'Nurses, are you? My daughter was a nurse before she got married, in one of the big London hospitals. She's talking about going back to it.'

'We're not nurses yet,' Patsy said. 'And we're not going to be real ones – just VADs.'

'What's that, then?'

'Voluntary Aid Detachment,' Thursday said proudly. 'We'll just help.' She remembered the bearded man and stopped abruptly, then got up and craned out of the window to see what the soldiers were doing by the engine. 'They must have cleared some of the track by now. They've been shovelling like mad.'

'But the snowdrift might go for miles,' Patsy said. 'We could be here all night.'

Thursday shuddered. 'I hope not. We'll freeze to death. Oh – they're coming back.' She drew back as the soldiers clambered back into the compartment, stamping snow from their boots and shaking it from their khaki great-coats. 'Have you managed to clear it?'

'Enough to move a bit further. We're just going into a cutting, see, and it's filled up with flipping snow. There was some blokes digging through from the other end. We're just coming into Guildford.'

'Guildford!' Thursday said in relief. 'That's our last change.' She looked at Patsy and then at the bearded man, wondering if even that was giving away too much.

The soldiers crammed themselves on to the seats again and several got out cigarettes and lit up. The compartment filled once again with smoke and after a few exploratory shudders the train finally gathered itself together and began to rumble along the track. They looked out and saw the white walls of snow, shovelled aside by the soldiers and some of the other passengers. The sky was still heavy with leaden clouds and the afternoon was already begin-ning to grow dark

Patsy had moved up next to Thursday. 'D'you know what a pinnace is?'

'A sort of boat, I suppose. It's to take us across the harbour.' She glanced at the man again, but he was at the other end of the opposite seat and the soldiers were talking too loudly for him to hear. 'Mind you, with this cold the harbour's probably frozen and we'll be able to walk across!'

Patsy giggled. 'I've heard people are skating on the Serpentine, and there's lots of ice on the river at Evesham.'

'There is at Worcester, too.' The Severn was too deep and fast-flowing to freeze over, but there were floes coming down like miniature icebergs. Thursday sighed and rubbed her hands together. 'I'm turning into an iceberg myself. I can't feel my toes at all.'

'You will, when we start to warm up,' Patsy told her. 'That's if we ever do get warm again.'

The scene outside had changed. Houses and other buildings could be seen, and in a few moments the train arrived in the station. Everyone got up stiffly and began to haul luggage down from the racks. The bearded man handed Thursday her suitcase. They'd be supplied with all the clothing they needed in their uniforms, and she had brought only personal possessions and a photograph or two of the family.

'There you are, my dear.' He spoke in a cultured voice, like someone on the wireless, and she felt ashamed of her suspicions. Not that that stopped him from being a spy, she reminded herself. She smiled at him anyway, just to give him the benefit of the doubt, and turned to climb down to the platform. Patsy was waiting, her own bags beside her.

'Got your gas mask?'

Thursday touched the brown cardboard box slung from her shoulder. 'I've got so used to carrying it now, I'd feel naked without it. Where do we go next?'

Patsy nodded across the station. 'That platform over there, and we'd better look nippy, the train's waiting to go. D'you think he really was a spy?'

Thursday grinned and shook her head. 'I reckon he was a vicar! He had a lovely voice. I expect it was one of those women who was a spy. We didn't give away any secrets anyway. Those soldiers talked more than we did.'

They hurried across the station and scrambled aboard the next train, which was already huffing and puffing in readiness to go. The compartments were even more crowded than on the last one, and the girls were forced to sit on their suitcases in the corridor. The train lurched into motion and began to rumble slowly through the silent landscape. The whiteness of the snow gave a glow to the empty fields.

'Just let's hope we don't get stranded again,' Thursday prayed as she tried to keep her balance on the small case. 'I feel as if I've been on trains all my life, and home is just a dream. All I want is a steaming mug of tea and a nice comfortable bed.'

'A hot bath would be nice,' Patsy said wistfully. 'And a cuddly eiderdown. What d'you reckon the chances are?'

'Just about nil, I should think!' Thursday glanced along the crowded corridor. There were two soldiers, but most of the men and women with them now wore naval uniform. She felt a sudden twinge of excitement. These might be the very sailors and Wrens she would be working with at Haslar. Never mind steaming mugs of tea and hot baths – the war work she'd been longing to do was just about to begin!

Portsmouth Harbour station, when they finally reached it in the late afternoon, was the strangest railway station Thursday and Patsy had ever seen.

'It's practically out at sea!' Patsy exclaimed, staring down through the boarded decking to where the murky harbour water surged below. 'It must be built on stilts, like a pier. D'you think it's safe, with all these trains on top?'

'Well, it's been here quite a while. I reckon it would have fallen down by now, if it hadn't been.' Thursday lifted her suitcase and looked around. 'Where do you suppose the pinnace is going to be?'

'It would help if we knew what it was! There are some boats at the end of the platform, see? Perhaps it's one of them.'

The two girls trudged along the platform. An icy wind sliced through the station, bringing a whiff of salt and seaweed. Clouds hung low and yellow over the grey water and although the snow seemed to have stopped for the time being it was obvious that there was more to come. Outlined against the darkening sky they could see the grey silhouette of a ship's prow, and beyond that a clutter of buildings on the opposite shore, dominated by a tall tower.

'I wonder what that is? It's not a church, surely.'

Thursday shrugged. 'I dare say we'll find out.' There were a few more people, mostly in naval uniform, making their way in the same direction. She glanced at a Wren walking beside her and said timidly, 'We're looking for something called a pinnace. D'you know what it is?'

The girl looked at her in surprise, as if not accustomed to being spoken to by a girl in a tweed coat and dark blue beret, carrying a suitcase. Perhaps I ought to have saluted, Thursday thought nervously.

'A pinnace? Yes, of course. It's a small naval launch. Why are you looking for one?'

'We're supposed to be reporting to Haslar Hospital.' Thursday gestured to Patsy. 'We're VADs. Only we've had terrible trouble on the trains and we got delayed. I'm afraid we might have missed the – the pinnace, and I don't know how else to get there.'

The Wren smiled. 'It's all right. I'm going there, too. Just follow me. The pinnace will be waiting at the pontoon.' She marched towards the station exit, smart in her navy uniform, and Thursday and Patsy fell in behind her, thankful to be almost at their journey's end.

'So it's a pontoon now,' Patsy whispered. 'It must be a railway platform where the trains come in and a pontoon where the boats tie up.'

They came out through the big doorways and down the icy steps. They seemed now to be on a wide bridge, with railings on the other side. There were crowds of people tramping through the frozen slush, some heading down the long slipway, others making for the town. Across the bridge was part of the harbour, with small boats rocking on the dark water, and beyond those they could see the great gateway of the dockyard, with the grey bulk of naval ships tied up alongside and mysterious buildings and towers inside the walls. A huge crowd of workmen was pouring out through the gate.

'That tower you can see is the Semaphore Tower,' the Wren told them as they stared. 'The whole harbour's controlled from there. The harbourmaster has his office up high so that he can see all that's going on. The gateway's called the Lion Gate. The dockyardmen are knocking off work – it's always busy then.'

'There's a ship inside,' Thursday said. 'Those masts and – what's it called? – rigging? What sort of ship's that?'

The Wren gave the masts a proud look. 'That's Nelson's ship, HMS *Victory*. You used to be able to go aboard it before the war, and they'd show you round. But no one's allowed in the dockyard now unless they've got an official reason to be there.'

She turned and joined the hurrying throng to stride down the slope towards the little jetty that floated at the bottom. The girls glanced at each other and followed her, lugging their cases. They seemed to have been dragging them about all day, Thursday thought. She had almost forgotten what was inside, but whatever it was it was a lot heavier than when she'd set out that morning.

'Gosh, what a crowd!' she exclaimed to Patsy. 'Where on earth are they all going?'

A man dressed in rough workmen's clothes heard her and grinned. 'We're going home, love, to Gosport. Where else d'you think we'd be going?'

'That's the town across the harbour, where Haslar is,' Patsy said. 'Didn't you look at the map?'

Thursday nodded, annoyed with herself. Of course she'd looked at the map before she'd left home, and seen that Gosport lay on the other side of the harbour, on a little peninsula surrounded by sea and inlets. Haslar itself seemed to be right on the beach, looking out across the Solent towards the Isle of Wight, with a long creek almost cutting it off from the town. Obviously people who lived in Gosport would need a ferry to take them to Portsmouth.

There were several boats fastened to the bollards on the floating pontoon. The dockyardmen were shoving aboard the largest, many of them pushing bikes which they piled on the bow. It didn't seem big enough for such a crowd, Thursday thought, watching in fascination, and wondered what it was like to go to work by boat every day. Nearly as good as working in Venice, she thought with a small giggle.

'Our boat's this way,' the Wren explained briefly, appearing again at their side. 'Come on – no time for staring.'

They turned away and found themselves looking down into a much smaller boat, already filled with sailors and Wrens. One of the sailors, who was obviously in charge, gave them an impatient look.

'Look lively, now. We ain't got all day. Mind how you come, now – we don't all want to end up in the drink. Blimey, ain't you never bin on a boat before?'

'Only a pleasure boat on the river,' Thursday said, scrambling down from the pontoon. The two rocked on the waves, now together, now apart, and she almost fell into the bottom of the boat in her hurry to get aboard before the gap between them widened.

'Strike me pink, you ain't going to make much of a sailor.' The seaman grabbed her arm to steady her. 'Sit down quick, for Gawd's sake. Let's hope they don't never put Wrens in charge of ships.'

'They aren't going to be Wrens,' the girl who had guided them down from the station said sharply. 'They're going to be nurses.'

'Oh, that's all right, then. They can soothe my fevered brow any time.' The sailor went forward to the bow and quickly unwrapped the painter from the bollard, then returned to the helm. The engine changed its note and the boat began to back away from the pontoon and then turned to head off across the harbour.

Bitterly cold as it was, the journey was all too short. Thursday and Patsy, huddled together, stared about them at the busy scene. The light was fading rapidly now but Thursday could see that the harbour stretched far beyond the dockyard jetty to a dim, snow-covered hill beyond. As well as the ships tied to the nearest jetty in the harbour, there were others beyond – great grey battleships with fearsome prows crowded with long-barrelled guns, smaller ones with odd-looking contraptions on their decks. There were other boats too, ferries and tugs, bustling about, each intent on its own business. And when she turned her head to look in the other direction, she gasped.

The harbour mouth, flanked on both sides by solid round bastions that looked as if they'd stood there for hundreds of years, looked far too narrow to admit ships of the size that had obviously come through it. Yet, even as they watched, another ship entered between the fortress-like walls. Huge and grey, it nosed through the gap, almost filling it, and everything else in the harbour slowed to allow it to pass.

'Whatever is it?' Patsy gasped, staring up at the broad, flat deck which overhung the ship's sides. It loomed above them, oddly lopsided yet grimly intimidating.

'Aircraft carrier,' a sailor beside her said briefly. 'That's the *Ark Royal*, that is. Biggest ship in the Navy.'

The very name seemed awesome. The girls watched as

it passed, a swelling wave surging away from its bow and lifting the little pinnace on its bosom. They slid down the other side and rocked a little, but the seaman at the wheel steered it expertly to avoid the worst of the motion.

'Nearly there now.' They turned again to find that they were heading away from the main harbour, into a creek filled with boats of all kinds, from naval launches to yachts and small sailing dinghies. On their left was the tall red brick tower they had noticed when they first arrived and they stared at it curiously.

'Water tower,' their mentor told them. 'And that place there, that's HMS *Dolphin*, where the subs are based.'

'Subs? You mean submarines? Is *that* a submarine?' Thursday gazed at the long, almost tubular shape berthed alongside the quay. Now that she looked, she could see a number of dark, sinister shapes beyond it. She shuddered. 'I'd hate to go down in one of them.'

The creek twisted round another bend and they found themselves alongside a further quay, with a few other launches tied up. The skipper brought the pinnace expertly alongside and another sailor jumped ashore with the painter and wrapped it quickly round a bollard. The passengers began to disembark.

'The hospital's straight on.' The Wren was beside them again. 'Where are you supposed to report?'

'To someone called Miss Makepeace. She's the Red Cross commandant.'

The Wren nodded. 'Well, that's the gate. Go through there and ask someone. Good luck!' She turned away and disappeared into the dusk, and the girls watched her go, feeling suddenly bereft.

'Is that really the hospital?' Patsy whispered as they stared up at the imposing gateway. 'It looks much too grand!'

Timidly, they approached the long brick wall. Through the big iron gates they could see a magnificent red-brick building with tall, very evenly spaced windows and an arched colonnade. Beside the gateway stood two sailors with rifles.

'Who goes there?'

'It's us,' Patsy said, as if they ought to know. 'I mean – we're supposed to be reporting here. We're VADs.'

'VADs? Sounds like something nasty you catch in a foreign port.' The sailors grinned at each other, then stared at them suspiciously. 'Where are your papers?'

'Here.' Thursday lifted her chin defiantly and produced her letter. 'You won't be so cheeky when we're giving you injections!'

'Injections? Yeugh – can't stand needles.' The guard glanced at the papers, then nodded. 'All right – you can go in. Straight through the main building and turn to starboard. D Block's straight ahead. If you get lost, ask a matelot, they'll tell you.' They hesitated and he added impatiently, 'Well, what's the matter now? Cat got your tongue?'

'It's just – what's starboard? And who are the matelots?' Patsy asked, and the two men roared with laughter.

'A matelot's a sailor, ducks,' the other one told her. 'Like us, see, in square rig. *Uniform*,' he added when they looked blank again. '*This* uniform, with bell-bottoms – bell-bottomed trousers – and a round cap and a square collar, see? *We're* matelots. But don't go calling anyone in a suit with a peaked cap a matelot, will you? They're *ratings* – that's if they ain't got scrambled egg on their caps, and then they're officers.'

'And starboard's on the right,' the other added. 'Port – left, starboard – right. Got it?' He grinned. 'Blimey, you ain't half got a lot to learn.'

'I thought we'd come to learn about nursing,' Thursday said, lifting her suitcase again. 'I didn't know we had to learn about the Navy as well.'

'Well, you're *in* the Navy now, or as good as,' the guard told her. 'So you got to learn the lingo, see? And one of the first things you'd better learn is not to distract the guards, or you'll be doing jankers before you even get as far as the door. 'Op it!'

The girls looked at each other and grinned. Once more, they picked up their cases and trudged along the straight, smoothly paved way beneath the arched colonnade. It was almost, Thursday thought, like being in the crypt she had once been allowed to go down under Worcester Cathedral. She felt a strong sense of history, of all the sailors who had come here in the past to be nursed, and a vision of all the sailors who would come here in the future.

'We're here,' she murmured, swept by sudden awe. 'We're actually *here*.'

Miss Makepeace was tall and thin, with a long, narrow face and brown hair pulled tightly back beneath her cap. She looked elegant and aristocratic, her belt pulled in around her narrow waist and her skirts swishing as she walked. Her back was very straight and her uniform looked as crisp as if it were freshly washed and ironed every morning. She had very bright brown eyes that seemed to see everything.

She was in her office when the two girls knocked on the door, as directed by the sailor – *matelot*, Patsy whispered with a nervous giggle. The office was large and cluttered, with maps and charts on the walls and a big square desk behind which Miss Makepeace sat. She regarded them with her bright brown eyes.

'You must be Tilford and Martin. The other girls have all arrived.'

'Our train was delayed. We kept getting stuck in snowdrifts.'

The thin face did not alter its expression. 'Naval time is five minutes *before* time. All naval establishments are treated as if they were seagoing ships, and being late by *even one minute* would mean that you missed your ship. That's the worst crime naval personnel can commit. You must always make sure you have allowed enough time for

77

all contingencies.' She paused to allow her words to sink in, then gave them a smile which lit her face with sudden warmth. 'However, today the ship hasn't sailed without you and I'm very pleased to welcome you aboard. I hope you'll be happy here.'

The smile became more severe, and her voice deepened. 'But the most important thing is that you should be *useful*. This is a major naval hospital, with a fine history. Haslar has cared for wounded servicemen from every major battle fought since Trafalgar and we expect to care for more during this coming conflict. You and your comrades will be in the front line, looking after men who have been injured fighting for their country. Always remember that this is a very great privilege, and always remember that from girls in such a privileged position we expect the *very highest standards*.'

There was a silence. Thursday wanted to look at Patsy but didn't dare. The bright gaze held their eyes, and then the smile broke out again and she knew that she would follow this woman to the ends of the earth.

'You will call me Madam,' Miss Makepeace continued. 'I am the Red Cross commandant here, and I have charge of over two hundred VADs. As you know, you're assistant nurses – the hospital is staffed by the Queen Alexandra Royal Naval Nursing Service, generally known as QARNNS – but you'll be kept very busy and you'll do real nursing. You'll be given training for this and I'll give you your lectures myself, assisted by naval doctors and qualified nurses – QARNNs. I'll also organise your duties and regulate your living conditions. If you have any problems, you may come to me at any time. I will support you and look after you, and in return I expect *complete loyalty*. Do you understand?'

The girls nodded. She'll get it, too, Thursday thought, fascinated. She's like Mr Churchill, she's only got to look at you and you'd do whatever she said.

'Which of you is which?' Madam asked.

'I'm Thursday Tilford, Madam, and this is Patsy Martin.'

Miss Makepeace looked at her. 'Thursday? Is that your real name, or a nickname?'

'It's my real name, Madam. I was born on Armistice Day and my parents wanted to commemorate it. It's my middle name, though – my first name's Rosemary. For Remembrance.'

'Very nice,' Madam said, 'but you'll be called by your surname when you're on duty.' She looked at Patsy. 'And you're Patricia, presumably?'

'Yes, Madam.' Patsy's voice was subdued, her nervous giggle silenced. She sounded close to tears. Miss Makepeace gave her a sharp glance.

'How long is it since you had any food or drink?'

'I can't remember. We had some sandwiches on the train—'

'You must have tea,' the commandant said decisively. 'We can deal with the details later. I'm speaking to all the new intake this evening, after supper. I'll get someone to take you to the mess now, and then you can go to your dormitory and unpack and have a rest. Supper will be at seven, and please don't be late.'

'Or it'll sail without us,' Patsy murmured as they followed her out of the office and, cheered by the prospect of tea and a rest, she gave Thursday a large wink.

The dormitory had about thirty narrow iron beds in it, in two long rows. Tall windows ran along one side but it was now completely dark and the blackout curtains were all in place. We'll have to wait till tomorrow to see if we've got a sea view, Thursday thought. She put down her case for a moment and surveyed the scene.

Each bed was covered with a counterpane, with a large, dark blue anchor embroidered down its centre. Just in case you forget you're in the Navy, she thought with a little grin. The beds themselves had plain black iron frames and the mattresses didn't look all that thick. And there were, of course, no eiderdowns. She hadn't really expected that there would be.

It was warm enough, however, with a big iron stove in the middle of the room, and some of the girls had already settled themselves around it on straight-backed chairs taken from beside the beds, and were drinking out of mugs which stood keeping hot on top of the stove. There was a large coal scuttle nearby, so at least the Navy wasn't mean about keeping its nurses warm.

The dormitory seemed to be full of girls, all wearing a variety of civilian clothes and all doing more or less the same things – writing letters home, sorting out their possessions or just lying on top of the counterpanes. I suppose they're all new too, Thursday thought, or they'd be in uniform. Some were quiet and apparently overwhelmed by their new surroundings, others chattering and animated. Small groups were already forming as they got to know each other. They looked up as Thursday and Patsy came in and some of them smiled. One gave them a friendly wave.

'Put the wood in the hole, you're letting all the fug out. There's some cocoa over here if you want some.'

'Oh, yes, please!' The two girls dropped their bags and went eagerly towards the stove. 'We're freezing – we had an awful journey. One of the soldiers in the carriage said it was like Siberia, and it jolly well was, too!'

'Well, you're here now.' The girl made room for them beside her. She was on the tubby side, with fair hair and very round china-blue eyes. 'My name's Elsie Jackson. You must be the last two – there are only two beds left. They're by mine, over there.' She nodded towards a bed with its counterpane already rumpled and a heap of possessions scattered over it. The two beds next to it were still neat and tidy. 'We get a locker each and we share the cupboards. Bit like being at boarding school!'

Thursday nodded. She was used to sharing a bedroom

with Jenny, but twenty-nine strangers was something different. I hope we'll all get on well together, she thought a little nervously, and caught the eye of another girl, sitting opposite. She was thin and sallow with mousy brown hair, and she looked away quickly when Thursday looked at her. Well, there was one that might be a problem, for a start.

Gratefully, she sipped the mug of cocoa Elsie had handed her. It was hot and rich and made a warming pathway down her middle. The cold that seemed to have got right through to her bones started to ebb a little, and she looked at Patsy and grinned.

'Well, here we are! And we've learned things already. What a pinnace is – and a matelot—'

'And which direction's starboard!' Patsy added. 'And in a minute we're going to find out something else, too. We're going to find out what naval food's like! My Uncle Sam was in the Navy and he says it's lousy.'

'Let's hope he's wrong, then,' Elsie Jackson said, patting her stomach, and Thursday laughed. If anyone looked as though she'd be interested in the food, it was Elsie Jackson!

Suppertime was announced by the ringing of a bell. Still uncertain of their way about, the girls trooped out on to the landing where, to their relief, a nurse in the uniform of a QARNN was waiting. She gave them a brisk smile and led them down to the mess where they were to eat their meals.

'It doesn't seem too bad so far,' Thursday whispered to Patsy. 'I mean, she seems quite friendly, doesn't she. I thought nurses were all dragons.'

'That's sisters. And matrons,' Patsy whispered back. 'In any case, this is just the first evening. You wait till tomorrow, when we get on the wards. I bet it'll be different then!'

Tomorrow. By then, I'll have been away from home for a whole day and night, Thursday thought. She pictured

81

what they'd be doing at home now – sitting round the table in the cosy living room, having their own supper and listening to the news. She thought of her own chair, empty for the first time, and her eyes prickled.

I'll write to Mum as soon as we get back to the dormitory, she thought. I'll write and tell her everything.

It seemed insulting to say that Miss Makepeace looked like a horse, even a friendly one. It made her sound ugly, and she wasn't. Thursday crossed out the last three lines in her letter and tried to find another way of describing their commandant.

'What on earth are you finding to write about?' Patsy enquired. She was lying on her bed in the long dormitory, having scribbled no more than a postcard to send home. 'All we've done is arrive, unpack and have supper!'

Thursday glanced at her locker, with the photo of the family standing on the top. Most of the girls had put photographs on show. Patsy had a photo of a young soldier beside her family. She'd told them it was her boyfriend.

'They'll want to know about the journey and what it's like here, and all about Portsmouth—'

'We haven't seen anything *of* Portsmouth! All we did was walk down the pontoon and come over the harbour in that boat.'

'Well, that was interesting, wasn't it? All those ships, and the submarines. My dad and brother will like reading about them.'

'I don't think you ought to write about those things.' Elsie rolled over and looked serious. 'Someone might think you're a spy.'

Thursday stared at her. 'But no one else is going to read it!'

'I wouldn't be too sure about that. I bet letters from here are censored. It's a naval establishment, isn't it. You don't want to get into trouble.'

Thursday looked down at the letter. She had covered several sheets of paper with her untidy scrawl, describing the hours they had spent stuck in the blizzard, the strangeness of Portsmouth Harbour station, the journey across the harbour and, finally, their arrival at the hospital. She'd tried to make it interesting and funny so that the family would enjoy reading it. Now it looked as if her efforts were wasted.

'Just tell 'em you've arrived, it's snowing just as much as it is at home and the food's lousy,' Patsy advised. 'That's all I've said.'

'I'm not sure I'll even get away with that,' Thursday said gloomily. 'Even the wireless isn't allowed to say what the weather's like.'

'And it's probably unpatriotic to complain about the food,' Elsie observed. She seemed tired out and ready to go to sleep. She must have had an even longer journey than they'd had, Thursday thought, but when they went to supper they'd got separated and there hadn't been a chance to ask.

'It was funny, coming over by pinnace instead of the ordinary ferryboat,' Elsie said thoughtfully. 'I felt quite important!'

'Have you been here before, then?' Patsy enquired, and Elsie laughed.

'I should think so! I'm Pompey born and bred. Portsmouth,' she added, seeing their blank faces. 'I've lived here all my life, and I've got a granny in Gosport, so we've always been back and forwards across the ferry.'

'You had the shortest journey of any of us!' Thursday said, laughing. 'I thought you must have come hundreds of miles, you seem so tired.'

'Well, of course I'm tired,' Elsie retorted with a grin. 'We had a bit of a beano last night at home, to give me a send-off. Didn't get to bed till three this morning.'

'But why do you have to live in?' Patsy asked. 'Couldn't you go home every night if you live so near?'

'Well, they want us on hand, don't they? Anyway, I wanted to live in. I'm a mobile really, it's just that this is where I've been sent. Doesn't mean to say I'll stay here.'

'Why not?'

'Well, we can get sent anywhere – abroad, even. My auntie was a VAD in the last war and she went to Malta. She said it was gorgeous, always hot and sunny, and they spent all their time off swimming and sunbathing. I'm going to volunteer if I get the chance – anything to get away from this sod-awful winter.'

Thursday glanced at her in surprise. She wasn't used to hearing women swear so casually. Mr Robertson, at the tailor's shop, discouraged even the men from swearing, at least when the girls were present.

'You were pretty late, weren't you?' Elsie went on. 'I thought we were all supposed to report at two o'clock.'

'We were, but the train kept getting stuck in the snow. The soldiers had to dig it out. We didn't think we were going to get here at all.'

Elsie shuddered. 'Did you notice those huge icicles under the platform at the harbour station? They must be about fifteen feet long – it's like Cheddar caves down there. And there's ice all along the sea wall.'

Neither Thursday nor Patsy knew what the sea wall was, but they were too tired to ask more questions. Thursday gave up any idea of starting her letter again and folded the sheets away. She picked up her soap and towel and slid off the narrow iron bed.

'I'm going to wash and then get into bed. We're not going to get much rest tomorrow.'

'Not if Miss Makepeace's – Madam's – "little talk" is anything to go by,' Patsy agreed. 'I didn't take in half she said. Except that if we're seen standing still we'll be given something else to do. Still, I dare say she'll go over it all again in the morning.'

'We get our kit in the morning.' Thursday looked at the long room with its narrow beds, its plain washstands and the one long cupboard which they were all to share as a wardrobe. The only sign that it was part of a naval establishment were the blue anchor emblems in the centre of each counterpane. Perhaps tomorrow, with their nurses' uniforms and capes and other bits and pieces scattered about, it would look more like the Navy. Or perhaps, with naval discipline, you weren't allowed to scatter things about.

In the washroom, queueing with other girls for a turn at one of the basins and then scrubbing her teeth with Gibbs' toothpaste from its little round tin, she listened to the chatter and felt suddenly homesick. I wonder what they're doing at home now, she thought. Just finishing supper – something on toast, and a cup of cocoa. Dad's giving Patchie a bit of toast with some fish paste on it and Steve's reading his *Hotspur*. And Jenny's just realised there's a hole in her stocking and she's just got to darn it before she goes to bed.

It all seemed very far away. She wondered if they'd be thinking of her too, noticing the empty chair at the table and missing her. Mum would, and so would Dad. Steve and Jenny would be just pleased to have some extra space. Yet at the thought of them her eyes filled with tears and she felt a sudden painful ache in her throat.

'If you've finished, there's a few more of us would like to use the basin,' a voice said in her ear, and Thursday moved out of the way with a muttered apology. She made her way back to the dormitory, feeling lost and uncertain.

The other two girls were already in bed. Elsie was asleep again, and Patsy did no more than open one eye and mutter goodnight. Within a few minutes the last girl came in and put out the light.

They lay in the darkness, listening to the muffled sound of waves on the shore. Thursday heard sobbing from a distant corner, and a long, trembling sigh from the next bed. She reached out a hand and felt about until her

85

fingers encountered Patsy's, and they held each other tightly.

'It'll be better in the morning,' she whispered. 'We'll all feel better in the morning.'

Chapter Six

'Haslar Hospital,' Miss Makepeace began, 'was opened in 1750. It was one of the first proper naval hospitals and the largest hospital in Europe at the time. Before that, sick and wounded sailors weren't treated in any proper way – they either died at sea or they were sent to local lodging houses or even alehouses to recover. There was a sort of hospital in Gosport, at the end of what is now Whitworth Road – it was called the Fortune Hospital, and the area there is still called Forton. But it was a shambles, no more than a clutter of tumbledown shacks, and I doubt if anyone actually got better through the nursing they received there. Things are very different today.'

She paused and fixed her piercing eyes on the forty or so girls who sat before her, like children in a classroom. They gazed back, already held in thrall by her personality and by the history she was giving them of the proud hospital of which they were now a part. That's nearly two hundred years old, Thursday thought. Sailors have been coming here for nearly two hundred years to be nursed and treated and made better.

'Not all of them recovered, of course,' Miss Makepeace went on, as if reading her mind. 'There are many thousands of men buried here at Haslar. For one thing, it had been used for some time already as a common burial ground, and then when it became a naval hospital a great many of its patients were already beyond help when they arrived. It's been recorded that in the years of 1779 and 1780 over seventeen hundred men died and were buried here. Then there were the six hundred men, including their admiral, who died when the *Royal George* capsized two years later. There were thousands of soldiers who came back from the battle of Corunna with Sir John Moore and died of typhus – doubtless, you all learnt about that in your history lessons at school – and it's also said that over three and a half thousand were buried in the paddock ten years before that. There was a Turkish colony in Gosport, who were also buried here—'

'Is that why it's called Turktown?' Elsie broke in, and then as Miss Makepeace stopped talking and everyone turned to stare at her, she added in some confusion, 'Well, that's what we call it in Pompey, and I've always wondered why.'

'Of course, you live in Portsmouth, don't you, Jackson?' Miss Makepeace observed. 'Well, I dare say that is indeed the origin of the term. And now, if I may continue . . .'

Haslar Hospital had, it seemed, a chequered history. The girls discussed it as they came out of the classroom and into the big quadrangle.

'Imagine all those bodies, buried under our feet!' Patsy shuddered. 'I tried to add them up as she went along but I lost count at five and a half thousand, and she didn't even say how many thousands there were who came back from – where was it?'

'Corunna,' Thursday said solemnly. 'We learnt about it at school. Miss Makepeace said so.'

'Well, *you* might have done! I never listened much in history lessons, all those kings and queens having their heads cut off. It was nothing but dead people and now we've got them here, under our feet.' She looked down at the ground. 'They must be crammed together like sardines.'

'It's a nice place, though, isn't it?' Thursday looked around at the long, rectangular buildings on each side of the big square. 'Smart, I mean. It doesn't really look like a hospital at all. Not like the one in Worcester, anyway.'

'A lot of places round here look like this,' Elsie

remarked. 'With those rectangular windows all separated into squares. It's called Georgian.'

'I suppose because one of the Georges was on the throne then. Let's have a look at the little church.'

They strolled across the quadrangle, only to be halted by a yell from a man standing at the edge. He waved his arms at them and they hesitated, then turned back the way they had come.

'No – come *here*! I want a word with you.'

'In trouble already,' Thursday murmured. 'Is he an officer, Patsy?'

'Must be, he's got a lot of gold on his cap.' Nervously, the girls approached and stopped a few yards away from the officer. He glowered at them.

'Don't you young girls know it's an offence to walk across the quad? Who are you, anyway?'

'We're VADs,' Patsy answered. 'We only arrived yesterday. We don't really know anything yet.'

'Hasn't your commandant given you any information at all?'

'Yes, sir, she told us about Haslar being built and how many dead bodies there are, and—'

'Don't be impertinent!' The officer had a full beard and moustache, and heavy brows that came right down over his eyes. He looked, Thursday thought suddenly, like a sheepdog, and she stifled a nervous giggle. His glance shifted to her at once.

'Something to say, gel?'

'No, sir,' Thursday answered hastily. 'Only – we're sorry, sir, we didn't know. We won't do it again.'

'Hmph.' He glared at them for a moment or two, then gave a small, impatient jerk of his head. 'Very well. On your way. Just remember in future, understand? And tell that commandant of yours to keep you in better order!'

'Yes, sir,' the girls chorused, knowing that they would never dare tell Miss Makepeace any such thing, and they turned and scuttled away.

'Whew!' Thursday said when they were out of earshot. 'I wonder who he is.'

'An admiral at least, I should think,' Patsy said. 'Did you see all that gold on his cap? Enough to keep me for six months! Where are we going? I thought we were going to look at the church.'

'We'll leave that for another day,' Thursday said. 'I'm not risking the quad again! Anyway, I want to see the sea. It must be this way.'

'We haven't got much time,' Elsie warned. 'We've got to be back in fifteen minutes.'

They walked quickly towards the wall which surrounded the hospital and found a gate. And beyond the gate was the sea.

'Oh!' Thursday exclaimed in delight. 'Oh, look at that!'

They stood still, looking at the sight before them. The hospital was built right to the edge of the shore, with a protective sea wall sloping down into the sea from the road that ran outside the walls. It was outside the harbour itself and looked across at the city of Portsmouth in one direction and to the Isle of Wight in the other. The clouds of the day before had cleared away and snow lay everywhere, covering the buildings with shimmering ice. There was a fringe of ice all along the sea wall.

'It's like fairyland,' Thursday said in awe. 'It's so pretty!'

'Is that a cathedral?' Patsy asked, looking at the dome that could be seen in the midst of the city buildings. 'I suppose Portsmouth must have a cathedral.'

'Course it does,' Elsie answered. 'It's a city, isn't it? That's the old part of Pompey you can see from here. It's a bit slummy but it's sort of interesting, too – quaint, you know.'

'Pompey?' Patsy queried. 'What's that? Is it part of Portsmouth?'

Elsie laughed. She had a loud, rather raucous laugh, but it wasn't intended to make Patsy feel silly. It was just

Elsie's laugh. 'Pompey's *Portsmouth*! Didn't you know that? I thought everyone did. It's a sort of nickname. They use it for the football team, too – we've even got the Pompey Chimes on the Guildhall clock.' She chanted the notes of a chiming clock. ' "*Play up, Pompey! Pompey, play up!*" '

'I don't know anything about football,' Thursday said, 'but my dad does the pools and my brother's football mad.' She gazed across the harbour again. 'We'll have to go over there some time. Mum'll want to know about Portsmouth and so will Dad and Steve. They're always going on about the football team.'

'Best in the country,' Elsie said. 'Well, they must be, they won the FA Cup last May, didn't they? You can get to Portsmouth two ways,' she went on. 'Either the ordinary ferry that goes to where the station is, or the floating bridge. It works on chains – they pull it from one side to the other, and it takes cars, too. It goes to Old Portsmouth, so you end up miles from Commercial Road, but it's handy for getting to Southsea. That's Southsea, where the pier is. We used to go out there on Sundays on the bus, and go swimming. It's good – there's a boating lake and rock gardens, and a fair at Clarence Pier, see?'

'Fancy being able to go swimming in the sea whenever you want to,' Thursday said enviously. She looked down at the sea wall. 'D'you think we could go swimming here in summer? Is it safe?'

Elsie shrugged. 'I think so. People do, but it's deep when the tide's up. It comes right up the wall, see, so it's deep straight away.'

'What are those big things out at sea?' Patsy asked. 'They look like forts.'

'They are. This part of the Solent's called Spithead, see, and those are the Spithead Forts. They were built about a hundred years ago when people thought France was going to invade us. There are forts all around here. You can see them up on the hill.'

'What hill?'

'Portsdown Hill. It's at the top of the harbour. You can see the forts on top of it, and there's lots more in Gosport. They've got moats round them.'

'Forts and moats all over the town,' Thursday said. 'Gosh, it sounds really interesting.'

Elsie stared at her. '*Gosport's* not interesting. There's nothing here at all. You want to see Pompey.' The girls turned and began to make their way back for Miss Makepeace's second lecture. 'Pompey's *much* better!'

The next lecture introduced them to naval routine and discipline. Although the VADs, being part of the Red Cross, were not strictly in the Navy, they were attached to it and subject to the same rules and regulations that ordered the sailors' lives. Some of them were quite incomprehensible.

'No cycling along the quarter-deck?' Thursday echoed in a whisper. 'What's the quarter-deck? I thought that was part of a ship.'

'Haslar Hospital *is* a ship,' Miss Makepeace said. She seemed to have ears that would hear the slightest whisper, as well as eyes that saw everything. 'To all intents and purposes, anyway. As I've already told you, all shore establishments are treated as if they were ships and the same regulations apply. They're given names like ships – for instance, we have HMS *Hornet* and HMS *Dolphin* next to us here at Haslar, and HMS *Vernon* over the water – and sometimes you'll hear them called "stone frigates". Then, when the men go to sea, they slip naturally into the routine. There's a good reason for everything in the Navy, you'll find.'

'Like not being late because the ship might sail without you,' Patsy said boldly.

Miss Makepeace nodded. 'But the ship *will* sail without you,' she corrected. 'There's no "might" about it. And don't forget there are good reasons for that, too. A harbour's a busy place, with a great many ships all carrying on their own business. And all subject to the tide. In a place like Portsmouth Harbour, with such a narrow entrance, only one ship can go in or out at a time. There are only certain states of the tide in which some of the larger ships can go through at all. You can see why every minute begins to count, and if we had half a dozen ships all waiting for personnel who were a few minutes late, there would very soon be chaos.'

The girls nodded. Put like that, it was easy to understand. And it wasn't fair for the sailors to have to obey those rules if the nurses were allowed to be lax. In any case, Thursday thought, patients were entitled to have their nursing treatment on time.

'And while we're on the subject of the patients,' Madam said, 'please remember that there's to be *no* fraternisation. That means no little romances. You're here to treat them, not flirt with them – even though the men themselves may think differently. A little bit of humour and a few pleasantries are perfectly acceptable to ease their burdens, but there are to be no assignations. That must be understood.'

The girls nodded, some a little ruefully. They'd all read stories in which hospitals were romantic places, with lots of opportunity for finding sweethearts.

'Shame!' Patsy whispered. 'I was looking forward to a bit of – what did she call it? – fraternising.'

At last the lecture was over and they were allowed to ask questions. Thursday put up her hand.

'I still don't understand what the quarter-deck is,' she said. 'And why we're not allowed to cycle along it. We haven't even got bikes!'

Miss Makepeace smiled. 'A lot of my girls do have their bicycles here. You'll soon find how useful they are for getting into Gosport and even over to Portsmouth. The quarter-deck on a ship is traditionally that part where the officers and rather superior passengers would take the air.

Sailors would only be permitted there to carry out essential tasks or wait upon the officers. It's still treated with great respect – and on a shore establishment the same respect applies. The quarter-deck at Haslar is the long avenue which leads to the chapel. You may walk along it, but that's all. No matter *how* much of a hurry you may be in,' she added, fixing Patsy with a gimlet eye.

'I don't know why she looked at *me* when she said that,' Patsy complained afterwards as they went for lunch. 'Do I *look* the sort of person who's always late for things?'

Thursday glanced at her and grinned. There *was* something about Patsy, with her curly hair already escaping from its pins and her stockings wrinkled, that looked as if she might have dressed rather hastily. 'I expect it was just coincidence,' she said solemnly. 'I don't suppose she really meant to look at you at all.'

Patsy looked at her suspiciously. 'All right. I know I'm not the tidiest person in the world. Anyway, we're getting our uniforms this afternoon, so then we'll all look the same.'

The issuing of uniforms had been intended to take place that morning, after the medical, but there had been some hold-up in the stores and it had been rescheduled for the afternoon. Thursday was quite relieved. The medical itself had been quite bad enough, she thought, what with having to strip off in front of everyone else and being examined for nits just as if you were a kid at school. Auntie Maudie used to do that, she remembered, go round the schools and examine children's hair with a fine-toothed comb. The children hated it, and Auntie Maudie hadn't been too keen either and had always had a good wash as soon as she got home, in case she'd caught any herself.

Thursday had had them once, when she was about eight, and she remembered the horrible black shampoo her mother had had to use, stinking of tar, and the way she'd combed through Thursday's hair every morning, pouncing on the tiny creatures and cracking their minute eggs. It had made Thursday feel sick to think of things living in her hair, and the thought of it made her want to scratch her head even now.

Lunch was in the mess, a big canteen where the meals were served by a long line of cooks. The whole place had been run by sailors until the war started, but now Wrens were starting to take over some of their domestic duties, to free the men to go to sea. They dolloped heaps of mashed potatoes, tinned peas and minced beef on the plates held out to them, and the girls found a table and sat down to eat. There were other new girls, too, and they introduced themselves – Vera Hapgood, a thin, sallow-faced girl with mousy brown hair, Jeanie Brown, pretty with a round, smiling face and light brown curls, Ellen Bridges, who was tall and bony but had nice eyes, and a rather aristocratic girl called Louisa Wetherby. In all, there were about forty new VADs.

'I'll be glad when we've got our uniforms,' Jeanie Brown said, tweaking her plaid skirt. She had a soft voice with a touch of a Scottish accent. 'We stand out like sore thumbs in civvies. I feel like a visitor!'

'They say we won't be allowed to wear our civvies at all then,' Vera said discontentedly. 'Not even to go out. I must say, I think that's going too far. It's not as if we're in the proper Navy or anything.'

'It's as bad as being back at school,' Louisa agreed. 'Impossible to sneak out at night to meet the boys because we didn't have anything to wear that didn't immediately shout out that we were from the Abbey!'

The others looked at her. 'Did you go to boarding school, then?' Patsy asked.

'Mmm. In Malvern.' Louisa reached for the salt.

'That's near where I live!' Thursday exclaimed. 'I come from Worcester, and my auntie lives in Ledbury. We used to go to the Malvern Hills for picnics.'

'Oh, it's a nice enough place,' Louisa allowed. 'It's just that we were never let out without a bodyguard. Well, they *called* her a matron but she was more like a prison warder. I suppose it was because of all those boys' schools down the road – the whole place is seething with boarding schools, girls' and boys'.'

'Is it really like the stories say?' Patsy asked curiously. 'Being at boarding school, I mean? Midnight feasts and all that?'

Louisa laughed. 'If only it had been! We were kept on the run so much we were always too tired to think about midnight feasts. Lessons, sports, prep – it never stopped. I tell you, nursing won't be any worse than that – nothing could be.'

'Well, at least you probably had decent facilities,' Ellen Bridges remarked. 'Bathrooms and things. Our school didn't even have proper lavs. We had to go down the yard to a privy with an earth bucket.'

'Where do you come from, then?' Thursday asked. 'You sound as if you're from Devon.'

'Dorset,' Ellen corrected her. 'A little village near Bridport. I thought I might get sent to Plymouth, there's a naval hospital there – I was quite surprised when I was told to come to Haslar.'

The other two girls both came from London. Vera Hapgood was from Wandsworth and Jeanie Brown from Chalk Farm. Her parents were Scottish, she said, which was why she had a faint accent.

'There are lots of other VADs here,' Thursday remarked, looking round. There was a table near them full of girls in the grey dresses and white aprons of the Red Cross, with the cross itself stitched prominently to the bibs. They were laughing and chatting with animation, and looked relaxed and sure of themselves. Thursday wondered if she would ever feel so confident. 'I feel a bit like I did on my first day at school!'

'Having uniforms will help,' Louisa confirmed. 'And finding our way around. It's like going to boarding school

– you think you'll never know which way to go, but you soon learn.'

The others looked at her. None of them had been to boarding school, but Louisa was clearly a 'posh' girl who lived in a big house and whose family had money. There were a number of VADs like her – Thursday had already noticed the accents of girls who came from similar backgrounds and would probably never have even been inside a two-up, two-down back-street house, or played out in the street. They were girls who didn't need to earn their living, girls who could have been officers in the women's services, but wanted to nurse and so had volunteered as poorly paid VADs.

'Taking jobs away from them that needs them,' Vera Hapgood whispered to Patsy, who was sitting next to her, but Patsy rounded on her.

'Doing jobs that need to be done, I'd say! They didn't *have* to volunteer, they just wanted to help, and they'll skivvy the same as the rest of us. I think it's good that they're not too proud to get their hands dirty.'

Vera looked down her nose and turned away. The other girls were chattering and nobody else noticed the exchange except Thursday, who was sitting on Patsy's other side. She raised her eyebrows at Patsy, and Patsy shrugged. There was bound to be one who was a cat, but what did it matter? There were plenty of other girls who looked nice.

Issued an hour or two later with their own grey dresses and white aprons, together with black lisle stockings, a navy petersham belt and sturdy black shoes, they began to feel almost like nurses. They giggled as they tried to put on their caps, setting them on each other's curls and regarding the results in a mirror.

'It looks like a water lily,' Ellen Bridges said, turning her head this way and that as she looked in the mirror. 'I think it's quite smart, really.'

'I think it looks more like a mating hen!' Patsy said, with a giggle. 'Look at the back – it's like a lot of feathers stuck up in the air! I just hope none of those male pigeons on the quad mistake me for a female.'

'You're disgusting,' Vera Hapgood told her. 'It's what comes from living in the country, I suppose. You see it going on all the time.'

'Go on, I bet you've seen dogs at it in the street! My auntie's bitch – *lady dog*, I suppose you'd call her,' she added, seeing Vera's shocked expression, 'got out once and half the dogs in the neighbourhood had a go before they managed to catch her. The puppies were lovely,' she added reminiscently. 'All fluffy. We reckoned it was the sheepdog from the farm that caught her. We found homes for all of them.'

'These shoes are a bit clumpy,' Elsie said, disregarding Patsy's stroll down memory lane. 'I like my high heels better. But the belt's nice, the way it pulls your waist in. You're lovely and slim,' she said enviously to Thursday. 'I wish I was slim like you.'

'You could be,' Vera said, 'if you didn't have so much mashed potato.'

Elsie ignored her. 'Anyway,' she said, 'I take after my mum, and my dad says men like a nice cuddly armful.'

Thursday reached into her bag and took out the little box containing the small watch Auntie Maudie had given her. She opened it and hesitated, feeling self-conscious about pinning it on. Elsie peered over her shoulder.

'Oh, isn't that smashing! Where d'you get it?'

'It was my auntie's. She's a registered nurse. D'you think I'll be allowed to wear it?' She held it up and some of the other girls crowded round to look as well.

Vera sniffed. 'I don't expect they'll let you. You know what Madam said about no jewellery.'

'It's a proper nurse's watch, isn't it?' Patsy said. 'I don't see why you shouldn't wear it.'

'Well, then, it'll be only sisters who are allowed to wear that sort of thing,' Vera said, but Elsie turned on her.

'You're just being nasty, getting your own back about

the *bitch*.' She emphasised the word deliberately. 'We'll ask Nurse Stanway. She'll tell us.'

Helen Stanway, the senior VAD who had brought them over to the clothing store, looked at Thursday's watch and nodded. 'Not many VADs do wear them, but there's no rule against it. So long as it keeps good time – a watch that gains or loses wouldn't be allowed. They're much better than wristwatches because you'll be forever putting your hands in water.' Elsie gave Vera a triumphant look, and Stanway turned away and clapped her hands for attention. 'Now that you're all ready, we're going on a tour of the hospital. You need to know all the wards, as there's no knowing where you'll be assigned at any time, and you also need to know where to go for supplies. Tomorrow you'll be on the wards. Remember that Haslar's a big hospital and there isn't time to go searching for girls who've got lost, so please pay attention.'

Outside, the clouds had begun to gather again and there were flurries of snow whipping like white sandstorms over the bleak expanse of the quadrangle. The girls wrapped their cloaks around them and scurried behind the older VAD. They stopped just outside the main entrance and looked in awe at the gracious buildings and grand façade.

'That is the coat of arms of George the Second,' Stanway said importantly. 'The lion and the unicorn. That's because it was in his reign that the hospital was built. That's why it looks as it does, because a lot of important buildings were built that way then. It was the fashion at the time.'

'See?' Elsie whispered. 'Georgian. Told you, didn't I?'

Helen led them at a brisk pace back through the entrance and they marched down the long, tree-lined avenue of the quarter-deck towards the chapel. It was just like a proper church, Thursday thought, and when she said so Stanway nodded.

'It *is* a church. It's dedicated to St Luke, because he's the patron saint of doctors.' She waved her hand around at the pews and the gallery with its organ. 'They have services every Sunday and during the week, and funerals when a patient dies. I think officers can get married here, too. You'll all be expected to attend divine service, of course, unless you're of some other denomination.' She led them back along the quarter-deck and under the arches again. 'We'll go down to the cellars next.'

'Ugh,' Patsy said. 'Do we have to? I don't like dark underground spaces.'

Stanway smiled. 'Well, you may be seeing quite a lot of these so you'll have to get over that, I'm afraid. But wait and see – you might be in for a surprise.'

The girls trooped down the steps, stopping to stare in amazement as Stanway opened the big doors and led them into the vast space beneath the hospital.

'But it's all done out like a hospital itself!' Thursday said at last.

Helen Stanway nodded. 'That's right. It's in case of air raids. If there's a red alert we'll be able to bring the patients down here, and quite a number of stretcher cases, too. The aim is to keep everyone safe.' She turned to lead them through into a further space. 'But this is the real showpiece. Do you know what this is?'

The girls stared around them. Like the rest of the cellars, the floor was of brick and the ceiling beamed with huge slabs of wood that stretched from wall to wall. Doorways led to other cellars, and beyond those could be seen even more doorways. But in the middle of the underground room in which they stood now was a long table, and at the sides were long counters and trolleys bearing sterilisers and other medical equipment.

'It's an operating theatre!' Thurdsay said. 'It's a bit like the one at the cottage hospital where my auntie works – only a lot bigger.'

'Haslar's a big hospital – we have to be ready for anything. Most hospitals just get in a few serious patients each day, unless there's a disaster of some kind – though that'll probably change when the air raids start. But Haslar is always ready for a disaster. Even in peacetime we always have to be on standby, in case a ship sinks, for instance, and we may get a sudden influx of patients with serious injuries. That's why before the war started, the hospital sometimes seemed quite empty – the beds were there for emergencies. But when there's a war on, the emergencies will be much more frequent. In fact, they'll probably become quite normal.'

She spoke quite unemotionally, but Thursday felt a shiver run down her spine at the words. She looked at the long table, and at the instruments and bottles ranged on shelves and in cupboards around the walls, and thought of operations taking place while aircraft thundered overhead, while an air raid raged all around. Would you hear the bombs dropping, down here under the ground? She thought of stretcher after stretcher of men being unloaded from ships – injured men, men with broken limbs, burns, bleeding wounds. She thought of the QARNNs, the male sick-berth attendants, the doctors and the VADs themselves, fighting to save the men while the men fought above their heads; while yet more men were injured.

The war was suddenly very real. And when she looked around at the faces of her fellow VADs, she could see that they felt it, too.

They came back up the stairs and Stanway showed them the smoothly paved way with its metal tracks that ran down the middle of the wide corridor.

'I noticed these before,' Patsy said. 'They're like a miniature railway.'

'They were for the carts that brought patients from the boats,' their guide informed them. 'Most of them came from ships that were coming back from war and anchored off Spithead. They had to be transferred to the hospital ships first – those were old ships, anchored in the harbour – and then brought to Haslar by another boat. Then they were loaded on to carts, like little trams, and brought straight into the hospital.'

'I bet they were glad to get here, after all that,' Thursday remarked feelingly. 'All that being carried from one ship to another, and tossed about by the sea!'

'From what Miss Makepeace – Madam – said this morning, a lot of them didn't live long anyway,' Patsy agreed. 'Seems it was more like a funeral home than a hospital!'

Helen Stanway gave her a severe look and for the first time her unemotional guide's voice began to show real feeling. 'Haslar has always had a fine reputation. It was the first and biggest hospital of its kind and it's going to be even more valuable during this war. We're in the front line here at Portsmouth Harbour, and you're very lucky to have been sent here. What we do here is going to be something to be proud of.'

They stared at her, taken aback by the sudden passion in her voice, and then Thursday said quietly, 'I think it will. And I'm proud to be here, for one. And I bet everyone else is, too.'

'That's right!', 'So am I!' and 'Three cheers for Haslar!' cried the other girls. 'Hip, hip, hooray! Hooray! Hooray!'

The corridor echoed to the sound of their cheering and heads popped out of side doors and wards to see what was going on. Miss Makepeace herself came striding around a corner, her brows lifted as she looked at the gathering in their brand-new uniforms and capes.

'Whatever's going on here?' She looked at the VAD. 'Stanway, have you any explanation for this extraordinary conduct?'

The senior girl blushed. 'I was just showing them round, Madam, and explaining what a fine hospital Haslar is, and how much it's going to do to help the war effort. And then they all just started to cheer.'

'I see.' The commandant's face was stern as she looked at the now silent girls, but Thursday was sure she could detect a twinkle somewhere deep in those bright brown eyes. 'Well, I'm pleased to see that you understand the value of our work here, and the privilege we've been given to be a part of it,' she told them severely. 'But please remember that this is a *hospital*. There are sick people here, people who need rest and quiet and care. People who do *not* want their afternoon's rest disturbed by what sounds like a football crowd applauding a goal. Is that understood?'

The girls nodded, subdued by her tone. 'Yes, Madam.'

'Good.' She looked them over for a moment and then her smile broke out, transforming her entire face. 'You may continue with your tour. I'll see you again after tea for another lecture, and then you'll be free for the rest of the evening. And tomorrow . . .' She surveyed them again. 'Tomorrow, you'll be on the wards.'

On the wards! The girls looked at each other and made faces of excitement and apprehension. Then they turned and trooped after Helen Stanway for their first glimpse of those wards and the patients they would be helping to care for.

There was so much to learn in that first week.

Like the other VADs, Thursday had done a course in first aid when she had joined the Red Cross. But knowing how to give artificial respiration to a friend who was pretending to have drowned and bandaging portions of that same long-suffering friend that weren't really bleeding were very different from dealing with the real thing. It hadn't prepared her at all for what she was to encounter on the wards of Haslar.

'Your job is to make the tasks of the nurses and SBAs easier,' Miss Makepeace told them. 'At this stage, that means the more mundane tasks – but always remember that these are *just as essential* as the more skilled ones. A patient who is desperate for a bedpan *feels* just as much in need as one who is waiting to have a dressing changed.

Possibly more. And the cleanliness of the ward is a priority. Hygiene is all.'

'And what that boils down to is that we're skivvies,' Elsie muttered as they collected dusters and brushes from the cupboard. 'Catch them letting *us* change dressings.'

'VADs do, though. And when the SBAs go to sea . . .'

The SBAs were sick-berth attendants, the naval term for male nurses. There were a number at Haslar, but there was always the chance that they'd be sent to sea, and the VADs were more or less on standby for that event. Until that happened, they worked together but the SBAs had varying attitudes to the young civilians.

'You're in the Navy now. Brightwork means *bright*-work. It's no good just giving them taps a bit of a wipe, you need to be able to see your face in them. Use a bit of elbow grease.'

'And don't let anyone send you to the stores for it,' Elsie advised with a grin. 'I knew someone who spent half an hour waiting for a tub and then got torn off a strip when they went back to the ward, just for being daft enough to believe it. The Navy's full of jokes like that – paint for the last post, that sort of thing.'

'It's the language I can't keep up with,' Patsy complained. 'I've managed to remember that the floor's always called the deck, and the kitchens are galleys, but I still forget to call the lavatories the "heads". Honestly, it's just like little boys playing games. I mean, I know a lot of it is so that when they go to sea they know all the proper names, but surely they can tell the difference between a building and a real ship. It wouldn't be that hard to remember the names. I don't see why they can't call the lavs "lavs" anyway,' she added. 'The world wouldn't come to an end just because they used the same words as the rest of us.'

They set to with their brooms and dusters in the never-ending task of keeping the wards clean. Thursday thought she had never seen a place which shone like Haslar. Every corner was swept daily, every floor scrubbed and every surface polished. She rubbed industriously at the wide window sills, chatting to the patients as she did so.

'You're not going to polish me as well, are you?' a young rating asked, pretending to cringe away from her. 'I don't think I'm well enough for that.'

'If you're well enough to get out of bed, you're well enough to be clean,' Thursday told him. 'The only difference is you've got to do it yourself. We don't have time.'

Once they were up, the patients did a lot for themselves. As sailors still officially on duty, they were expected to help keep the wards clean and polished, and they took round food and drinks to fellow patients and helped them wash and shave. But for the VADs, blanket baths loomed ahead and it was difficult to know who dreaded them most, the patients or the girls.

'Who d'you think Sister Burton will pick to use as a demonstration model?' Patsy asked as they ate fried bread and sausages for breakfast. They had been at Haslar for two weeks now and it felt like years. 'Hope it's that young leading hand in bed one, the one with the fair curly hair. I rather fancy seeing him in the altogether.'

'Patsy! We're not supposed to *fancy* the patients. You know what Madam said about no fraternisation. Anyway, he's got a girlfriend – I've seen her picture on his locker.'

Patsy winked. 'I wonder if she's seen as much of him as we're going to.'

'We're giving him a wash,' Thursday told her severely. 'That's all. Not asking him to marry us.'

Elsie giggled. 'By the time we've finished with him, he might *have* to marry us!'

'I'm not listening to this,' Thursday said. 'You're just wicked, the pair of you. I don't know what my mother would say if she knew what sort of girl I'm having to mix with these days.'

The three of them collapsed in giggles, but their hopes

were doomed to disappointment. When they trooped into the ward for their lesson, they were led straight past bed one with its curly-haired occupant, and along the length of the ward to the far end. They glanced at each other and made rueful faces, then gathered round the bed.

'You have six minutes for each patient,' Sister Burton, the senior QARNN in the ward, told them. 'We expect you to take a little longer at first, but by the end of the week you ought to be up to speed. Now, gather round and watch while I bath Stoker Davis.'

Stoker Davis's bed had been surrounded by screens. His pyjamas were removed, revealing him to be a large, hairy man with a beer belly, although his lower half was covered modestly by a white towel with the usual naval anchor embroidered in one corner. He lay watching them through eyes almost hidden by a foliage of shaggy brows, his malicious grin similarly shrouded by a heavy grey moustache and beard. Thursday wondered why Burton couldn't have chosen one of the younger, better-looking patients as an example. Probably it was because he was so repulsive, she thought, and unlikely to excite anyone's feelings. Even his wife wouldn't be excited by this mass of blubber, she thought, looking with distaste at his hairy belly.

'Blimey,' Elsie murmured in her ear, 'if this don't put us off nothing will. And he knows this is our first time, the old bugger.'

The QARNN fixed her with a cold look. 'Did you say something, Jackson?'

'No, Sister,' Elsie said meekly. 'Only that I think this is going to be very interesting.'

Burton gave her another suspicious look and turned to the bowl of hot water which had been placed on the locker beside the bed. She dipped an old and rather grey flannel into the water and squeezed it out, then rubbed it with a lump of carbolic soap. She began to rub it briskly over the hairy bulk on the bed, explaining what she was doing.

'You might not think a patient could get dirty, lying in bed in a clean ward, but there's always dust in the air and where there's dust there are germs. Patients are in a vulnerable condition, open to infection, and must be protected from these germs. Hot water and good carbolic soap are our best weapons in this war.'

'That's right,' the stoker agreed. His voice sounded like coal being shovelled into a furnace. 'That's what we oughter do against the Jerries, chuck hot soapy water at 'em. They wouldn't wanter invade us then!'

The Sister gave him a look as cold as the one she had bestowed upon Elsie. 'I'll do the talking here, Stoker, if you don't mind. Lift up your arm. The armpits are a particularly important area,' she went on. 'Sweat gathers here, as it does in all the crevices, and can result in soreness and raw skin, where germs can easily enter. It's especially important to make sure these areas are perfectly dry.'

'Hey, there's no need to rub as hard as all that,' the patient protested. 'I'm as tender as a baby's bottom under there.'

'Bedsores are another thing to watch out for,' Burton continued, ignoring him. 'Patients who can't move much will get sores just from lying in one position all the time. That's why they must be turned as often as possible. Look out for these sores as you carry out the wash.' She beckoned to Thursday to help her turn him over. 'No, Tilford, not like that. Hold him this way, you see? Then you won't pinch his flesh. That's right. Now, ease him up carefully – you're not flipping a pancake. Now, slowly, carefully – and over he goes. Well done, Stoker.'

What about well done, Tilford? Thursday wondered. All he did was lie there. Then she looked at the body that lay before her and gasped.

The sailor's body was tattooed from shoulder to hip – and probably well beyond, she thought, wondering what lay under the strip of towel that covered his most intimate parts. Apart from his most intimate parts, of course. She gazed, marvelling, at the intricate patterns and knew from the stifled giggles she heard behind her that the other girls were as startled and impressed.

A serpent that would have frightened Eve herself wound its way around his shoulder blades and down his spine, while on either side, perfectly symmetrical, crouched two lions, so lifelike that you could almost see their tails lashing. In between were various smaller tattoos of other creatures – hawks, dragons, scorpions – and spread across his buttocks, the body hidden in the cleft, she could see the wings of an enormous butterfly.

Sister Burton gave them all a few moments to recover from their shock and then spoke tartly.

'I don't know what you think you're all gaping at. I presume you've seen tattoos before?' She gave them a stare that dared them to laugh. 'Well, I can tell you, you'll certainly see a lot more before you've finished at Haslar. They're a great favourite with sailors, and these are especially fine ones, aren't they, Stoker?' The man on the bed gave a grunt, muffled by the pillow, and Sister Burton continued briskly, 'Now then – you, Jackson – there are no sores, thanks to our care, so you can wash his back. A brisk rub with the flannel, please, though of course you'd be much more gentle if there were any injuries. And now we'll turn him back again – so . . .' Elsie heaved until the stoker lay once again on his decorative back. 'And that's all. I'll leave you to finish off,' she said to the man, and ushered the girls back through the screens. They looked at her questioningly, and she said, 'There are certain parts of a man's anatomy that it isn't suitable for female nurses to handle. Unless he's too ill to manage it himself, we leave that to him. If he can't manage, an SBA will deal with it. The men themselves prefer this.'

'Bet they don't,' Patsy muttered as they made their way to the next bed. 'Bet there's nothing they'd like better than a pretty young VAD handling their—'

'Patsy! Stop it!' Thursday bit her lip hard to keep a straight face. Burton walked ahead of them, straight-backed. She was a small woman, dark-haired, thin and wiry and, as they'd already found, surprisingly strong. She had dark eyes in a thin, humorous face, but when it came to blanket baths she made it quite clear that she'd heard all the jokes before and no longer found them funny. That was supposing she'd ever found them funny in the first place.

'Mind you, she must be thirty if she's a day,' Patsy had observed when they had been discussing this at breakfast. 'Past it, poor old soul.'

Thursday didn't think she was past it. She'd seen Sister Burton last night setting out for an evening off duty, wearing a turquoise wool dress that showed her slender figure in quite a different light from the QARNNS uniform. Her hair had been twisted into a pleat instead of its usual severe bun, and her lips had been touched with bright red. She looked excited and happy, and quite unlike the brisk figure now expertly turning an injured torpedo-man on to his other side.

'Torpedoman Smith has back injuries,' she explained. 'His dressings have to be changed three times a day and he must be bathed with extra care. He must be turned every hour. His whole body feels uncomfortable and tender, and we don't want to cause him any more pain or discomfort than we absolutely have to.' Her fingers moved gently over the maimed body and Thursday could see the tension in the wasting muscles dissolve under her touch. She could make him better just by doing that, she thought, and her respect grew.

They made their way round the whole ward and by the end of the morning each girl had carried out at least one blanket bath. Their early nervous giggles disappeared as they ministered to the injured men, and their embarrass-ment was forgotten. Their only worry was that they didn't think they would ever be able to do it at the required speed.

'Six minutes for each one!' Patsy said later as they walked across the quad. The snow had stopped at last and lay in deep drifts around the edges of the big square, swept into piles by the groundsmen. The clouds had peeled away and a pale winter sun lit the walls of the hospital with a russet glow. 'I'll never be able to do it in that time.'

'It's no wonder VADs run everywhere,' Thursday said. 'They've forgotten how to walk.' They went out through the gate and gazed out over Spithead. The tide was out and the sea wall sloped away below them, a steep descent towards the narrow strip of shingle. The sunlight sparkled on dancing waves and the Spithead Forts, capped with a layer of snow, looked like iced cakes. A warship was steaming slowly past the Isle of Wight.

'I wonder where they're going,' Thursday said. 'And what will happen to them. Everyone's expecting Hitler to invade as soon as the weather's better.'

'They say it's been even worse in Europe,' Patsy said. 'Terrible storms, and snow up to the roofs. Some of the Russian soldiers have been frozen to death, and they just had to stop fighting in Norway. I had a letter from my boyfriend this morning, he says they haven't been able to dig trenches for weeks in Belgium.'

'Should he be saying that kind of thing?' Elsie asked. 'Don't their letters get censored?'

'Well, this bit was left in. I suppose they know we must've all noticed the snow and ice. It's the same everywhere. Tell you what, when the weather's better I'm going to get my mum to send my bike down. It can come on the train. Why don't you get yours too, Thursday? We'd be able to get round better – go into Gosport when we're off duty.'

'I haven't got a bike,' Thursday said. 'I could get one though, second-hand. There was one advertised on the noticeboard in the mess, ten bob they wanted for it. Or I could go to that shop in the high street, Clarence Cory's, they've got a lot on show.'

'I'll bring mine over too,' Elsie said. She was able to go home for her half-days. 'I wouldn't mind going for a ride sometimes, along Lee or up to Hillhead. I could pop round and see Gran, too, when I've got an hour to spare.'

Their short break over, they turned away from the view and walked back to the buildings. Miss Makepeace was giving them another lecture, on bleeding and bandages, and they had learnt by now that 'Madam' expected every girl to be in her place well before the lecture was due to begin.

After all, as Patsy remarked as they hurried to hang up their cloaks, it wouldn't do for the lecture room to sail without them!

Chapter Seven

Steve's papers arrived on the same day as Thursday's first letter home. Mary looked at the two envelopes and put his up on the mantelpiece, her heart sinking. It would be a long wait until he came home to open it but at least there was Thursday's letter to take her mind off things. She opened it, smiling at the close-written pages.

'Sounds as if she's enjoying it all,' she told Walter when he arrived home that evening. 'Plenty to do, lots of company, and some nice girls. And the area sounds really interesting. It must be nice to be so near the sea. Lovely in summer.'

'Well, so long as she feels she's doing some good.' He sat down in his armchair and rested a moment before taking off his boots. 'Blimey, I'm worn out! The roads are just ice, and half the streets are blocked with snow. And we've started the change-over in the shop. Putting in all sorts of new contraptions.'

For over two hundred years, Royal Worcester Porcelain had been making beautiful objects in bone china – dinner services, figurines, lovely decorated bowls or china flowers – but now they were to make something different – something to do with the war, he said, but if he knew more he wasn't telling even Mary.

'And our Steve's call-up's arrived,' Mary said, indicating the brown envelope on the mantelpiece.

Walter looked at it. 'Well, we knew it'd come. I don't suppose they'll send him off straight away.'

'Oh, Walter,' she said, 'it's all come so sudden. Our Thursday gone, and now Steve . . . And we're not going to be able to keep our Jenny here much longer, you know. She's just itching to be off.'

'Well, there we do have a bit of say. She's not seventeen till next December, and she can't join anything till then. And maybe by that time there'll be no need.'

'I wouldn't put it past her to try anyway,' Mary said. 'I'm not at all sure they check up on ages when these girls volunteer.'

'They still need their father's signature, and she'll not get that till the proper time.' Walter pushed his boots away from him and lay back in his chair. 'There wouldn't be a cup of tea going, would there?'

'Sorry. I was thinking about these letters. I did put the kettle on, it ought to be coming to the boil any minute.' A shrill whistling from the scullery announced that it was and she hurried out. 'I had a note from our Maudie this morning, too,' she called through. 'The postman had something to say, I can tell you, with all these letters. Anyway, I thought I might ask her over to tea on Sunday if the trains are running.'

'They won't be, if this weather keeps up. It was snowing again when I come in. It'll be Easter before you see your Maudie again at this rate.' He accepted the cup of tea that Mary brought through and took a grateful sip. 'That's better.' He looked up at the mantelpiece again. 'Where *is* our Steve, anyway? Surely he ought to be in by now.'

The back door opened at that moment and Steve stamped into the scullery. He shouted out cheerfully and they heard him take off his boots and coat and then pour himself a cup of tea. He came into the back room, his hair wet with melting snow, grinning.

'You'll never guess what—'

'Your papers have come,' Mary interrupted, unable to wait any longer. 'They've been here all day.' She handed him the envelope. 'Open it, for God's sake, Steve, and tell us the worst.'

Steve put down his cup and took the envelope, staring at it. He looked up at his mother.

'I was going to tell you—'

'Tell us in a minute. I want to know when you're going. I want to know where you'll be.'

'They won't tell us that.' Slowly, he slit open the envelope and drew out the sheet of paper. He read it quickly. 'Well, that's all right, then.'

'What is? What's it say?'

'I'm going in the Royal Worcesters. I'm to report to Norton Barracks in three weeks' time. That gives me time to give in my notice at work. Mr Rogers has already said he'll keep my place for me.'

'I still think it's a pity you couldn't finish your apprenticeship first,' Walter said. 'It wouldn't have made all that much difference, carrying on till December, and you'd have got your indentures then. It would've stood you in good stead, having a trade behind you. Probably made a difference to where they send you.'

'I'm more or less finished now,' Steve said. 'A few months won't make that much difference. I've still got the knowledge and experience, though I don't know what use an apprenticeship in chinaware will do me in the Army. I don't suppose I'll be making posh plates for brigadiers. Anyway, never mind that, what I was going to tell you was that I met our Leslie on the way home. And he was telling me he's volunteered for the RAF! What do you think of that?'

'*Leslie?* But he's not old enough – he's not seventeen till March.'

'No, but he's put his name down and he can join up then. He wants to learn to fly – be a pilot. And they like them young, say they learn faster.'

'And what's our Flo got to say about this?' Walter demanded. 'And her Perce? They won't be best pleased, I can tell you.'

'Leslie says it doesn't make any difference what they

say. He's set on it. He says he'll never get another chance like this.'

'If Perce refuses to sign—' Walter began, but Steve interrupted him.

'He won't. What's the point? You know what Leslie's like, he's just as likely to forge his father's signature. If he's made up his mind to do something, he'll do it, no matter what.'

'But that's against the law! He could go to prison.' Mary stared at them aghast, but Steve shrugged.

'And who's going to report him? The authorities won't care, and Uncle Percy isn't going to get him sent to prison. I don't reckon there's a thing he can do about it.'

Walter stared at his son. Then his shoulders sagged and he turned away and stared into the fire. Mary took his cup and poured fresh tea into it and at last he spoke again.

'I tell you what. This war's started already. And it's not just fighting. It's what's happening in people's homes. Our Steve here, going off to be a soldier. Young Leslie, going against his father's wishes, set on getting his own way, and him still only sixteen. Our Thursday, left home. Kiddies sent away to live with strangers. It's breaking up homes, that's what it's doing, breaking up homes and families, and that's the worst thing that can happen. Because the country's *built* on families, and when they go, everything else goes, too.'

'But that's what we're fighting for,' Mary said. 'So that we can go on living the way we always have. So that families *can* stay together.'

Walter lifted his head and stared at her, and she saw the hollowness of his eyes, and behind them the dread and the knowledge that he had carried ever since his own days in the Army, when he had seen and experienced all those horrors he never talked about and had tried so hard to forget.

'Well, let's just hope the families are still there when all the fighting is over,' he said in a flat, dead voice. 'Let's just hope we can pull them all back together again. Them that are left.'

'You've done *what*?' Percy demanded. His face flushed and the veins on his neck stood out. He'd been filling his pipe when Leslie made his announcement and he held it in his hand, shreds of tobacco still trailing from the bowl.

'You heard.' Leslie spoke in his cheekiest voice, knowing it would enrage his father still more, but inside he was quaking. He felt almost amazed by what he had done, and was wondering how he'd had the nerve to go into the RAF recruiting office and sign his name. 'I've signed up for the RAF.'

'And there's no call for back-answering,' Percy snapped. 'You know very well what I meant. You had no right. And they won't take you anyway. You're only sixteen.'

'I'm old enough to register. I put down my name for when I'm seventeen. You can join then, and be trained as a pilot. It's what I want to do, Dad. You know I've always wanted to fly, and this is my chance. I don't want to get called up for the Army, like our Mike.'

'And that's another thing. What's this going to do to your mother? You know she worries about Mike, and if you go off too – flying *aeroplanes* – she'll never have a minute's peace. And you don't even know there'll *be* a war by the time you get to seventeen. It could be all over by then.'

'Won't matter then, will it?' Leslie said sullenly. 'And why shouldn't I do what I want, just because of Mike? *He's* doing what he wanted. You never stopped him going in the Territorials when he was my age.'

'That was different. There was no war then.'

'No, but you knew if there was he'd have to go. And you never said he couldn't go when it did break out—'

'I couldn't, could I? Territorials had to go—'

'And if I'd been one, so would I, soon as I got to the proper age. So what's the difference in signing up for the

RAF?' Leslie stared at his father. 'Anyway, I've done it now, all legal, and you can't do a thing about it. It's the law.'

'And I'm your father. I could go down the office and say you did it without my authority.'

'It's King and country now,' Leslie said. 'That's what the authority is these days.'

Percy took a deep breath. His face was almost purple. He stepped forward and Leslie saw that his fists were balled. He backed away, but at that moment the door opened and Flo came in, with Denise close behind her She stared from one to the other.

'What in the name of goodness is going on here?'

Percy stepped back and uncurled his fists. He looked at his wife and shook his head. 'It's this boy. You'll never credit what he's been and gone and done.'

'What?' Flo turned to her son, her face pale. 'What have you done, Leslie? You've not got in trouble with the police, have you?'

'Course I haven't! It's nothing like that, Mum. I've just put my name down for the RAF, that's all. I haven't joined up – not yet. But I will, soon as they'll take me,' he added in a determined tone. 'I just wanted to make sure of it, that's all. I didn't want to find myself shoved into the Army or the Navy.'

'There's nothing wrong with the Army—' Percy began, but Flo interrupted him.

'Let's get this straight. Let's sit down and talk about it.' She sank into her armchair and after a moment Percy followed suit. Leslie and Denise sat on the upright chairs and looked at each other. There was a moment's silence.

'Right,' Flo said. 'Now tell me what this is all about, Leslie. You've signed up for the RAF, is that right?'

'Yes.'

'But you aren't actually joining? You're too young. I hope you haven't lied about your age,' she added sternly.

'No, I haven't. It's just a sort of waiting list. But I'm not waiting to be called up,' he added swiftly. 'They're not taking men till they're twenty and I'm not waiting that long. I'm going in soon as I'm old enough, as a regular.'

'A regular? And how old d'you have to be for that?'

'Seventeen,' he muttered, looking at the floor.

'*Seventeen*! But that's in March – it's only a few weeks away.' Flo stared at her son. 'You say it's not now, but you could be gone in six weeks' time! Oh, *Leslie*.' She covered her face with her hands.

Percy gave his son a look. Leslie stared at the floor again. Denise, looking bright-eyed from one to the other, spoke up.

'Well, I think it's smashing. Our Leslie, a pilot! You ought to be proud of him, Mum and Dad, that's what you ought to be. Not going on at him like he's committed a crime.'

'And you needn't stick your oar in,' Percy snapped, rounding on her. 'None of this concerns you.'

'It does. Leslie's my brother.' Denise faced her father defiantly. 'Anyway, it won't be all that long before I'm old enough to help the war effort too, and it's time you faced up to it. The war's going to be won by young people, like Mike and Leslie and me, and old people like you have got to realise it. I don't know what you've got against us all, anyway. Look at the way Auntie Mary went on when Thursday said she wanted to be a VAD. And Steve, volunteering. We've *got* to do our bit. You can't keep us tied to your apron strings and let other people go and do the dirty work.'

'We know all that,' Percy retorted. 'We've been through one war already, just in case you've forgotten. We know what it's like. And we don't like the idea of kids like you and Leslie going through what we went through. What's so wrong with *that*?'

'I didn't say there was anything wrong with it. I just said you can't keep us in our prams. Anyway, what about you? Didn't you volunteer to go in the last war?'

Percy flushed again. He seldom spoke about the Great War, but Flo had told the children time and time again how he'd gone to the recruiting office the minute they'd opened in 1914 and signed up for the Army. And it wouldn't take a brilliant mathemetician to know that, having been born in 1898, he must have lied about his age to do so.

Fortunately, he and Flo had never told their children exactly how old they were. They'd married young, in the last year of the war, and he wasn't even sure that Flo had realised he must have lied.

'Well, there's no use arguing about it all,' he said gruffly. 'What's done's done, and I'm sure we don't want to stand in your light, any of you. But you've got to realise, you two, that all this is very hard on your mother. She thought she'd have you home a few more years yet, and here you are all going off, leaving home, and goodness knows what's going to happen to any of us. The world's upside down, and it's not easy.'

Denise was silent. She moved a little closer to her mother and laid her hand on Flo's arm.

'Don't worry, Mum. I dare say they'll take one look at our Les's ugly face and send him straight back anyway. Pilots are supposed to be good-looking. And you're still stuck with me for a while.'

'And that's supposed to make her feel better?' Leslie asked, risking a joke now that his father seemed to have backed down a bit. He glanced at his mother. 'I'm sorry, Mum, but I really do want to do this. And I didn't want any arguments – that's why I went to the office without saying anything first.'

'Well, you shouldn't have. You should have talked it over with us.' But Flo stretched her hand out to him and pulled him close. 'I'm proud of you all the same, son. Proud of you all. And if all the youngsters in the country are like you and Mike and our Denise – well, we'll show Hitler what he's up against, that's all.' She gave him a quick kiss and then straightened her shoulders. 'And I'd be obliged if someone would set their hand to laying the table now. Denise, you get the kettle on and, Leslie, you can go up the street and get some fish and chips. All I could get at the butcher's was hearts, and you know they need soaking overnight and then half the day in a casserole to get them tender.'

Denise and Leslie jumped to do as she told them and Flo looked across the fireplace at her husband. Percy had started to fill his pipe again, tamping down the tobacco as if it had done him an injury, and she reached her hand out and touched his arm.

'Don't be angry with him, Perce. He's doing what he thinks is right, and if he was a year or two older you'd be patting him on the back. They're children we can be proud of, all of them.'

'I know,' he said. 'It's just that – well, I know what war's like, Flo. I've seen it in the trenches. I never thought we'd be sending our own children off to that. I never did.'

They sat together gazing into the fire, troubled by their memories and their fears. But they knew that their part now was to support their children in whatever path fate might lead them. In a country at war, nobody had any other choice.

Chapter Eight

The girls were allocated to their wards almost at once. Apart from Miss Makepeace's lectures, the best training was on the job. In any case, Haslar wasn't a teaching hospital and there wasn't time for the doctors and QARNNs to conduct classes, even if they'd been able to.

'Not that we need much training to empty bedpans,' Thursday remarked, carrying a pile of big metal ovals out of the sluice room. 'Or to scrub floors. My dad was right, we're just skivvies.'

'We'll have more interesting things to do later, though,' Patsy said. 'I mean, I've heard that VADs are actually allowed to roll bandages sometimes. If they're very, very good.'

'Well, at least it won't be so smelly.' Thursday set off along her side of the ward, distributing pans as she went. Some of the men could sit on them unaided, some had to be helped, some needed to be held in position. It didn't matter what rank they were, when it came to basic functions all were equal. It didn't matter what their attitude was either. They were all patients and deserved equal care.

'Ouch! Do you have to be so bloody clumsy?' the tattooed stoker complained bitterly as Thursday slipped her arm under his shoulders to heave him on to the pan. 'You've got my skin all caught up. It bloody *hurts*.'

'Sorry. It's just that you're heavy—'

'That's the trouble with getting sodding girls to do the job,' he grumbled. 'Ain't got the muscle for it. Bloody daft idea, if you ask me.'

'Now then, Stoker, mind your language,' said a passing SBA. He came to give her a hand and between them they heaved him on to the bedpan where he sat looking like Humpty-Dumpty on his wall, only hairier. He glowered at them both.

'You'll have to mend your manners a bit now we've got ladies on the wards,' the SBA went on cheerfully. He had dark, curly hair and didn't look much older than Thursday. 'None of that effing and blinding you're used to on board.'

'Ladies!' the stoker said contemptuously. 'These ain't ladies! What lady'd want to do the jobs they're doing, eh? Wiping a lot of blokes' bottoms for 'em. Scrubbin' floors. Cleaning jobs. They'd never get proper ladies doing that kind of work.'

'Women do all sorts of work now,' Thursday said indignantly. 'And all sorts of women do it, too. Some of our VADs are real upper-crust.'

'Well, I ain't come across none of 'em.' He scowled ferociously. 'Don't distract me now. I got to concentrate.'

Thursday and the SBA grinned at each other and left him to it. Within a few minutes, the men were all enthroned and the VADs went to collect the bowls of warm, soapy water for their washes. By the time they came back some of the men were ready, while others were still wearing their looks of anxious concentration. She started to collect the pans and take them to the sluice for emptying and washing out, until finally the stoker was the only man left.

'I just don't seem to be able to manage it this morning.'

'I'll put you down for a dose of syrup of figs tonight,' Thursday said, reaching for the pan.

The sailor clung on to it. 'No, don't take it away yet! It'll only be a few more minutes. I don't want none of that jollop, it turns me bowels to water.'

'Well, that's the idea, isn't it. They're like rock at the moment. You'll have to go soon. It's three days now.'

'It comes from being a submariner,' he said. 'They don't encourage it on the boats.'

'That's rubbish and he knows it,' Sister Burton said when Thursday reported this conversation. 'Tell him it's syrup of figs tonight or an enema tomorrow, he can take his choice.'

'Just make it an enema anyway,' one of the other SBAs suggested. 'This lot haven't seen one yet. It's time they learnt how to give them.'

Patsy and Thursday gazed at him. Thursday wasn't even sure what an enema was, but Elsie had told them that her grandmother had to have them to help her go. 'It's horrible,' she said. 'They stuff all this rubber tube up your bum and then pour soapy water down it, see, till you're all full up, and then it washes everything out. Gran sits on the lav all day Monday in the hopes that she won't need one. It's Tuesday the nurse comes round,' she added in explanation.

Thursday and Patsy looked at each other. 'Is she having us on?'

'I hope so,' Patsy said. 'I can't see any of this lot even letting us start to shove rubber tubes up them.'

'They don't have no choice,' Elsie said, in a tone of satisfaction. 'They have to let us do it.'

It sounded more like a punishment than a treatment, and from Elsie's tone Thursday suspected that it might even be used as one. She thought of the stoker receiving an enema, and couldn't picture him exhibiting the docility that must be required.

She had her opportunity to see next morning. True to the SBA's threat, the syrup of figs had been 'forgotten' that night, and when the bedpan round had been completed next morning the stoker had still not 'managed'. Sister decreed an enema and the new VADs were summoned to watch.

'He's going to hate this,' Patsy whispered as they all trooped down the ward, Thursday pushing the trolley with all the equipment laid out on it and Elsie pushing the screens. The rest of the patients watched with a mixture of apprehension and interest, which turned to relief on the faces of all but the stoker. He stared at them in dismay, which changed rapidly to fury.

'Here! Nobody never said I 'ad to 'ave one of them! I was supposed to 'ave syrup of figs. That's what they told me yesterday.' He fixed Thursday with a glowering eye. 'You heard that bloke, you heard him say so.'

'You said you didn't want syrup of figs,' the dark-haired SBA said innocently. 'Didn't he?'

Thursday nodded. 'He said it turned his bowels to water,' she confirmed.

'Well, they're going to be water anyway now, ain't they? Give it me now, I'll take it straight away. I'm not 'avin' yards of bleedin' 'osepipe stuffed up me arse. I'll put in a complaint, that's what I'll do. Take it away.'

'Sorry,' Sister said, reading the stoker's notes. 'You haven't had a movement for four days now, and that's too long. It'll be all the worse for you if we don't do something to clear you. You'll be getting a blockage, and that'll mean another operation.'

'Well, at least they gives you knock-out drops for that.' The stoker watched in growing alarm as the screens were pushed round his bed. 'Look, I'll take a double dose. I'll sit on the bleedin' bedpan all day. I'll do anything, only don't put that bloody tube in me. I hates it. I *hates* it, I tell you.'

'Everyone hates it,' the SBA said calmly. 'But it's only uncomfortable, it doesn't really hurt. Now, come on, Stoker Davis, don't be such a coward. Worse things happen at sea, you know.'

'No, they don't,' the stoker retorted. 'Nothing worse than this happens at sea, and I been there and I know.' With utmost reluctance, he allowed himself to be pushed back on to his pillows and then rolled to one side. He turned his head and squinted at the VADs, standing just inside the screens. 'Are these bleedin' girls going to watch?'

'They've got to learn, Stoker Davis.'

'Why 'ave they? You're not going to let *them* start doin' this? Bits of girls, rammin' 'osepipe up decent men's backsides? It ain't right.'

'And what's going to happen when all the SBAs are at sea? You'll give yourselves your own enemas, will you?'

'We won't 'ave bleedin' enemas! That'll be one thing that'll be against the law.' He cringed and yelped as the cold rubber touched his anus. 'Here, couldn't you 'ave warmed it up a bit first?'

Nobody answered. The girls watched, embarrassed but transfixed as the rubber tubing was pushed further and further into the man's back passage. Then the dark-haired SBA picked up the jug of soapy water.

Sister Burton nodded. 'All right, West. Ready to go. You can time this, Tilford,' she added to Thursday.

The SBA's dark eyes caught Thursday's and he gave her a solemn wink. She felt her lips twitch and folded them firmly together. She lifted her watch with one finger and watched its hands intently. The stoker moaned in anticipation.

The girls watched, fascinated, as half a gallon of water disappeared into the stoker's nether regions. There was a deep groan from the bed and then a howl of misery. The SBA took no notice, but picked up a second jug. Davis began to swear.

'That's enough of that!' Sister said sharply.

'And I've 'ad enough of that!' Davis shouted. 'Gorblimey, it'll be coming out me ears if you puts in any more. Stop it, for Gawd's sake.'

Sister nodded. The younger man stopped pouring and they waited for a moment. Then the stoker was heaved back into a sitting position and placed hastily over the bedpan.

'You'll need a bloody sight more than one,' he groaned,

and Thursday couldn't help feeling sorry for him. He looked the picture of misery, crumpled over his full and aching belly. 'Oh, my Gawd, 'ere it comes . . .'

'Well,' SBA West said a little later, when he and Thursday were in the sluice with the bedpans and the draught from the open windows had blown away most of the stench, 'he won't refuse his syrup of figs next time.'

'Did you really have to pour all that water into him? *Two* jugs?'

He grinned. 'Well, we wanted to make sure of it, didn't we? Don't want to waste the surgeon's time with an operation. Sorry about his language, but you'll hear worse before you've finished here.'

'But what a baby he is,' Thursday said. 'What a coward. I mean, I know it's not very pleasant – well, I've never had one, thank goodness, but it does look horrible – but what's he going to be like in action if he's going to kick up a fuss like that about an enema?'

'Oh, he'll be all right in action. He's used to that.' West glanced at her. 'He was on the *Grenville*. They reckon he's been put in for a medal.'

'The *Grenville*? Wasn't that sunk a few weeks ago? Patsy Martin had a cousin on board her. They think he went down with the ship – she said the whole family were really cut up when they heard.'

He nodded. 'Eighty-odd blokes went down with her. In the North Sea. Davis managed to get out from the engine room and into a lifeboat. He brought two other blokes with him. They reckon he nearly drowned getting them in the lifeboat.'

Thursday looked at him in silence for a moment. 'You mean he's a hero.'

'Pretty near. But there's a lot of heroes about in wartime. They'd run out of medals if they gave them to everyone who deserved them.' He finished sluicing out and turned away. 'Come on. Back to the ward. There's work to be done.'

126

Thursday followed him thoughtfully. She glanced down the ward to where Stoker Davis was now lying against his pillows, his colour returning as he sipped cocoa from a large mug. It was hard sometimes, when you were scurrying about with urine bottles or mugs of cocoa, to remember that most of these men had been injured through the war, that many of them – perhaps all of them – might be heroes. It was hard, when you looked at a man in pyjamas perched on a bedpan, to remember that he lived a tough and dangerous life outside.

Anyone who thought there was nothing happening in this war ought to come here, to Haslar, she thought, and see what had happened to these sailors. The burns, the broken bones, the injuries from explosion when some German missile had hit and perhaps sunk their ship. The man whose back had been almost stripped of flesh; the boy of no more than seventeen who had lost his right arm. The thirty-year-old who had been blinded and could only walk in a shuffle, and whose young wife couldn't bear to visit him.

'I don't mind if they swear,' she said to Patsy. 'They can say what they like. What's the use of fighting for freedom if you can't at least say what you like?'

The best way out of Haslar was across the narrow bridge, which led across Haslar Lake and into the town of Gosport. One afternoon, about a fortnight after they had arrived at Haslar, the three girls set off to explore. Most of the snow had now been swept away from the pavements, but there were still patches where it had hardened into ice. The piles at the side of the road were dirty and unattractive, and there was grey slush in the gutters.

'It's like being in a flipping fort itself,' Patsy remarked as they walked under the huge archway that led out through the ramparts. 'Look at this great high wall all round the hospital. It's like a prison. Is everything round here built like this? There's those Spithead Forts, too, and the ones you can see on top of the hill, and there's others all over Gosport – what were they all for?'

'They're queer, these forts,' Thursday agreed. 'I've never seen anything like them before.'

'They told us at school that they were built by Lord Palmerston when he was prime minister in Queen Victoria's reign,' Elsie said. 'They were supposed to defend us against the French, but they never invaded so they got called Palmerston's Follies and everyone laughed at him for wasting all that money on something that would never be needed. I don't reckon he was so far wrong, though – they're all being used now. It's just that this time it's the Germans who're going to invade us instead of the French.'

'Not *going* to,' Thursday corrected her. '*Trying* to. They're not going to succeed. They'd have to get past our lads first, over in France.'

Her cousin Mike was in France now. He'd had a few days' leave at Christmas, and now he'd gone back as part of the BEF. *More* initials, Thursday's grandmother had said disgustedly, and refused to call it anything else than the British Expeditionary Force, even though her false teeth were in danger of falling out when she struggled with the words.

Thursday's mother had written to tell her how upset Auntie Flo had been when Mike departed. There would be real fighting over there, as soon as the weather got a bit better, and meanwhile he must be living in a tent amidst all the snow and ice. Flo had always gone on about Mike's chest and never even liked him going camping with the Scouts as a boy, and on top of that she now had Leslie to worry about as well. She was sure he'd be called up to the RAF the minute he turned seventeen, and nobody had been able to persuade her that even if he had volunteered they would probably take the older boys first.

They walked down the road to the bridge and stared at it. There were actually two bridges – an older one which could have taken cars, and a narrower one which stretched steeply above it. The lower bridge was unusable, since the middle span had been removed.

'Blimey,' Elsie said, staring at it. 'No wonder it's called Pneumonia Bridge. You're halfway to heaven at the top of that.'

'Why have they taken away part of the lower bridge?' Thursday wondered. 'It looks perfectly all right. Did it get damaged somehow?'

'Must have done,' Patsy said. 'So now we've either got to climb up there like mountaineers or go miles round, unless we get the boat to Portsmouth. And there's a toll to pay, too!'

'Not for us,' Thursday reminded her. 'Hospital staff don't have to pay. I tell you what, we'd better get those bikes. Otherwise we're going to be stuck out here. It's like being on a desert island!'

They began the climb up the steep span of the bridge. It swayed with the bitter wind that scoured across the harbour and they wrapped their capes round them, forgetting that they had complained about not being allowed to wear civvy clothes outside. At the top, they paused and stared at the long creek that twisted from the harbour and inland to the village of Alverstoke, cutting Haslar off from the town.

'Why did they build the hospital in such a queer place?' Patsy asked. 'It seems daft, when it's so hard to get to. It must have been even worse when it was first built and there was no bridge at all.'

'Probably they didn't want the sailors to escape,' Thursday said. 'I expect that's why they built the wall so high, too. They were all pressed men in those days, weren't they?' She looked at Elsie for corroboration. 'And didn't Madam say most of the patients came by boat from ships out in the Solent? It was easy enough for them to get to.'

'That must be why it was built in Gosport,' Elsie

remarked. 'Pompey would have wanted it on their side really, but Haslar was just as easy for them and meant they didn't have to use anywhere in the harbour.'

'You talk as if Gosport wasn't really entitled to have anything so important as a hospital,' Thursday teased her, and Elsie shrugged.

'Well, it's just a dead end, isn't it? Nobody goes to Gosport, not unless they've got to. There's nothing much here, apart from all these forts and a few naval bases. Pompey's where everything is – the shops and the dance halls, that sort of thing.'

'*You* come to Gosport. You know it quite well.' They started the descent down the other side of the bridge and waved at the toll-house keeper in his little house at the bottom.

'I come to see my gran. I wouldn't bother otherwise. Most of the people I know at home have never been to Gosport at all, or only come over on the ferry for the ride and just walked up the high street. That's enough to show there's nothing here!'

They left the bridge behind them and walked along the causeway and past the tall red tower of Trinity Church and down to the Hard. From here, they could see the city of Portsmouth across the harbour, the ships at the jetties and the stubby little ferry boats bustling to and fro from the wooden floating pontoon.

'Shall we go over?' Elsie suggested, with longing in her voice, but the other two shook their heads.

'There isn't time. It'll be dark by half past four. Let's walk up the high street and see what's there.'

'I can tell you that,' Elsie said disparagingly. 'Nothing.'

They turned and walked past the pub at the end of the high street. 'The Isle of Wight Hoy,' Thursday remarked. 'Funny name. It's like being in a different country – sea and forts and queer names. And look, there's a Woolworths. And a Littlewoods. We can get most of what we need there. It's not that bad, Elsie.'

'It's just not Pompey,' Patsy said teasingly. 'I tell you what, there's only one thing wrong with this place and that's not enough men! I thought there'd be plenty of sailors in a place like Haslar Hospital, but they're either doctors that won't look twice at common little VADs, or else they're patients and too sick to bother.'

'There's plenty of sailors around Pompey, and Gosport too,' Elsie said, 'but I don't know as I'd go out with one. They've got a reputation, you know – girl in every port, that sort of thing. You couldn't ever depend on one staying faithful.'

'I'm not bothered about them being faithful,' Patsy said. 'I've got a boyfriend anyway – my Jeff. But we're not serious. I don't want to be serious about anyone yet. I just want someone to have some fun with. Go to dances and the pictures and things like that. But with the ones we've got, the minute they're fit to take a girl out they're sent away again. And we're not supposed to get friendly with them anyway.' She shivered. 'I tell you what, I wouldn't mind a cup of tea. Is there anywhere we can get something that's not hospital food?'

'There's the Swiss Café,' Elsie admitted. 'I've been in there once or twice with Gran. It's not bad. Or there's the Dive – that's a sort of cellar under the Market House, over the road from the Isle of Wight Hoy. It looks all right but I've never been in it – not the sort of place Gran would go!'

They walked a little further, past an assortment of small shops – a grocer's, a bookshop, a sweetshop – and then came to the Swiss Café. It looked warm and friendly and they went inside and looked around with interest.

There were only half a dozen tables inside, and one was already occupied by three naval ratings. The girls sat down at another, pulling off their gloves and rubbing their cold fingers together. A middle-aged waitress came to serve them and when they had ordered tea and toast Thursday looked around and caught the eye of one of the young men at the table in the window. It was the dark-haired SBA.

'Hullo,' he said, staring at her. 'You're from the hospital.'

'That's right,' Thursday said, remembering that his name was West but feeling awkward about using it. She couldn't just call him by his surname but she didn't really feel that using the initials SBA sounded right, outside the hospital.

'We did that enema on Stoker Davis together.'

'Well, I didn't, I just watched. You gave it to him.'

He grinned. 'And he didn't like it much, did he?' He indicated his two companions. 'Doug Brighton and Roy Greenaway, and my name's Tony. The Three Musketeers, we are. Doug and Roy are from different wards but you'll see 'em loafing about. These are some of our new slaves,' he told the other two sailors.

The girls looked at them assessingly. Patsy's complaint about the lack of men had been heartfelt, but here were chaps they'd been actually working with yet had never seen as possible boyfriends. Maybe we just haven't been looking properly, Thursday thought. And it wasn't as if they were bad-looking. The one called Tony had nice dark brown eyes – she'd already noticed those, while they were giving Stoker Davis his enema – and curly brown hair, while Roy Greenaway had auburn hair and blue eyes and Doug Brighton reminded her of the film star Gregory Peck. He looked as if he knew it too, as his eyes moved slowly over each girl as if deciding which – if any of them – would be suitable as a girlfriend.

'So what are your names, then?' he asked, and his voice sounded smooth and silky, but more as if he'd practised sounding like that than as if it came naturally.

'I'm Elsie Jackson,' Elsie told him, preening a little. 'I come from Pompey, but I'm living in at Haslar because I'm mobile.' She grinned at Doug Brighton. 'I nearly went mad when I found I was coming all the way to Gosport!

Hope they'll send me somewhere a bit more exciting when my training's finished.' She didn't seem to think there was anything wrong with his manner, Thursday thought. Perhaps it's just me.

'And I'm Patsy Martin. I'm from Evesham, in Worcestershire.'

They all looked at Thursday. 'And how about you?' Doug asked after a moment. 'Haven't you got a name?'

'Of course I have,' she answered, irritated. 'It's Thursday – Thursday Tilford.' She met his eyes, knowing he would comment. Nobody ever heard her name without at least looking surprised.

'*Thursday*?' he repeated, as she'd known he would. 'You're kidding!'

'I told you, it's Thursday.' She heard the edge in her voice and saw the other girls glance at her in surprise. 'Not Monday, Tuesday, Wednesday or Friday – *Thursday*. What's so odd about that?'

He raised one eyebrow. Again, it looked as if he'd practised it and Thursday felt even more irritated. He's nothing but a show-off, she thought, thinks he's God's gift to women.

'Well, you've got to admit it's unusual.'

'Oh, yes,' she agreed, 'I admit that. But there's nothing wrong with being unusual, is there? Or perhaps you think everyone should be just ordinary – like you.' She turned her eyes away from him and spoke to Tony. 'I suppose you'll all be sent to sea soon. Once the VADs are trained.'

'That's the general idea. That's where we're needed.' Tony West flexed his muscles. 'Can't wait to see some action!'

'Even after you've seen what happens?' Thursday asked, thinking of the burns, the injuries, the missing limbs and blindness. So far, Haslar's patients had come mostly from ships like the *Grenville*, damaged at sea, and the new VADs hadn't seen the worst cases, but she knew

133

that some of the patients they had seen were recovering from serious injuries.

'All the more. That's what we're for, isn't it – to see the enemy off. Don't want 'em marching up Gosport High Street and taking over the Swiss Café, do we!' He grinned and the others laughed.

'They couldn't,' Patsy said with a grin. 'The Swiss are neutral.'

'You mean they could take over everything else but this place'd have a sort of special dispensation to stay the same? We could all come in here and have tea and toast just as if we weren't under Hitler's jackboot?' The three young men laughed. 'And the Jerries'd have to stand outside with their noses pressed against the glass, wishing they could come in, too.'

'No, they'd be allowed in as well. That's what neutral means, you're friends with everyone.'

'I don't think the Swiss are friends with everyone,' West said. 'They might be neutral but they're all trained, and they've all got guns. They're not going to fight in someone else's war, but they won't let anyone take them over.'

'That's just being cowards,' Roy Greenaway said. 'They're not true friends at all. *We* are – we joined in to defend little countries like Czechoslovakia and Poland, not ourselves. Switzerland'd come in quick enough if they were being threatened, and then they'd expect everyone else to fight for them as well.'

'Like the Yanks,' Doug Brighton nodded. 'They're keeping well out of it, but I bet if they got attacked they'd jump in all right. Be different then.'

Thursday said nothing. She half agreed with the boys, but felt dimly that there must be more to it than that, and she didn't really take to Doug Brighton. He was just too good-looking, and knew it. As she studied him, he turned his eyes on her and she blushed and looked away quickly, but not before she'd seen a faint grin on the chiselled lips.

The tea and toast arrived and the girls sorted out the cups and saucers and poured their tea. The toast was hot and although the 'butter' was really margarine, it warmed them after their cold walk. They went on talking to the three SBAs and learnt a bit more about the town.

'The quickest way back's through Bemister's Lane. It takes you more or less straight to Pneumonia Bridge.'

'How did the other bridge get damaged?' Thursday asked. 'It must have been much more useful to be able to get cars and trucks and things across to Haslar that way. Why didn't they repair it instead of building that little footbridge over the top?'

'They knocked it down deliberately,' Tony West told her. 'So that they could get bigger vessels in and out of Gun Boat Yard. It's a big creek, Haslar Lake, there's all kinds of stuff up there. And then there's *Dolphin*, of course – you've seen the submarines?'

Thursday nodded. She felt that she could spend hours just wandering the waterfronts and hards of the little town, staring at the unfamiliar sight of ships and boats. There was so much going on – ferries and tugs bustling about, the white paddle steamers churning their way to the Island, the grey bulk of the naval ships looming through the narrow harbour entrance. And across the water, in Portsmouth, the jetties and buildings of the dockyard and the black-rigged masts of HMS *Victory* as a symbol of Britain's greatness at sea.

And the everlasting fascination of the sea itself. It was always different – grey and ominous, as it had been when they arrived, blue and sparkling as on the first morning when they'd looked over from the sea wall at the Solent and the gleaming dome of Portsmouth Cathedral, with the tree-covered Island like a fairyland across the channel. The tides, washing in and out, so that when you looked out in the morning it was high and deep against the slope of the sea wall, and a few hours later barely reaching the beach at its feet. The creeks, winding mysteriously through the town so that you could walk down a narrow street a mile inland and find yourself on yet another shingly beach, with the tide washing the end of people's back gardens.

Thursday thought she had never been in such an interesting place, a place that could change with the weather, even with the time of day. She wanted to explore it, to get to know it, and she made up her mind that this was what she'd spend her off-duty time doing.

'I tell you what,' she said, unconsciously copying Patsy, 'I'm going to see about buying that bike the minute we get back to the hospital.'

They walked back together through the lane that led from the high street to Walpole Park. It was so narrow that they could only walk in pairs, and Thursday, walking behind the others, found Doug Brighton beside her.

'I'm glad we met you in the café,' he told her. 'I've seen you around the hospital. You're pretty.'

'Thanks,' Thursday said a little shortly. She glanced up at him and saw that he was smiling down at her. Perhaps he was waiting for her to say how good-looking he was. Well, he can wait on, she thought irritably. He doesn't need telling anyway, he knows it already.

'Maybe we could slip away from the others,' he murmured, sliding his hand round her waist. 'Get to know each other a bit better, hmm?'

'No, thank you,' Thursday said, even more tersely, and shrugged his arm off. 'I think you may have got the wrong idea about me.'

'Hoity-toity!' he said, and moved away. 'Well, you won't get another chance. I don't ask a girl twice.'

'Good,' she said, and watched him step forward to walk beside Elsie. Tony, who had been beside her, glanced over his shoulder and dropped back. He gave her a wink.

'Doug hasn't been bothering you, has he? You don't want to take any notice of him. He's all right really.'

'I'll take your word for it. He's just not my type.'

Tony looked as if he were about to ask what her type was, but at the look on her face he seemed to think better of it. A few moments later, they emerged from the lane and crossed South Street to find themselves by the boating pool. There were a few small rowing boats and canoes tied up at the far end and Tony told Thursday that you could hire one for sixpence an hour.

'The other part's for model yacht racing. It's quite famous – supposed to be one of the best in the country. They have regattas here. And just over there's the swimming baths – salt water, of course, they get it from the moat.'

'*Another* moat? Right in the middle of the town?'

'Oh, yes,' he said, grinning, 'there are moats all over Gosport. All the forts have got one. People here don't think they're anything unusual.'

They passed the tall red church tower and climbed the steep span of Pneumonia Bridge. Once again, as they reached the top, Thursday huddled her cape more closely around her. The wind whipped her skirt around her legs and threw tiny spikes of ice against her face. She hurried along, her head down, and skittered after Tony down the narrow, slippery slope, looking forward now to being back in the warm hospital. The other two couples scurried along beside her and the six of them dashed along the road, past the high wall and through the gate, past the sentry. Once inside the sheltering walls, they slowed down, laughing, and the three ratings walked to the door of D Block with the girls.

'Let's do that again,' Tony said to Thursday. 'Not the last bit, I don't mean – but let's go out and have a cuppa some time when we're off duty. And maybe we could go for a walk, or a bike ride. Didn't I hear you say you were getting one?'

Thursday nodded. 'We're all going to. Perhaps when the weather's better we could go on rides and picnics and things. I want to see more of the seashore.'

'We could go swimming in the summer,' he said, and she nodded again.

They stood for a moment looking at each other. Then Patsy called from the doorway and Thursday turned away, feeling her heart skip a little.

Since she'd parted from Sidney, she'd hardly been out with a boy again. There hadn't really been time, and she had been too taken up with her new life as a VAD. But now, with two girls as friends and three chaps for them to go around with in a group, it was nice to think that there might be someone special for her.

Could Tony be special? She thought of the two of them, heaving the big, hairy stoker about on his bed, giving him enemas and wiping his bottom, and giggled. It wasn't exactly romantic. But that didn't mean romance couldn't blossom away from the ward.

'He's nice, isn't he?' Patsy said as they made their way to their dormitory, and Thursday nodded.

'Mind you, I've never gone so much for the dark ones, but my last boyfriend had fair hair so maybe it's time for a change.'

Patsy looked at her in surprise. 'Dark hair? I was talking about the red-headed one – Roy Greenaway. I thought he was smashing.'

'And *I* quite fancied the good-looking one – Doug,' Elsie said, grinning. 'So that's one each! Things are looking up, girls.'

Laughing and pushing each other, they ran down the corridor to the dormitory. Madam would have a fit if she could see us now, Thursday thought with a giggle. But life had been difficult and serious enough in the past few weeks. It was time they started having fun.

Chapter Nine

The weather began to improve at last and the roads were cleared of their covering of ice. Patsy's bike arrived and Thursday had bought the one that was for sale. Elsie brought hers back from a visit home, so they were now able to go further on their afternoons off and one Saturday afternoon the six of them cycled out through the big gateway, feeling as if they'd been set free. They rode all the way along the road that ran along the top of the sea wall to Gilkicker and past the big red-brick fort that had been built almost on the beach.

It was the first time they'd all been out together since the day they'd met in the Swiss Café. It wasn't often that their time off coincided and Thursday and Tony had only seen each other on the ward, but Patsy had been to the pictures with Roy Greenaway a couple of times and Elsie had been to the Forum cinema in Gosport with Doug Brighton, and told Thursday it was like sitting next to an octopus. 'You never know where his hands are going to be next!' she said, but her grin told Thursday she hadn't objected much.

'I wouldn't trust him further than I can throw him,' Thursday said, but Elsie just laughed and said she could handle Doug Brighton. He already knew that he only had to go an inch too far and he'd get a slap.

The road led inland for a little way and then past a row of big, elegant houses and out to the beach again, where it stopped. Away on either side ran the sweep of Stokes Bay, with only a rough track running along the top of the shingle.

'It's all stones,' Patsy said in a disappointed voice. 'There's hardly a patch of sand anywhere.'

'There isn't much sand anywhere along this coast,' Elsie admitted. 'It's all shingle.'

'What, even at Southsea?' Thursday asked teasingly.

'Even at *Brighton*, and nobody seems to complain about that!' Elsie retorted, making a face at her. 'It's good for swimming, though. I've come out a few times, when I've been over to see my gran. Mind you, there's no amusement arcade or fair, like there is at Southsea and Clarence Pier. Not even a prom. It's just beach.'

'There's a pier,' Patsy pointed out. 'But it looks as if something's happened to it – it's all broken down at this end.'

'That was done deliberately,' Tony told her, 'so that the Germans couldn't use it for landing when they invade.'

'*If* they invade,' Thursday corrected him automatically. 'But you can see this would be a good place for them to try.'

It was almost like a spring day, still cold but bright with a pale sun shining, and the sea glittered blue all the way over to the green hump of the Isle of Wight. Gulls swooped on the water, calling in raucous voices, and there were a few people walking their dogs along the shoreline. One black Labrador was rushing in and out of the waves, and a Jack Russell that reminded Thursday of her Auntie Maud's Nipper joined it, barking hysterically. Thursday felt a sudden pang of longing for Patch, who had never even seen the sea. He'd love it here, she thought, and wished she could see him again. But except for girls who lived nearby, like Elsie, none of them had been able to go home yet. They'd been promised some leave at Easter and she was looking forward to it. Only a couple of weeks now.

It must be nice, living by the sea, she thought. She looked at the beach and imagined it crowded with families in the summer, their bikes leant up against each other while the children scrabbled for enough sand to build a castle and the parents lay back on an old blanket in the sun.

Wooden groynes had been built running down the beach to break up the waves and prevent the storms that could blow up along the Solent from doing too much damage. It was almost as if the beach had been divided up into compartments. Probably people had their favourite places and looked on them almost as if they owned them.

'I suppose lots of people come out here in summer,' she remarked. 'Families and so on.' She gazed along the sweep of Stokes Bay. 'I bet it's lovely here on a sunny day.'

'Oh, yes, it's all right,' Elsie conceded. 'It gets quite crowded at weekends. Mostly Gosport people, of course.'

'Well, it's not crowded now,' Doug commented, taking off his round matelot's cap to smooth back his hair. 'There's not another soul to be seen, apart from those people with their dogs. Pretty bleak, if you ask me.'

'Nobody did ask you,' Thursday said a little sharply. 'I think it's nice like this.'

Doug looked at her and raised his eyebrow in the way that always annoyed her. 'Well, pardon me for breathing. Somehow I thought we were all allowed to talk this afternoon, but maybe I was wrong. Maybe we had to have special permission from her ladyship.'

Thursday flushed. He was right, of course, and she shouldn't have snapped at him. But he'd only said it to annoy her. Whatever she said, he had to say the opposite, just because she wasn't taken in by his good looks.

They continued on along the path that had been worn along the top of the beach. Rough, tussocky grass stretched on their right between the beach and the village of Alverstoke with its grey church tower. They turned inland again to cycle on to Lee-on–Solent and stopped to look at the pier and the tall white tower.

'What's that for?'

'It's a sort of entertainment place. You can go up to the top and look at the view in summer, and there's a tea-place and a ballroom. They have quite good dances.' Roy Greenaway looked at them, his blue eyes twinkling. 'We could come to some.'

The girls brightened. 'That'd be good. But it's a cup of tea we could do with now. Is there a café or anything here?'

There was a small café opposite the tower and they parked their bikes and went inside, giving little exclamations of relief at the cosiness. The early March sun, cheering though it was, didn't do much to warm things up. The boys took off their caps and stacked them on the table. Doug once again smoothed back his hair, which Thursday thought had obviously been given a liberal dose of Brylcreem, and Tony ran his fingers through his tousled dark curls.

'Tea and toast all round, I reckon,' he said. 'And I'll have cheese on mine.'

The waitress shook her head. 'No cheese today, love. We've got Spam or Marmite. Or you could have a sausage.'

'Just the one?' he asked, and she nodded and said, 'They're a bit short today.'

'And there's nothing worse than a short sausage,' Doug quipped, and gave Elsie a nudge and a meaning look. 'Isn't that right, Elsie?'

The other two boys grinned and the girls looked at them reprovingly.

'I hope I don't understand that joke,' Thursday said, tossing her head so that her hair swung like a chestnut bell against her cheeks. 'We're not on the ward now, you know.'

'Bit of a prude, are you?' Doug said with a faint sneer in his voice. He lifted his eyebrow.

'I don't think so.'

'Not much good being prudish when you're nursing sailors,' he went on as if she hadn't spoken. 'No such thing as private parts in a hospital. No such thing as privacy.'

'I said, I'm *not* a prude.'

'Not much fun for Tony here if you are,' he said, looking her in the eye.

Thursday flushed scarlet and started to get up. Tony put his hand on her arm and spoke to Doug.

'That's enough, Doug. Thursday's a nice girl, she doesn't like that kind of talk.'

'Shouldn't have joined the Navy then,' he said. 'You know what they say. If you can't stand the heat, get out of the kitchen.'

'I didn't volunteer to make stupid jokes about men's private parts or to be called a prude,' Thursday said tightly. 'I volunteered to help nurse people who were injured in the war. So that people like you could go back to sea and nurse them on board ship. And if you ask me, it's a pity that's not where you are now.'

'Here, hang on a minute, Thursday,' Elsie said. 'It's not Doug's fault he hasn't been drafted. They're waiting till we're properly trained.'

'They'll wait a long time then,' Doug said, still looking at Thursday. 'Some of the VADs I've seen still haven't found out how to scrub the brightwork.'

'And some of the SBAs I've seen still haven't learnt any manners.'

'All right, you two, all right, that's enough,' Patsy said. 'There's no need to get all aeriated. It was just a joke, that's all.'

'Yes, come on, Thursday, calm down,' Elsie said. 'He didn't mean anything.'

'He did. He's been needling me all afternoon. He never stops.'

'I haven't said a word—' Doug said in an injured tone.

'You don't have to say anything. It's the way you look at me.'

'Well, I won't look at you again,' Doug said. 'Will that be better?' He turned his chair away and gazed across the café at the far wall. There was a large mirror fixed to it and

143

Thursday, following his gaze, saw that his reflected eyes were meeting hers. He put on a soulful expression and then winked at her. She struggled for a moment with her annoyance, and finally burst out laughing.

'Oh, you're impossible!'

'No, I'm not,' he said, still looking at her in the mirror. 'I'm just unusual. Like you, Thursday – remember?'

Thursday sighed and gave in. 'All right, I'm sorry. I shouldn't have reacted like I did.'

'Well, maybe I shouldn't have said what I did. And I shouldn't have laughed at your name the first time we met.' He turned back and reached his hand across the table, his eyes twinkling as he looked directly at her. 'I'm sorry, Thursday. I think it's a nice name – honestly.'

'Well, thank goodness for that,' Patsy said as they shook hands. 'It's not much fun for the rest of us, I can tell you, having to listen to you snipe at each other. Perhaps now we can settle down and be friends.'

Thursday met Doug's eyes across the table and grinned a little unwillingly. After all, what had he really done to annoy her? Put his arm round her waist, that was all. And said something a bit smutty that she shouldn't even have understood. And what if he was too good-looking? He couldn't actually *help* it, could he? And maybe anyone who looked like Gregory Peck was likely to be a bit conceited about it!

'Yes, and keep the party clean,' Roy said. 'Just because we work together on the wards doesn't mean the girls find the same things funny outside.'

'I know,' Doug said. 'But they're going to hear a lot worse jokes than ones about sausages before this lot's over, and see a lot worse, too.' He looked at the three girls and his voice was suddenly serious. 'All you've done so far is take a few bedpans round and wipe a few bottoms. All the patients you've seen are getting better. You wait till we get a crew straight off a ship that's been blown up. You wait till you've got a bloke with no arms landing in your lap, screaming for his mother. You wait till you see some poor bugger with his face burnt away. You wait till you see raw nerves and flesh and a muscle hanging out by its strings. You won't worry about a few smutty jokes then. You'll be glad of *anything* to raise a grin.'

The girls gazed at him. None of them could think of a thing to say. It was quite clear that Doug had seen all these things and more, and that he thought they would be seeing them, too. Thursday looked at the others and felt sick.

'I'm sorry,' she said quietly. 'It's just that it's all new to us, see. We haven't got the hang of things yet. I know we've got to learn to be more broad-minded.'

'You'll have to,' he said grimly. 'None of you will be much use at Haslar if you don't.'

Thursday and Tony cycled without speaking through the lanes of Rowner. The others were slightly ahead, their laughter floating back towards them, but Thursday felt subdued. Mum and Dad always did tell me I was too touchy, she thought.

There were woods and commons on either side, and she thought it would be a good place for picnics later on in the year. There was a golf club, too, but there was still plenty of room for anyone who wanted to come out and enjoy the countryside. I bet there'll be bluebells in those woods soon, she thought. And blackberries in the autumn.

Tony rode along beside her and glanced at her face. 'Feeling a bit better now?'

She nodded. 'I suppose I shouldn't have flown off the handle like that. I can take a joke as well as the next person, I just don't like smut, that's all, and Doug does get under my skin a bit, I don't know why.'

He nodded, then said, 'But you are going to have to get used to it, you know. People like Doug – well, he's seen a lot of nasty things. A few off-colour jokes don't seem very important when you've been through what he has.' He paused. 'He was on the *Grenville*, too, you know.'

Thursday looked at him. 'The *Grenville*? The ship that stoker was on? The one that sank?'

Tony nodded. 'He wasn't hurt but he was brought to Haslar with the rest of the crew. He'll get a new draft soon but he wanted to be with them as long as possible. Haven't you noticed he comes and has a yarn with Stoker Davis most days? He was one of the blokes Davis dragged into the lifeboat. If it hadn't been for Davis, he wouldn't be here now.'

Thursday didn't speak for a moment. Then she said, 'I wish I'd known that before.' She glowered at the gorse bushes they were passing. 'I'm too flipping prickly, that's my trouble,' she said bitterly. 'I've always been like it, but if I'd *known* that about Doug—'

'It's the same with a lot of the blokes,' Tony told her. 'Almost everyone you meet in Haslar's been through something like that. And it'll be true more and more as this war goes on. They might all be heroes, but that doesn't mean you have to like them all.'

'No, but not liking them doesn't mean I've got to make my own judgements on the sort of people they are,' Thursday said. 'Anyway, we're not supposed to let that sort of thing get in the way of the work, are we? They're *patients* – or they're like you and Doug and Roy, people we've got to work with. Maybe that's why we're not supposed to "fraternise",' she added thoughtfully.

'Well, never mind all that,' Tony said, cycling close beside her. 'I've been wanting to get you on your own. I wanted to ask you if you'd got a boyfriend at home. I bet you have – a girl like you's probably got a boy for every night of the week.'

'Hey, what's that supposed to mean?' Thursday demanded indignantly, and he grinned.

'Not what it sounded like! Sorry – what I meant was, you'd have plenty of boys wanting to go out with you. But is there anyone serious?'

'Not at present, no.' Thursday hesitated. 'Well, there

146

never was really. Only a chap I used to knock about with a bit, go to the pictures and that sort of thing. But it wasn't serious, and he took the huff when I told him I was volunteering for the VADs.'

Tony raised his eyebrows but said nothing. They had reached the town again now and were cycling through the built-up streets. The others had got well ahead, Patsy with Roy, Elsie with Doug. Thursday noticed a small cinema on their right. 'We could go to the flicks some time.'

'Yes, I wouldn't mind,' Thursday agreed. 'I expect the others would like to go, too.'

'Well, it's a free country.' He gave her a grin. 'That's what we're fighting for, isn't it! But I don't want to go round in a gang all the time, Thursday. I'd like us to be on our own sometimes. Like now. We can talk better.'

'We can't do much talking in the pictures,' Thursday pointed out, and he gave her another grin, with a wicked glint in his eye.

'Well, maybe it's not just talking I had in mind.'

Thursday tried to look exasperated. 'You sailors! You're all the same.'

'And aren't you glad of it,' he retorted, and they both laughed.

Thursday glanced around for something to say to change the subject. 'What's this place we're passing now? It looks a bit like Haslar, with that long wall and all those square windows. And that big gateway.'

'It's HMS *St Vincent*. It's a training place for boy seamen. If you look through the gateway you'll see the mast with rigging, just like on a sailing ship. They send all the sprogs up there and one has to stand right on the top. They call him the button-boy.'

Thursday turned her head to peer through the gateway at the tall mast. It seemed impossibly high to send young boys up. 'How old are they?'

'They start at about thirteen.'

Thursday stared at him. 'Boys go into the Navy at thirteen?'

Tony nodded. 'They start us young, you see. I mean, there's a lot to learn when you go into the Navy. All about ships, and girls, and the sea, and girls, and—'

'All right, all right, I get the message. Every nice girl loves a sailor, and all that.' She grinned at him. 'We don't have much chance to do anything else round here – there's nobody else around! And it's harder to tell which ship they're off, now that you can't wear the name on your hatbands. So we don't know whether the chap we're going out with is likely to be around next week or whether he's going to love us and leave us. I thought that was supposed to confuse the enemy, but I reckon it's more confusing for the girls!'

The others had stopped and were waiting for them, their bikes propped against the kerb. 'Doug says why don't we go in the Swiss Café before we go back?' Patsy said, looking at Thursday. 'He said he'll stand us a penny bun each to make up for upsetting you.'

Thursday looked at Doug. 'You don't need to do that. It was my fault as much as yours.'

'Well, I'll do it anyway. Come on, we've just got time and it was a cold ride all the way from Lee.'

Their eyes met and she knew he was genuinely sorry he had upset her. Maybe he's not so bad after all, she thought, and smiled at him. They mounted their bikes again, turning towards the high street, and went into the little café where they had first met. It was as warm and welcoming as ever, and they sank on to chairs and ordered tea and penny buns. Tony sat next to Thursday, pulling his chair a little closer, and they talked quietly together, their voices muted under cover of the chatter all around them.

'I love these,' Thursday said, taking a bun. 'When I was a kid I used to pick off the brown shiny top and save it for last.'

'I did that, too.' Their eyes met and Thursday felt a little shiver brush across her skin. Tony smiled. 'Where's your home? Gloucester, isn't it?'

'Worcester. It's quite different to this.'

'Almost in the middle of the country. Had you ever seen the sea before you came here?'

'We went to Weston-super-Mare a couple of times. But you're lucky if you see the sea there – the tide goes out for miles!' Thursday glanced around the little café. All the tables were taken, and at almost every one there were men in uniform. There were women, too – Wrens in their dark blue, a few khaki-clad ATS and a couple of VADs she recognised from Haslar. 'You're not so aware of the Services in Worcester. We've got an Army regiment – my brother's joining them – but you don't see them around in the city as much as you see people here. Gosport seems to be one big barracks in itself.'

'Well, it was meant to be, I suppose.' Tony reached for another bun. 'It was built like a fort with bastions all around it, so that it could be defended in any direction. And that would defend Portsmouth Harbour.'

'I haven't been over to Portsmouth yet,' Thursday said. 'We haven't had much time off so far, and the weather's been so awful . . . Elsie's asked me and Patsy to go home with her some time. She lives somewhere called Fratton.'

'*Somewhere called Fratton*?' Tony exclaimed in pretended shock. 'You can't say that – Fratton's famous. It's where Portsmouth football team have their ground. You must have heard of the Pompey football team.'

'Well, yes. My dad listens to football on the wireless and does the pools, and Steve's football mad. But I never take much notice.'

'And you look such a nice, intelligent girl, too.' Tony said, shaking his head sadly.

Thursday giggled. 'Do you have to be intelligent to follow football?'

'You be careful, my girl. People have been pushed off the top of Pneumonia Bridge for less than that.'

'Ooh, I'm really scared,' she whispered, putting her hands up to her face in mock terror. Their eyes met again and she felt a shiver touch her skin. There was a moment of silence.

'Come on, you two,' Patsy broke in suddenly, and Thursday glanced up in surprise. She had almost forgotten the others were there. 'It'll be getting dark soon. It's not much fun cycling with no lights in the blackout.'

'Speak for yourself!' Elsie said, with a glance at Doug. 'I think it could be a *lot* of fun!' She gave Thursday a mischievous glance. 'And going by the way you two have got your heads together, I reckon you might think so, too.'

Thursday looked sideways at Tony and blushed at the twinkling look in his eyes. Well, maybe it will be, at that, she thought, and gave another shiver of excitement. I never felt like this with Sidney, she thought, not even when he kissed me. I never felt anything much when he kissed me.

She wondered what it would be like if – *when* – Tony kissed her.

Chapter Ten

Easter came early that year. The week before the end of March, with the snow and ice gone at last from the streets and still no sign of German bombers, everyone wanted some fun. The girls had all got the weekend off but before they went home there was a dance on at Lee Tower ballroom and they were all going, to celebrate.

'Though I'm not sure what we're celebrating,' Elsie remarked, smoothing the golden hairs off her legs with a piece of sandpaper. 'We're still stuck in this hospital and there's still a war on, even if we haven't got all that many new patients coming in at the moment. We can't even wear pretty frocks, we've got to go in uniform. I mean, who's going to want to dance with a girl in uniform when all the local girls can wear their frocks?'

'Well, there's nothing we can do about that. Some men like uniforms, anyway. And we're celebrating spring coming.' Thursday peered into the scrap of mirror over the washstand as she polished her chestnut hair with a silk scarf. ' "*The winter is over and gone, the time of the singing of the birds is come and the voice of the turtle is heard in the land.*" '

The others stared at her. 'What on earth are you on about? Is that poetry?'

'I think it's from the Bible, actually. Our English teacher used to say it to us at school.'

'I didn't think turtles made a noise,' Patsy said, filing her nails. 'A sort of gurgling, perhaps. And do they really come back in spring, like swallows? Anyway, the Bible happened on land, not at sea.'

'There was the Sea of Galilee,' Elsie reminded her.

'That's not a proper sea, it's an inland sea – a big lake.'

'I don't think they were really turtles anyway,' Thursday said, wishing she'd never started it. 'It means turtle *doves*. I'm not ever going to quote bits of the Bible at you two again, you're just philistines.'

'Don't you mean Pharisees?' Elsie asked, and Thursday threw a hairbrush at her.

'Never mind all that. Look, Patsy, have you made up that row with Roy yet? It's going to be a bit miserable if we go to the dance and you two are still at loggerheads.'

'I don't have to go with Roy,' Patsy said. She finished her nails and picked up a black lisle stocking. 'Just look at this hole, it's enormous! Anyway, there are other fish in the sea.'

Elsie groaned. 'Now we're back to turtles again!'

'Yes, but the trouble is,' Thursday said, ignoring her, 'if you don't go with Roy you can't come with us either, because the other two won't go without him.'

'Flipping heck! They're not chained together, are they? They can go out without each other.'

'They won't, though. No more than we will. And it's nice, going round in a group. Come on, Patsy, promise you'll make it up. It wasn't anything serious, was it?'

'S'pose not,' Patsy said reluctantly.

'Well, then. Get up off that bed and do your hair.' Thursday looked at her own in the mirror. It shone like a conker polished on a small boy's trousers. She clipped it back at the temples and let it fall in a shimmering bell to her shoulders. 'And you can use my new lipstick if you like. You know you'll enjoy it when you get there.'

The whole dormitory seemed to be going to the dance at Lee Tower. There would be plenty of young men there – sailors from *Hornet* and *Dolphin*, Fleeties from *Daedalus*, and lots of local girls to supplement the VADs and Wrens. Even Madam had promised to put in an appearance, though none of the girls could imagine her dancing.

'Which just goes to show how wrong you can be,' Thursday remarked a few hours later as they watched Miss Makepeace whirl by in the arms of the Surgeon Rear Admiral. 'She's a smashing dancer.'

'I wouldn't mind being able to foxtrot like that,' Tony admitted. He slid his hand down Thursday's arm and took her hand. 'Let's go outside for a minute.'

Thursday got up and followed him. It was part of the evening to nip outside for a few minutes with your partner, and everyone studiously avoided looking at you as you went – though they were quick enough to notice smudged lipstick when you came back! She felt in her pocket to make sure she had a hanky to wipe any tell-tale stains from Tony's cheeks.

Hand in hand, they walked slowly along the promenade, passing other couples who were standing at the rails gazing out over the whispering sea. The full moon had thrown down a glimmering pathway which seemed to lead directly to the mysterious bulk of the Island. We could walk across it, Thursday thought, we could walk across it into a magic land where there's no war and nothing to do but be happy.

Tony stopped and took her in his arms. They kissed gently and she sighed and laid her head on his shoulder.

Since the day a couple of weeks before, when they'd all cycled out to Lee together, she'd been feeling different about Tony. Before that, he'd been no more than one of the SBAs she worked with, a pleasant fellow with dark curls and friendly eyes who tipped her the wink when Sister Burton or Matron was about to come into the ward, and sometimes offered to sluice out the bedpans for her. It had been nice to run into him and his mates at the Swiss Café that day but there hadn't really been time to take the friendship any further, although she'd hoped they'd get the chance some time. But as they'd pushed their bikes back in the dark past Trinity Church that evening, he'd stopped suddenly and pulled her against him. She'd felt his lips against her cheek, and then on hers, and she'd felt a great surge of excitement. I never felt like this with Sidney, she thought, I never felt anything like this with Sidney . . . And she'd pressed herself close to Tony and found herself returning his kiss, wanting it to go on.

Since then, they'd found quite a few odd moments to slip away into a dark corner of the hospital grounds for a few more kisses. They'd been to the pictures, too, as Tony had suggested, though they hadn't seen a lot of the film. He'd managed to get seats in the back row, right in the corner, and they'd cuddled close together in the dark, blissfully aware that all those nearby were similarly engaged. Nobody in the back row took any notice of anyone else – or of the film. That wasn't what the back row was for.

'You wouldn't think there was a war on at all,' Thursday murmured. 'It's all so peaceful. And everyone seems so happy, enjoying themselves in there.' She shivered a little. 'I feel sort of excited because summer's coming, and there ought to be so much to look forward to – and then I remember that now the weather's better Hitler will probably start the air raids and we could be bombed or invaded at any minute, and I feel scared instead. What's going to happen to us all, Tony?'

He said nothing for a moment. Then, laying his face against her hair, he said quietly, 'I can tell you what's going to happen to me, Thursday. I'm going away.'

A cloud drifted across the moon, suddenly throwing the promenade and the sea into darkness, blotting out the silver pathway. Thursday lifted her head and stared at him, trying to make out his expression. 'What do you mean? Have you had a draft?'

'Yes. It's partly your fault.' He tried to speak jokingly. 'You're all so well trained now, us poor SBAs aren't needed any more, so we've all got to go to sea. I'm joining a ship at the end of next week.'

'Next *week*?'

'Yes,' he said. 'But I'll be leaving Haslar before that –
I've got a few days' embarkation leave. I'll have to go
home, see my mum and dad and everything.'

There was a silence. Thursday stood very still in his
arms. I knew this would happen, she thought, I knew he'd
have to go away. We're not serious about each other.
We've just been having fun. We haven't even known each
other more than a few weeks. I *knew* he'd have to go away.
But . . .

'Oh, *Tony*,' she said, and tears crept down her cheeks.

'Hey,' he said, feeling the wetness against his face.
'What's all this? You're not going to go all soppy on me,
are you, Thurs?'

She tried to laugh, but it choked in her throat.

'No, of course not. I just felt – well – you know – it took
me by surprise, I suppose.' She felt for her hanky. 'Sorry.'

'It's all right,' he said quietly. 'I feel a bit like crying
myself.'

'Oh, Tony.' Now she did laugh. 'You don't!'

'I do. Half of me doesn't want to go away, Thursday.
Not now we're just getting to know each other.'

He paused and she said, 'And what about the other
half?'

'Oh, the other half can't wait,' he said with a grin.
'Going to sea again – getting the chance to give old Hitler
a bloody nose. It's what we all want, isn't it, we blokes?'

'So you don't want to cry too much.'

'Not too much, no,' he said honestly. 'This past
fortnight or so's been good, Thursday, and I don't want to
leave you. But I can't honestly say I wish I wasn't going.
It'll be good to get back to sea, and I've been itching for a
crack at the Huns.'

'But you won't actually be fighting. You'll be in the sick
bay.'

'When we're in action,' he said, 'we're all fighting. You
can't be on board ship and not be part of it.'

Thursday was silent. Then she said, 'You haven't told me which ship you're joining.'

'The *Rodney*,' he said. 'It's a battleship. I can't say where we'll be going.'

'No, I know. Walls have ears and all that.' She shivered against him. 'Oh, Tony . . . Tony, if you want me to wait for you, I will. It doesn't matter that we've only known each other a few weeks—'

'No,' he said. 'It wouldn't be fair to ask you to wait, and not go out with other blokes, and then come back and find we didn't feel the same any more. Look, we don't know how long this war's going to last, or what's going to happen to any of us. It's better not to be tied.'

Thursday felt the tears burn her eyes. 'But I want you to know that when you come back—'

'We don't know that I *will* come back,' he said sombrely. 'Look, I told you about the *Grenville* and what the blokes were like that came off that. You've seen some of them in the wards – they're better now, but there's still that poor blighter who lost both his legs, and the one who was blinded. And I told you about some of their girlfriends – they can't cope with it. They don't know what to do. Some of them stick by their boys, but some of them just walk away. I don't want you to have to make that sort of decision, Thursday. I don't want you to feel tied.'

'I wouldn't feel that.'

'You don't know what you'd feel,' he said soberly. 'Those girls didn't know they'd feel like that either. It's not their fault – they just weren't ready for that kind of thing. Maybe they got engaged without really being sure. Without knowing each other well enough. That's what I feel about us, Thursday. We don't know each other well enough. We haven't had time. I don't want you to feel tied to me. It's too soon.' He kissed her ear. 'It's not goodbye,' he whispered. 'I'll come back, and maybe we can start again. And I'd like you to write to me.'

'I will,' she said. 'I will write. Oh, Tony—'

'It's been fun,' he said firmly. 'It's been smashing, knowing you. But now I've got to go away. Give me a kiss, Thursday, a proper kiss to remember you by.' He bent his head and touched her lips with his.

Thursday clung to him. Their lips met again and she felt him shake. She pressed her lips against his, trying to feel the surge of desire she'd felt when they first kissed, but all she could feel was sadness.

'Don't let's go back inside,' she said. 'Let's just stay out here. Let's find somewhere to sit down and be together.'

'We'll go back for the last waltz,' he said, and with their arms wound tightly around each other's waists they walked slowly along the moonlit prom. 'Let's have one more dance to remember.'

Easter leave for the VADs started on the day before Good Friday. They had the whole weekend off, and didn't have to be back until they went on duty on Tuesday morning. It was their first home leave since they had arrived at Haslar, and they were all wildly excited at the idea of seeing their families again.

Tony came to the railway station to see Thursday off. She and Patsy were catching the same train and Patsy scrambled aboard, taking Thursday's bag with her.

'You two say your fond farewells here and I'll find seats.' Patsy winked at Tony. 'Good luck. See you again soon.'

Left alone on the platform, the two stared at each other. For a few moments, Thursday could think of nothing to say. She glanced down at the wooden platform, with the sea surging beneath it.

'It seems ages since Patsy and I first came here, back in January,' she said with a laugh. 'But it's only just over three months – no time at all, really. And it's even less than that since we first met – you and me.'

'I know,' he said quietly. 'Not long. But long enough to know . . .'

'Know what?' she whispered, when he stopped.

Tony looked at her gravely. 'Long enough to know that I meant what I said last week. I like you too much to want to tie you down, Thursday. If we had a bit longer . . .'

'Oh, Tony,' she whispered. 'I meant what I said, too. I would wait for you – if you wanted me to.'

'No,' he said, and bent his head to her face. 'No, I'm not going to ask you to do that. It isn't fair – not after just a few weeks. But – oh, Thursday, I *wish* we had longer. I wish so *much* that we had longer . . .'

The whistle of the train shrieked in their ears. A puff of steam billowed around them and they clung together and kissed. If we had longer, Thursday thought desperately, if we really did have longer – what would happen? Would we find we loved each other – or would it just fizzle out, like it did with me and Sidney? And will we ever get the chance to find out?

'Thursday, get in the train, for heaven's sake!' Patsy shrieked, leaning out of the window. 'You'll get left behind – come *on*!'

Thursday tore herself out of Tony's arms. 'I'll have to go. Oh, Tony, take care. Please take care. And I'll write – I promise I'll write.'

Between them, with Tony pushing and Patsy dragging at her arms, they got her into the train. The porter came along and slammed the door and Thursday leant out of the window, waving wildly. Her cheeks were wet with tears, and she was half laughing, half crying as the train puffed out of the station and she watched him dwindle away in the distance. Then the train rounded a bend and he was gone, and Patsy hauled her into the compartment where she had saved two seats.

'Well, that's that,' she said, pulling Thursday into the seat beside her. 'Fun while it lasted, but he's gone now and you'll have to look for someone else to go around

158

with. It's no good looking at me like that,' she added, catching Thursday's shocked expression. 'You weren't in love with Tony, any more than I am with Roy.'

'How do you know that?' Thursday demanded. 'You don't have any idea whether I'm in love with him or not.'

'Well, more fool you if you are,' Patsy remarked. 'It's no use falling in love these days, Thurs. Not seriously, anyway. *I* don't intend to – not with Jeff, nor Roy, nor anyone else. I'll be friends with them, I'll have a bit of fun and a few kisses, there's no harm in that – but I'm blowed if I'll let it go any further. You just get hurt if you do that, Thursday, believe me.'

Thursday said nothing. She looked out of the window and thought of Tony, left behind at Portsmouth to join his ship. By the time she came back off leave he might be anywhere. He might even have been sunk.

'I don't know whether I loved him or not,' she said honestly. 'We didn't have time to find out. I just know I *might* have done – if we'd had longer.' She turned to Patsy. 'I don't think I want to just have fun. I want to love someone – really love someone.'

Patsy looked at her shrewdly.

'Well, I expect you will, one day. But don't go looking for it in every chap you meet, Thursday, and don't try to force it either. Just wait till it comes of its own accord. And in the meantime—' she grinned wickedly '—just do what your Auntie Patsy says and have fun. It's good practice, if nothing else!'

It was strange to be at home again. Thursday arrived at the front door, fumbling in her bag for the key she'd been given on her birthday and remembering the big red wooden one her father had given her, but before she could do anything else, the door swung open and her sister Jenny stood there, beaming with delight.

'Thursday! Gosh, you're doing your hair different!'

'It's to get it under my cap more easily.' Thursday

stepped through the door and gave her sister a hug. 'And you've got taller, surely.'

'I've grown another inch and a half,' Jenny said proudly. 'I'm taller than Mum now.'

'*Everyone's* taller than Mum.' Steve, who had just completed his first six weeks' training in the Army, was behind her, grinning. 'Hiya, Thurs. How's tricks?'

'Okay, thanks.' She made a face at him and was then nearly knocked off her feet as her mother came flying through from the kitchen and enveloped her in a tremendous hug. 'Oh, *Mum*! Mum, it's so good to see you again. Oh, and here's Patch too!'

'It seems years since you went away. Let me look at you.' Mary's eyes ran over her assessingly. 'Are you sure you're eating enough? They're feeding you properly, are they?'

'Mum, we never stop eating! We probably get more than you do. How are you getting on with the ration books?'

'Oh, they're dreadful. You should hear our Jenny go on about them at the shop. Well, you probably will.' Mary took Thursday's bag from her and pushed her into a chair. 'I'll make a cup of tea. What sort of journey did you have? At least there's no snow now, not like when you went. What's Haslar like? And Gosport? Have you been to Portsmouth yet?'

'Don't you read my letters?' Thursday demanded, getting out of the chair and following her mother to the kitchen. 'I've told you all those things.' Patch was leaping at her, and she lifted him into her arms.

'I know, but it's not the same as hearing it from your own lips. What about the other girls – and Patsy and Elsie? They sound nice girls. Have they gone home, too?'

'Never mind them,' Jenny said wickedly, poking her head round the door. 'What about the *sailors*? Have you got a boyfriend yet? And what about that stoker you mentioned, the one that had all the tattoos – is he still there? Is he really tattooed *everywhere*?'

'Jenny, don't be disgusting,' her mother said sharply. 'I don't know why you had to tell us about that, Thursday, it's just given her a lot of silly ideas. Tattoos, indeed! I don't know what that girl's coming to.'

Thursday laughed. 'Well, it did give us all a surprise when we first saw them, but we've got used to them now. A lot of the men have them. They get them done abroad mostly, but there are places in Portsmouth as well – there's one quite close to the harbour. It's a sort of naval tradition, I suppose.'

Mary made the tea and brought it into the living room. The best biscuit tin was produced, with biscuits in it that Jenny said she'd got from the shop specially, and Thursday was made to sit in the best armchair while they plied her with questions. She told them about everything she could think of – the hospital, the town of Gosport and the city of Portsmouth, the harbour and ships, the sea and the cycle rides she'd enjoyed with the other girls. Finally, she told them about the dance and about Tony.

'So you *have* got a boyfriend!' Jenny exclaimed. 'I knew it!'

'Don't be daft,' Thursday told her sharply. 'It's not serious and anyway, he's going away. We said goodbye this morning,' she added with a forlorn note in her voice as she remembered their parting on the station platform.

'Oh, Thursday. I am sorry,' her mother said. 'But still, if it wasn't serious . . . Young Sidney's home, too, you know. I saw his mother in the street the other day, she said he'd got a bit of leave. Maybe you could pop round and—'

'No,' Thursday said firmly. 'No, Mum, I couldn't. It wouldn't be fair. And, anyway, I don't suppose he'd even be interested now.'

'No, he wouldn't,' Jenny piped up from the floor. 'I saw his sister last week and she told me he's got a new girl.

Dorothy, her name is, and he's ever so sweet on her, so there wouldn't be any point in you going round.'

'Oh.' Thursday looked at her sister. So Sidney had a new girl. Well, there was no reason why that should bother her, was there? She'd always said there was nothing serious between them. She hadn't even given him a thought for weeks.

All the same, the news, coming only hours after she had said goodbye to Tony, gave her a cold, lonely feeling and she remembered her words to Patsy. It *would* be nice to have someone to love.

Patsy was right, though. You couldn't go looking for it. And you certainly couldn't force it to happen.

The Tilfords had organised a family party for Easter Day. Everyone was coming to Walter's and Mary's house for tea. Flo and Percy were there with Denise, Albert and Ada had walked round from the next street, and Maudie had come over on the train from Ledbury, bringing Nipper. He and Patch were sent straight into the garden.

'I've brought some flapjacks, too,' Maudie said, taking a tin from her shopping bag. 'Thought they'd do for tea.'

Mary took them, smiling her thanks. 'Oh, yes, we all love your flapjacks. I've made some rock buns and a Victoria, and Flo's brought a beautiful fruit cake. She'd got some sultanas and currants saved up since Christmas. Mum's brought some scones and Jenny's made a pink blancmange in that rabbit mould and put green jelly all round it – looks lovely, it does.'

There was an atmosphere of celebration. Thursday had spent the morning making hot cross buns and Steve had brought bars of chocolate from his allowance. He lounged in his mother's armchair in his new khaki uniform, talking to his father and uncle about his 'square-bashing' while his grandfather sat listening. Like the other men, he had already been through a war, but his had been fought in Africa, against the Boers.

'Thursday's been telling us all about Haslar,' Mary said as the women made tea. 'Says it's a beautiful hospital and in a lovely spot, right by the sea. They'll be able to go swimming in the summer. And Portsmouth's a nice place, too, lots of good shops, like Worcester. Not that you've got much money to spend, have you, Thursday?'

'Not by the time they've deducted most of our pay for rations and uniform,' Thursday said ruefully. 'And we have to pay for any breakages, too. Jeanie Brown was nearly in tears the other day when she dropped a thermometer, but the patients all had a whip-round to pay for another one. I don't know what she'd have done, else.'

'Well, us nurses never do get paid much, do we?' Maudie commented. 'But there's always the chance of marrying some nice young doctor! We'll have to have a bit of a chinwag all to ourselves later on, Thursday. Mary, I've finished this sardine and tomato paste – what d'you want me to use next?'

'There's a pot of bloater over there, look. I managed to get a bit of luncheon meat, too – the men will like that. Pity those pullets Flo and Percy have bought haven't come into lay yet, we could have had a few boiled eggs as well. Still, I think it's a pretty good spread, all things considered,' Mary declared, looking at the piled plates.

Thursday looked at her aunt. 'How's Mike, Auntie Flo, have you heard from him lately? And what about Leslie? I was sure he'd be with you today.'

Flo's mouth turned down at the corners. 'He'll be along later, in time for tea. He stayed home to sort out his things, ready for Tuesday. You know he's been taken in the RAF? Minute he turned seventeen, they took him in. We did our best to stop him, your Uncle Perce laid the law down proper, but there was nothing we could do. He said he'd go whatever we did, and he's so headstrong we knew he meant it. Says he'll never get a chance as good as this, and you know he's always been mad about aeroplanes.'

163

'Well, they'll never let him fly, surely, a boy of seventeen,' Mary said. 'I mean, he's barely old enough to drive a car.'

'I hope not. But it's out of our hands now, see. This is war, and once their lads are in the Services what parents want just doesn't come into it any more.' She stood with her hand on a pile of sandwiches, ready to slice them into squares, and sighed heavily. 'As for our Mike, he's off to France with the BEF. Looking forward to it, too. Says Hitler doesn't stand a chance against the whole Army. Well, maybe he's right, but it stands to reason *some* of them are going to get hurt and killed. I just pray every night it won't be him – and then I think of all the other mothers praying for their boys, and I feel guilty for doing it.'

'You don't have to feel like that. We're all bound to think of our own.' Mary took the knife from her sister's hand and cut the sandwiches. 'There, put those on that meat-plate – goodness knows when it'll see a joint of meat again – and we'll start laying the table. Tell those men to get up off their backsides and go outside. Walter can show them the garden, he's got all sorts of veg growing out there, planted a lot of stuff over the weekend, he has – beans and carrots, and I don't know what else. If it all comes up, we'll not need to bother the greengrocer all summer.'

Thursday looked at her mother and aunt and thought of the young sailors she had seen at Haslar. Boys no older than Leslie in the wards, brought in off ships that had been sunk by enemy action. The eighteen-year-old who had lost both legs, the one who was blind. As yet, she hadn't seen men with fresh wounds, but she knew it would come, and she knew that many of them would be no older than her cousin and would have had just as responsible jobs.

Of course they would let Leslie fly. They'd let anyone go to war who was willing and soon they would be conscripting even those who weren't. And then they'd be filling the hospitals, too, with their own injuries – broken and torn limbs, shattered bodies, burns. Why else would the Government be recruiting so many VADs?

She went into the back room where the men were now discussing the RAF raid on the German seaplane base at Hornum, in reprisal for the German bombing of Scapa Flow. Maudie was there, too, and she turned and gave Thursday a look which showed that she also understood what it meant. She also knew that youth was going to be no bar to responsibility and to action.

'Fifty bombers!' Walter said. 'You ought to be proud of your Leslie, Perce, volunteering to join that lot. I know he's jumped the gun a bit, going so early, but you can't say his heart's not in the right place.'

'Oh, he's got the right idea,' Percy agreed unwillingly. 'I just hope he'll take a bit more notice of his officers than he takes of me. He'll find Service discipline a bit strict for his taste, I'm afraid.'

'Well, he'll soon get used to that,' Maudie said briskly, and turned to Steve. 'You'll know all about that, won't you? And I hear you've been learning to wash and iron your own clothes. I thought you were supposed to be training to be a soldier, not a washerwoman!'

'A smart soldier's an efficient soldier,' Steve said, obviously repeating what one of his officers had said. 'And the enemy wouldn't be very frightened by a crowd of scruffy oiks.'

'So how are you enjoying it, then? Think you'll like being a soldier?'

'Yes, I do, as a matter of fact. I didn't think I would, really. I volunteered because it seemed the right thing to do – but I'm in with some really good blokes, and once we're through our training and we can get out there and start putting the Jerries to rights, we'll be able to feel we're really doing something. And it's interesting learning to fire a gun and use a bayonet and all that. We were throwing grenades the other day. I tell you what, you don't make any mistakes with those.'

'Real grenades?' Mary asked in horror, coming in from the kitchen. 'You mean they could have exploded?'

He nodded. 'That's the idea of them! Once you've pulled out the pin, you throw as hard as you can. This is the Army, Mum, not a Boy Scout camp. We're going over the Channel soon and we'll need to know what we're doing if we're going to beat Hitler's men.' He finished his cup of tea and looked at his father and uncle. 'Let's go for a walk, over the allotment. You can show me what veg we're having for Sunday dinner.'

The men went out, obviously wanting to get away from the women to talk properly, and the women looked at each other.

'I suppose he's right,' Mary said sadly. 'There'll always be wars. It's human nature, isn't it? But I don't suppose there's ever been a mother yet who's really wanted her own boys to go and fight.'

And they'd want it even less if they could see what I've already seen, and what Doug Brighton says we'll see, Thursday thought. But she couldn't say so. What was the point of upsetting her mother and aunt even further? What was the point of telling them the truth?

Jenny and Denise had gone upstairs to the bedroom Jenny shared with Thursday. She thought of it as hers now, even though Thursday's bag was in one corner, her nurse's uniform hung in the wardrobe and her pyjamas were laid on her pillow. Denise held them up in front of herself.

'Proper passion-killers, aren't they? I suppose they're to put the sailors off.'

'Don't be daft, the sailors never see them. They're all in different buildings. I like that green jumper, Dizzy. It's new, isn't it?'

'Well, sort of. Mum unravelled one of hers and knitted it for me. It's all right, but I'd rather have had that pink one she wears.' Denise picked discontentedly at the lacy pattern, then reached into the new handbag she'd persuaded her brother Mike to buy her before he went away. 'Look, I've got some nail varnish! Crimson Lady, it's called – want to try it?'

'Coo, yes, it's smashing!' They stared at the little bottle of scarlet fluid. 'I've got some remover here – we'll have to take it off again before we go downstairs.' Jenny began to paint her nails, holding them out to gaze at them. 'It's ever so bright, isn't it?'

Their nails painted, they lounged on the beds and compared notes about their jobs, the boys they'd met or would like to meet, and the films they'd seen.

'I know *Pinocchio*'s a kids' film really,' Jenny remarked, looking into the mirror as she fiddled with her dark curls, 'but it was good all the same. And there's some really scary bits in it, too. I heard quite a few kiddies crying when he got swallowed up by that whale.'

'I didn't like the bit where his nose grew,' Denise said. 'It seemed a bit cruel to me. I went to see *Wuthering Heights* last week with my new boy. It was lovely. Laurence Olivier's a real heart-throb.'

'*What* new boy? You never said you had a new boy. What happened to Brian?' Jenny sat up, agog. Denise was younger than she was, yet had already had a string of boys, all willing to take her to the pictures *and* pay for her to go in, while Jenny had only been out with one boy, and he'd suggested they meet inside. She stared jealously at her cousin.

Denise combed her fair hair with her fingers and looked nonchalant. 'Oh, he's still around. I just decided I didn't want to see him for a couple of weeks, that's all. I dare say I'll go out with him again some time.'

'He might not hang about.'

Denise shrugged. 'Doesn't matter. Plenty more fish in the sea.' She glanced sideways at Jenny and started to take the nail varnish off again. 'You work in the wrong place, that's why you don't get anyone. What boy's going to come into a grocer's shop?'

'I know, but Dad won't let me get a job at the factory. He says the girls are a rough lot and he doesn't want me associating with them. You'd better give me that remover, they'll be shouting for us in a minute. He wanted me to do a tailoring or dressmaking apprenticeship like our Thursday, but even he can see I'd be no good at that – I can't even thread a needle. And he wouldn't let me work in a hairdresser's either, said the premium was too high.'

'That's daft. He'd have had to pay a premium for you to do dressmaking. Anyway, you wouldn't have had any more chance of meeting boys there than at the grocer's.' Denise preened her hair again. 'I get a lot coming in the garage, of course.'

'I thought you were sweet on that mechanic with the curly hair?' Jenny said with a touch of malice. The dark-haired mechanic was at least twenty and had never shown the slightest interest in Denise. About the only boy who hadn't, Jenny thought, rubbing her nails with a scrap of cotton wool and wondering what her cousin had that she didn't.

'Oh, him,' Denise said dismissively. 'He's going out with that redhead from Larksley's. Talking about getting engaged, she is. I don't think he's so keen, mind. Anyway, he'll be called up soon, bound to be.'

'There won't be any boys left to go out with at this rate,' Jenny said gloomily. 'They're all either getting called up or volunteering. The only ones left will be the ones with flat feet or glasses, and who wants to go out with them?' Denise nodded and made a face, and they sat in silence for a moment before Jenny said, 'Anyway, you still haven't told me who this new boy is. Come on, Dizzy, spill the beans.'

Denise grinned. 'Well, you won't believe it, but it's that fellow from the post office. The one on the parcels counter. Vic Pearce, he's called. I take the post down every afternoon, see, and there's usually a parcel or two to send off – parts for other garages, stuff like that. Well, he's been on that counter for the past couple of weeks and we've got chatting and – well, you know. He asked me out on Saturday and we went to see *Wuthering Heights*.' She rolled her eyes. 'It was ever so romantic.'

Jenny stared at her. 'But he must be over twenty! I saw him when I took that parcel down to send to our Thursday.'

'Twenty-two,' Denise said with some pride. 'He told me.'

'Does he know you're only fifteen?'

'No, and you're not to tell him! He thinks I'm eighteen. Well, I look it, don't I? 'Specially when I've done myself up.' She tossed her head defiantly. 'And don't you tell our dad or mum neither, nor yours. They'd go up the wall if they knew I was going out with someone that old.'

'Yes, but – well, you know what boys are like when they get that old.' Jenny spoke doubtfully, not sure herself what she meant, but knowing that older boys spelt trouble. 'I mean – he'll have had other girlfriends, lots of them.'

'Well, I've had lots of boyfriends. It doesn't matter.'

'Yes, but suppose he wants . . . I mean, what happened? Did he put his arm round you or kiss you or anything? In the pictures, I mean.'

'We sat in the back row,' Denise said shortly. 'You've got to have a cuddle if you sit in the back row.'

'And what about afterwards? You want to be careful, Diz.'

'He saw me home like a perfect gentleman and kissed me goodnight at the door,' her cousin retorted. 'I don't know what you're getting at, Jenny. Vic's a decent boy.'

'He's a man,' Jenny said, feeling that as the older of the two she ought to be responsible.

'Man, then. What difference does it make? You're turning into a proper old woman.'

Jenny had an idea it made a good deal of difference but

she said no more. She wasn't sure she knew what the difference was or what the dangers were, she just felt that there must be some in her fifteen-year-old cousin going out with a man seven years older than her. That was nearly half her age again, she thought, aware that her uncle and aunt would have a fit if they had any suspicion. At the same time, she was wildly envious and knew that she would have given her eye teeth to have gone to see *Wuthering Heights* – or any other film – with Vic Pearce from the post office.

'Tell you what,' Denise said generously. 'I'll get Brian to take you to the pictures next week. He won't be doing anything. They're showing *The Lion Has Wings*, it's about the RAF. We saw the trailer.'

'No, thanks,' Jenny said shortly. 'I'll find my own boys. I don't want your cast-offs.' She got up and stared into the mirror on the wall above the chest of drawers. 'Did you get any new lipsticks this week?'

'Yes, I was going to show you. Here.' Denise produced the familiar Ponds tube. 'Cupid's Bow. It's a lovely bright red. Try it.'

'And have my dad see it when we go down? You know what he's like about make-up.'

'Well, so's mine, but I manage. You can wipe it off before we go down. Come on, I'll show you how to make your mouth into a proper Cupid's bow. And it wouldn't hurt you to go to the pictures with Brian, you know. Boys are much more interested in a girl who's already got a boyfriend. They think she's worth going after, see?'

'I can't see any boy being interested in a girl who's going out with Brian Jones,' Jenny sniffed. 'They'll just think she must be desperate. Anyway, I don't want to see a picture about the RAF. I shouldn't think you do either, what with your Leslie joining up.'

Denise, gazing into the mirror as she began to apply her lipstick, grinned. 'We don't need films at our house! It's all he can talk about – flying aeroplanes. Dad keeps telling him they won't let him train for a pilot, but he's dead set on it. And Mum's almost in tears every time she looks at him. I tell you what, Jenny, the minute I'm old enough I'm going to join, too. They're talking about letting women fly as well.'

Jenny stared at her. 'What, Spitfires and Hurricanes? They never are!'

'Not for fighting. It's transport – taking the new planes from the factories to the airfields. They say Amy Johnson's going to be doing it.'

'The one that flew to Australia all on her own? But she's a really good pilot. She's famous.'

'That's right, and now she's flying for the RAF,' Denise said. 'And there's one who's only twenty-two, and she's an instructor as well. She learnt to fly when she was seventeen.'

'Yes, but they're people who can already fly,' Jenny said. 'They won't train new ones.'

'Who says? Anyway, they'll let women work on planes – be mechanics, and all that.' Denise, who was never happier than when grubbing about helping her brother with his motorbike, finished painting a Cupid's bow on her mouth and gave Jenny a radiant smile. 'Look, this is our *chance* – our chance to get away and do something *interesting*. You know what'll happen when it's all over, don't you? We'll have to get married and settle down and live dull, dreary lives like our mums, doing what our husbands tell us all the time. We'll never have another chance like this. I'll do your mouth now.'

Jenny opened her mouth and stretched her lips as her cousin directed. There was silence until Denise had finished and then they both looked into the mirror.

'There,' Denise said. 'Doesn't that look smashing? You could also pass for eighteen now.'

'I could, couldn't I,' Jenny said, staring at herself. 'Maybe I will go out with Brian after all. I like the way you've made it turn up at the corners.'

'Makes you look sort of smiling and cheeky,' Denise agreed. 'Tell you what, there's a dance on at the Oddfellows next Saturday. Why don't I get Vic to ask one of his friends to make up a foursome? That's a better way of meeting other boys than going to the pictures. Come on, Jen, it'll be fun. And our dads won't mind if we say we're going together.'

Jenny turned her head this way and that, still admiring the red Cupid's bow of her lips. She felt a quick tremor of excitement. 'All right. But I'll need to borrow your pink blouse. I haven't got anything else to wear.'

'That's OK, I was going to wear my spotted one anyway.' The ring of the doorbell sounded suddenly, and there was a sudden hubbub of voices. 'That'll be our Leslie arriving.'

Mary's voice sounded from the bottom of the stairs. 'Are you two coming down now? Leslie's here and we're all going out for a walk.'

'Better take this lipstick off,' Jenny said with a grimace. 'Dad'll go mad if he sees it. Says it makes a girl look cheap.'

Denise giggled. 'Well, if it does, I bet she has more fun than an expensive one! Most of the boys I know can only just afford the price of a ticket at the pictures. Except for Vic, of course,' she added with some pride. 'He's getting a good wage, being older and in the post office.'

Jenny scrubbed at her mouth, finding with some panic that the stain was more difficult to remove than she'd expected. There was still a trace of scarlet around her fingernails, too. She hoped her father wouldn't notice. She needed to keep in his good books now, if she was to be allowed to go to the dance next week with Denise and Vic, and Vic's friend. The excitement tingled through her again.

'Will you do my lips when we get there?' she asked. 'And can I borrow your black belt as well?'

Chapter Eleven

It seemed to Thursday, in those first weeks after Tony went away, that it was at sea that the war was fought the most bitterly. All through the winter the Navy had been battling it out, from the River Plate in South America to the North Sea, and now Scandinavia was being drawn in as well. There was a sense that the 'phoney' war, as it had come to be called, might be drawing to an end and the real war beginning. The winter might be over and gone, but with the time of the singing of birds came the threat of invasion.

The hospital, too, was imbued with a sense of waiting. Patients arrived in a fairly steady stream, but there had been no further sudden influxes. As the men got better, they got out of bed and sat round the big iron stoves in the middle of the wards, drinking cocoa and strong tea and swapping tales of life at sea. They always fell silent as the nurses came near, not realising that most of the girls had very good hearing and knew exactly what they were talking about. Thursday thought of Doug's joke about sausages and smiled wryly, wondering how she could ever have been offended by such an innocent quip. I didn't know the half of it! she thought with a grin.

The training of the VADs went on, with the girls learning how to take pulses, give injections and apply drips. It wasn't likely that they'd be expected to undertake these skilled tasks as a general rule, the QARNN who taught them explained rather dismissively, but in times of emergency anything could happen.

'You'll all be having your inoculations tomorrow,' she

informed them as they ended their duty. 'Don't expect to be let off duty if you feel a bit off-colour. The patients must always come first.'

The girls stared at her. 'Inoculations?' Thursday asked. 'What for? I had my smallpox when I was a baby.'

'Yes, but you have to have more now you're in a hospital. You may come into contact with all kinds of diseases, brought in from abroad, besides which you may go abroad yourselves. Cholera, diphtheria, yellow fever—'

'Yellow fever? But that's from China, isn't it?' Elsie exclaimed. 'We're not going to China, surely?'

The QARNN gave them a cold look. 'You don't know where you might go. Anyway, whatever you have, you're having it tomorrow, so be prepared and *don't expect time off.*'

'I can't say I like the idea of this,' Elsie muttered as they went off duty. 'I never did like needles.'

'You didn't say that when you were giving that poor artificer his injection!' Patsy said. 'You told him not to be a big baby.'

'Well, of course I did. I didn't have to tell him I was even more scared than he was. I wonder if they'd let me off if I said I had a cold?'

'No, they wouldn't, they'd give you a double dose,' Thursday said unkindly, but she wasn't really looking forward to the injections any more than Elsie was, and when her turn came to hold out her arm next day she closed her eyes and turned her head away. Later on, when she started to feel shivery and hot, she wondered if she was getting flu, but one look at Sister Burton's face told her that there was no use in saying anything. She finished her duty feeling groggy and went without supper to crawl thankfully into her bunk as soon as the night staff took over.

'If this is just the inoculation,' she heard Elsie groan, 'I hope to God I never get the real thing. Yellow fever must be absolutely *horrible.*'

They felt a little better next day, and on the third day were back to normal. Some more patients had arrived from a trawler which had had an encounter with a mine in the Solent, and Thursday was able to forget her troubles in looking after them. It was when she came off duty that she found herself thinking of Tony, feeling a mixture of sadness and guilt. Did I really love him? she wondered. Or was it just a passing flirtation? She wrote to him every day, trying to keep his cheery face alive in her mind and feeling angry with herself when she couldn't do it.

'Why don't you come home with me this weekend?' Elsie suggested, coming into the dormitory a week or two after Easter to find Thursday sitting despondently on her bed, staring at a blank sheet of paper. 'There can't be anything to write to Tony about – you only posted a letter yesterday. And you haven't been out since we came back off leave.'

'I know. It just makes me feel better. Closer, somehow.' She sighed and closed the writing pad. 'Thanks, Else, but I don't really feel like it. I'll just stop here.'

'No, you won't.' Elsie went across to the mirror and pushed back her yellow hair. 'Stopping in on your day off won't do nobody no good. You'll come with me. I've told my mum all about you and she thinks you sound the sort of girl she wants me to be friends with. So you come and show her how wrong she is, all right?'

Thursday grinned reluctantly. 'Why don't you take Patsy? I'm no company for anyone at the moment, Else, honestly.'

'Because Patsy's all right. She's going out with Roy, anyway. They've made it up again – till next time they have a row. Come on, Thurs,' she wheedled. 'We can go to Commercial Road and look at the shops on the way.'

'We'd have to go on our bikes,' Thursday said. 'I haven't got enough money for the bus. I spent this week's wages on new stockings for the dance.'

'That's all right, I don't mind the ride so long as it's not raining. And if it is, I'll lend you the fare.'

On Saturday it wasn't raining and the two girls set off as soon as they came off duty, cycling down to the jetty to catch the pinnace. They settled themselves on the wooden seats, gazing down at the water churned by the propeller into a pale, sudsy blue. As the boat chugged on its five-minute journey across the harbour, they looked up at the green rampart of the hill that enclosed it, pockmarked by the white chalkpits, and at the naval ships tied up to the jetties in the dockyard.

They stared at the sharp grey prows looming above as the pinnace circled round to approach the Portsmouth pontoon. Thursday thought of Tony, somewhere at sea, and felt the ache of tears in her throat. She turned deliberately away and thought instead of the day she and Patsy had first come to Haslar. They'd caught the naval pinnace then and it had been getting dark as they crossed the harbour. There had been snow and ice on the ground and a bitter wind scouring across the water, bringing yet more snow, while underneath the station platform had hung enormous icicles.

Now spring was coming – the time of the singing of the birds – and the tender blue of the sky was reflected in the dancing waves. And apart from the evidence of the warships – some of which were always present in Portsmouth anyway – there was still little to show that the country was at war.

Little – except for the sandbags piled outside every shop doorway the girls passed as they cycled up Queen Street. Little, except for the strips of brown paper criss-crossing every plate-glass window. Little, except for the cardboard gas-mask boxes hung on every shoulder, the tin hats of the ARP wardens, the posters everywhere reminding gossipers that 'Walls have ears' or that they should 'Be like Dad – keep Mum'. Little, except for the recruiting posters, the air-raid regulations, the public shelters on street corners, the sailors with no ship's name-band on their caps, the nervous glances skywards whenever an aircraft passed overhead.

'Blimey,' Elsie said as they came into Commercial Road. 'It's like a flaming army camp. Don't let's bother with the shops, Thurs. We've got no money, and it's too flipping depressing anyway. Let's just go straight home and see if Mum's managed to make any cakes.'

Thursday nodded. They pedalled through the streets and on to Fratton, where Elsie's family lived in a small house in a quiet back street.

She banged loudly on the front door. 'Dad put in a bell but it's stopped working. Hello, our Eddy,' she greeted the small boy who opened the door. 'I've got something for you.'

The boy was about seven. He stared at Thursday and then backed away, shouting over his shoulder. 'It's our Elsie, and she's brought a lady with her.'

'Lady!' Elsie said, laughing. 'He must mean you, Thurs. I thought for a minute someone else had come in behind us. Hello, Mum,' she added, stopping to kiss a tiny, birdlike woman who had popped out of the kitchen like a wren from a nestbox. 'Looking as good as ever. This is Thursday, that I told you about.'

'It's not,' Eddy said. 'It's Saturday.'

'Her *name's* Thursday, silly. Thursday Tilford. She's a nurse with me at Haslar.'

Eddy stared at her suspiciously. 'How can a person have a day's name?'

'My mum and dad liked it, that's how,' Thursday told him. She smiled at Mrs Jackson. 'I hope you don't mind Elsie bringing me home.'

'Mind? Of course I don't mind! You being miles away from your own home and all. You're welcome. Now . . .' she bustled back to the tiny kitchen '. . . you'll be wanting a cup of tea after that long ride. I'd have had the kettle on ready but I didn't think you'd be here yet. Thought you were going round the shops.'

'We were, but it's so flipping miserable. All those sand-bags and things.' Elsie wandered out after her. 'Where's Dad?'

'Down the shed, mending my shoes. Go and give him a call, there's a duck.' Thursday heard the clatter of teacups being arranged on a tray. 'I made a few rock buns 'specially, supposed to be fruit buns but the currants look as if I chucked them in from the top of the hill. There just aren't any to be had, even on ration.'

Thursday looked around the room. It was small and cluttered, with a dining table in the middle and an armchair each side of the fireplace. On the wall was a big map of Europe which had been given out by the *Daily Express*, with blue pins stuck all over it showing where the Allied forces were and red ones where the Germans were. There were an awful lot of red ones, she thought.

Elsie came back in, followed by a large bald-headed man wearing a dirty shirt and braces. He wiped his hand down the shirt before shaking hands with Thursday and gave her a broad smile then jerked his head towards the map. 'Been looking at my arthritic efforts, then?'

'It's all right,' Elsie said. 'He knows it's supposed to be "artistic". Not that a few pins stuck in a map are anything to do with art.' She looked at the map. 'Blimey, it don't half bring it home to you what's going on. We think it's bugger all just because we're not getting the air raids they were on about, but there's plenty of fighting really, isn't there.'

'Language, Else,' her mother said, coming in with a tray of tea. 'You can see Thursday's a decent girl – she doesn't swear and nor should you. She used to work in a laundry,' she told Thursday, setting the tray on the table. 'Learnt a bit more than washing clothes, she did, and none of it much good to her.'

'They were a pretty rough lot,' Elsie acknowledged.

'But hearts of gold, all the same.' She looked at the map again. 'What d'you think's going to happen next, Dad?'

Mr Jackson was filling a pipe. He tamped down the tobacco, set a match to it and drew in deeply before answering. 'Well, it's up in Scandinavia mostly now, see. The Germans going into Denmark took the Allies by surprise a bit. It'll be Norway next, if I'm any judge, and then us.'

'But they were supposed to be neutral,' Thursday objected. 'They shouldn't have been invaded.'

'It's for their "protection",' Mr Jackson said with heavy sarcasm. 'Mind you, they've turned the tables on the Germans a bit by not putting up a fight. That means they're not at war and the Germans can't take over. They've got to recognise their government, see?'

Thursday didn't really see but she nodded. Elsie was more sceptical.

'I don't see Hitler taking no notice of that. He hasn't bothered too much about rules so far.' She passed Thursday a cup of tea and looked at her mother. 'Is our Dave going to be home tonight?'

'Far as I know. You know he's broken up with that Eileen?'

'He never has! I thought she'd got her claws into him proper.'

'So did I, but he came home last weekend and said they'd finished. Wouldn't say why, but I reckon she'd been a bit sharp with him once too often. You know what she was like.'

'She was a real little cat,' Elsie told Thursday. 'Treated our Dave like dirt. Thought he was a little puppy dog, and so he was for a while, but it wasn't ever going to last. Dave's not the sort to be ordered about.'

They sat chatting as they drank their tea, and then Mr Jackson went back to his shed at the bottom of the garden to finish his cobbling. Eddy took another bun and ran outside to play, and Elsie's mother got out some sewing.

She was doing piecework for the marine barracks at Eastney, she said. Lots of the women in Pompey and the surrounding towns were sewing various items of uniform. They got paid a bit for it, but it was war work as well and you knew that some sailor or marine was going to be glad of the stitches you put in.

'I wonder if my brother will get something you've made,' Thursday said. 'He's gone into the Army. But his regiment's in Worcester, so I suppose it'll be people round there who do the uniforms.'

'Oh, your poor mother,' Mrs Jackson said, laying down her work for a moment. 'She must be so worried. Has he gone away yet?'

'He's just finished his training. He'll be going soon – to Belgium or France, I suppose, that's where most of them seem to be going. Or maybe Norway.'

'Our Dave can't join up,' Elsie observed. 'He's got a bad leg, see – had infantile paralysis when he was a nipper and it left him with one leg a bit short. He has to wear a surgical boot.'

'I never thought I'd be glad he had that,' Mrs Jackson said. 'Poor little chap, he was only five, and stuck in bed ill for months – but now look, it could have saved his life. It's funny how life turns out.'

'Here he comes now,' Elsie said as the back door opened and a young man appeared in the doorway. He had fair hair, a few shades darker than Elsie's blonde, and very dark blue eyes. He came into the room, limping a little, and gave Thursday a shy grin.

'This is my friend Thursday,' Elsie said, 'and this is our Dave. He's a bit of a nuisance but we can't get rid of him.'

Thursday grinned, recognising the same brother–sister banter that went on between herself and Steve. She thought Dave looked rather nice. He was a couple of years older than Elsie and although he wasn't very tall his illness didn't seem to have left him badly crippled. The built-up boot was barely noticeable and his limp no worse than as if he'd turned his ankle. He had the sort of face that creased easily into a grin, and the creases stayed afterwards so that he looked permanently amused and friendly.

'They tried,' he told Thursday. 'Elsie's been trying all her life. Put me in the rubbish bin once, she did, nearly drowned me in the bath, left me outside in the snow . . . But you can't keep a good man down.'

'It's all lies,' Elsie said, getting up. 'I couldn't help you slipping when I was washing your hair, and I didn't know that old pram had been left out for the dustmen. And it was you wanted to make a snowman.'

'I didn't want to *be* a snowman,' he retorted, and they both laughed. Elsie went out to help her mother get supper ready and Dave and Thursday were left alone.

'So how d'you like Pompey?' he asked, sitting down in his mother's armchair.

'I haven't seen much of it yet. The weather's been so awful, and we've been going to Lee on our half-days, or round Gosport. Elsie's talking about going to a dance-hall in Southsea some time.'

'Kimballs,' he nodded. 'It's quite good. Or there's South Parade Pier. I don't go dancing much myself,' he added.

Thursday felt awkward. She said, 'What d'you like doing?' She could only think of things he probably couldn't do at all – roller-skating, walking, playing football. She wondered what it had been like for him as a small boy, growing up with one leg shorter than the other. Had the other children picked on him or had they been kind?

'I can ride a bike,' he said, guessing her thoughts. 'I go miles. Over the other side of the hill – there's lots of nice places to go to. Southwick, Hambledon, Rowlands Castle. You ought to get Elsie and your other friend to come, now the weather's getting better.' His eyes were bright and friendly. 'We could go for a whole day somewhere.'

It was a nice idea. But Thursday thought of Tony and

shook her head. 'I don't know. I've got a boyfriend, you see—'

'That doesn't stop you having a day out,' Elsie said, coming back into the room to lay the table. 'And Tony told me he didn't want you stopping in. You're not engaged, are you?'

'No, but—'

'Listen,' Elsie said, spreading a blue cloth on the table and getting a set of home-made cork mats out of the cupboard, 'there's a war on. We don't know where we'll be this time next year. We've got to have fun while we can.' She looked at the map on the wall, at all the pins clustered in France, in Belgium and in Scandinavia. 'I reckon Dad's right. Once Hitler's got all that lot under his thumb, he'll be looking across the Channel at us. There won't be much time for bike rides then.'

Mrs Jackson appeared in the doorway with an enamel casserole dish held in a cloth between her hands. 'Have you got that table laid yet, our Else? I've made a nice Lancashire hotpot, with plenty of veg. And there's a bottle of plums for afters, with some custard.'

'Lancashire hotpot!' Dave said, getting up to help Elsie with the knives and forks. 'My favourite. Must be because you're home, Elsie – all we get these days is corned beef. Corned-beef hash, corned-beef fritters, curried corned-beef balls – you wouldn't believe the number of different things our Mum's found to do with a tin of corned beef!'

'Oh, I would,' Elsie said feelingly. 'I can tell you, I would. I reckon the cooks at Haslar could give her a few tips, and all.'

It was getting dark when the girls finally returned to Haslar after an evening spent playing cards and listening to the wireless. They cycled in through the big gateway, waving their passes at the guard and keeping a careful eye open as they rode illicitly along the quarter-deck. As they parked their bikes in the shed, Elsie gave Thursday a sideways look.

'Feel a bit better now?'

'Yes, I do,' Thursday admitted. 'Thanks for taking me with you, Else. It was nice, meeting your family. It was nice being in a home again, if you know what I mean.'

Elsie smiled. 'I think our Dave fancied you a bit.'

Thursday shook her head. 'There's nothing like that. I can't just forget about Tony. We were just starting to get fond of each other.'

'That doesn't stop you going out and having a bit of fun with friends,' Elsie pointed out. 'You can't stay indoors all the time or just go for bike rides on your own. Tony wouldn't want you to do that.'

They walked away from the bike sheds towards the dormitory building. Thursday looked up into the sky. It was quiet, with no aircraft, but she could see the dim shapes of the barrage balloons that floated above them. For an hour or two, while they'd played hilarious card games – Chase the Ace, 99, Devil's Poker – she'd been able to forget the war. But now, back at the hospital, knowing that behind the blacked-out windows men were lying injured and ill, she knew that it couldn't be forgotten for long. And she knew that Elsie and Tony were right – nobody knew what was going to happen next. You couldn't live your life as if you had years and years ahead of you and all the time in the world to enjoy yourself.

You had to have fun while you could. You might not get many more chances.

Chapter Twelve

The war was spreading. Denmark surrendered only a day after being invaded, yet remained neutral despite being occupied by German forces. The newspapers explained this at length, but Elsie complained that she still didn't properly understand it. It was all to do with 'politics', she thought, and ordinary people like her just weren't expected to understand them.

Thursday didn't agree.

'You ought to try to understand them,' she said. 'Ordinary people can change politics. Look at trade unions. Look at the Labour Party.'

'My dad's Labour, always has been,' Elsie said.

'That doesn't mean to say you've got to be one. You can think for yourself, can't you?'

'Of course I can. But how do I know what to think if someone doesn't tell me?'

'Oh, for Pete's sake!' Thursday exclaimed, and Elsie laughed.

'Well, you know what I mean. I can't make up my mind just like that. I need to know a bit more about it.'

'Read the papers, then,' Thursday said, and picked up the crumpled *Daily Mirror* that Elsie had tossed aside once she'd looked at 'Ruggles' and 'Jane'. 'But don't just take what they say as gospel. Think about it.'

'You'd better come over our house again and listen to our dad,' Elsie told her. 'He's a shop steward, and he knows what he's on about.'

Thursday wondered what her own father would say if he knew that she was going to the home of a shop steward.

He hated Labour politics and trade unions, despite working in a factory himself. Worcester Porcelain had always dealt fair with its workers, he said, and you didn't need to go calling strikes when you had a fair employer. But Thursday could see that not all employers were fair, and what else could the workers do but withdraw their labour? What other weapons did they have? She sympathised with Elsie. It was very hard to know what was right and what wasn't, where politics were concerned.

Thursday had been over to Elsie's home twice more now. She felt at home with the Jacksons. Mr Jackson reminded her of her own father – even though his politics were so different – and Mrs Jackson treated her like another daughter. Eddy, having decided that her name was the only interesting thing about her, left her alone, but she got on well with Dave and they'd been for a bike ride together, pushing their cycles up the steep, chalky slopes of Portsdown Hill to coast down the other side to Boarhunt and Southwick. Dave had suggested the three of them take a picnic and make a whole day of it next time they got a Saturday or Sunday off.

'We could go up through Hambledon to Soberton or Droxford. The Meon Valley's nice, you'd like it.'

'Hey, don't get too ambitious,' Elsie warned him. 'We've got to ride back to Gosport afterwards, remember.'

On a bike, you couldn't tell that there was anything wrong with him. He had put wooden blocks on one of his pedals to make cycling easier for his shorter leg, and could cycle much further uphill than either Thursday or Elsie. When they had puffed their way as far as they could and finally dismounted, he would look over his shoulder at them, his face creased with his grin, and ride on to the crest of the hill. Portsdown was the only one he couldn't manage, and even then he was almost at the top before he was forced to give in and limp the rest of the way.

Patsy didn't come to Elsie's. She was spending all her free time with Roy Greenaway. They continued to quarrel but always made up again, and Patsy swung between moods of fury and elation. One day, Roy was a rat and she was never going to speak to him again; the next, she was blissfully in love again. The other girls got used to it and merely shrugged their shoulders and rolled their eyes.

Roy was the only one of the 'Three Musketeers' still at Haslar. Doug had been drafted to the *Rodney* with Tony and they were now somewhere off Scandinavia. Thursday and Elsie had been alarmed to hear that the ship had been damaged in an air attack but letters came soon to tell them that both boys were all right, though it had been 'a bit busy' down in the sick berth for a while.

'They take it so lightly,' Thursday said. 'As if it's a big game.'

'I don't suppose they thought so really. It's just the way they talk. To tell you the truth, I was surprised to hear from Doug at all. There was never anything between us. I suppose they just like to get letters from home. He always asks after you, by the way.'

'Can't think why. He never had a good word to say to me when he was here.' Despite Tony's assurances that Doug was a 'good bloke', Thursday had still never managed to get on with him. 'Anyway, I dare say they'll have both forgotten us by the time they come home again.'

Elsie cocked an eye at her. 'Absence not making the heart grow fonder, then?'

'It's nothing like that! Tony and me weren't serious either. We just write – you know, like you said, they like getting letters from home.' She turned away so that Elsie wouldn't see her colour rise.

Thursday had been dismayed when she first realised she was thinking less of Tony as the days and weeks went by. Missing him at first, she had gradually found her life and thoughts filling with other things. They were busy at the hospital, their training almost complete, and she'd even been allowed to help with one or two minor operations, flushing with delight when the surgeon told her she would make a good theatre nurse. With the spring weather improving every day, a cycle ride with Elsie and her brother was more attractive than staying in the dormitory writing letters and although she still sent him a letter every other day, they were shorter and talked less about 'missing him'.

She felt guilty, but reminded herself that Tony hadn't wanted her to wait. He'd known they hadn't had time to get serious. And she'd still be his friend when he did come back, of course she would. She wasn't serious about Dave either. Probably, she thought, Patsy was right and it was best not to get serious about anyone, the way things were.

I'll go on writing, she decided, but not so often. And I won't sign off with kisses. He won't mind, and we can just be friends.

The Allies landed in Norway, only to depart after no more than a fortnight. It seemed as if the German army was too powerful for them. People began to get anxious about an invasion again. Suppose the BEF, now in Belgium and France, couldn't hold out against them? What was to stop the Germans from crossing that frighteningly narrow strip of water? There were only twenty miles between Dover and Calais. Not much further than it was from Portsmouth to Southampton.

The word *blitzkrieg* was once again on people's lips. Air raids. Bombs. The unthinkable. The unimaginable.

And then, on 10 May, it became all too real.

'They've invaded the Low Countries. Belgium. And Holland. They're *bombing* them.'

Dave came rushing in with the *Sunday Dispatch* soon after Elsie and Thursday had arrived for their bike ride. The girls stared at each other and Mr Jackson snatched the paper.

'They've bombed the harbours – almost all the ships have gone. And they've sent in parachutists, and troops in gliders. And tanks – Panzers. They're overrunning *everywhere*.' He lowered the paper and looked at them.

'You know what this means, don't you. It's the end of the phoney war. It'll be our turn next.'

Thursday felt a cold trickle of fear down her spine. She looked at Elsie, and saw the same dread in her friend's eyes. Dave slapped his leg in frustration.

'Blast this thing! I wish I could go. What use am I, a flaming cripple?'

'Don't talk like that!' his mother said sharply. 'You're doing a useful job at home. I'm thankful you can't go.' She looked at her husband. 'What d'you think's going to happen, next, Bill?'

He was reading the paper again. 'They'll go for France next. Let's hope Churchill will do a bit better than Chamberlain. At least he's got a bit of fire in his belly, for all he's a Conservative.'

'It's going to be a coalition, though, isn't it? That's what they're saying. He'll put the best men in the jobs. Politics isn't going to matter.'

'Well, let's hope so.' He looked again at the paper and shook his head. 'It's looking bad. Mind you, we've got a lot of men in France and they might be able to hold 'em off – but if they can't . . .' He shook his head again.

The cold trickle of fear shivered further over Thursday's body. She thought of her brother Steve and her cousin Mike, both now in France. She'd been anxious before, of course she had, everyone was anxious all the time – but it was more of a background anxiety, something you were aware of but lived with. Now, it seemed sharper and more frightening. Now, it seemed horribly likely that they might get hurt. Now, it seemed horribly likely that they might not even come home.

Blitzkrieg.

If they could do it to Holland, they could do it to England. Thursday glanced out of the window, almost as if she expected to see parachutes descending at that very moment. All she could see were the blue sky and the silver, floating barrage balloons. But she could imagine the puffball shapes of parachutes. She could imagine the aircraft and the falling bombs.

'Well,' Dave said, sounding subdued, 'it's not going to help anyone if we just sit here staring at each other. We might as well still go for our bike ride.'

He stopped, as if he'd been about to add something else but thought better of it. But everyone could finish his words in their minds.

It might be the last chance they'd have.

Blood, toil, tears and sweat.

It seemed to Thursday afterwards that that Sunday bike-ride was the last carefree day of the war. The three of them, their sandwiches already made and an apple each in their saddlebags, had set off uneasily, feeling almost guilty that they could still enjoy themselves while the people of Holland were suffering so much, but after they had puffed their way up to the top of Portsdown Hill and were coasting down through the narrow, primrose-spattered lanes to Denmead, their spirits lifted. It was impossible to be entirely gloomy on such a lovely May day, with the sun smiling out of a sky of tender blue and the hedgerows bursting into fresh green life. Amongst the soft gold of the primroses were purple splashes of violets, the fields were full of ambling cows and a stream sparkled between drooping willows. The thought of war seemed very far away and the three of them tried to set aside their fears and concentrate on enjoying this day, which seemed to have been handed to them as a gift.

'It's no good everyone being miserable,' Dave said as they sat on the bank of the little River Meon to eat their picnic. 'We've all got to go back to work tomorrow, and you two have got to be cheerful for your patients. Days off are meant to help us stay strong.'

'I know. I just can't help thinking about those poor people ... What must it be like to be bombed and invaded?' Thursday looked around the peaceful fields, at the flowers in the grass, the trees with their leaves curling out from buds. 'I keep thinking – what if it happens here? How would we manage? The Army's all in France. It would be just us.'

Her answer came a few days later, when the new prime minister made his first speech to Parliament which was reported on the Home Service news. He offered little hope, only *'blood, toil, tears and sweat'* – yet somehow his speech, gloomy as it was, gave them heart. It was his determination that shone through – his determination not to be beaten. Without denying that the country faced an *'ordeal of the most grievous kind'*, without offering any easy solution, he drew everyone to him by his confident assumption that the country was with him, that victory would be achieved by every man and woman working together. He made no apology for declaring that his policy was to wage war – war against monstrous tyranny. And that without victory there would be no survival – either for the British Empire or for mankind itself. And somehow he managed to covey his belief that victory was held in the hands of ordinary people, and not something to be left to those in power. And – what was more – his belief that together they could achieve it.

'I take up my task with buoyancy and hope,' he ended. *'I feel entitled to claim the aid of all, and I say, "Come then, let us go forward together with our united strength".'*

'He's got a wonderful way with words,' Thursday said soberly when the news ended and Helen Stanway switched off the wireless in the D Block mess. 'What he says makes you feel you really can win.'

'And so we can,' Helen said. Her father was an army major and in France now, and so was her fiancé, a captain. She looked pale and anxious, but the light of determination was in her eye and the set of her jaw. 'And we've got an important part to play. It's up to us to get the wounded men fit and ready to fight again.' She looked grave. 'I've got a feeling we're going to be seeing quite a few of them from now on.'

Again, Thursday felt a small shiver of premonition trickle down her spine. She glanced at Patsy, who had been subdued all day because Roy had been suddenly drafted to a ship – a 'pierhead jump' he'd called it – because of an attack on the convoy it was in, which had resulted in a number of injuries. The sick bay itself had been damaged and two of the SBAs killed. The ship had stayed at sea, helping others which had been struck, and Roy and another SBA had been sent out at less than an hour's notice. But where they were and when they would come back, Patsy had no idea.

Patsy really did love Roy after all, Thursday thought, never mind all her talk about not taking it seriously. She was still writing to Jeff, but – as Thursday wrote to Tony – as no more than a friend. But from the look on her face now, it was obvious to everyone that Roy had become far more than a friend.

His ship might be next, Thursday thought. And there'll be other ships sunk, too. How many of the wounded will make it back to Haslar? Are we really going to be as busy as Stanway thinks?

The atmosphere on the wards was tense. The recovering patients paced up and down, staring out of the windows, obviously itching to be back at sea. Some of them badgered the doctors to let them return to duty, and some succeeded in getting themselves discharged. The other men, not fit to be out of bed, were equally restless. 'How can we win a war when we're stuck here like bloody old women?' one demanded fretfully. 'Blimey, they got sick bays and sawbones on board, ain't they? All I needs is me dressings changed. I could still do me job, couldn't I?'

But as fast as the beds were emptied, new patients arrived to fill them. Ships were still being attacked and sunk in the Channel, and Haslar was the nearest hospital. The patients arrived by launch, ferried from the ships that came in to tie up at the jetties, or lay at anchor in the Solent. Thursday got used to helping them disembark at the hospital jetty and loading them on to trolleys to wheel them along the old, polished tramway. Sometimes she handed them over when they reached the ward, sometimes she came in with them and helped the QARNNs tend to their injuries. Usually, they had been more or less patched up by the doctors and SBAs on the ships that had brought them there and, so far, she had seen few fresh wounds. All the same, the sight of their gashed and broken bodies was enough to subdue her normally bubbling spirits, and she went to bed at night tired and dispirited.

'No use letting it get us down,' Elsie said. 'Remember what our Dave said, we've got to be cheerful for the patients. They don't want long faces round them, do they.'

Thursday smiled ruefully. 'You're right, and so's Dave. It's just – well, I can't help thinking about Steve, and my cousin Mike, in France. Hurt, and away from home.'

'And wouldn't you want them to be looked after by someone bright and cheerful?' Elsie asked. 'Course you would!'

A day or two later, Elsie opened a letter from her mother and told them that her brother Dave was joining the newly formed Local Defence Volunteers. 'It's for all the men who can't join the regular Services to be part of the armed forces. It's a sort of home army. Anyone between seventeen and sixty-five can join and they'll get proper uniforms and guns and things.' She read a bit further. 'They're just getting armbands to start with, but they can start training straight away. Then if we get a parachute invasion like Holland, they'll be ready for them.'

'Well, that's something,' Thursday remarked. 'I bet Dave's pleased.'

'He is, Mum says. He's been fretting at not being able to do anything. Now he'll be as good as anyone else.'

On the following Sunday they were able to hear Mr Churchill's voice for themselves when he made his first broadcast. His rolling voice boomed through the mess, calling the Nazis the *'foulest and most soul-destroying tyranny that has ever darkened and stained the pages of history'*. We must win, he told the listening nation. Together, we *would* win.

'We will,' Thursday said, gripping Patsy and Elsie by the hand. 'We *will*.'

Yet it was only days later that they heard that France and Belgium had begun to fall. The Germans were sweeping through to the Channel coast. Amiens was taken. Arras was surrounded. Boulogne was evacuated. And as Britain watched and held its breath, the BEF, pride of the Army, was forced to retreat to the beaches. Their backs were not even against a wall; only the sea lay behind them.

'What are they going to *do*?' Patsy asked, as she and Thursday walked back to D Block from the ward for breakfast after their night duty. She was almost in tears. 'They'll never get back – they'll all be killed. It's going to be a massacre!'

It had been a bad night on the ward. One of the patients, a young sailor who had been badly burned in an explosion in the engine room of his ship, had died as Thursday helped the QARNN to change his dressings. They had known he was near the end, and had felt almost relieved that his suffering had stopped at last, but as Thursday had stared down at the young face, raw and reddened by fire, deeply pock-marked by shards of white-hot metal, she had felt a grief that seemed to foreshadow the horrors that were to come. I don't know if I can do this, she'd thought with sudden fear. I don't know if I can stand seeing more and more men come in like this, only to die . . . But the senior nurse, seeing her hesitation, had spoken sharply.

'Stop it, Tilford! You're here to help them, not to think about yourself.'

'I wasn't—' Thursday began, but the QARNN shook her head.

'Yes, you were. You were thinking about what *you* feel. You've been told before, over and over again, you must not, *ever*, allow your own feelings to get in the way of your work. Now, this poor boy needs attention even if he's gone beyond medical help. You can see to the body.'

She marched away down the ward, her back straight, and Thursday looked after her and then down at the still, ravaged body in the bed. She knew that the QARNN was right, and that she must not allow her own feelings to interfere with her work. But she knew too that the QARNN herself had been upset by the boy's death. Otherwise, Thursday thought as she began the task of laying out the wasted body, she would not have used the word 'poor'.

None of the nurses, however hardened they seemed, was totally immune from pity and emotion. And once again she thought of the men who were being driven to the beaches of France, the men who were being beaten back by the enemy they had been sent to conquer.

'I don't know what they're going to do,' she said miserably in answer to Patsy's question. 'I don't see what they *can* do.' She stopped and looked at her friend. 'D'you think – d'you think this is going to be the start of the invasion?'

They stared at each other. Then running footsteps sounded close behind and Elsie, who had been working in the Zymotics Block, panted up to them. 'There's something going on. I saw it from the upstairs windows. Come and look.'

She set off, still half running, for the gate leading out to the sea wall. The other two glanced at each other and followed. There was already a small crowd of VADs, QARNNs and sailors crowding through the narrow opening, and the girls joined them, pushing their way through to stand in the long line forming at the top of the sloping wall.

'Boats,' Patsy said in wonder. 'Boats of all sorts. But what . . . ?'

'They're going to France,' Thursday whispered. 'They must be. They're going to bring the soldiers back.'

It was still early. Dawn had broken, but there was still a pale rosy tinge to the sky, and the tower and dome of the cathedral glowed softly like mother-of-pearl. Mist lay in gauzy shreds on the water and muffled the engines of the boats that slid across its surface. There was something ghostly about the long procession of boats, as if they were from another world.

Silently, they watched as the flotilla slid through the narrow neck of water between Sallyport and Blockhouse. Half of Haslar Lake must be there, they thought, as well as all the other creeks and inlets around the edge of the harbour. Boats of every description: family motor boats and small yachts, used more often for Sunday jaunts in the Solent than for longer voyages; larger boats, owned by wealthy people who kept them pristine and polished but were offering them now on a journey from which they might come back – if they came back at all – battered and bloodstained. And tugs and ferries – one of the Isle of Wight paddle steamers, and even one of the stubby little Gosport ferries.

'It's the *King*,' Thursday said, staring. 'It's the *Ferry King*.'

'It never is!' Elsie strained her eyes. 'I wonder who's on board. I know the skipper, Ted Chapman – he lives down April Grove, not far from my auntie. And Sam Hardy, his mate, my dad knows him, and their apprentice – Ben something – surely they've never taken him as well. He's only a boy.'

'But why are they going anyway?' Patsy asked. 'They're only little boats – they won't be able to bring many men back. Look at that one, it's not much bigger than a dinghy. What good will that be?'

'It'll be able to get close inshore,' said a sailor with his arm in a sling, standing nearby. 'That's what it is. They must be getting them off the beaches. The ships'll have to stand off, see – too shallow to get close in. So they'll need the little 'uns to ferry them over.'

'But how did they know to go? It hasn't been on the news.'

'Didn't people who owned small boats all have to register them a couple of weeks ago?' Thursday asked. 'I seem to remember something about it. Maybe this was why.'

'You mean they knew the Army would get caught? They knew, and never did anything about it?'

'What could they do? They couldn't bring them back till they got to the beaches, could they? And they did do something – they got all these little boats lined up ready to go and help. And made sure the Navy was ready, too. And the hospitals, like Haslar. I don't see what else they could have done.'

'They could have never sent them there in the first place,' Patsy said bitterly, staring at the passing fleet. 'They could have not had a war.' She was silent for a moment and Thursday saw tears slipping down her cheeks before she burst out again. 'It's not fair! All these boys having to go and fight, and get hurt and killed – their lives ruined, their families pulled to pieces. And why? What for? Because of some horrible man in another country who wants to take over the world. It's not *fair*!'

Thursday put her arm around Patsy's shoulders. 'We know it's not fair, Patsy. But you can't just stand by and let a man like Hitler walk all over people. It'd be us next. We had to stop him.'

'We haven't, though, have we? We haven't stopped him at all. He's taken over Norway and Denmark. He's bombed Holland and Belgium and taken them over, too.

And now it's France. He's driving our boys out of France and we've got to send a lot of – of *dinghies* to go and get them back. He's *winning*, Thursday. He's winning, and it *will* be us next. We just haven't got a chance.'

The sailor turned on her. His eyes were angry, his face red. 'And if he wins, whose fault will it be?' he demanded. 'Yours, that's who. And people like you who give in. It's people like *them*, out there—' he jerked his head towards the apparently endless procession '—who're going to win the war. People who *won't* give in. People who're ready to stand up on their hind legs and give him what for, no matter what it costs. Not people like you, staying safe on shore and whining about things being *fair*.'

He drew in a breath and Patsy, her face scarlet and her eyes filled with tears, opened her mouth to answer, but he began again, drowning her voice, '*Nothing's* fair, didn't nobody never tell you that? It ain't *fair* that I broke my bloody arm falling down a companionway so that I can't be going, too, to do my bit. It ain't *fair* that my old dad got killed in the last war, so that my poor mum had to go charring and take in washing to bring up five kids. It ain't *fair* that there's thousands of poor bleeders over there now, waiting for someone to go and fetch 'em home. But *fair* don't have nothing to do with it. We got to forget *fair* and just get on with the job. And the sooner I can get my arm out of this bloody sling and get back to sea, the better. I'll be out of the way of you snivelling VADs for a start.'

Patsy stared at him. Her face was working with her efforts not to cry. Thursday tightened her arm around her shoulders and spoke equally angrily.

'We're not snivelling VADs! We've been up all night looking after patients, and we'll do the same tonight and every night as long as we've got to. And when they start bringing men back from France we'll work night *and* day to look after them. And we're not going to give in to anyone. But you can't blame Patsy for being upset. Her boy's over there somewhere, on a ship, and she's already lost a cousin on the *Grenville*. It's not always easy to keep hoping, 'specially when you're dog-tired.'

He looked embarrassed and shrugged. 'Well, maybe I did come on a bit strong. But you hear of these fifth columnists and so on, trying to lower morale. I reckon it's up to all of us to keep it up, that's all. We've bin through other wars and come out all right. We'll get through this one, too.'

'But not before there's a lot of people killed,' Patsy said in a shaky voice.

The sailor looked at her and made a face of wry sympathy. 'I know, love. But that's war, innit? There's always people killed. We just got to remember that most of 'em volunteered, one way or another. So far, anyway. And it's winning in the end that counts.' He paused and then said, very quietly, 'I reckon most of us'd be ready to give our lives so that the world can be free again. That's what it's for, innit.'

For a moment or two, nobody spoke. Then Elsie, who had been unusually quiet, said cheerfully, 'Well, that's as maybe, but I'll tell you what I *ain't* ready to give up, and that's me breakfast! And a little bird told me it's sausages this morning, so let's go and get our share before them other greedy-guts snaffles them all.'

The news broke on Monday. Hundreds of requisitioned boats, from ferries to fishing smacks, cockle boats to barges, yachts to drifters, had already left and now others joined the fleet. Dinghies, pinnaces, even rowing boats all came flocking out of hidden creeks and little harbours. If they were too small to make their own way, they were towed by bigger ships; some of them were swamped by the wash of the bigger boats, some were damaged by the stanchions to which the tow ropes were tied being ripped away from their bows. But most of them got there, and joined in the great rescue, driving right into the shallows on the beaches of Dunkirk, and ferrying crowds of exhausted, wounded soldiers to the ships that waited to take them home.

The hospital radios were switched on for every news report. Anyone who had time would race to hear it, then report back to the wards so that nurses and patients alike could hear the latest. They heard the call for small ships, for steamers and ferries and motor boats. Portsmouth Harbour, like every other harbour in the country, became alive with vessels, all setting forth on their mission of rescue. The girls went up to the sea wall whenever they had the chance, to watch.

'A lot of them are going to be coming here, you know,' Elsie said quietly.

The other two nodded. Patsy had recovered from her moment of despair and was even more determined that Hitler would be defeated – here at Haslar Hospital, if she had anything to do with it. They gazed at the procession of boats and then turned their eyes to the south, to stare past the Isle of Wight to the smudge on the far horizon.

Perhaps it was cloud they saw there; perhaps it was the smear of smoke from the burning town of Dunkirk. But each girl felt a shiver as she watched it, and each girl felt that now the war had truly begun.

From this moment on, nothing would ever be the same again.

Chapter Thirteen

Soon the patients would begin to arrive.

Madam had called all the VADs together and told them that they were to stand by for a huge intake. Her eyes sombre, she had warned them that they must not expect these new patients to be as well presented as those they were accustomed to receiving from ships. There would be severe injuries to deal with, worse than anything they might have seen before.

'These men are coming straight from the beaches of Dunkirk,' she said. 'There are going to be thousands brought home, as fast as they can be shipped across the Channel. There won't be the facilities or the time to give them the treatment they need before they arrive here. We must be ready to do whatever is needed, and we must be ready to work all the hours we can. There will be no time off, except for essential eating and sleeping – and not too much of that either.' Her brown eyes moved slowly over the faces of the silent girls. 'I know I can rely on every one of you to give of your best.'

The girls went back to their duties quiet and a little nervous. Thursday and Patsy found themselves together in the sluice, washing out bedpans. They paused for a moment, unsure of what to say.

'This is it, isn't it,' Patsy said at last. 'The real beginning.' She looked at Thursday a little fearfully. 'I know we've seen plenty of wounds before, but it sounds as if this is going to be just awful. I just hope we can cope with it, Thurs.'

Thursday nodded. 'I hope so, too. But we will, Pats.

We will. We've got to, haven't we? It's what we've been trained for all these months.'

She went back to the ward, thinking of her brother and her cousin, both in France. Were they even at this moment waiting on the crowded beaches? The thought made her feel sick. Perhaps they were on their way back already, she thought. Perhaps tomorrow she'd get a letter telling her they were safe.

The wards had been cleared of all who were fit to leave. Neatly made beds, the blue anchors on their counterpanes all perfectly in line, stood in rows waiting for new occupants. The operating theatres were ready, the medical staff on standby. All leave had been stopped. Thursday, who had been planning to have a few days with the family in Worcester, wrote to tell her mother that she wouldn't be coming.

She received an answer that told her that Steve and Mike were both in France and that nobody knew what had happened to them. Her heart sinking, she read the letter out to the others as they sat in the mess.

'My cousin's hubby's there, too,' Elsie said. 'And the boys – Tony and Doug, and Roy – they're probably mixed up in it somewhere as well, on the ships. And poor Stanway, her dad's a major and he's out there – I reckon nearly everyone's got somebody to worry about.'

'We've just got to do our best for the ones we get here,' Patsy said. Her face was white and the other two realised again just how much she thought of Roy Greenaway, despite their squabbles. 'And hope there's someone, somewhere, doing their best for our boys.'

'They won't *all* be injured,' Thursday said, trying to inject a positive note into the conversation. 'There'll be plenty that are still all right.'

'That's right,' Elsie said. 'No news is good news, that's what my mum always says. And we just got to pull together, like Mr Churchill told us. We can't give way. Mind you,' she added, 'he promised us blood, sweat and tears, didn't he? So I suppose we got to expect to cry a bit as well.'

Thursday thought of her brother, somewhere in France. Somewhere on the Dunkirk beach, perhaps, or already at sea and on his way home. Alive and unhurt, she prayed, and realised for the first time just how much Steve meant to her. She thought of their childhood, of growing up together. Squabbling over who had the skin on the custard, who would lick out the bowl of cake mixture, whose turn it was to have the cat on their lap. Walking to Sunday school together, stiff and clean in their best clothes, arguing under their breath; scrambling for the best biscuit in the tin. I've been greedy all my life, she thought. I've always wanted the best for myself, but if Steve comes back all right he can have everything. Custard skin, biscuits, cake mixture – they were all things for kiddies. But if he comes back from this, I'll give him the world.

There wasn't time to think any more. Between listening to the wireless, scanning the newspapers and getting the wards ready – as well as caring for the patients still in hospital – there was barely time to think at all.

'Will we be getting soldiers?' Patsy wondered. 'I mean, there won't be that many sailors hurt, will there?'

Almost before the words were out of her mouth, reports were coming in of ships being blown up and sunk. HMS *Wakeful*, torpedoed by a German E-boat – six hundred men lost from below decks, those on the upper decks thrown into the sea to be rescued or drown. Then a drifter, fired on by her own side who mistook her for an E-boat as she picked up some of those survivors. And the Isle of Wight paddle steamer ferry, *Gracie Fields*, launched by the singer herself only three years ago, sunk with eight hundred men aboard as she plied her way back across the Channel.

The news grew worse with every bulletin they heard. The Luftwaffe were out in force, strafing and bombing.

They machine-gunned men on the beach and in the water. They attacked the ships as they stood off, waiting for the men to be brought to them. And then they were forced to defend themselves as the RAF swooped in like a cloud of angry bees and waged battle in the skies, above the heads of the soldiers and sailors struggling in the sea.

Brief as the news items were, they were enough for Thursday's vivid imagination to picture the details. As if she were there herself, she could see the sky which had been so blue and tender obscured by a pall of oily black smoke – smoke from the inferno of Dunkirk, smoke from the bombed and burning ships, smoke deliberately created to block the view of the bombers. She saw the sea, which had been so calm and blue, churned into seething, blood-reddened soup; the beaches strewn with the bodies of dead and wounded soldiers, in grotesque parody of the sun-bathers who had once lain on the golden sands, and the boats which came and went a bitter reminder of the pleasure craft of a different world.

News filtered through each day, and each day Thursday felt as if she were living it with the men. She seemed to stand with them during those endless days, as they waited patiently for hours up to their necks or waists in the flowing tide. She seemed to watch them as they stood in the water because there was nothing else to do; as they queued because there was no other way. When the little boats came, she felt the cold, hunger, thirst and exhaustion of the men as they climbed aboard, almost dead with it, and fell into the arms of the sailors who had come for them. She felt their dulled relief as they heaved themselves into the ships and lay on the decks, crammed together, speechless and dazed, some unable to understand what was happening, since so much had happened to them. Some of them were wounded, some barely scratched. Some died.

Others, she knew, waited without patience. Their nerve had broken, their minds gone, and they screamed and panicked, pushing to climb aboard the boats, almost sinking them in their clumsy panic. All reason gone, they clawed at the sailors who shoved them back into the water, knowing that their small craft were too overloaded to float. They fought and raged, and in some cases were threatened with pistols before they would cease. Some were shot, to save the rest. Some simply fell back into the water and drowned.

'The poor bloody blighters,' Elsie said, in tears as they listened to the news late that afternoon. 'Oh, the poor, poor bloody blighters . . .'

'Listen!' Patsy exclaimed, holding up her hand. 'It's the siren! It's an alert!'

'They're coming!' Thursday was on her feet as the wail of the siren rose into the air, almost drowning out her words. She shrieked to make herself heard. 'It must be them – they're arriving already!' She grabbed up her cape and flung it round her shoulders. 'Come on – down to the jetty!' She was out of the door, followed by the others, and as they ran they could see VADs and QARNNs pouring out of every building in the hospital. Doctors and SBAs were there too, running as fast as their legs would carry them for the jetty where the men must land. And as they ran, they could see the boats – the little boats that had not gone to Dunkirk but could now play their own part, going out to the ships or across to the harbour railway station and ferrying the wounded men to the jetty where, for the past three hundred years, such wounded men had been brought to Haslar Hospital to be healed.

Thursday and the other two girls were amongst those receiving the first intake. They stood on the jetty, their capes and headdresses fluttering in the breeze, watching as the first naval pinnace ploughed through the choppy waves towards them. The men could be seen lying in the bottom of the boat and, as they drew closer, Elsie gave an exclamation of pity.

'Just look at the poor devils! They haven't seen a wash in weeks. And those *bandages* . . .'

'We'll soon have them right,' Thursday said stoutly, but her heart quailed as she began to catch a glimpse of the injuries they must deal with. And the *numbers* – for beyond the first boat she could see another; and, beyond that, another and another and another. A whole line of them, stretching across the harbour. And she knew that as the first was unloaded of its wretched cargo it would turn and go back for more. It was like Dunkirk all over again – in miniature. Not thousands, but hundreds, all coming to this one hospital.

And, she thought, the same scene was being enacted in other naval and military hospitals all over the country. Not hundreds, but thousands.

The pinnace drew alongside. A matelot jumped ashore with the painter and wrapped it swiftly around the bollard. The nurses moved forward, ready to take their patients, and the sailors helped them lift the broken bodies carefully out of the boat.

'Go easy with this one. Got a broken back . . . This 'un's not so bad, just his arm smashed and a few grazes . . . This feller's eyes are all bandaged up, look, can't see nothing, the ship's doc says he mustn't be moved too rough . . . This one's bad. Burnt all over. Tell you the truth, we didn't think he'd make it across. He don't even like being touched . . .'

The man's screams proved the sailor's words. Thursday flinched as she tried to lift the body without hurting him, but it seemed impossible. She felt a sob rise in her throat as she tried to find a place where she could touch him without causing him searing pain. In the end, she gave up and steeled herself to lift him without paying attention to his cries, praying that once he was in the ward he could be given relief from his agony.

There was no time to think about him again. The stream of casualties was swift and apparently endless. In the next few hours, Thursday found herself faced with injuries such as she had never seen before – torn and broken bodies, their limbs wrenched away, sightless eyes, heads swathed in rough, bloodstained bandages. There were broken bones, burns and bullet wounds, there were great bleeding cuts tied with hasty tourniquets or heavily padded, there were broken backs and pelvises and once, to Thursday's enduring horror, a man so badly slashed that the dark mass of his liver protruded from his abdomen. Surely, she thought, such a wound could not be survived – but even as it entered her head she thrust the thought savagely away and knew that even the faintest shred of hope must be seized on and used for the patient's recovery.

She didn't know how many hours had passed, sometimes with Patsy and Elsie at her side, sometimes with Vera Hapgood or Jeanie Brown or one of the other VADs. It didn't matter who it was: they all worked with equal determination and equal care in all the tumult. Around them was a cacophony of noise – boats coming and going, men and women shouting orders, patients crying out and screaming. The trolleys rattled back and forth along the paved way, their wheels clattering on the smooth stones. Above them, the late afternoon sky faded into evening and then darkened to night. The blackout was ignored. They had to have light and surely the German planes were too occupied in trying to prevent the rescue from Dunkirk. Occasionally, they were dragged away to swallow a hot cup of tea and a sandwich, but nobody wanted to stop for long and as soon as they had finished they were back at their posts back with the endless stream of wounded men.

It seemed to Thursday as if she had been working almost for ever when Patsy spoke suddenly in her ear.

'Oh, Thursday,' she muttered, 'look at this.'

The sailor they were lifting had a loose bandage over his entire face. He'd groaned, but the groan had had a strange sound to it and, alarmed, Patsy had lifted the bandage.

Thursday looked. The face was so badly damaged that it was almost unrecognisable as human. The nose had been smashed, the mouth torn and most of the the teeth knocked out. One cheek was bruised almost black, and as swollen as if the man had mumps. But above the damage the dark brown eyes were miraculously untouched and as she stared into them she saw recognition and caught her breath.

'*Tony* . . .'

'I thought it was. I couldn't be sure,' Patsy whispered, horrified, but Thursday nodded and so, grotesquely, did the man they were lifting. He groaned again and his torn lips twisted. 'Oh, my *God* . . .'

'He's in agony,' Thursday said. 'You can see. Oh, Tony, *Tony* . . .' She stared at him and felt a strange, twisting agony in her own breast. In the months since he had left, she had come to realise that she hadn't really loved him – but he'd been the first boy she'd felt real desire for, the first boy who had kissed her properly, the first boy who had found a place in her heart. And now, seeing him torn and bleeding and in pain, her heart went out to him in sorrow. 'Oh, *Tony* . . .'

'Come on, you girls,' Helen Stanway snapped, materialising beside them. 'Keep going. We've got to get these poor fellows up to the wards as quickly as possible. What's the hold-up?'

'It's Tony West. SBA West, who used to be on our ward,' Patsy explained rapidly. 'He was Tilford's boyfriend.'

'Oh.' Stanway looked at the mutilated face and it was clear that she was wondering how they could tell. 'Well, all the more reason to get him to the ward quickly. Get him on the trolley and then come with me. There's another pinnace coming in.'

Between them, the girls lifted the stretcher on to the waiting trolley. Tony's eyes were still fixed on Thursday's face and she bent towards him and spoke softly beneath the tumult all about them.

'You'll be all right now,' she said softly. 'You really will, Tony. Haslar's a marvellous place.'

He knew that, of course. He had worked here himself, nursed men through their own injuries. He had seen men recover, he had seen men die. And he knew too, as Thursday knew, that he might – along with so many of the other men who had been brought this far – have come to Haslar only to die. The deaths of Dunkirk had not ended on the beaches, or in the sea.

The phoney war was truly over. The real war was well under way.

It was over at last. The stream of patients slowly came to a stop. There were no more boats. On the ninth day, the doctors and nurses went down to the jetty and received the last few broken men; there was no one left alive to bring back. They walked slowly and heavily back to the crowded wards.

The beaches of Dunkirk were strewn with the last of the dead, some thrust into hastily shovelled graves, some left to the waves and the gulls. Some, who had died before it began, had been buried in the dunes and the fields behind the beaches. Some would be found and identified, some would never be known.

And yet, even in this darkness, Winston Churchill could find words to hearten his countrymen. The girls listened to his next broadcast, weighed down with exhaustion and the grim horror of all they had seen, and heard the words that were to carry them through the rest of the war, the words that once more stiffened the resolve of so many worn and weary people.

'If the British Empire and its Commonwealth last a thousand years,' Winston Churchill declared, 'men will say, "This was their finest hour".'

Their finest hour? To Thursday, thinking of the

exhausted men, travelling dazed and bewildered by ship and train to hospital or home, it was difficult to believe. Yet somehow, as he always managed to do, Mr Churchill managed to point to those who had worked so hard and with such courage to bring the men home. This was the spirit of Britain, he seemed to say, this was the spirit that would, despite all setbacks, eventually win the war for Europe and for the world. Once again, he inspired hope, defiance and determination, and as Thursday and the other girls listened, none had any doubt but that he would lead the country to victory.

'We shall fight on the beaches, we shall fight on the landing grounds, we shall fight in the fields and in the streets, we shall fight in the hills; we shall never *surrender . . .'*

There was little rest for the VADs, for those first few weeks after Dunkirk.

The hospital was packed with wounded – soldiers as well as sailors, for they had simply been brought to the nearest hospital at first. As their conditions improved they were transferred, until eventually all the patients were naval once more. The girls worked ceaselessly, often continuing long after their duties should have ended, to help the casualties and each other. They tottered back to their mess and dormitories only when they were too weary to carry on, ate without noticing what was on their plates and then fell into bed for a few hours' sleep. Then they were up and ready to go back again.

Thursday could never even have imagined some of the injuries she saw. Dressing them was difficult, sometimes impossible. The men lay awkwardly in their beds, some piled with pillows, some with none at all. Their exhaustion delayed healing and they seemed dazed and stunned by what they had endured. As they slowly got better, some of them talked about their experiences; others turned their faces aside and tried to forget.

'It was the queues in the water that got me,' one sailor

told her as she changed his dressings. 'I was in charge of one of the boats, see, that was ferrying them off. Hundreds of them, there was, long queues of men just standing there in the water, waiting. Bin there for hours, tide coming up round 'em, going down again. Gawd knows what state they was in under their clobber. Must've had skin like sponges.' He flinched as Thursday removed the last pad of lint and began carefully to bathe the wound beneath. His little boat had been strafed, several of the men in it killed outright and two or three others, like himself, injured by bullets. 'Them at the front was almost swimming,' he went on. 'And as the blokes behind tried to get near the boats, the poor buggers at the front got pushed in even deeper. Just bloody bad luck if you couldn't swim.'

Thursday paused and looked at him. 'Do you mean some of them couldn't?'

'Stands to reason, dunnit. Not even all sailors can swim – reckon that if they get sunk, they'll be so far out at sea it wouldn't do 'em no good, just prolong the agony. So it stands to reason soldiers won't be no better.'

'But what happened to them?'

'What usually happens,' he asked, 'if you're in deep water and can't bloody swim?'

Thursday felt sick. She went on bathing the wound and then folded a dressing to go over it. The man went on talking. It was almost as if he had a festering boil, she thought, that must be lanced so that the pus could ooze out. The pus of his memories needed to be released or it would remain inside him, poisoning his mind. And she, as a nurse, had to listen, just as she had to bathe the wound to stop it going septic.

'That wasn't all,' he said. 'If you ask me, they was the lucky ones. It was the poor bleeders on the beach I felt sorry for. Just waiting till they could even get near the water, knowing they didn't have a chance. And even when they did get to a boat, they wasn't safe. None of us was safe. Bloody bombers overhead, ships blown to bits as you climbed aboard. I saw one, just taken a big ferry-boat load on, the ferry boat was just pulling away when a bomber flew over and dropped the lot. I never saw nothing like it. Just a huge mass of black smoke and flame, and bits flying everywhere. And the poor bleeders aboard . . .' He shook his head. 'Nothing left. Nothing to speak of. Just bits and pieces. The sea was full of 'em. Arms and legs and Gawd knows what, flying through the air and then floating past.' He was silent for a moment, then said quietly, 'I saw a bloke's head. Just his head, nothing else. His eyes were still open – it was as if he was looking at me. As if he was *asking* . . . I tell you, nurse, I don't never want to see nothing like that again.'

Thursday finished the dressing with shaking hands. Her legs were trembling and she wanted to sink down on the bed beside the man and put her arms around him. She wanted to cry with him, to hold him and feel his warmth against her; two human beings, bewildered and terrified by the reality of war.

Sister Burton's voice cut sharply into her thoughts and she jumped. 'If you've finished that dressing, Tilford, there are other patients waiting.' She was standing at the foot of the bed, her face severe. 'Bed number three needs a bottle, and number five has been asking for his water jug to be refilled for the past ten minutes. You know it's vital that burn cases have their liquid levels kept up.' Her eyes rested on the sailor for a moment. 'You really mustn't keep the nurses gossiping. They've got important work to do.'

Thursday hurried to fetch the urine bottle, and then to fill the water jug. As she passed Sister again on her way to the sluice, the older nurse detained her for a moment.

'I know the men have been through a terrible ordeal,' she said quietly, 'and as nurses it's our duty to give them whatever care we can. But it mustn't be at the expense of either other patients or ourselves. And we must never,

never break down in front of a patient. You do understand that, don't you, Tilford?'

Thursday nodded, feeling a sudden lump in her throat. She knew that she had been dangerously close to tears as she'd listened to the sailor's tale, and she knew that Sister must have heard at least some of what he had been saying, and seen the effect it was having.

'Yes, Sister,' she said. 'Thank you, Sister.'

Sister Burton's eyes rested on her face for a moment. 'They all have terrible tales to tell,' she said gently, 'and it's only right that we, safe here at Haslar, should listen to them. But we must never let it interfere with our duties. Whatever happens, we must always be able to carry out our work.'

'Yes, Sister,' Thursday said and, perilously close to tears again, escaped to attend to another patient who was calling for a bedpan. I can take it better when she's telling me off, she thought, scurrying round the ward seeing first to this man and then to that. It's when she's being nice to me that she almost makes me cry.

Sister was right, though. The stories the men had to tell, the experiences they recounted, were so horrific that if you dwelt on them you wouldn't be able to cope. And nurses had to be able to cope.

'It's like you've got to grow another skin,' Elsie said when they talked it over later that night. 'Or put on a suit of armour whenever you go in the ward. I can see now why sisters and matrons turn into such dragons. They've been doing it so long they can't stop.'

'But Sister was kind to me really,' Thursday said. 'She knew I was getting upset and she came to put a stop to it. And I could see she was upset, too, inside herself. She'd heard the bit about the head, I'm sure. Anyone'd be upset by that.'

She went to see Tony whenever she had a chance. He was in a different ward and, as a patient, she wasn't really supposed to 'fraternise' with him. But the ward sister knew they'd been friends and allowed her in, on the strict understanding that it was only for a few minutes. 'The poor boys need all the comfort they can get,' she said. 'Just sit and talk to him about happier times. It's all any of us can do.'

Thursday approached his bed the first time with trepidation. She couldn't forget his horrific injuries and didn't know quite what to expect. She knew he'd had an operation and would therefore be bandaged, but was unprepared for the grotesque sight which greeted her.

'His head's all swollen!' she whispered to the VAD who had come with her. 'It's enormous.'

'No, it's just the dressings,' the girl reassured her. 'They've built a sort of wire cage round his face, you see, and then bandaged over that. So that it's kept sterile but the bandages don't actually touch him. It's all raw flesh, you see. The next operation he has, they're going to try taking some skin from his thigh and put it on his face. It's a new procedure but it's been quite successful so far.'

'Skin from his thigh? But that'll leave—'

'A raw patch there, yes. But it'll be very carefully done and looked after. And it doesn't matter if his thigh's a bit scarred, does it – not if it saves his face.'

Nothing was said about his life being saved. But Thursday had seen that appalling injury, and knew just how deep it had gone. She didn't know how Tony had managed to go on breathing, let alone living, during that terrible journey from Dunkirk to Haslar. Someone, she thought, had already saved his life. Now Haslar was continuing with the task, making every effort to ensure that he kept on living.

And Tony was just one man. One sailor, amongst so many.

She crept to the bedside and sat down on the straight-backed wooden chair, looking at the bandaged body. She hadn't realised before that Tony had many other injuries, too, but now she could see the splints and the dressings that covered him. Only one hand seemed unhurt, and she touched it softly, afraid that, however gentle she was, she might be sending ripples of pain through his body. But Tony didn't move. She didn't even know if he were aware of her presence.

She thought of the day she had first seen him on the ward, the day they had done Stoker Davis's enema. She thought of the day they had met in the Swiss Café, the day they'd cycled out to Lee, the night so soon after that when they'd gone to the dance together and he'd told her he was leaving. I'd just begun to fall in love with him then, she thought, but it was too soon to know if it was going to last. And then, while he was away, I began to see that it wasn't real, lasting love – not the sort you need for a marriage. But it's a sort of love all the same. We stayed friends and always will. And she felt the tears burn her eyes and brim over on her cheeks.

'Tony,' she whispered. 'Tony, it's me – Thursday. I'm here with you. You remember me, don't you? Thursday – Thursday you went dancing with, and cycling? Thursday you used to take to the Swiss Café? You remember me.'

There was no movement. The fingers lay limp in her hand. She swallowed back tears and started again, trying to bring back to him all the memories that had been in her mind.

'Remember the day we went out to Lee, and I had that row with Doug? Remember the day we gave Stoker Davis the enema? Remember Pneumonia Bridge and Bemister's Lane? You're back at Haslar now, did you know that? Back here, safe and sound. And nothing more's going to happen to you. Nothing bad. They're going to mend you and put you together again and you'll be as good as new. Everything's going to be all right, Tony. Everything's going to be all right.'

The other VAD came quietly to stand beside her. 'You'll have to go now, I'm afraid. Sister said only a few minutes.'

Thursday bit her lips. 'Does he know I'm here? Does he know anything at all?'

'We don't know.'

'He's in a coma, isn't he?' Thursday said. 'He's not responding at all.'

'It's better that way,' the girl said, her eyes full of pity. 'At least we know he's not suffering.'

Thursday turned and looked down at the still figure on the bed. The eyes were hidden by the cage of wire and bandage. The unbandaged hand lay still and limp. The man on the bed was undoubtedly unconscious, but who knew what was going on in his mind? Who knew for certain that his sleep was peaceful?

'We don't know that,' she said. 'We don't know that at all. But I hope – I really do hope – it's true.'

Chapter Fourteen

Not all men who came back from Dunkirk were injured. Some, like Helen Stanway's father and Roy Greenaway and Doug Brighton, were unscathed.

Others, like Thursday's brother Steve and her cousin Mike, didn't come back at all.

'Missing!' she said to Elsie when she received her mother's letter. 'That's all they know. Missing, both of them. They could be dead, or prisoners – we just don't know. They don't even know how to find out.' She was white-faced, dazed. She looked at the letter again, as if it might say something different this time. Steve, missing. Mike, missing. It couldn't be true. She felt sick.

'Here, sit down,' Elsie said suddenly. Her voice seemed to come from a distance and her face loomed close and then receded. Thursday stared at her, felt herself sway and then felt Elsie's hand on her arm, pressing her down into a chair. 'Put your head between your knees. Take a deep breath. That's right. And another. No, don't try to sit up, just stop there a minute . . .' She heard Elsie's voice talking to someone else. 'Just had bad news about her brother. And her cousin, too. Both at Dunkirk – didn't come back . . .' The voice faded amidst a concerned murmur of voices. She could make out Jeanie Brown's soft tones, and Ellen Bridges's louder Cockney, and then Louisa's commanding voice. Someone pushed a cup of water under her nose and she sipped it, choked a little and then lifted her head, staring at them with bewildered eyes.

'Our *Steve*. He hadn't been in the Army five minutes. He'd only just finished his basic training—'

'Oh, *Thursday*.' Patsy was beside her, putting her arm round her shoulders. 'Thursday, I'm so sorry.'

'It doesn't say they're dead.' Louisa had taken the letter from her fingers and was reading it swiftly. 'It says missing. They might be prisoners of war.'

'The army'll find out,' Elsie said. 'Don't you know where they were, or anything? Didn't they say in their letters?'

'You know they're not allowed to. All we knew was that they were in France.' Thursday stared at the scrap of paper, already stained by her mother's tears. 'Mum must be going mad, worrying, and so must be poor Auntie Flo. And there's her Leslie too, he's in the RAF, training to be a pilot. Oh, if *only* I could go home, just for a couple of days . . .'

'Ask Madam,' Louisa suggested. 'She might give you a couple of days. I'll come with you now.'

They went up the stairs to Madam's office together and knocked on the door, always left ajar so that the VADs felt at liberty to go to her at any time. Madam was at her cluttered desk, working on some papers. She listened with sympathy to Thursday's hesitant request, and then shook her head regretfully.

'I'm very sorry, Tilford. You know as well as I do how busy we are. With so many patients, we're at full stretch. I can't spare anyone, even for a moment, unless for the gravest emergency. If your brother had been killed, for instance . . . But it seems that there's still hope for him. I'm afraid there's no chance of any leave.'

Thursday knew she was right. There was far too much to do on the wards. The girls were kept busy running to and fro all day, at the beck and call of the QARNNS nurses. Their tasks were still mostly menial but they were, during especially busy periods, allowed to do more of the skilled nursing work that they had practised, like changing dressings or administering medicine, even injections. In the present emergency, they took on more and more, and

Thursday was especially grateful for the extra responsibilities.

'It makes you feel you're really doing something,' she said to Patsy as a group of them sat in the office rolling bandages during what was supposed to be their time off. 'I don't know why I didn't go in for nursing years ago.'

'Probably because your dad said you had to be a tailor's apprentice,' Patsy said shrewdly. 'Dads have got a lot to answer for.'

'Well, he wanted the best for me, I suppose.' Thursday rolled in silence for a moment or two before returning to the subject that seemed to occupy so many of her thoughts these days. 'Oh, Patsy, I *wish* we knew what had happened to our Steve, and Mike. I had another letter from Mum this morning. She says Dad's written to the regiment but there hasn't been any answer yet. She's frantic.'

'They must be in an awful muddle,' Patsy said. 'There were men all over the place. Nobody knew who was where. It'll take ages to sort them all out.'

'Yes, but you'd think the men themselves would be able to get in touch somehow. I mean, if they're prisoners. Aren't there rules about that sort of thing? Aren't the Germans meant to let our authorities know, and let them write home?' Thursday sighed despondently. 'The longer it goes on, the worse it seems. Sometimes I think they must be dead, and sometimes I think maybe they got away and they're wandering round France, lost and starving . . .' The tears came to her eyes again and a picture came into her mind of Steve, aged about three, sitting on the floor with a chocolate biscuit in one hand and getting it smeared all over his face. 'I can't *bear* to think of our Steve like that, I just can't.'

'Perhaps the Germans are in a muddle, too,' Jeanie said. 'They must have taken an awful lot of men prisoner. It's probably taking them a long time to sort them all out.'

They sat in silence for a while. Thursday wiped her eyes and drew a deep breath, determined not to start crying again. She seemed to have done so much of that lately, either about Steve and Mike or about poor Tony, still swathed in his cage of bandages. But she'd managed, on the whole, to stay more or less dry-eyed when on the wards and she didn't want to break down now.

'Well, they're doing their best to get the Army together again,' Louisa said, trying to sound more cheerful. 'At least we're not going to let ourselves be beaten.'

'And how long's that going to take?' Vera Hapgood demanded. 'Months, maybe years – and meanwhile Hitler just marches in and takes us over. It's just the chance he needs, isn't it, while we've got no army to speak of. What sort of defence have we got against all those great big Panzers and things?'

'What do you mean, great big Panzers?' Patsy enquired. 'What d'you think they are?'

'Well, they're tanks, aren't they? Huge big tanks that can go over anything.'

'I don't think so. They're soldiers – German soldiers. What they call crack regiments.'

'Well, whatever they are,' Vera said, irritated, 'they can just march in and take over now, and there's not a thing we can do to stop them.'

Thursday lifted her eyes from the bandage she was rolling. Her jaw was set. 'There is. We can fight them. Like Mr Churchill said – on the beaches, in the streets, in the hills. We shall never surrender.'

'You'd surrender all right if half a dozen German soldiers were holding you down and raping you,' Vera said bluntly. 'Didn't they surrender in Czechoslovakia and Poland? And Belgium, and Holland, and all those countries in Scandinavia? It'd be the same here, too. You can't fight against the sort of army he's got.'

'But we're *British*. We don't get invaded. We haven't been invaded since – since—'

'Since 1066,' Elsie supplied. 'William the Conqueror. We did it at school.'

'Yes, that's right, so did we. Since 1066. That's nearly a thousand years ago.'

'Doesn't make any difference,' Vera said, occupying herself with a fresh bandage. 'Nobody's ever sent such a big army against us since, that's all that means. Look, *nobody* wins against Hitler. It's obvious.'

'And it's also unpatriotic to talk like that!' Elsie said angrily. 'You're as bad as a fifth columnist, trying to make us all miserable. I wouldn't be surprised if you're a spy!'

'Don't be daft,' Vera began, but the other girls were joining in, too, shouting at her and getting to their feet. One even threw a bandage at her. Patsy was almost in tears. The office was in pandemonium when into the midst of it all walked Miss Makepeace herself.

'Girls! Girls! What in heaven's name is going on?'

Her voice cut through the uproar, and the girls stopped shouting and stared at her in dismay. One or two began to cry. Vera looked defiant, and Elsie furious.

'We were just rolling bandages, Madam,' Patsy began uncertainly, and faltered to a stop under the icy glare.

'*Rolling bandages?* It sounded more like a bear garden. And this bandage looks distinctly *un*rolled.' She bent to pick up the bandage someone had thrown at Vera. 'You realise this cannot be used now that it's been on the floor? A whole bandage wasted! I don't know *what* you were all thinking of.' Her brown eyes snapped with anger as she turned them on each girl in turn. 'Will someone please explain to me exactly what was going on? Tilford, you're a sensible girl – usually.'

Thursday bit her lips, wishing that Madam hadn't singled her out. Whatever she said now, she was going to get someone into trouble, and experience had taught her that she wouldn't be thanked for it. She looked down miserably.

'It was just a silly argument,' she muttered. 'It got a bit out of hand, that's all. I'm sure it won't happen again.'

'*I'm* sure it won't, too,' Madam said cuttingly. 'But I'd still like to know what it was all about.'

'It was Hapgood,' Elsie began furiously. 'It was all *her* fault, she—'

But Miss Makepeace cut her off with the lift of a hand. 'I was asking *Tilford*, if you don't mind.' She looked again at Thursday. 'Well? And just what was this silly argument about?'

'It was about the invasion,' Thursday said desperately. 'If one happens – and whether we could fight them – and what's happened in other countries. Some – someone said we wouldn't be able to and the rest of us said – well, we said what Mr Churchill said—'

'Very well. I think you've given me the gist of it.' Madam looked at Vera Hapgood, who was looking sullen, and at Elsie, who was still red with anger. 'Would I be correct in saying that you suggested we wouldn't be able to resist, Hapgood, and that you, Jackson, said we would?'

'She as good as said we'd let them rape us!' Elsie burst out. 'She's no better than a traitor!'

'*That's enough*!' Madam's voice cut through the hubbub as the other girls joined in, each eager now to give their own version. 'I've never known such disgraceful behaviour. This is a *hospital*. There are sick men here, needing your care. How can you shout and scream at each other like fishwives, when there are men only a few yards away who may be *dying*? Have you forgotten everything you've been taught – everything you should know without *having* to be taught? I'm ashamed of you all. Every one of you.' She paused for a moment, giving each girl in turn a scathing glance so that they wilted before her like flowers. 'You will all sign your names in the book as soon as you go off duty, and none of you is to go outside the gates of the hospital for a week. Is that understood? And if you find yourself bored with all the free time you'll find on your hands, you can go to each ward in the hospital and offer to do whatever tasks they allot you. They may have their own bandages to be rolled.' She turned to Elsie and Vera. 'Hapgood and Jackson, come with me. The rest of you, get on with your work. Without talking *at all*.' She gave them all another severe glare and turned to stalk out, followed by the half mutinous, half frightened figures of Elsie and Vera. The others looked at each other, anxious and embarrassed, and sat down again slowly, picking up their half-rolled bandages. Thursday glanced sideways at Patsy.

'I wonder what she'll do to them.'

'Not let them out again for a fortnight, I wouldn't wonder,' Patsy muttered back. 'Not that it makes much difference, when we're working all the hours God sends as it is. And we'd better not say any more. I wouldn't put it past her to be outside the door now, listening to hear if any of us dares speak.'

Madam did not return, however, and when they had finished their task the girls returned to the ward, where it was clear that Sister Burton knew all about their misdemeanours and was as angry as Madam. She received them coldly.

'You realise that your behaviour reflects directly upon me? And I imagined that I had a ward to be proud of. I thought I could rely on every one of you to be responsible and to carry out tasks usually allotted to trained nurses. Instead, you've shown yourselves to be no better than raw recruits, and as such you'll be returned to orderly duties.' Her icy glance was like a scratch across their faces. 'I hope you understand that this means the QARNNs will be even more hard-pressed, and that you needn't expect any sympathy from them.'

'We're really sorry, Sister,' Thursday said. 'Honestly, it won't happen again.'

'I should hope not, but I'm glad of your reassurance. However, such promises don't mean you won't be punished. I understand that all shore leave is to be stopped for the next week? Well, we'll find you plenty to do here, and if we can't, I dare say they've quite a few potatoes waiting to be peeled in the kitchens. I'm sure the time will fly!'

Her heels clacked away across the polished floor and the girls made rueful faces at each other. They dared not say any more, though, but went about their tasks as efficiently as possible, hoping desperately that their efforts would be noticed. Unfortunately, Sister Burton seemed to have developed the ability only to notice the things that weren't done properly, and for the next few days the wards echoed to her voice as first one VAD and then another fell victim to her irritation.

'What are you doing in the sluice, Nurse? Bed three needs changing . . . What are you doing with those sheets? The blanket baths should have been finished a quarter of an hour ago . . . What are you standing there for? The poor man in bed six needs a bedpan at once . . . Nurse, come here immediately – what sort of a dressing do you call this? Didn't you take in one single word of your training?' She stood with arms akimbo, shaking her head in despair. 'Really, I sometimes wonder what the Red Cross is thinking of, sending us such dim-witted girls. If you ever saw a dream walking . . .'

Her sarcasm reduced the girls to tears. Even Elsie, returning to the ward after her dressing-down in Madam's office, was subdued, while Vera looked at everyone as if it was all their fault and she hated them. Never a popular girl, she now withdrew into her shell completely, carrying out her work with just as much effort as was necessary to keep her out of trouble. She went through the day without the vestige of a smile on her thin, sallow face, and the men began to call her Nurse Sourpuss.

'It doesn't help,' Patsy said as they sat in the mess eating their supper towards the end of that dreadful week. 'She does her work, but she never puts anything extra into it. Sister's bound to have noticed.'

'It's not the men's fault we got into trouble,' Thursday agreed. 'And they're a good bunch – it cheers me up, too, to smile at them and have a little chat. It's about all that's got me through this.'

'You're lucky,' Elsie said morosely. 'You can go out again on Saturday. I've got another week of it, along with that long-faced little cat Vera. And to cap it all, Sister's put us on duties *together*. I won't be able to get away from her for a minute. Pass the bread and marge, Pats, I need a bit of comfort.'

'Perhaps she thinks you'll make friends with each other,' Patsy suggested, sliding the plate along the table. 'Here, have a spoonful of jam as well.'

Elsie snorted. '*Nobody* could make friends with that scaremonger. I still can't get over what she said. It was almost as if she thought we'd *enjoy* being raped by Germans!'

'Oh, I don't think she really meant that—' Thursday began, but Elsie broke in, shaking her head vigorously.

'She jolly well did! You didn't hear what she said to me while we were on our way to Madam's office. She as good as said I was looking *forward* to it!'

The others were silent. Then Patsy said uncomfortably, 'Are you sure of that, Else? You didn't – well, misunderstand her?'

'No, I flipping well didn't. She said it plain. "Of course, they wouldn't have to hold *you* down, would they, Jackson?" I couldn't misunderstand that, now, could I?'

Patsy and Thursday glanced at each other unhappily. Elsie was right, you couldn't misunderstand that. And after Vera's other remarks, it really was almost enough to have her branded as a scaremonger – the sort of talk that could get you into serious trouble.

'Did you tell Madam she said that?' Thursday asked after a moment.

Elsie shook her head again. 'What's the use? She won't want one of her VADs branded as a traitor. She just wants us all to get on with being nurses. She wants us to be a credit to her.'

'Yes, but if Vera goes on saying that sort of thing—'

'If she does,' Elsie said darkly, 'I'll deal with her in my own way. You don't need to worry about Vera-blooming-Hapgood. Vera *No*good, that's what I'm calling her from now on. And if she dares say another word about me, or about us giving in to the bloody Germans, she'll wish she'd never been born. *I'll* see to that.'

Despite all the extra duties, Thursday managed to get in to see Tony at least once a day. She sat beside him, holding his lifeless fingers and murmuring into his ear, reminding him of the fun they'd had together and the things they'd done. The trouble was, there hadn't been all that many of them and so she found herself repeating the same things over and over again. Not that it seemed to matter, she thought, gazing sadly at his face, still swathed in bandages. He didn't seem to hear her, didn't seem to know she was there. In fact, every day he seemed to slip a little further out of her reach.

'He isn't doing well, is he?' she said to Jeanie Brown, who was the VAD on duty when she left on the fifth day.

Jeanie started to deny it, then caught the look on Thursday's face and bit her lip. 'No, not very well. The captain's worried about him.'

The doctors were all officers, most of them lieutenant commanders or captains. Their rounds were conducted like 'rounds' on ships – an inspection to see that all was in order as much as to treat the patients. Nobody was ever allowed to forget that Haslar was as much a ship as any that went to sea, and that patients were effectively on duty. But this didn't affect their treatment – unless it was to make it even more thorough. The naval doctors' code of behaviour was as strict as the men's, and their driving aim was to get them back on active service.

'What does he say?' Thursday asked, and Jeanie looked awkward.

'Well, you know they don't tell us anything much . . .

225

But I heard him tell Sister he thinks there's some brain damage. You can't tell until the patient wakes up – but the longer he stays in a coma, the poorer the outlook is.'

Thursday knew this, but her heart sank at hearing it confirmed. She turned back to look at Tony's still figure, and tears burned her eyes. He'd been so pleasant, so friendly, such good company. And even if they hadn't been really in love, they'd been good friends and he'd made her feel special, just for a while.

'There's still a chance, though,' Jeanie went on determinedly. 'We're doing all we can to bring him round. I sit beside him, too, and talk to him like you do – except that I didn't know him so well before,' she went on hurriedly. 'But I can tell him about what's happening here. He was an SBA so he'd understand about hospital news. I talk about that, and what I do when I'm off duty – that sort of thing.'

Thursday nodded and tried to smile. She went out of the ward and crossed the broad square towards D Block, trying to blink back the tears that stung her eyes.

Poor Tony, so bright and cheerful, so full of jokes, yet so tender on that last night at Lee, when he'd told her he'd got a draft. Poor Tony, his face torn apart, his body wrecked, lying there in a coma, perhaps never to wake – and even if he did, what would life be like for him? What could life be like for a man with a ruined face and a damaged brain?

Oh, Tony, she thought, Tony. It would almost be better if you never did wake up . . .

Chapter Fifteen

Mary Tilford, her greying hair hidden beneath the turban she wore for housework and her everyday frock hidden by a flowered pinafore, opened the front door to find her sister-in-law standing there. They stared into each other's eyes for a moment, each asking the same question and each reading the same answer.

Mary turned away and went indoors, and Flo followed her. She was wearing a cardigan she'd knitted from one of Percy's old pullovers. It was grey and a bit shapeless, not one of her best efforts, and in ordinary times she wouldn't have been seen outside the house in it. Now, Mary knew, she hardly cared what she looked like.

'There's no news, then,' Mary said, going out to the kitchen to fill the kettle. She got two pale green cups and saucers out of the dresser and set them on the small wooden table with its covering of checked American cloth. She'd been making corned-beef rissoles and the ingredients were just ready for mixing – the corned beef flaked into small pieces, the potatoes mashed with carrots, a bowl of breadcrumbs and a bottle of OK sauce. She fetched a pint of milk from the shed, which was the coolest place, and poured some into each cup.

'No news,' Flo agreed heavily. She stood in the doorway and watched as her sister-in-law finished mixing the rissole ingredients together and shaped them into balls, placing them on a baking tray and patting them flat. The gas stove was already hot, and just as Mary slid them in the kettle began to whistle. She poured some hot water into the brown teapot, swished it about and then tipped it out before measuring two level teaspoons of tea into the pot.

'One for each person and *none* for the pot,' she said ruefully. 'That's what Lord Woolton says, isn't it? I must say I don't like it much. I like tea to *look* like tea – and taste like it, too. But we've all got to save wherever we can. Come and have a sit-down for a minute, Flo.'

'I wouldn't mind so much,' Flo said as they went back to the living room and settled themselves in the two armchairs, 'if we'd got any idea where they were. But we don't know anything at all. All we've had about Mike is that one telegram – "Missing". It could mean anything.'

'I know. We've had the same.' The crumpled scrap of paper was on the mantelpiece now, behind the marble clock that had been Mary's mother's, and Mary got up and took it down, staring at it as if it might say something different this time. 'I just dread that telegram boy coming again. I dread it.' She put the paper back behind the clock.

'I know, and yet you *want* him to come as well. You want to *know*, don't you? And it could be good news next time, that's what you've got to think of.' Flo dropped a couple of saccharin tablets into her tea and took a sip. 'What I keep telling myself is there must be hundreds of soldiers in hospitals who've been wounded and aren't properly conscious yet – can't say who they are. Our boys could be like that. It's not that I want them to be wounded, of course it isn't – but they'd be *alive*, wouldn't they? That's the thing.'

Mary sighed. Flo was clutching at straws, but they were straws Mary wanted to clutch as well. If only Steve could be in hospital somewhere, peacefully asleep, wounded in some way that he could recover from – something that didn't hurt too much . . . But her common sense told her that although there must be boys who were like that, and that both Steve and Mike could be amongst them, there were also many more who were dead or taken prisoner. And her mind would not stop seeing the beaches of

Dunkirk – beaches she had never seen but imagined as long stretches of sand – crowded with the waiting men, and strewn with the bodies of those whose wait was over.

'They'd have their dog-tags, though, wouldn't they?' she said to Flo. 'If they were in hospital, they could be identified.'

'They could have lost them.' Flo wasn't ready to give up hope. 'They could have taken them off—'

'They're not supposed to take them off, ever.'

'But they *could* have. We don't know. Nobody knows.'

Mary was silent. She wanted to cheer Flo up – heaven knows, she wanted to cheer herself up – but this was a straw that was too fragile for anyone to clutch for long. The boys wouldn't have taken off their identity discs. Walter had told her there were circumstances in which the discs could have been damaged and unreadable – if the wearer had been shot, or blown up, for instance, without actually being killed – but she didn't want to think of Steve or Mike being shot or blown up. The only real possibilities were that they'd been either killed or taken prisoner.

'We'll hear before long, I'm sure,' she said at last. 'They'll have to let us know soon. They're calling all the men in again, those who had leave, so they'll be sorting them all out. They'll know who's still missing. And if they're prisoners, don't the Germans have to tell our people? We'll get some news soon.'

'I suppose so.' Flo sipped again and pulled a face. 'I don't like these saccharin tablets as much as sugar, do you? They're much too sweet. It's a horrible taste.'

'Well, don't put two in, then.' Mary was glad of an excuse to smile. 'Just use one!'

'I suppose I could do that,' Flo said, with the ghost of a smile. 'Funny how you don't think of the obvious, isn't it. I'll just rinse out this cup, Mary, and have another one, only don't tell Lord Woolton, will you. But, you know, I reckon I'll give up saccharin as well as sugar. Percy's always drunk his tea without. He says it's more thirst-quenching that way.'

'I suppose you'd soon get used to it. And how's your Leslie? Jenny said she'd seen Denise at that dance last Saturday and she said he was learning to fly. I told her I was sure she'd got that wrong.'

'No, it's true. They're training all those that have got an aptitude. I don't know what that means, I'm sure, our Leslie's never shown an aptitude for anything much, bar laying in bed on a Sunday morning. He's cock-a-hoop over it, of course.'

'But he's only just seventeen!'

Flo shrugged. 'Old enough to drive a car, old enough to fly a plane, it seems. I don't reckon they'll let him fly in action, though, not so young as that. It'll be a few years yet. No, it's not him I'm worrying about. It's our Denise.'

'Why, what's she been up to?'

Flo pursed her lips and leant forward as if she thought she could be overheard. 'She's been stepping out with a young man from the post office. Thinks I don't know about it, but Mrs Hawkins up the road told me her Rosie had seen them. Those dances she and your Jenny go to, she sees him there, and they've been to the pictures together too.'

'From the post office? Well, what's wrong with that? It's a good job, the post office is – civil service.'

'It's not the job I object to. It's the fellow. Twenty-four if he's a day, Mrs Hawkins says, and I went down to see for myself and she's right. He works on the parcels counter. Nice enough looking chap and a nice smile, but he's a bit free with it. Flirting with a girl from one of the offices, he was. I don't like it, and nor does Percy, and we're going to have it out with Denise tonight. He's too old for her.'

'Twenty-four!' Mary repeated. 'That's nine years older than Denise.'

'I know. I don't even like her having a boyfriend, not a

regular one. It's all right going to a local hop, a crowd of boys and girls together, and I didn't mind when she said she was going with your Jenny, but going out steady with a boy – no, not a boy, a *man* – that age, well, that's a different kettle of fish altogether.'

'And what about my Jenny? What's she doing while your Denise is canoodling with this fellow?'

'You'd better ask her that yourself,' Flo said grimly. 'Is that those rissoles I can smell?'

'Oh!' Mary jumped up and ran out to the kitchen. 'Caught them just in time,' she called, lifting the tray from the oven. 'Good job you remembered them, Flo, we can't afford to waste food these days.' She came back into the room. 'I'll have a word with Jenny tonight. See what she's got to say about this chap from the post office – and see what she's been getting up to as well. The trouble with these young girls is that they can make themselves up to look so much older. I know for a fact she's been wearing lipstick and powder, and I'm almost sure I saw stuff on her eyes when she came in the other night. She wipes it off before she comes in, but it won't *all* come off on a hanky.'

'I know. Denise is the same, and she's painting her nails, too. I saw flecks of bright red varnish all round the edges of them the other day. Her dad's told her he won't have her looking cheap, but she takes no notice. It's this war, Mary. It's giving them all ideas.' Her mouth turned down as she thought again of Mike. 'I'll go now. I don't like to be out too long, in case – well, you know what I mean.'

In case a telegram comes. Mary knew exactly what she meant. She, too, was anxious every moment she was out of the house, in case the boy came sweeping down the street on his red bike with that dreaded brown envelope in his bag. She saw Flo to the door and they both looked up and down the street anxiously, as if he might be coming at this very minute.

'We'll hear soon,' Mary said, giving her sister-in-law a kiss. 'I'm sure we'll hear soon.'

'Yes. Yes, I know. And in the meantime . . .' Flo gave her a crooked smile. 'We've got plenty to worry about at home, haven't we?'

Mary watched her go, giving her a wave as she turned the corner, and then went thoughtfully indoors. She stood looking for a moment at the rissoles, cooling on their tray.

Denise, going out with a man of twenty-four. And her Jenny, supposedly out with her but apparently somewhere else instead. So who was she really spending her time with?

I'll have a word with that young lady when she gets home, she thought grimly.

'He's not twenty-four,' Jenny said. 'He's twenty-two.' She tossed her dark curls and faced her mother defiantly. 'And he's really nice.'

'That's still too old for a girl of fifteen,' Mary said sharply, slapping a rissole and some mashed potato on her plate. Jenny was the only one who came home for dinner now that both Thursday and Steve were away. 'It doesn't matter how nice he is. And your Auntie Flo's been down the post office and seen him. She said he was flirting with all the girls.'

'Well, what if he was? Anyway, I don't believe it. He loves Dizzy, he said so.'

'*Loves* her?' Mary repeated in shock. 'What do you mean, loves her?'

'What I say. He told her he wants them to get engaged.' Jenny put her hand to her mouth and gazed at her mother with wide brown eyes. 'Only it's supposed to be a secret. You're not to tell Auntie Flo.'

'Not tell Flo! Of course I'll tell Flo. She's got to know. Denise is only fifteen – she can't be thinking of getting engaged. Her father would never allow it anyway, not till she's at least nineteen. And then only when he's sure the man's the right sort.'

'Well, Vic is the right sort. He's ever so nice-looking, and he's got a good job. What else do you want?'

'There's a lot more than that to getting married,' Mary said. 'And what I want to know is—'

'They're not talking about getting married. Just engaged. *Secretly* engaged. Nobody else would even know.'

'Half Worcester will know, if you've got anything to do with it,' Mary said. 'You've never been able to keep a secret. And getting married is what being engaged is all about, you silly girl. Anyway, Flo and Percy will soon put a stop to all that nonsense. What I want to know is what *you've* been getting up to.'

'Me?' The colour ran up Jenny's face. 'What d'you mean? *I* haven't been getting up to anything.'

'Oh, no? Then why have you gone as red as a turkey-cock? Come on, Jenny, out with it. What have you been doing while Denise and this Vic have been off spooning? Sitting all by yourself in the moonlight? Or did she get him to bring along a mate?'

Jenny's colour deepened. 'We haven't done anything we shouldn't—'

'Who is it, Jenny? What's his name? And how old is this one? About the same age as Vic, I should think, if they're friends.'

Jenny's eyes dropped. She scraped the rug with her toe. 'He's called Sam. Sam Hayward. He's in the post office as well, he's a sorter.' She lifted her eyes. 'He's nice, Mum, he really is. You'd like him.'

'And how old is he? Same as Vic?'

'He's twenty-three,' Jenny muttered, casting her eyes down again.

'Twenty-*three*? Oh, *Jenny*.'

'I don't see what's so awful about that! Why's age so important? Uncle Percy's five years older than Auntie Flo.

233

Vic and Sam are only seven years older than me and Denise. It's not that much different.'

'Your Uncle Percy and Auntie Flo knew each other for a long time before they got married. And Flo was nineteen before they even started going out together. There's a lot of difference.'

'I don't see why,' Jenny muttered.

Mary looked at her. The girl's cheeks were still scarlet. 'You do know why. You know very well why. Now, be truthful with me, Jenny. Have you done anything you shouldn't? I want to know.'

'No! I've already *told* you! What do you think I am, some sort of a – a tart? Sam *respects* me, he said so, and he wouldn't do anything I didn't want him to. He – I – we—' Jenny floundered, and then burst into tears. She turned and pulled open the door, running from the room. 'Oh, it's not *fair*! You always think the worst of me – it's just not *fair*!'

Mary heard her footsteps on the stairs and then her bedroom door slammed. Overhead, she could hear noisy weeping and knew that Jenny had flung herself on the bed. She bit her lips ruefully, feeling tears in her own eyes.

So he 'respected' her, did he? And he wouldn't do 'anything she didn't want'? And Jenny couldn't even look her in the eye when she said so. Her only way out was to burst into tears and cry that it wasn't fair, like a small child caught out, and then run away.

I'll have to talk to Walter about this, she thought. And we'd better go round and see Flo and Percy, too. If we don't put a stop to this straight away, one or the other of those girls is going to be bringing trouble to the house. And Denise isn't even sixteen yet.

Just as if we haven't got enough to worry about.

'I knew this would happen,' Denise said furiously. 'I *knew* some old cat would see us and tell Mum. Why can't people mind their own business?'

Jenny shrugged. She had met Denise from work to warn her that there was trouble waiting for her at home and they'd gone into a teashop to discuss the matter. Denise was wearing a new pink blouse, she noticed a little jealously. It was funny about Denise, even with all the shortages she always seemed to have something new – a blouse, a jumper, a lipstick. She smoothed down her own green frock. It was her favourite and she'd set her hair only last night, but she felt shabby beside Denise in her pink blouse, and with her fair hair done in Marcel waves. 'You know what old people are like. Nosy and spiteful, just because their lives are practically over. Can't stand seeing younger ones having a bit of fun. The question is, what are we going to do about it?'

The waitress, a girl of about fifteen, appeared at their side with a notebook. 'You can have chips and Spam or chips and one egg, but you can't have chips and Spam *and* egg, or—'

'For goodness' sake!' Denise snapped. 'We just want a pot of tea, all right? And a slice of cake between us.' She turned back to Jenny. 'Do about it? Why, nothing. We'll just go on same as usual. They can't stop us seeing Vic and Sam. They'd have to lock us in our bedrooms to do that.'

'My bedroom hasn't got a lock,' Jenny said. 'But I wouldn't put it past our Dad to put one on.'

'They can't do it,' Denise said impatiently, smoothing one hand over her waved hair. 'We've got to go to work, haven't we? They can't come with us. They can't watch us every minute. They can't even stop us going out in the evenings. This is the twentieth century, Jen, not Victorian times.'

'There'll be awful rows, though.'

'So what? I'm not scared of a row or two.'

Jenny chewed her lip doubtfully. She'd been in trouble with her dad before, of course, but never seriously, and they'd always made things up with a kiss and a cuddle.

She'd never defied him in the way that Denise was suggesting now.

'I don't know . . .'

'Well, I do! I love Vic and he loves me, and we're not going to let anyone stop us seeing each other. We're secretly engaged. We'll be getting married one day. We've got to see each other.'

'Uncle Percy's never going to let you get married, 'specially when he finds out you've been going out with someone seven years older than you.'

'We can wait. We'll wait till I'm twenty-one. He won't be able to stop me then. Or we'll go to Scotland.' She became aware of the young waitress at her side, holding a tray and listening in fascination to their conversation. 'All right, you can put it down.' She poured two cups of tea and looked at her cousin. 'Well, what are you looking so pop-eyed about?'

'*Scotland*?' Jenny gasped. 'Why Scotland?'

'Because you can get married there when you're sixteen, without having to ask anyone. There's a place – Gretna Green. I read about it in a magazine. People who want to get married run away and they get married in a blacksmith's forge.'

'In a *blacksmith's* forge? You're making it up, Dizzy.'

'I'm not. It's true, I tell you, I read about it.' Denise put a lump of sugar in her tea and stirred it aggressively, her reddened lips pushed out in defiance.

'Anyway, you're not even sixteen yet, so you can't even do that.' Jenny looked at her cousin. 'Diz, I'm not sure about all this. I mean, I know you love Vic and he says he loves you—'

'He doesn't just *say* it, he does love me. Are you going to have a bit of this cake?'

'Yes – no, you eat it. Look, you won't do anything daft, will you? I mean – you don't want to take any risks. He *is* a lot older, and—'

'I can look after myself, thank you very much,' Denise

said, biting into the slice of dry sponge. 'And Vic's promised me nothing'll happen. Anyway, what about you and Sam?'

'We don't – we haven't – we've never gone all the way.' Jenny's colour scorched her cheeks. 'But he wants to, I know he does, and I – I'm not sure I—'

'Well, me and Vic are in love,' Denise stated. 'And what we do is our business. And I might not be sixteen yet but I will be in a couple of months, and no one – not even my dad – is going to stop me doing what I like. Things are different now, Jen. There's a war on. Vic could get called up and go away, and I might never see him again. Why shouldn't we have what happiness we can while we've got the chance? What right does anyone have to ruin our lives by making us wait?'

'So what will you do? I mean, Scotland's a long way away and you know we're not supposed to travel if we don't have to. There's those posters: "Is Your Journey Really Necessary?" And I don't know what the fare would be, though I suppose Vic's getting a good wage. And where would you live? You couldn't stop at home, and—'

'Oh, for goodness' sake! I didn't say we *would* run away – just that we *could*. Vic hasn't said anything about getting married – not yet, anyway – just engaged. *Secretly* engaged.' She stopped and looked at Jenny. 'You never said anything to your mum about that, did you?' Her eyes widened as she saw Jenny's colour deepen again. 'Oh, Jen, you *didn't*!'

'I didn't mean to! It just sort of came out. I wanted her to know that you and Vic were serious. I'm sorry, Diz. I really am.'

'Oh, that's wonderful, just wonderful,' Denise said bitterly. 'Now everyone'll know. *Dad* will know. And all the old cats in the street will know. They'll all be looking at me. Honestly, Jenny!' She looked round for the waitress. 'We want to pay now.'

'I'm ever so sorry,' Jenny said humbly, looking at her

cup of tea. She hadn't even touched it so far. She picked it up and sipped, but it was cold and she put it down again.

'Sorry's not going to help much, is it.' Denise brushed crumbs from her lips and got to her feet. 'Well, better go and face the music, I suppose. And I don't fancy being in your shoes, neither, when your dad hears about all this. And you and Sam aren't even engaged, not even *secretly*.'

Nor going to be, Jenny thought as she walked slowly home. She'd already begun to have doubts about Sam. It had been fun at first, going out with an older boy, but his kisses had scared her a bit. She'd only been kissed once or twice before and those had been fumbling attempts, with lips firmly closed. And Sam had wanted to touch her a bit more than she liked, even though it was exciting, too. She'd been sleeping badly, her body itchy and restless, and she'd worried quite a bit about whether she might be going to have a baby. Someone at school had told her you only had to kiss a boy to find yourself in the family way, and although she hadn't thought this seemed very likely, the way Sam had kissed her had brought the idea back into her mind. Suppose it was true . . .

'Don't neither of you girls never bring trouble to this house,' Mary had warned her and Thursday more than once. 'We've never had nothing like that in this family and we're not starting now.' And Jenny had thought of a girl she knew a few streets away, who'd had to get married suddenly and had a baby five months later. She lived in two rooms with her young husband now, and people said they argued all the time and the baby never stopped crying. Their landlady had given them notice, and her mum and dad still wouldn't speak to her or let her in the house.

I wish Thursday was home, she thought miserably. She could tell me if it's true, what with her being a nurse.

Perhaps it would be better not to see Sam again. Then, whether it was true or not, he wouldn't be able to get her into trouble. If he hadn't already.

She walked the last hundred yards down Waterloo Street slowly and reluctantly. Whatever she and Sam had or hadn't done, there was going to be trouble anyway. Mum would have told Dad about Sam, and about Vic and Denise, and he'd be waiting with a face like thunder. There was going to be a really horrible row.

As it happened, she needn't have worried. By the time she reached home, her mother and father had other things to think about.

'There's been a telegram!' Mary said the minute Jenny walked through the door. 'Oh, Jen, there's been a telegram about Steve – and your Auntie Flo's had one, too, about Mike!'

Chapter Sixteen

'You can have a forty-eight-hour leave pass and a rail warrant,' Miss Makepeace said to Thursday. 'That's all I can give you, I'm afraid. You know how busy the hospital is.'

'I know, Madam. I'm really grateful. It's my mum I'm worried about, you see, she must be so upset. She and my auntie are really close.'

'Of course. And I'm very sorry to hear about your cousin. You've a brother missing, too, I believe?'

'Yes, Madam. He's *believed* killed – we don't know for sure. But we know Mike – my cousin . . .' Her voice choked on the words.

'Yes, I see. It's a very sad and anxious time,' Madam said. 'Well, you can go tomorrow morning. There's an early train from Portsmouth, you should be able to reach Worcester by the afternoon if all the connections work. You'll have to be back on duty on Monday morning, so you'll have to leave on Sunday afternoon at the latest. It doesn't give you very long at home, but it's the best I can do.'

'It'll be good just to have a few hours, Madam. Thank you.'

Thursday left the office and walked slowly down the stairs. She paced out to the sea wall and stood gazing across the Solent to the Isle of Wight, thinking of Mike.

It didn't seem possible that he was dead. He was too young. He was her *cousin*. He'd only been in the Army for five minutes. It couldn't be true that he would never come home again, never come round to see Steve and sit in

Dad's chair laughing at her, never kick a football about with his mates or play charades at Christmas. It couldn't be true that he would never sit at the dinner table again, pouring OK sauce over his meal until Auntie Flo took the bottle away from him, never go to the pictures at the Scala, never have a proper girlfriend, never get married.

His whole life's gone, she thought, watching a frigate steam out through the neck of the harbour. His whole life's gone for ever.

And what about Steve? Had his life gone for ever as well? Wasn't he ever going to come home again to tease her and argue with Jenny, and go up to the pub with Dad? She remembered how they used to go on the train to Malvern and climb up Worcester Beacon to fly the kite Dad had made him, how they'd go down to Upton-on-Severn on a pleasure steamer on Sunday afternoons, how they'd go on Sunday school outings to Bredon Hill by charabanc. I didn't realise how much he meant to me, she thought. He was just Steve, my brother, a pest and a nuisance – except that he wasn't really a nuisance at all and I'd give anything to have him come home again.

The journey seemed endless. Thursday sat in the hot, stuffy carriage, staring out of the window and thinking of the last time she had travelled on this line, on her way to Haslar for the first time. She'd been excited, nervous, looking forward to her new life and the independence of being away from home. And at the same time, Steve had been starting on his new life, too, joining the Army and setting off for his basic training.

And now he was missing, and Mike was dead.

The train was full. Trains always were these days. Her compartment was filled with soldiers, all talking in loud voices. They tried to draw her into their conversation but she shook her head and they noticed her reddened eyes and left her alone. She sat in the corner, staring out of the window, trying not to feel bitter that they were alive and

Mike was dead. Their own lives might not last much longer anyway. They'd come back safe from Dunkirk, but who was to say where they would be sent next?

She stood on the platform at Worcester station at last, her kitbag at her side. There was nobody on the platform to meet her – but she hadn't expected anyone, she told herself valiantly. Trains were so unreliable these days, you couldn't say for certain when you'd arrive anywhere, you couldn't expect people to hang about waiting on railway platforms. She made her way to the exit and handed over her ticket.

'Thursday! *Thursday*!'

'Jen!' Thursday exclaimed, feeling a surge of pleasure and relief. 'Have you been waiting long? There was a hold-up—'

'Only about an hour,' her sister declared with a grin. 'I got some time off from the shop. Oh, *Thursday* . . .'

Their momentary pleasure at seeing each other vanished in the sudden remembrance of grief. They stared at each other, tears welling from their eyes, and Thursday opened her arms to her sister.

'Oh, Jen, Jen . . . I still can't believe it. Our *Mike*. It doesn't seem possible.'

'I know. We can't believe it either. Auntie Flo can't stop crying. I wonder where all the tears come from, I really do. Dizzy says she keeps making cups of tea for her but she lets half of them go cold. She just looks at that photo he had took of him in his new uniform and then she keeps looking at the telegram as if it might say something different, but it never does. And Mum's nearly out of her mind over Steve.'

'There hasn't been any more news?' Thursday asked, knowing that if there had been Jenny would have told her at once. Her heart, momentarily lifted in hope, sank again as Jenny shook her head.

'No. Nothing. We don't know what to think. One minute Mum's convinced he's dead, the next she says she

242

knows he's alive. She thinks he's in a hospital somewhere with a lost memory.'

'Well, I suppose he could be.' They walked to the bus stop. Thursday wanted to get home to her mother as quickly as possible and it was already nearly four o'clock. She fidgeted impatiently as they stood there, waiting. 'Oh, Jenny, I've felt so awful, being all those miles away.'

'I know. We just want to be together, somehow. Only we – we won't be, will we?' Jenny's eyes filled with tears again. 'Oh, Thursday, it's just *horrible*.'

The bus lumbered along and they climbed aboard and found seats upstairs. The air was filled with cigarette smoke. Thursday tried to find something more cheerful to talk about. 'Did you hear Mr Churchill's broadcast on Monday evening?'

'Yes. We all did.' Jenny sighed. 'We didn't know about Mike or Steve then, but it still made Mum cry. She said it made her feel proud that he'd been there. Now – she just can't stop thinking how cruel it all is. Why can't they go and fight it out between them, Churchill and Hitler and everyone? Why do they have to send boys like our Steve to do their dirty work? Why can't they just sit down and *talk* about it?'

'Well, I suppose they tried. That's what Mr Chamberlain did, wasn't it? But it doesn't do any good with people like Hitler.'

Jenny sighed and nodded. 'I suppose that's it.' Her voice wobbled. 'And Dad – I've never seen Dad so upset. He was crying the other day, I saw him. Our Dad, *crying*, Thurs.'

'Don't say any more,' Thursday begged her, unable to bear the thought of her father in tears. 'You'll start me off again. Let's talk about something else for a bit. Have you got a new boyfriend?'

Jenny wrinkled her nose. 'You could have picked something a bit more tactful! There was going to be a proper shindig if all this hadn't happened. I suppose there still will be, once they start thinking about it.'

'Thinking about what? What sort of shindig? What are you on about, Jen?' Thursday stared at her sister.

'Me and Sam Hayward. I've been going out with him for a few weeks now. Denise fixed it up for me when she started going out with Vic Pearce. He's one of Vic's mates at work, see.'

'No, I don't see,' Thursday said. 'Who's Vic Pearce, and who's Sam Hayward? I've never heard of either of them. Is he any relation to Mrs Hayward up the road?' She frowned at Jenny. 'What do you mean, you've been going out with him?'

'Well, what do you think I mean? Going out – going to the pictures and things. And I don't think he's any relation of Mrs Hayward. He comes from near Powick. Anyway, they both work in the main post office, him and Vic, and Denise got talking to Vic when he was on the parcels counter and they started going out together, and then she fixed it for me to go, too, with Sam. He's a sorter.'

'Well, what's wrong with that? They're both good jobs.'

'It's not their jobs. It's – well, Vic's twenty-two and Sam's twenty-three.'

Thursday stared at her. 'Twenty-two and twenty-three? No wonder Mum and Dad don't like it! Have they met these chaps?'

'No, but Auntie Flo went down the post office when she found out, and she said Vic was flirting with all the girls. The thing is, Dizzy says they're secretly engaged, only I let it out when Mum was on at me and of course she went and told Auntie Flo. And Dizzy was talking about running away to Scotland to get married, and – well, that's how it was when we got the telegram, so I don't know what'll happen now.'

'Dizzy's talking about getting *married*? But how can she? She's only fifteen. And why in *Scotland*?' Thursday put a hand to her head. 'I can't make all this out. Are you sure it's not some daft story?'

'No, of course it's not. And Dizzy says you can get married there without your parents' say-so when you're sixteen, and she'll be that in a few weeks. Honestly, Thurs, I don't know what to make of it all. She's got some story about a blacksmith's forge, you can get married over the anvil or something. It can't be true, surely.'

'I think I've heard something about that,' Thursday said doubtfully. 'But Auntie Flo and Uncle Percy will never let her go.'

'Well, that's the point, isn't it – she'd be running away.' Jenny shook her head. 'She's really fallen for this Vic. I – I'm a bit worried about her, to tell the truth.'

Thursday glanced at her. 'Why?'

Jenny turned her head away and Thursday's glance sharpened. 'Jen! You don't think . . . ?'

'I don't know.' Jenny gazed unhappily out of the window. The bus was just crossing the bridge. In a few minutes they'd be home and all the talk would be of Mike and Steve. She lowered her voice. 'Thurs, there's something I want to ask you. You know what they say about when a boy kisses you – I mean, is it true you can have a baby from that?'

Thursday stared at her. 'Just from kissing? No, it's not. Of course it's not.' She glanced around the bus, wondering if anyone could overhear their conversation, and felt a sudden twinge of panic. The whole thing sounded like a dreadful muddle and she wondered how her mother was coping with it all, on top of Steve's disappearance. 'Jenny, you and Sam haven't—'

'No more than that,' Jenny said hastily. 'Honestly. But it's the way he does it – sort of deep, if you know what I mean. I just wondered – I mean, people do say – and you being a nurse, I thought you'd know.'

'He'd have to go pretty deep for that to happen!' Thursday said. 'It's all right, Jen, if that's all you've done

245

you're OK. But don't go any further.' She looked at her sister. '*You're* not thinking of getting secretly engaged, or married or anything, are you? Because if you are, I've got to say I think you're being really, really selfish. What about poor Mum, with all she's got to worry about – have you thought about her feelings? I mean, I'm not surprised about Denise, she's always been one for getting her own way, but I thought you had a bit more sense. I hope you're not thinking of running off to Scotland as well.'

'No. In fact, I've more or less decided to stop going out with him. I only went because Dizzy fixed it up for me. It scares me a bit. I don't want that sort of thing yet.'

'Well, all you've got to do is tell Mum and Dad that, then, isn't it.' Thursday stood up. 'Here's our stop.' The memory of her brother flooded back into her mind and she thought of her mother, sitting at home with Steve's photograph, waiting for another telegram, and Jenny's tale was pushed once more to the back of her mind. They were just silly girls, the two of them, she thought impatiently.

She pushed her way down the bus and dragged her kitbag out from the luggage space under the stairs. Jenny joined her on the pavement and they walked in silence the last few hundred yards to Waterloo Street and the house where Mary Tilford sat, gazing at a photograph of her son in his stiff new khaki uniform and the telegram that told her he was missing, believed killed.

'I can't believe it,' Mary said dully for the fifth or sixth time. 'I just can't believe it. My Steve. My *boy*.' She shook her head. 'I just can't believe it's true.'

'I know,' Thursday said gently. She and her mother had fallen into each other's arms, weeping, when she first arrived, but now the initial storm was over and they were sitting with cups of tea and a slice of cake brought in by Mrs Harting next door. Jenny, still subdued, had slipped out to the kitchen where she was scraping potatoes and carrots for tonight's meal.

'He was too young,' Mary went on, talking almost to herself. 'He was just a boy. He had all his life before him, and now it's gone, all gone. I just can't believe it.'

'We don't know yet what's happened to him,' Thursday reminded her, trying to convince herself that Steve could still be alive. 'He could still turn up. Just try to keep your mind fixed on that.'

She was having to try very hard not to cry again herself. The only way she could manage, she found, was to think of herself as a nurse, with the mother of one of her patients. She'd dealt with that often enough in the past few months, she thought sadly. Weeping mothers and sisters, wives and girlfriends, even brothers and fathers. They'd all needed a calm, reassuring presence, someone who would sympathise without becoming too involved in their tragedy. She'd been able to provide it, even though she had often wept afterwards, and it was what her mother needed now.

'Remember what the telegram says,' she went on. '*Missing believed killed.* They could be wrong. It was chaos over there, they didn't know half of what was going on.' But she had a dreadful, aching feeling that it was true. Steve was dead, just as Mike was dead, and he was never coming back.

Patch came and put one paw on her knee. She stared into his anxious face and her control broke. 'Oh, Mum. Oh, *Mum.*' Her heart was a fierce twist of pain against her ribs, spreading upwards into her throat and eyes and tightening across her skull. Tears were the only relief and, unable to hold them back any longer, she sobbed, 'Oh, Mum. *Steve* – our *Steve* . . .'

Jenny slipped back into the room, white-faced. She brought fresh cups of tea and she set them on the table and patted her mother's shoulder. Thursday felt for her handkerchief and wiped her wet face and blew her nose. She gave her sister a shaky smile of thanks and thought how Jenny had grown up in the few months since she'd last seen her. Probably she'd grown up most of all in the past few days.

'Sorry, Jen,' she murmured. 'I'm not being much help.'

'You *are*,' Mary said, hearing her. 'You're all the help in the world – both of you. I don't know how I'd have managed these past few days without our Jen, and it's so good to have you here now, Thursday. I just wish you could stop a bit longer.'

'So do I. But we're so busy in the hospital.' She stopped abruptly, remembering that many of the patients were men who had been brought back from Dunkirk, wounded but alive. 'I couldn't get more than a forty-eight-hour pass,' she finished lamely.

'I know. There's other mothers' sons need you. It's all right, Thursday, I know that. And I want you to go back and look after them. There's got to be *some* good come out of all this.' She wiped her own face and looked at Thursday. 'I'm glad you went to be a nurse. I really am glad.'

Thursday felt her eyes fill again and picked up her cup hastily. 'Drink your tea, Mum. Jenny's made some fresh, look. And she's out there now, getting the vegetables ready for tonight. What a difference! She didn't even know what the potato peeler looked like when I went away.'

'I heard that!' Jenny called. 'And I don't remember you doing all that much in the kitchen, our Thursday.'

'I did! I always helped cook the Sunday dinner, and wash up after it. You made yourself scarce then, if I remember right.'

'I had to go to church,' Jenny said with dignity. 'I'm in the choir.'

'Now then,' their mother said, 'don't you two start squabbling the minute Thursday gets through the door.' But she spoke fondly, as if it was good to hear their banter again. There was a small silence as she drank her tea and then, as if she'd remembered her anxiety all over again,

248

her eyes brimmed over. 'But why did they send all those poor young men to France?' she cried. 'Why didn't they realise Hitler was too strong for us? They must have *known* most of them would be killed. Why did they ever do it?'

'I don't know, Mum. But you heard Mr Churchill on the wireless the other day. Jen said he made you feel proud. Remember what he said about Dunkirk? "*Their finest hour.*" Our boys are heroes. Maybe thinking that will make you feel a bit better.'

'Nothing'll make me feel better,' Mary said, dully. 'Nothing's ever going to make me feel better, except our Steve coming home again.'

When Walter came home half an hour later, Thursday felt her tears flow again as she embraced him, but this time she didn't try to hold them back. Dimly, she understood that although the mothers of her patients needed a nurse who would stay calm, her own parents needed to share their anxiety and grief with their daughters. And she needed to share hers, too. It wasn't right to hold it all back.

Jenny made him a cup of tea and announced that supper would be ready soon. She'd made a meat pie, with mince and carrot and onion, and the savoury smell was filling the house. She started to lay the table.

'I'll do that,' Thursday said, getting up. 'You've been slaving away ever since I arrived.'

'No, you sit and talk to Dad.' Jenny set the knives and forks beside the plates. 'You've only got a couple of days.'

Walter sat down heavily in his chair and received his tea. Thursday saw how drawn he looked, and felt a pang of sorrow. He's aged ten years, she thought. Poor Dad. He thought the world of Steve, and now he doesn't even know if he's still got a son.

'Are we going round to see Flo and Perce?' he asked his wife. 'We said we would, if Thursday managed to get home.'

'Yes, we'll go round about seven. We won't stop long, though. I don't like to be out too long in case – in case a telegram comes.' Her voice shook.

'Perhaps he's been taken prisoner,' Thursday said hopefully, but Walter shook his head.

'I reckon we'd have heard by now if he had been. Bill Brown at work, his boy's a prisoner and they heard last week. Mind, it must have been a real mess out there, with all the men separated from their units and everything. It'll take time to sort it all out.'

'Well, then, he *might* be a prisoner. Or he might even be hiding somewhere in France. Someone could be looking after him. They're on our side, after all.'

'So they say,' Walter grunted. 'I don't know as the French have *ever* been on our side. And they're giving in now, you can see it. Why, the Germans are in Paris now – how can they stand up against them? 'Specially now we're not there. They're being overrun.'

'They haven't surrendered yet. They haven't signed anything.'

'They will. They'll have to.'

Jenny brought the pie and vegetables in and they all sat round the table. Thursday was hungry after her long journey, and Walter, too, after his hard day's work, but Mary only picked at the food and then pushed her plate away.

'You've got to eat, Mum,' Thursday said gently. 'It won't do our Steve any good for you to starve yourself.'

'I can't fancy it. I can't fancy anything.'

'You'll get ill. You've still got Jenny and Dad to think about. What good is it going to do them if you get ill? They'll have to worry about you as well as Steve. And there's Auntie Flo, she needs you, too. And at least you've still got some hope for Steve – it's more than they've got. It's *selfish* to let yourself get ill, Mum. It's *unpatriotic*.'

Mary stared at her daughter and Walter made a movement as if to stop her.

'Don't talk to your mother like that, Thursday.'

'She's got to eat, Dad. She's got to.' Thursday turned back to her mother. 'Come on, try a little bit and it'll give you heart to eat some more. Never mind whether you fancy it or not – just eat some. That's it. And a bit more. It's not so bad, is it, even if our Jenny did get it ready!'

Mary gave a small, shaky laugh. She put some more into her mouth, chewed and swallowed. 'It does make me feel a bit better,' she admitted.

'Of course it does. Now try some more. You don't have to finish it, just eat as much as you can manage.' Thursday watched as her mother slowly ate the pie and vegetables. 'And eat something every mealtime, all right? It doesn't have to be much – just so long as you keep on eating. You mustn't stop.' She finished her own plateful and smiled at her sister. 'That was good, Jen. You're turning into a good little cook!'

After the meal, when the girls had washed up, they all walked round to Flo's and Percy's house. Mary and Walter walked behind and the two girls in front, just as they'd done when they were little. But when they were little, Steve would have been there too, scampering on ahead. Now, there was a gap where he had been.

'I don't know how you dared talk to Mum like that,' Jenny said. 'I've been treating her with kid gloves, frightened of making her cry even more.'

'You have to be cruel to be kind sometimes,' Thursday said. 'I learned that in my training. You can be really gentle with the men sometimes, but other times you have to just buck them up. You should hear the way we talk to the sailors!'

Jenny laughed. 'Don't they swear back at you?'

'Yes, sometimes. They get really narked. But it's better for them to be angry than sorry for themselves and they're usually OK after a bit.'

They arrived at their aunt's house. The blinds were drawn and inside the front room it was quiet and dim, the summer sunshine shut out. But at the back, the window was open and Flo was washing up the tea-things. In the garden, they could see Percy with his sleeves rolled up, hoeing his vegetables.

Mary kissed her sister-in-law. 'How are you feeling, Flo? I didn't think I'd find you doing the chores.'

'Oh, I'm not so bad.' Flo tipped the water down the sink and dried her hands on the roller towel behind the back door. 'I'm better doing something. And it's no use giving way, is it? Life's got to go on. Perce needed his tea, and there's no one else to get it. Our Denise has gone out somewhere – said she'd only be half an hour, but that was over an hour ago so goodness knows when she'll be back.'

'Denise has gone out?' Mary exclaimed, while Thursday and Jenny gave each other rueful glances. 'Well, that's not very thoughtful of her, in the circumstances. I dare say she's off out with that chap of hers?'

'Must be, I suppose.' Flo spoke wearily. 'I can't blame her for going, it's miserable here and she's as upset about Mike as we are.' She looked at Mary. 'I haven't said nothing to Percy about the feller. About how old he is, and all that talk about being engaged. What with – with Mike and everything – well, I couldn't bring meself to even think about it, let alone do anything. I just hope it'll blow over.'

'Well, let's hope you're right. And I won't say anything either. Now, you come and sit down and let me make you a cup of tea. Thursday's here too, look, she's got two days' leave to come and see us all, so we'd better make the most of her. She's done me a bit of good already, I can tell you!'

'Your mum's lucky to have you,' Flo said, giving Thursday a kiss. 'Just a shame you've got to be so far away. While I think of it, Mary, there's half a dozen eggs in that pudding basin, you can take 'em with you when you go. The hens are laying really well. And it'll be currant time soon, too, we must think about going and picking a few for jam and bottling. Mind, I don't know where we're going to get the sugar from – they do say we'll get extra sugar for jam-making, but I'll believe it when I see it. Oh, and I've got a knitting pattern for you, that one out of *Woman's Weekly* for a pullover, I'll look it out now—'

'Come and sit down,' Mary said again, gently. 'We can see to all that later. Come and have a rest and a cup of tea now. It'll make you feel better.'

Flo looked for a moment as if she were going to agree. Then she sagged, her momentary unnatural brightness dimmed. 'Oh, Mary,' she said, sinking into a chair and putting both hands over her face. 'Oh, *Mary*. I don't reckon *anything's* going to make me feel better. I don't reckon I'm ever going to feel better again.'

Chapter Seventeen

There was no funeral for Mike – there couldn't be, without a body to bury – but perhaps one day he'd be given a proper marked grave in a special cemetery in France, like the soldiers who had been killed in the Great War. But on Sunday morning they all went to the little church at the end of the road and the vicar said a special prayer for him, and all the others who had been killed at Dunkirk, and then for those like Steve who were still missing. And they sang 'He Who Would Valiant Be' as a special hymn for them. And afterwards, people who knew the family came up and shook Flo's and Percy's hands and said how sorry they were, and a few went back to the house for a glass of sherry. It was the nearest you could get to a proper ceremony and somehow it did seem to help.

'I can sort of believe it a bit more now,' Flo said afterwards, as she put away the plates and glasses that Mary and Thursday were washing. 'All those people being so nice about it. It makes it seem more real.' She paused. 'Not that I want it to be real. I don't, I don't at all.'

'I know, Auntie. None of us wants it to be real.' Thursday put down the glass she was drying and put her arm around her aunt's shoulders. 'But we've got to go on living, somehow.'

Flo nodded and rubbed her nose with the back of her hand, leaving a tiny moustache of bubbles. 'That's it. There's the rest of the family to think about as well. I wish our Leslie could have got leave, too, but he said it was impossible, they're all on standby even when they're not flying. I suppose you'll have to be going back tomorrow.'

'First thing,' Thursday said regretfully. 'We're so busy. And everyone's expecting the invasion to start any time.'

'Oh, Thursday, and you're right in the front line down there. It's one of the places they'll come, isn't it – the south coast.' Mary's voice shook. 'What will you do? Have they got places for you to go if there's bombs? And suppose they send in ships and troops – how will we ever stop them now that all our boys have been brought home? I can't bear—'

'Well, that's the good thing about it, isn't it,' Thursday said cheerfully. 'All our boys are back here—' her voice shook as she remembered that not all the boys were back, but she went on determinedly '—so they'll be on the spot straight away. They won't let the Germans set a single foot on the beach. Remember what Mr Churchill said. *"We'll fight them on the beaches."* That's what we'll do. And we'll know when they're coming, too, because the bells will be rung to warn us, and Alverstoke church is only just round the corner from Haslar.'

'But where will you go?' Mary asked again. 'Have they built shelters?'

'There are huge cellars all underneath the hospital. It's all organised, Mum, they've even got operating theatres down there. Honestly, there's no need to worry.'

Mary sighed. 'Well, if you're sure.' She washed a mark off one of the glasses. 'That Mrs Hoskins, fancy wearing bright red lipstick to church! And it's all smeared on this glass. I don't know what the vicar thought. Still, she's a nice enough body.' She was silent again for a moment, waiting as Flo carried a tray of the best glasses through to the front room, and went on in a lowered voice, 'I just wish we could get some news of our Steve now, that's all. And I'm worried about poor Flo. She's bearing up ever so well, but she's got all that worry about with her Denise, too. Has our Jenny said anything to you?'

'About this boyfriend?' Thursday said cautiously. 'Well, yes, she has. He's a lot older than Denise, I gather.'

'Him and his pal, yes. The two of them ought to know better, going around with girls Jen and Denise's ages. Denise isn't even sixteen, you know. And talking about secret engagements, if you please! Well, stands to reason they must know it's wrong, or they wouldn't want to keep it secret, would they? And what's our Jenny been up to? She won't tell me a thing. I don't know what's to be done about it. Me and your dad were going to come round here and have a talk about it, and then the telegrams came . . .' Her voice faded, then she went on despondently, 'I suppose we'll have to think what to do about it now. Only I can't somehow. I can't seem to put my mind to it, and yet I can't stop thinking about it either. Our Jenny always seemed such a level-headed girl. I don't know what she's thinking about, going with a feller so much older, and encouraging her cousin as well.'

'I don't think you need worry, Mum,' Thursday said. 'Jenny told me she's stopped seeing Sam. She didn't really like it, him being so much older. And I don't think she was ever as keen as Dizzy.'

Mary tipped away the water. 'Is that true? Oh, that's a relief! At least she's got a bit of sense. Let's hope Denise sees it the same way. I dare say Flo will be round to see us later on, she said she'd call round before you went back. Perhaps we could have a word about it then. Anyway, we'd better go home now and have a bit of dinner, it's going to be late enough as it is.'

Sunday dinner was liver and bacon without the bacon. It wasn't much of a Sunday dinner, Mary said disparagingly, especially for Thursday's first time home, but there just hadn't been any meat at the butcher's, and what with everything else . . . Thursday declared that it was her favourite meal anyway, and if she'd been asked what she wanted it was just what she'd have chosen. And afters of stewed apple and blackcurrants from the allotment made it a feast. Her voice broke a little as she almost added that with Steve not there, she could have all the skin off the custard, and tears came into her eyes as she thought of why he wasn't there. But luckily her mother didn't seem to notice, and the moment passed. Jenny, however, seemed to realise why Thursday stopped so abruptly and reached beneath the table to give her hand a squeeze. The two girls looked at each other with understanding and Thursday thought again how much her sister had grown up in the past few days.

'You'll look after Mum, won't you,' she said privately afterwards. 'You won't give her anything to worry about.'

Jenny shook her head. 'I know what you mean. And I'm definitely going to finish with Sam. I'm seeing him tomorrow to tell him.'

'And stick to boys your own age, right?'

'Don't think I'll bother with them at all,' Jenny said with a shrug. 'I'm going to join the Red Cross, like you, and learn first aid and nursing. I might even go down the Infirmary and see if I can get in there.' She looked at Thursday with a gleam in her eye. 'And how about you? You haven't said much about what you get up to. I bet you've got a few boyfriends, haven't you, what with all those sailors and doctors around?'

Thursday coloured. 'Don't be daft! Doctors wouldn't look at someone like me. There's plenty of VADs that are quite upper-class, you know. Helen Stanway, her father's got a title of some sort, and someone told me she's an "Honourable" herself, only she never says so, she doesn't put on any side at all. And there's Caroline Stoddart, she's a bishop's daughter, and Louisa Wetherby's father was a general in the last war and got a chest full of medals. I don't think the doctors are going to look at girls like me when they've got people of their own class.'

'It's not what their fathers do that they're interested in,' Jenny observed. 'It's what the girls'll do.'

'Jenny! And you were asking me if you could get in the family way by just kissing!' The girls dissolved into giggles and their mother came out to see what was going on.

'Honestly, I thought you must have got Arthur Askey out here.' She looked at them as they tried to straighten their faces, guilty at having found something to laugh at. 'Don't look so worried! It's good to hear you laugh. I don't think Mike would have wanted us to be miserable all our lives. Anyway, what I came out to tell you was that Auntie Flo's come round and she wants to see you before Thursday goes back.'

Jenny looked alarmed. 'I think I ought to go upstairs and do some mending. My stockings are all holes—'

'You've got to talk to her some time,' Mary said. 'You're the only one that knows about this fellow she's been going around with. Your auntie's worried.'

'I don't like telling on Denise,' Jenny began, but Mary shook her head.

'This isn't a kiddies' game, Jen. It's serious. If Denise is talking about getting engaged, they've a right to know. She's only fifteen.'

'I don't see why that matters so much—'

'Of course it matters! If they've been doing anything they shouldn't . . .' Mary hesitated, her colour rising. 'It's *against the law*, Jenny. Kissing is all right, though I'd rather you didn't even do that till you're a bit older, but anything more is *against the law* with someone under sixteen. This Vic could be in serious trouble, and so could Denise.'

Jenny stared at her mother. 'Against the law?'

'Yes.' Mary was clearly embarrassed. Such subjects were never discussed, or even mentioned, normally. Thursday herself hadn't known the 'facts of life' until some older girls had told her at school, and when she'd started nursing she'd discovered that half those were wrong. Like Jenny's fear about kissing . . . She knew that her mother was finding this conversation difficult, but it was something that had to be made clear. Jenny was over sixteen, but Denise wasn't, and if things had gone further than kissing – well, the 'trouble' that would be brought on

Auntie Flo's house might be even worse than what was usually meant by that phrase – an illegitimate baby.

Jenny looked ready to burst into tears.

'But I don't know what Denise and Vic have done! She hasn't told me anything, honestly – only that they wanted to get engaged. I can't tell Auntie Flo anything more than that. I really can't.'

'Well, you'd better come and tell her that, then. Come on, Jen, you can't skulk out here in the kitchen for ever. And she wants to see you, too, Thursday.'

Thursday looked at her sister. 'Come on. You haven't done anything wrong. And Mum's right, you can't lurk out here every time Auntie Flo comes round.'

Reluctantly, Jenny followed her mother and sister into the living room. Flo was sitting in Walter's chair, looking at the empty fireplace, and when Jenny saw her, tears came to her eyes. She ran forward to kneel beside her aunt, covering her hands with her own and looking up into the worn face.

'Oh, Auntie Flo, I'm ever so sorry. I really am. I never realised – I never knew all that about – about it being against the law and all that. But I don't think they – they *did* anything. I honestly don't.'

'You weren't with them all the time, though, were you? You and the chap you were going with?'

'No,' Jenny admitted. 'But I still don't think they did.'

'Have you asked her?' Mary asked, and Flo shrugged.

'With all the upset about Mike, I haven't had much chance. And when I did, she just flounced out of the room. I don't know what to do with her, Mary, I really don't.'

'I'm sorry,' Jenny said miserably. 'It just seemed fun and – and sort of glamorous, going out with someone older. And they had plenty of money, too, they could afford to pay for nice seats at the pictures – not like when that Freddy Billings asked me to go and then said he'd meet me inside! I never thought about it being against the law.' She looked up with sudden horror. 'We won't have a policeman coming round here about it, will we?'

'Of course not!' Thursday said at once. '*You* didn't do anything wrong, Jen.'

'But Denise? I mean, how would the police know? You wouldn't tell them, Auntie Flo?'

'That depends on what they did,' her aunt said grimly. 'And on whether I can calm your uncle down. He's in such a state about it, he might do anything.'

'But you couldn't have Dizzy put in *prison*!'

'Denise wouldn't go to prison, she wouldn't go anywhere. It's the man who'd be in trouble.'

'But it wasn't Vic's fault!' Jenny cried. 'He's a nice boy, he is really. He'd never do anything to hurt her. And she told him she was eighteen! How was he to know?'

There was a brief silence.

'She did *what*?' Mary said.

'She told him she was eighteen. She told me she had, and he said something about it, too. He didn't know she was only fifteen, he really didn't.' Jenny hesitated and then said in a rush, 'She – we used to put make-up on before we met them. Lipstick and powder and – and eyeshadow and mascara. Dizzy even had some red nail varnish. She *looked* eighteen. She looked older than eighteen.'

The silence this time was longer. Then Mary and Flo looked at each other and Mary lifted her shoulders.

'I reckon that's it, then, Flo. You can't really blame the chap. Denise does look older than her age, and if she made herself up and then told him that – well, I don't see as how we can say it was all his fault.'

Mary folded her mouth and sighed. 'No, nor do I. Not that it helps much when it comes to this so-called secret engagement. I mean, we're going to have to tell them they can't see each other any more. Perce will have to see this Vic and tell him the truth. But we can't watch her all the time.'

'Perhaps when he knows, he'll be scared off anyway,' Thursday suggested. 'He won't want trouble.'

'And what's our Denise going to say about that? You know what she's like. She's so headstrong, she's as likely as not to go off with him anyway. Scotland, they're talking about. We can't go chasing her to Scotland.'

'They'll never do that. Vic'd lose his job for a start, and he could probably get into trouble for taking her away as well.' Thursday shook her head. 'That's just Dizzy talking, Auntie Flo, you mustn't take any notice of that.'

'I suppose you're right.' Flo got up. 'Well, I'm glad we've got a few things sorted out, anyway. I'd better go home and talk to Perce. Denise is up in her room, sulking, and he won't let her go out, so we can have it out with her, too.' She looked at Thursday. 'Why don't you walk back with me, if you've got a minute? It might help to have you there, you having been away from home. And thanks, Jenny – I know you don't like telling tales. But, like your mum says, it's not a game.'

Jenny nodded, subdued. But when her aunt and Thursday had departed and Mary came back into the room, she saw that her daughter's eyes were full of tears.

'What is it, Jenny?' she asked. 'What's the matter? There isn't anything else you ought to tell us, is there? If there is, you'd better say so.'

Jenny shook her head. 'No. Honestly, Mum. It's just that – well, me and Dizzy have always been best friends. And now – now I don't suppose she'll ever want to speak to me again!'

Thursday walked back with her aunt, not quite sure what was expected of her. Being away from home didn't seem much of a qualification for taking her aunt's and uncle's side against her cousin. I hope they don't think I've already forgotten what it's like to be nearly sixteen, she thought, and I hope they don't think that because I've been away from home I'm somehow more 'experienced'. And I hope Denise doesn't think I've turned against her.

All in all, she would much rather not have been involved. But she knew all too well how strained everyone was just now. Mike missing for so long, then confirmed dead. Steve, still missing. And now this problem with Denise and Jenny. It was too much to cope with, all at once.

'It's not that we don't like her having her fun,' Flo was saying as they trudged along. 'Your Uncle Perce and me, we've always taken the view that youngsters should be allowed to do what they like and enjoy themselves, within reason. But it's got to be *within reason*. And going out with a boy seven or eight years older and talking about getting secretly engaged and running away to be married – well, that's not within reason. It's not, is it?'

'No, it isn't,' Thursday admitted. 'But I'm sure it is just talk, Auntie. I don't really think Denise would do it.'

'I don't know so much. She's always been a headstrong little hussy. I wouldn't put anything past her, 'specially if she's really keen on this boy. Boy! I keep saying that. He's a *man* – and he's too old for her.'

'Maybe if they waited a while—'

'Well, I said that, but your Uncle Perce wants them to stop seeing each other right away. He won't have it. He's really angry, Thursday.'

Thursday could see this was true, the minute they walked into the house. Her uncle was sitting by the fireplace with the newspaper held in his hands, but he wasn't reading it. He was glowering at the pages and when Thursday and her aunt walked into the room he turned the glower on them. Thursday stepped back a little.

'Now, there's no need to look at us like that,' Flo told him sharply. 'It's not Thursday's fault all this has happened. She's come round to see if she can help us talk sense into Denise, that's all.'

Thursday couldn't remember having said any such

thing but she couldn't really say so. She gave her uncle a doubtful smile and was relieved to see his expression soften a little.

'I'm not blaming you, girl,' he said heavily. 'It's just that everything's such a mess. Your Steve – our Mike – and now this. And worrying about an invasion and bombing and whatever's going to happen next. It's not *knowing* anything, that's the trouble. Not knowing what Hitler'll do, what's going to happen to us all. I mean, suppose he uses gas? We've got our masks, but half the people don't bother about 'em. They carry the boxes, yes, but is there gas masks inside 'em? Sandwiches, that's what half of them use their boxes for! Sandwiches! Bloody fine use they'll be if the Germans drop gas on us all.' He stared at Thursday and she saw with dismay that his hands were shaking. The newspaper rattled. 'I went through the last lot,' he said. 'I *saw* people with gas. It's not funny. It's not funny at all. And just as if we didn't have enough to worry about with all that, our Denise goes and springs this on us. It's selfish, that's what it is. Selfish.'

'Well, I suppose she hasn't been in love before,' Thursday ventured, and he snorted with disgust.

'*In love*! She's not in love! She's just a silly girl who's had her head filled with nonsense out of all those daft love stories she reads. Mills & Boon! Barbara Cartland! I've seen 'em. She's forever got one in her hand, when she ought to be helping her mother round the house. She thinks some tall, dark, romantic hero's going to come along and sweep her off her feet. So what happens? She falls for the first bloke that gives her the eye and believes every word he says. And because he's a few years older and got a bit more money to spend, she thinks he's bloody Clark Gable. If you ask me, she ought to be still playing with her dolls.'

A sound at the door made them all turn. Denise stood there, her eyes red-rimmed but defiant. She stared at them all.

'I heard you talking. You're talking about me, aren't you? You're planning what to do with me. Well, you're not doing anything, because I'm going away. I'm going to Vic, that's what I'm doing, and you won't need to worry about me any more!'

Flo gave a little cry and put her hand to her mouth. Percy flung down his newspaper. Thursday stood by, uncertainly, wishing she hadn't come. This wasn't her quarrel and she didn't see what she could do to help. And she wanted to be back with her mum, using the little time she had left to comfort her.

'Going away? Denise, you *can't*—'

'And she's not going to!' Percy said grimly. 'You're not going anywhere, my girl. You're under age and under my jurisdiction, and if you go out of this house I can get the police to bring you back. And it won't be just you in trouble, it'll be that boyfriend of yours, too, and he'll be in *serious* trouble.'

'Oh, but there's something else,' Flo broke in before Denise could shout back at her father. 'Something Jenny told us.' She looked at Thursday. 'Tell your uncle what she said, Thurs.'

Thursday glanced unhappily at Denise, who was staring at her as if she were a traitor. She shrugged apologetically and said, 'Well, I honestly don't know much about it, but what our Jen said was that Denise told Vic she was eighteen. And he believed her.' She gave her cousin another apologetic look. 'Honestly, I don't think I can be much help, I ought to go home—'

'No, wait a minute.' Percy stared at his daughter. 'Is this true, Denise? Did you tell him that?'

'Yes, I did. I didn't think he'd want to go out with me if he knew I was only fifteen.' Denise stared back at him. 'What difference does it make, anyway?'

'It makes a hell of a lot of difference, you silly girl! It means we can't take him to court if – if he's done anything he shouldn't have done. And it means—' He stopped

264

abruptly. 'Well, never mind what else it means. Let's just hope it doesn't come to it.'

'I don't know what you're on about,' Denise said crossly. 'All we've done is love each other. What's so awful about that?'

'Love each other!' Percy repeated contemptuously. 'At your age! Well, let me tell you this, my girl, you won't "love each other" any more. You're not to see him again, understand? It's over.'

Denise stared at him. 'You can't do that. You can't stop me.'

'I'm telling you,' he stated. 'You're not seeing him any more. You'll be walked to work every morning and you'll be met every evening. You'll stay in every night. And I'll go down the post office myself and tell this Vic he's not to see you either. I'll put the fear of God into him. *And I'll tell him how old you are.*'

Denise's face whitened. 'You won't! You can't!'

'I will. You see.'

She stared at him, then at her mother, who was looking ready to cry. Finally, she turned to Thursday.

'Tell him he can't do this. We love each other, Vic and me – we'll *always* love each other.'

'Well, you can wait for each other, then, can't you,' he said. 'When you're twenty-one, you can do what you like.'

'But that's years away! Anything could happen!'

'If he can't wait, it means he doesn't love you, and you'll be better off without him. And it might be you who can't wait.'

'It won't be.'

'Your dad's right,' Flo said persuasively. 'You're very young, Denise. I know you think you love him, but you haven't had a chance to meet other boys yet—'

'I don't want to meet other boys. They're stupid.'

'Just give it time. That's all we're asking. A bit of time.'

Denise gave them a withering glance. 'And just what time do we have? There's a war on, in case you've forgotten. Vic'll get called up. *He* could be the next one to be missing, or killed. What time does anyone have these days?'

There was a short silence. Then Percy said, 'You didn't have to say that. Upsetting your mother. And Thursday here, not knowing what's happened to her brother. You didn't have to rub that in.'

Denise bit her lip. Then she said, 'I just wanted you to know how much it matters to me, too. I'm just as upset about Mike as you are, and just as worried about Steve. But I love Vic, and he matters to me just the same way. If you stop me seeing him now – and he gets called up and goes away – and I never see him again – well, I'll never forgive you, that's what. I'll never, ever, forgive you.'

She turned and walked out of the room, and they heard her going upstairs. Flo looked at her husband and sat down abruptly.

'Oh, Perce. Oh, *Perce* – what are we going to do?'

'I don't know,' he said heavily, shaking his head. 'I just don't know, Flo, and that's the truth.' He picked up the newspaper, stared at it for a moment, then dropped it again. 'I'd better go and feed the hens. Won't do any good to let them starve, on top of everything else.'

'Would you go and have a word with her?' Flo asked Thursday appealingly. 'She might talk to you, you're nearer her age. I know you want to get back to your mum, but if you'd have just a quick word.'

'Well, all right.' Thursday moved unhappily towards the stairs. 'I don't really think it'll do any good, but I'll try.' She went up the stairs and tapped on Denise's door. 'Dizzy, it's me. Can I come in a minute?'

Denise opened the door. She had been sitting on her bed and Thursday saw a photograph lying on the pillow. A thin, friendly face, topped with dark, curly hair, grinned out at her and she had to admit he was attractive.

'Is this Vic? He looks nice.'

'He is.' Denise looked at her. 'I suppose they've sent you up to talk sense into me.'

'Something like that.' Thursday sat on the bed. 'I don't know that I can, though.'

'Nobody's going to change my mind,' Denise told her. She looked down and drew a pattern with her finger on the counterpane. 'I really am upset about Mike. It's awful.'

'I know.'

'But I keep thinking – what if it happened to Vic? They wouldn't even *tell* me. His mum doesn't know me. I just – wouldn't know. I couldn't bear it, Thurs.'

'I know, but you can't get married, you know that. Not even in Scotland.'

'We could soon. It's not that long till my birthday.'

'Think about it, Dizzy,' Thursday said gently. 'What would happen if you ran away together? Vic would lose his job – what would you live on? Where would you live? And if he did get called up – what would you do then? You'd have cut yourself off from your family and everything. You know what your dad's like – he'd probably refuse to have you back. And you'd break your mum's heart.'

'They're breaking *my* heart.'

'They're not. They're trying to look after you.'

'I might have known you'd be on their side,' Denise said bitterly.

Thursday sighed. 'I'm not on their side. I'm not on anyone's side. I'm just trying to see reason. They love you, Dizzy—'

'They've got a funny way of showing it!'

'No, they *are* showing it. They're trying to look after you—'

'I can look after myself!'

'Can you?' Thursday asked. 'When you're somewhere in Scotland, away from everyone you know, with a man you've only known a few weeks or months, who's got no job and has cut himself off from *his* family as well – and might start to blame you for everything going wrong? Will you be able to look after yourself then?'

'It won't be like that.'

'It might be. And in any case, he's bound to get called up sooner or later. You'll be on your own then.'

Denise was silent for a while. She twisted her fingers in the counterpane and said at last, 'What am I going to do, Thurs?'

'Well . . .' Thursday had been thinking about this question. 'Why don't you ask your mum and dad if you can bring Vic to meet them? Ask him to Sunday tea or something?'

'They'd never agree! You know what Sunday tea means. Dad would go mad.'

'All right, then, one evening during the week. Just ask if you can bring him round. They ought to meet him before they decide what sort of chap he is.'

'I know, but they won't. I've tried.'

'Try again,' Thursday advised. 'I think maybe they'll agree now. They're in a sort of corner, you see – you all are. Nobody will back down or make the first move. But if you say you're sorry you've worried them, and promise you won't do anything like get secretly engaged or try to run away and get married, and if they can see for themselves that Vic's a nice chap—' she looked at the photograph '—and he does look a nice chap, I can see that, well, maybe they'll let you go out together again. And if you're still keen on each other in two or three years' time, they might let you get engaged. Or even married. People do get married at eighteen.'

Denise chewed her lips and stared frowningly at the creased counterpane. 'Well, I suppose I could try. But—' she looked up at Thursday again '—suppose – suppose we *have* to get married?'

Thursday stared at her, feeling cold. 'What do you mean? Dizzy, you don't think – you haven't—?'

'I didn't come on this week,' Denise said in a small

268

voice. 'That's the first sign, isn't it? I asked someone at work and she said it was. And – and yesterday I felt sick.' Her face crumpled. 'Oh, Thursday, I've been so scared. I didn't know what to do. And what with Mike – and then hearing about Steve – I don't know which way to turn. I can't tell Mum, I can't. It would break her heart. And Dad would kill me! Thursday, what am I going to do? I can't have a baby! I *can't*!'

Chapter Eighteen

Thursday, sat on the train and gazed out of the window at the passing countryside. She felt, she thought, as if she had been wrung out through her mother's mangle. The two days at home, which would have been hard enough to bear if there had only been her cousin's death to think about, had been a nightmare, and she felt guiltily thankful to be returning to Haslar.

At least Jenny seemed to have seen sense and decided to finish with her boyfriend, but Denise was in a very difficult position. If she really was expecting, she was going to have to tell her parents, as well as Vic. Thursday had no way of knowing whether Vic would stand by her – the photograph showed a nice enough looking young man, but you never knew what anyone would do when things got tricky. It wasn't his fault that Denise had lied to him about her age, but the fact was that she *was* under age and not knowing might not be a proper defence. And Thursday had an idea that a doctor, once he knew about it, would have to report it to the police. Even if he didn't – and she knew there were rules about confidentiality – she still wouldn't put it past Uncle Percy.

'If you're only a few days overdue, it might not mean anything at all,' Thursday had told her cousin. 'It could be just that you've been upset. Are you always regular?'

'Not always, no. But suppose it is?'

'You'll have to tell your mum. That's the first thing to do. And Vic,' she added.

'And how do I do that, if they won't let me see him?'

'You can write to him. Anyway, you're going to ask if

you can bring him round, aren't you? Look, you don't know that anything's happened, and you won't know for a few more weeks yet. Feeling sick yesterday isn't anything to do with it.' Thursday had only a hazy idea of what went on in pregnancy – it wasn't considered necessary to give detailed information to VADs who were going to nurse sailors – but she was doing her best to dredge up from her memory any scraps of knowledge that had come her way. 'You'd better just hope for the best,' she concluded at last. A clock struck downstairs. 'Look, I've got to go now. I'm catching the six o'clock train. Write and let me know how you get on, and for heaven's sake, don't do anything silly.'

Denise nodded tearfully and Thursday gave her an awkward kiss. She went downstairs and shrugged at her aunt's and uncle's questioning looks.

'I don't think she'll run off, or anything like that,' she said, hoping it was true. 'But she's got something to ask you. And – and I hope you'll agree.' She caught her uncle's look and flushed, knowing that he was about to say something caustic about being advised by a 'bit of a girl' even though she was a nurse. She went on hastily before he could speak. 'I've got to go now. Mum'll be wondering where I've got to. And – and I really am sorry about Mike.'

Her aunt nodded and gave her a kiss. 'Thanks for coming round, Thursday. You've been a real help.'

'I don't know that I have really,' Thursday said. 'But I dare say it'll turn out all right in the end.'

I hope it does, Thursday thought as she hurried away. And again, staring out of the train window a few hours later, I really do hope it does.

Leaving her mother had been even worse. Mary was tearful again when Thursday had got back to Waterloo Street, and her father didn't seem to know how to comfort her. He had his own feelings to deal with, and he and Mary had never faced anything like this before and weren't prepared for it. How did you prepare yourself for the death of your child?

'It just doesn't seem right,' Mary said sadly. '*You* expect to be the ones to go first, not your children. I know it's different in war – but we've already been through one lot in our lives. We didn't think it was going to happen all over again.'

'You don't know it is going to happen,' Thursday said. 'Steve's only missing – nobody knows for sure he's dead.'

'Not yet. But the longer it goes on . . . We've got to face it, Thursday. We've got to admit it's possible.' She sighed. 'It doesn't seem fair.'

'I don't think "fair" comes into it,' Thursday said. 'It's not up to people like us to decide when there's going to be a war. And we couldn't just stand by and let Hitler walk all over Europe.'

'Hitler never ought to have been allowed to get so much power in the first place,' her father said. 'He ought to have been stopped years ago.'

'But the Germans thought he was so good,' Mary said. 'Setting up the youth movement, and getting the country back on its feet. And nobody seemed to realise what he was doing to the Jews.'

'They didn't want to realise. They shut their eyes to it.'

'Well, we're doing something now,' Thursday said. 'And whatever's happened to Steve, we know he was doing something. He was doing his best for us all.'

'I'd rather he was at home,' Mary said, but the weeping seemed to be over, for a while at any rate, and she gave Thursday a shaky smile. 'You're a good girl, Thurs. I'm sorry you've got to go back, but at least you're safe where you are. And you're doing a good job.'

Jenny had been sitting quietly on the rug at her father's feet. They seemed to have made up their differences, Thursday thought thankfully, and got back to their old relationship. Jenny had always been her father's favourite

– perhaps that was why he'd been so angry and upset about Sam. Now she looked up.

'I'm definitely going to see about nursing, too. I'm going round to see the Red Cross lady tomorrow, and ask about training for first aid, and I'm going to go down the hospital as well and see if I can train as a proper nurse.'

'I don't think you're old enough,' Thursday began doubtfully, and Jenny made an impatient noise.

'I'm not old enough for anything, it seems! But I will be soon. And there's no harm in finding out. There must be *something* I can do.'

'You can do first aid. It's nursing I think you have to be seventeen for, and they're not taking VADs till they're twenty-one. But you could probably get a job as an orderly or something, in the meantime.' Thursday hesitated. 'It's hard work, mind, and not very nice. Cleaning floors people have been sick on, taking round bedpans and washing them out, scrubbing the sluices – you'd get all the worst jobs.'

'I don't care. I'd be learning as well. And I'd be doing something to help – I'd be getting ready to do better things.'

Walter put down a hand and ruffled his daughter's hair. 'You're a good girl, Jenny. You go and do your nursing, if that's what you want. It's good training and it doesn't seem to have done our Thursday any harm. You might even end up in the same hospital together!'

'And talking of ending up in hospitals,' Thursday said, getting up and looking round for her kitbag, 'I'd better get moving or I won't be ending up in Haslar tonight. And if I'm late back, the ship will sail without me and Madam will have my guts for garters!'

Mary looked alarmed. 'What ship? You never told us you were going to sea!'

Thursday laughed. 'It's just the Navy, Mum. Haslar's a naval hospital, so it's counted as a ship, and Navy time's five minutes early, wherever you are, because if it was

273

really a ship it would have gone. They don't wait, you see. It's a real crime to be adrift – late, I mean.'

They all followed her to the door and kissed her goodbye. 'You'll be careful, won't you, love,' Mary said, holding her tightly. 'You won't do anything silly.'

'Don't worry, Mum. We're safe as houses there, and they really look after us.' She hugged her father. 'Look after Mum, won't you.' She saw that his eyes were full of tears, and she buried her face against his shoulder for a moment. 'Oh, *Dad*—'

'Go on,' he said gruffly. 'Time to go. And don't worry about your mother or me, we'll be all right. It's your Auntie Flo I'm bothered about now, what with Mike and young Denise and all.'

'I know.' Thursday looked at her sister. 'You go and see about the Red Cross, Jen. You'll be all right. They're crying out for girls like you. And – don't do anything daft. You know.'

Jenny grinned a little crookedly. 'I won't. Don't you either.'

'Cheeky!' Thursday said with a grin, and hefted her kitbag on to her shoulder. She walked away and strode with a firm step to the corner of the street before turning back to wave.

They were all there – her mother, her father, her sister. But there was a gap where her brother should have been and, for a moment, as her eyes misted over she seemed to see him there, tall and proud in his stiff new khaki uniform, smiling and waving. And then he was gone, like a ghost vanished, and she had a dreadful, heartbreaking feeling that she would never see him again.

The train pulled in at last at Portsmouth Harbour station. Thursday dragged her kitbag out on to the wooden platform and made for the steps and the pontoon. The pinnace was there as usual and she scrambled aboard.

'Been home on leave?' the sailor asked. She knew him

slightly, a big, broad-shouldered matelot with a cheery grin, and she nodded and smiled. 'Family OK?'

'Yes,' Thursday said. There was no point in regaling him with the troubles she had left behind. 'Anything happened here?'

He shrugged. 'They reckon the French are going to surrender any day now, and Mussolini and Hitler are going to get together. But I dare say you heard that anyway.'

Thursday nodded. None of it was good news. With France occupied and submissive, the threat of invasion was very real indeed. And with Italy – who had been their allies in the 1914–18 war – joining forces with the enemy, it didn't look as if there was anyone left to fight on Britain's side.

'We're on our own,' she said. 'And it's only twenty miles across the Channel – not much further than from here to Winchester. How can a little island like us stand up to all that?'

'Same as we did before,' he said stoutly. 'Show 'em what Britain's made of. Land of hope and glory, they say, don't they? Well, that's what we are and what we'll always be. And don't forget the Navy.' He tapped his chest. 'Best navy in the world, we are. Britannia rules the waves. It's being an island that keeps us safe. It might be only twenty miles – but it might as well be a thousand, for all the good it'll do Hitler. We'll never let him in!'

Thursday looked at his sturdy body and cheerful, determined face, and smiled. With men like him to fight, and men like Churchill to lead them, maybe a little island like Britain *could* stand up to the might of the forces that were massing across that narrow strip of water. Maybe Britannia could still rule the waves, and maybe Britain would once again be a land of hope and glory.

Hope and glory. Two words that seemed to express what Britain stood for. The hope that all would once again be well with the world. The glory of knowing that it was true.

Her grief for Mike and Steve was no less. Yet when she walked into the dormitory at Haslar and dumped her kitbag on the floor, she was still warmed by the glow that the sailor's words and cheery grin had given her. She looked at the other girls, who were lounging on their beds, mending stockings, knitting, reading or writing letters, and smiled.

'I'm back! And what have you lazy lot been doing while I've been away?'

They turned and stared at her. She saw the stillness in their faces, and the sadness in their eyes, and a terrible premonition gripped her heart. She opened her mouth to speak, but no words came.

Elsie got off her bed and came towards her, and Patsy followed and reached for her hand.

'What is it?' she whispered. 'What's happened?'

'Oh, Thursday,' Patsy said in a voice full of tears. 'Oh, Thursday – it's Tony.'

'Tony? What do you mean? What's happened to Tony?' But she knew already. There was barely any need for them to say the words.

'He died,' Elsie said in a small, flat voice. 'He died last night. It was very sudden and he didn't suffer, they told us. But – his heart gave out – he just *died*.'

Chapter Nineteen

It hadn't been entirely unexpected, the naval surgeon told Thursday. Tony had been very ill and his treatment had necessitated several operations. Each one had been a danger to him, yet there was nothing else they could have done. And, finally, his heart had given out under the strain.

'He fought a brave battle.' Surgeon Commander Kirkpatrick looked at her. 'Was he your sweetheart?'

'I don't really know,' Thursday said honestly. 'We went out together when he was stationed here, but when he was drafted he said he didn't want me to wait for him, he didn't want me to be tied. And we hadn't known each other all that long anyway. I don't know if it would have got more serious or not. But we were fond of each other – and we had fun – and I'll miss him.' Her voice quavered.

The surgeon nodded. He looked about thirty-five, tall, with curly light brown hair that gave him a boyish appearance. He looked tired, as if he'd worked a long time to try to save Tony and the other sick sailors under his care, and she felt suddenly sorry for him. How many other wives and sweethearts had he had to talk to like this?

'I'd better go,' she said. 'I'm due on my own ward in five minutes.'

He nodded again. 'I've seen you there. Miss Makepeace says you're a good nurse.'

Thursday blushed with surprise and pleasure. The girls always supposed that the doctors didn't even notice them, except as pieces of equipment standing ready to do their bidding on their rounds. She couldn't imagine that such

277

august beings actually bothered to talk to Madam about the girls.

'Madam's wonderful,' she said. 'We all think the world of her.'

'And we think the world of you,' he said. 'All you girls, coming here and turning to doing all the worst jobs and never complaining. It makes a big difference to the hospital, having VADs here.' He gave her a sudden grin that made him look more boyish than ever. 'Mind you, I shan't talk to you like this when I'm on your ward! I shall be all stiff and starchy again then.'

Thursday met his eyes and saw the twinkle in them. She smiled back and wrinkled her nose.

'Yes, sir,' she said demurely, and turned to walk away. But as she passed the bed that had been Tony's and saw a different sailor there, her sadness returned and she felt a surge of misery and resentment.

Her mother was right. It *wasn't* fair that all these young men should suffer and die. It *wasn't* fair that their lives should be snatched from them before they'd had a real chance to live at all.

Land of hope and glory? She shook her head, and wondered if it would ever really come about. And how many more young men would have to suffer and die before it did.

Gradually, the Dunkirk wounded recovered and were sent to convalesce at home or in other hospitals, or went back to their ships or to other drafts. There was no lack of new patients, however. The Luftwaffe were in the skies every day, bombing convoys and ports, with the RAF on constant alert, ready to 'scramble' their aircraft to go and do battle overhead. Ships were sunk, some of their crews to be recovered and some to be lost. Of those who were saved, a large number came to Haslar.

'We may get patients of all nationalities,' Madam told the girls as they attended one of her lectures. 'Dutch,

German, Italian – anyone who needs treatment will be brought here. Obviously—' she fixed them all with a stern eye '—they will receive the same care, *whatever* their nationality. They are our patients, and we will not engage in hostilities. Our job is to care for the sick – not fight a war.'

'But suppose they've sunk one of our ships?' Elsie asked doubtfully. 'Suppose they've shot down one of our pilots? I don't know as I can feel the same about looking after a man that might have done that, Madam.'

'You must try, Jackson. You *will*.' Madam was quite unequivocal about it. 'I say again, these men will be our patients, they'll be brought here for our care. We're nurses, and ours is not to question or do anything else but our utmost for the patients, whoever they are and wherever they come from. Is that understood?' She swept her gaze around the rows of scrubbed faces. 'Very well. And there will, of course, be absolutely *no* fraternising. You don't have to talk to them – even if you can. All you have to do is care for their bodies.'

'So no getting friendly,' Patsy muttered as they filed out. 'Not that we'd want to, if they're the enemy.'

'I still don't feel right about it,' Elsie said. 'I mean, there's poor Tony, with that awful injury to his face, dying right here in Haslar, and there's Thursday's brother Steve missing, and her cousin dead, and all the others we know about – and now we're expected to look after Jerries and Eyeties. It just doesn't seem right. One minute we're trying to kill them, next minute we're trying to make them better. Just so they can go back and do it all again!'

'Well, they won't be able to do that,' Thursday said. 'They'll be POWs, won't they.'

'I suppose so. I still don't see why—'

'It's the rules,' Patsy said. 'The Geneva Convention and all that. You'd want them to look after our boys, wouldn't you?'

'Well, yes, but—'

'Well, then. We've got to look after theirs. And I bet that's all they are, too, lots of them – just boys, made to go and fight like our lads being called up. I bet they don't know what it's all about, half of them.'

They walked out to the sea wall and stood looking out towards the Spithead Forts and the Isle of Wight. As usual, the broad strip of water was busy with ships and tugs. The girls sat down and gazed at the smooth blue sea.

'It still doesn't seem possible there's really a war—' Patsy was beginning, when Elsie gripped her arm and exclaimed, 'What's that?'

They stared where she was pointing. A small cloud of black objects, not much bigger than houseflies, had appeared on the horizon. They approached rapidly, growing to the size of bluebottles, then bumblebees. And that was what they sounded like, too. A low, snarling buzz, and then a drone. A rising, falling drone, like the snores of an evil man.

'It's German planes,' Thursday whispered. 'It's bombers. Patsy – Else – it's the invasion!'

They clutched each other's arms, staring. The planes came nearer and although the girls had no real idea of what the difference was between German and British planes, they were certain that these were the enemy. Transfixed with horror, they watched, waiting for the bombs to fall.

'We ought to get under cover,' Elsie whispered. 'We ought to get back inside somewhere—'

'No – wait. Look at that! There's another lot coming from inland somewhere. Who are they?'

'It's our boys,' Patsy cried, leaping up and down. 'It's the RAF! They're coming to see them off. Hooray, hooray, hooray!'

'It *is*. It must be. There's an airfield not far away, isn't there? Near Chichester?'

'Tangmere,' Elsie said briefly. 'Oh, look at that, *look* at that! They're starting to fire. They're all over the place, look. See, those little puffs, that's smoke from the guns. They've got them in the tails of the planes. Oh, *look*!'

'One's been hit,' Thursday whispered. 'One of the planes has been hit.'

There was a silence as they watched one of the aircraft drop away from the mêlée and fall towards the sea. A stream of thick black smoke billowed from one wing, and then there was a sudden burst of flame and the whole plane was engulfed and spiralled in a black and orange ball towards the sea. It hit the water in a huge spray of boiling steam.

The girls were silent, and then Elsie said in a shaking voice, 'Was that one of ours or one of theirs?'

'Whichever it was,' Thursday said, 'there was someone inside it. I didn't see anyone bale out, did you?'

The others shook their heads. They looked again at the spot where the plane had hit the water, but there was nothing to be seen from this distance but a slight surge in the glassy surface. Whoever had been in the plane must be dead by now. Probably, they'd been dead even before the plane reached the sea.

The air battle was still going on. Aircraft were swooping and diving, performing all the aerobatics that once they'd performed for entertainment at air shows. They twisted between each other, jockeying for position, and all the time guns were firing. Another two planes went down, and then the raiders seemed to vanish. Two or three could still be seen as diminishing black dots, and then they were gone. The remaining aircraft circled around for a few minutes, then headed back inland, a couple doing victory rolls as they disappeared.

'We beat them!' Elsie exulted. She punched Thursday on the arm. 'We *beat* them! *We* saw 'em off, we showed 'em, *we* sent 'em packing all right. *They* won't come back in a hurry.'

'They will, you know,' Thursday said. 'They won't be put off that easily. Anyway, they don't have a choice, do they?' She looked at the sea, smiling under the June sunshine, and shuddered as she thought of what lay beneath it. 'And we still don't know if it was ours or theirs that went down. It could be our lads down there.'

'Yes, it could,' Elsie agreed soberly. 'But even so, Thurs – we did send 'em off with a flea in their ear, didn't we? They never got anywhere near Pompey.'

'No, they didn't.' The girls turned and walked back through the gate into the hospital grounds. 'What was that name you said, the place near Chichester where the airfield is?'

'Tangmere. Why?'

'I think that's where my cousin Leslie is,' Thursday answered quietly. 'He's been training as a pilot. Mum told me at the weekend he'd passed out. I was just wondering if he was in one of those planes we just saw.'

Dogfights became part of everyday routine. The raiders would appear as black dots, their droning sound increasing as they approached, and then the RAF defenders would swoop on them and the battle commence. There were nearly always two or three aircraft destroyed, some RAF and some Luftwaffe, and if the pilots were lucky they could be seen baling out, their parachutes appearing to rise from the falling plane to drift down like pale, floating mushrooms to the sea beneath where – if they were even luckier – they might be picked up by a fishing boat or perhaps a naval ship.

Some were, as Madam had foretold, brought to Haslar.

'He's got terrible burns,' Elsie reported when a young German pilot had been brought into her ward. 'All his hair and eyebrows have been burnt away, but mostly it's his hands. He's got to have operations or he'll never be able to use them again.'

'Is he going to stay here for them?'

'Seems like it. For the time being, anyway. He's in that little side room at the end of the ward.'

'Poor chap,' Thursday said. 'It must be awful, being away from all your own people in an enemy hospital. I bet he wonders what we'll do to him.'

'Poor chap nothing,' Elsie retorted. 'He shot down one of our planes before he went down, and our boy was lost. He's bloody lucky we're looking after him. I bet the Jerries wouldn't bother with our lads the way we're bothering with him – washing his face for him, spoonfeeding him, wiping his bum and all. I'm surprised at you, Thursday, what with losing your brother and Tony. And with your cousin one of the pilots at Tangmere too.'

'I don't think he's actually flying yet. Not in operations.'

'Well, he will be soon,' Elsie said grimly. 'There's a hell of a lot being lost.'

Thursday knew that was true, but she didn't want to think about it. She didn't want to think about Steve either. He came into her mind every night when she went to bed, and the realisation that he surely must be dead hit her afresh every morning when she woke up, and she was afraid that if she thought about him during the day as well she just wouldn't be able to do her work. The only way she could manage was by putting him out of her mind, and then she felt guilty, as if she didn't care as much as she ought to. And she felt guilty, too, when she thought of Tony, who seemed to be no more now than a part of a distant past. Too much has happened too soon, she thought, and I just haven't got time to think about them all . . .

There was nothing she could do about it, and no point in talking to anyone else. Everyone had the same griefs and worries these days. You could help each other, but when it came down to it, in your bed at night, in your mind and in your heart, you were on your own and had to find your own way through.

Denise and her parents had declared an uneasy truce over Vic. As Thursday had suggested, Denise had asked if she could bring him round one evening and her father had eventually agreed, saying that he wanted to have a word with the young man anyway. The problem then had been persuading Vic to come. She tried the next evening as they sat by the river, eating two pennyworth of chips out of newspaper.

'He's going to knock my block off. You said he was really up the pole about us.'

'I know, but I do think he'd calm down if he met you. He'd know what a nice boy you are then, he'd be able to see for himself. And Mum'll love you, I know she will. You've only got to smile at her!'

Vic wasn't so sure, but he couldn't see any way out of it. If he refused to come, Denise's father would be round at the post office like a shot, demanding to know why he was letting his precious daughter down. It didn't seem as if Vic could win. He took another chip and chewed thoughtfully.

'Maybe they're right. Maybe we ought to stop seeing each other for a while. Make sure of our feelings, like.'

Denise stared at him. 'But we *are* sure! *I* am.' Her lip quivered. 'I thought you were too. You said you loved me.'

'I do,' he said hastily. 'I do love you, Dizzy. It's just that – well . . .'

'Just that what?' She stared at him suspiciously. 'Has anyone been talking to you about me, Vic?'

'Talking to me? No, why? What would anyone have been talking to me about?' He poked about in the newspaper for a last chip, but could find only scraps of batter. 'D'you want these crispy bits, Diz?'

Denise shook her head impatiently. She said nothing for a moment, then she sighed and said, 'You might as well know. Mum and Dad'll tell you anyway. It's just that – well, there's something I told you when we first started going out together. Something that wasn't quite true.'

'What wasn't true? What are you talking about, Diz?'

'It's about how old I am,' she said uncomfortably. 'I told you I was eighteen, and I'm not.'

He looked at her. As usual, she was wearing lipstick and powder, with a touch of eyeshadow. Her hair was done in the latest Marcel waves. She could have passed for twenty-one, easily.

'What are you, then? Forty? Fifty?'

'Don't be daft! I'm younger – not older.' She looked at him appealingly, in the way that had first melted his heart.

'You're not!' He stared at her in astonishment. 'How much younger, then? Seventeen? That's not much. *Sixteen?*'

Denise shook her head. 'I'm fifteen,' she whispered. 'I'll be sixteen in August, but—'

'*Fifteen?*' His exclamation made her jump. 'You're *only fifteen?*'

Denise nodded. She saw his face whiten, his eyes grow dark. She put out her hand to touch him, but he flinched away. He screwed the newspaper into a tight ball and flung it into the water. His hands were trembling.

'Vic—'

'You told me you were eighteen and you're only *fifteen?* What the hell did you do that for?'

'There's no need to swear—'

'There's every need! I'm entitled to swear! Don't you realise, I could be had up for rape?'

'*Rape?*'

'Yes. Rape. *Statutory* rape, they call it. I could be put in prison.'

'But surely it's rape when the girl doesn't *want*—'

'Not when she's under sixteen,' he said grimly. 'She can want it all she likes, she can flaming *beg* for it, but it's still rape and it's still the poor bloody bloke who gets sent down for it.'

Denise was silent for a moment. 'Well – but it was you kissed me and – and touched me – and—'

'And you're telling me you didn't like it? You didn't exactly stop me, did you?'

'Well, I didn't know what you were going to do, did I? I've never been with a boy before – not like that. I didn't know you were going to – to . . .' She blushed crimson and floundered on. 'And I've been so worried ever since.'

'Worried?' he said, suddenly still. 'What about?'

'Well – about babies. Someone told me you could get a baby from kissing – a special sort of kissing, she said. And someone else said it was if you were out after eleven o'clock at night, and that was why fathers always wanted their girls in by ten. And then, when we – when *you* – did that, I thought that must be the way. I asked my friend and she said it was, but not the first time. And she was right, because I came on the next week, but then we did it again – three *times* – and – and, Vic, I haven't come on again and I'm over a week late now and I'm scared stiff! Suppose I'm having a baby? What am I going to do? My mum'll kill me, and so will my dad. You've got to come and see them, Vic!'

He stared at her. 'And they won't kill me, I suppose! Diz, I've told you, they'll get me put in prison.'

'No, they won't, not if we tell them we're secretly engaged and want to get married.' She grabbed his arm and shook it. 'Vic, they'll have to let us get married! They'll *have* to!'

Vic shook his head.

'They don't *have* to do anything, Dizzy. They'll never let us get married – not that we can, anyway, till you're sixteen.' He drew in a shuddering breath. 'I'll tell you what they'll do. They'll go to the police for a start and get me had up in court and put in prison. Then they'll find some nice quiet home for unmarried mothers, out in the country somewhere, and put it about that you're going away to work. You'll be sent there before you start to show, and you'll have your baby there and . . .' He stopped and looked at her white face, then continued in a ragged voice, 'And then they'll make you give it up for adoption. And that'll be that.'

Denise stared at him. 'Give it up for adoption? But why not just let us get married?'

'Because everyone would *know*,' he said. 'We couldn't get married for at least three weeks – that's even if they agreed to it straight away – and the baby would be born seven months later at the very most – more likely six, or even five, by the time they'd agreed to it – and everyone would know you were expecting when you got married. Your mum would never get over the shame and, come to that, nor would mine.' He rubbed his hand across his eyes. 'God, what a mess.'

Denise's eyes filled with tears. 'But I don't want to give my baby up. I want to get married to you and be a *family*.'

'I told you, they won't *let* us.'

'We could go to Scotland—'

'*No*. We couldn't. What would we live on? I'd lose my job, don't you realise that?' He sighed again. 'I'm going to lose it anyway. And what sort of a job am I going to get after I've been in prison? Nobody'll have me then – not for anything decent. Oh, God, why did I have to be so bloody *stupid*?'

'You didn't know I was only fifteen,' she said in a small voice. 'It's not your fault, Vic.'

'It's my fault I went with you,' he said roughly. 'It's my fault I never used anything. I took a chance. And now I'm paying for it. I'll go on paying for the rest of my life.'

'We can still get married. After you come out of prison—'

'For God's *sake*, Denise! Don't talk as if it's a foregone conclusion!' He took a deep breath. 'Listen. How sure are you that you've fallen?'

'I don't know. I don't know anything about it – what happens and all that. But my friend says that if you don't come on – that's the first sign. And then there's morning sickness, and I did feel sick last Saturday morning, so that's the second sign, and—'

'*I* felt sick on Saturday morning, too. I thought it was the fish and chips we had on Friday.'

'Oh. Well, it did taste a bit funny.' She gazed at him hopefully. 'D'you think I might be all right, then?'

'How the hell do *I* know?' He rubbed his forehead again. 'Look, it seems to me it's a bit early to tell. Aren't you ever – you know, a bit late?'

'Well, sometimes,' Denise said, blushing. She had never discussed this sort of thing with anyone except her mother and a few friends – never with a boy. 'And I've missed a whole month once or twice.'

'Well, maybe this is just the same. It might not be anything to do with – with us.'

'But how am I going to *know*?'

'You'll have to wait and see.' He put his arm round her. 'Look, it's no use worrying till we know for certain, is it? There might be nothing to worry about. Let's just try and forget it for a while, shall we?'

'*Forget* it?'

'Well, you know what I mean,' he said. 'Wait another two or three weeks. It might be perfectly all right. And if it isn't – well, we'll get something sorted out then, I promise.'

Denise stared at the water flowing past.

'Doesn't that make sense?' he persisted gently.

'Well, I suppose so. But you'll come round and see Mum and Dad?'

'Yes, sure. Only not this week, because I've got to go and see my auntie in Birmingham.'

'Your auntie? You never said.'

'No, well, you were so upset over your brother, and then this, I couldn't, could I? But she's not well and I've always been her favourite, and – well, she wrote to Mum yesterday asking me to go and stop for the weekend, and I couldn't think of any way out of it. I'm sorry, Diz, I'll have to go.'

'Well, you'll come next week, then, won't you? Just for a cup of tea. They will like you, Vic, I know they will.'

Vic wasn't so sure. Fifteen! He looked again at the girl beside him and saw past the make-up and the hairstyle to the naive child she truly was. I ought to have seen it in the first place, he thought. I ought to have been more bloody careful.

Chapter Twenty

The invasion was expected any day. Nobody was allowed on the beach any more – even the sea wall was out of bounds, although the inmates of Haslar Hospital could still look out from the windows and see the activity in the harbour and on the Solent. There were gun emplacements all along Gilkicker and Stokes Bay, and the golf course was strewn with rubbish – old bedsteads, broken prams, even a car with no wheels. It was to stop enemy gliders landing, someone said. Apparently they had really big ones that could carry troops, not like the little two-seaters you used to see soaring up from Lee airfield on Sunday afternoons.

'They've taken down all the signposts along the roads, too,' Elsie reported after she had been home for her afternoon off. 'Our Dave went over to Southwick on his bike and he said if he didn't know the roads so well he'd never have got home. And the nameplates on the railway stations are all painted over, so the Germans won't know where they are.'

'That's daft,' Patsy said. 'The stationmaster always shouts the name out.'

'Well, he won't when the Germans are in charge, will he?' Elsie said in exasperation. 'Honestly, Pats, you are a twerp sometimes!'

'The Germans aren't going to *be* in charge,' Thursday said stoutly. 'We're going to fight them on the beaches, remember? And in the streets, and in the hills—'

'And on the railway stations,' Patsy said with a grin. 'And since they won't be able to find their way anywhere, with all these signs taken down, all we've got to do is point them in the wrong direction – back to Germany!'

The hospital was braced for the invasion. Although it wasn't a civilian hospital, it would have to take in local casualties if the Gosport War Memorial Hospital couldn't cope and people were too ill to be taken on the long journey round the harbour to Portsmouth. And there were always naval patients coming in, from ships that had been in action or sunk.

The girls were becoming more proficient at their work and found themselves with added duties. Sometimes they were given patients who were their special responsibility. Thursday found herself assigned to look after the young German pilot with the burnt hands.

'I've got to treat him as my own special patient,' she reported, bringing a tray of food to the table where the others were eating lunch. 'Me and that young Nurse Petty, turn and turn about. So that we get to know him without having to talk to him.'

'I never heard anything so daft,' Vera Hapgood said. She had taken the last vacant seat at the table. 'As if any of us would *want* to talk to him, even if we could!'

'Well, I feel a bit sorry for him,' Elsie said. 'All on his own in a strange country, with nobody to care about him. I shouldn't think he's a day over nineteen – just a kid, really. What's his name, Thurs?'

'Schmidt – Sister told me it's German for Smith. And his Christian name's Heinz – sounds like a tin of baked beans, doesn't it?'

'I think it's a cheek, calling it a Christian name,' Vera said. 'How can a German be a Christian?'

'Well, they are, aren't they. Not the Nazis, I know, but the ordinary Germans. They're not so different from us.'

'Not different from us? Of course they are! My dad says the only good German's a dead German.' Vera stirred her tea fiercely. 'It's unpatriotic, talking like that.'

'He's quite nice-looking,' Elsie said, just to annoy her.

And Patsy chimed in with, 'I don't see why he has to be horrible just because he's a German. I mean, they can't *all* be bad.'

'Why not?' Vera demanded. 'They're taught to be – it stands to reason.' She gave them a defiant look. 'He's the enemy, and if it was me looking after him, he'd soon know what *I* thought about it. You don't have to be able to speak the language to let a man know what you think.'

'And that's just why Madam didn't assign you to be his special nurse,' Thursday told her bluntly. 'You'd torture him, that's what you'd do.'

'I wouldn't. I just wouldn't put myself out for him, that's all, and if you do it's as good as collaborating.'

Thursday drew a deep breath. 'Take that back!'

'Shan't. And it's not just you, it's her as well.' Vera pointed her fork at Elsie. 'Saying he's good-looking and all! You're nothing but tarts, the pair of you.'

Elsie jumped to her feet. 'And you're nothing but a spiteful little bitch—'

'Stop it, both of you!' Patsy grabbed Elsie's arm. 'You know what happened last time, we all got our shore leave stopped. Just calm down and don't be so daft.'

Elsie glowered but sank slowly back into her seat. Vera speared a piece of fried bread with her fork and put it into her mouth, glancing coolly around the table.

'I'm not saying a word,' she said. 'I just think you all ought to be more careful what *you* say, that's all.'

'And I think *you* ought to shut up,' Elsie muttered. 'It's all right, Thurs, I'm not going to scratch her eyes out, even if she does deserve it. Someone else'll do that for her one day, and I'll be there to cheer 'em on.'

'Me, too.' Thursday gave Vera a withering look and then got up and marched out of the mess to go to the ward. It was time to change the young German's dressings. She collected everything she needed on a trolley and wheeled it into the small side room where he'd been put. He was lying on his pillows, staring out of the little window at the bright summer sky. He turned his head as Thursday came in and gave her an uncertain look. She smiled at him.

'Hello. My name's Thursday. I'm going to look after you during the day from now on.' She had no idea whether he could understand her or not, but Vera's words rankled. Collaborator, indeed! Just because she talked to the man like a human being. And Elsie was right, he was a nice-looking boy, and probably had a nice home with a plump, loving mother and a dad not so very much unlike her own . . . She gave him another grin and lifted up his hand.

'Now then, how's this burn getting along? You haven't been doing anything you shouldn't, have you? No dirty work, no shovelling coal or gardening? Got to look after burns, you know, mustn't let any infection in. That blister now, that doesn't look so good, but as long as you don't let it burst you'll be all right. Let's get this nice clean dressing on it – and then a bit of bandage. I spent all yesterday afternoon rolling these bandages, I did, just for you . . . that's right, that's it, that's more comfy, isn't it? Now the other hand . . .'

She chattered away as she changed the dressings and gently washed the boy's face. He had been burnt about the forehead but his cheeks were unmarked, a smooth golden brown as if he had been sunbathing before he was shot down. There was a faint golden fuzz, as if he'd only just begun to shave, and she wondered again just how old he was. She met his blue eyes. He was just a kid, no older than her cousin Leslie, she thought. Probably longing for his mum or his girlfriend. For anyone who would be able to talk in his language, anyone who would be friendly and warm and loving towards him. He must be scared stiff here in England, not knowing what was going to happen to him when his hands were better.

'There,' she said at last, and stood back a little to beam at him. To her dismay, she saw his eyes fill with tears and he lifted his bandaged hands helplessly, as if to brush them away.

'Hey, what's all this, then? You don't have anything to cry about. You're safe here – no one's going to hurt you. And I bet they've let your family know where you are, so you'll be getting letters from home soon. Here . . .' She picked up the towel and wiped his eyes gently. 'It's all right,' she whispered. 'Thursday's here. Thursday'll look after you.' And before she knew what she was doing, she bent and kissed him on the smooth, golden cheek.

The German made a soft sound in his throat and Thursday jumped back as if he had stung her. She covered her mouth with her hand and stared at him, biting her lip against the nervous giggles that threatened to bubble forth.

'Oh, I'm sorry! I shouldn't have done that. I don't know what came over me. It was just seeing you, so – so sort of helpless, not even able to wipe your own eyes.' She backed away, pulling the trolley with her. 'I'm sorry – I really am sorry.' Without looking to see if anyone was coming, she fled out into the ward, then paused to draw in a deep breath and glanced around anxiously. Suppose anyone had seen her. Suppose *Sister* had seen her . . .

But apart from the patients in the nearest beds, who were both too concerned with their own troubles to worry about those of a German, no one else was taking the slightest notice. Instead, they were all engrossed by something that was happening by the window at the far end of the ward, where some of the up-patients were gathering around and reporting on what was going on. Another dogfight, she thought, and heaved a sigh of relief.

You'll have to be more careful, Thursday Tilford, she thought. Vera Hapgood would have had every right to call you a collaborator if she'd seen that. *And* a tart. Kissing a patient – any patient – was bad enough. But kissing a *German* patient! Thank God no one had seen, or heard.

'What are you all looking at over there?' she called,

pulling herself together and wheeling her trolley down the ward. 'I've got a load of dressings here to do. What's going on, another dogfight?'

The men turned and the nearest shook his head. 'We thought it was at first. But it looks more like a raid. It's bombers – Jerry bombers – and they're coming in fast.'

'Jerry bombers? But why hasn't there been an alert?' Thursday left the trolley and ran to the window. She stared at the black shapes, rapidly approaching, and saw the cloud of RAF planes rise from the Sussex coast to intercept them. And as she gazed, she heard the first wail of the siren split the air. 'Oh, my *God*!'

A raid. An air raid.

'It's the invasion . . .' she whispered.

It wasn't the invasion, but it was the first of the real air raids. The hospital was placed immediately on yellow alert, and then purple. That meant that everyone must be indoors and anyone not on duty was to take cover. If a red was announced, the up-patients would have to be moved down to the cellars, and a double red meant that everyone must take shelter, and the bed patients taken down below as well.

'I don't know how you're going to get us all down there,' a sailor who had his leg in traction said fretfully. 'I mean, you only got to loosen it off a bit and I go through the roof.'

'We'd better give you a gun, then, and you can shoot down a few Jerries while you're up there,' the man in the next bed suggested. 'You can be our secret weapon.'

The yellow alert stayed yellow, and no one was required to leave the ward. It seemed as if most of the action was over Portsmouth. They were probably targeting the dockyard, Thursday thought as she continued to change the dressings, trying to ignore the cacophony outside. She could hear the snarl of the German bombers wheeling over the harbour, and the lighter sound of the Spitfires and Hurricanes attacking them. Every few moments a tremendous crash signified yet another bomb hitting its target, and there was a constant rattle from the anti-aircraft guns dotted all around the two towns. The floor shook, and she tried not to glance too often towards the rattling windows, knowing that the sky was filled with swooping and diving aircraft. I wonder if Leslie's up there, she thought, frowning as she endeavoured to concentrate on her work. I wonder—

A cheer went up from the men who, contrary to all orders, were still clustered round the window. 'There goes one! He's hit, he's on fire! Bloody hell, what a sight, what a *sight*! Look at the flames – cor, bet his pants are feeling a bit warm!'

Thursday turned and stared. There, spiralling down into the stretch of water between Haslar and the Isle of Wight, was a ball of flame. Transfixed, she stood as still as a rock, both hands clutched to her chest. She saw a tiny puff of white lift itself from the fiery mass and float slowly down in its wake. The pilot, she thought, he's baled out. I wonder if he's badly burnt . . . And then the burning aircraft hit the water in a great, boiling plume of steam and spray, and the parachute disappeared.

The men burst into laughter and thumped each other's shoulders.

'Did you see that? Thought he'd got away with it, didn't he? Thought he'd parachute all the way back to bloody Germany! I bet he couldn't believe his eyes when he found himself landing in that lot. Couldn't believe his bloody luck!'

Thursday stared at them. She thought of her cousin Leslie, who might even now be circling up there, waiting for his chance to attack. Who might be the next one to be shot down in a ball of fire. She thought of the young German pilot with his bandaged hands and his smooth golden-brown cheeks. She thought of her other cousin

Mike, caught and killed on the beaches of Dunkirk, and her brother Steve who was probably dead, too.

'Stop it! *Stop it!*' Her voice startled everyone. They turned and stared at her and she faced them, too angry to remember that they were her patients, too furious to care. 'What do you think you're doing – laughing and cheering when you've just seen a man *die*? Don't you realise, that was a man on that parachute, probably no more than a boy – like that poor boy back in the ward here – and he was *burning to death*. Can't you imagine what that must be like? Hasn't any of you ever burnt himself? It *hurts*. Even a burnt finger hurts. And he was burning all over. And you're *laughing* about it.'

They gazed at her, then at each other. One or two dropped their eyes. A burly torpedoman glowered and spoke up.

'It's all very well for you to talk like that, Nurse. You never bin in action. We have – that's why we're here now. *We* got hurt, too – by blokes like that one you're so sorry for. We got shot and bombed on our ships, yeah, *and* burnt, too, some of us at Dunkirk. You don't have to tell us nothing about getting hurt, we does it for a bloody pastime.'

Some of the men murmured their agreement and Thursday bit her lip. She bowed her head a little in acknowledgement.

'I know. I'm sorry – shouldn't have said that. But I still don't see why you have to laugh. It isn't funny, whoever it happens to.'

'Yeah, but look at it this way.' The torpedoman seemed to have become spokesman. 'We don't think of them like human beings, see. We can't, can we? We got to go out there and kill people. We can't feel sorry for them.'

'But *laughing*—'

'It's not that we think it's funny,' another sailor said. He was smaller, with untidy fair hair and large ears. 'It's just that it's a fight and we're winning. We're pleased – aren't you? Aren't you glad when you see one of our blokes winning? They're risking their lives up there.'

Thursday bit her lip again. 'Yes, I know. Yes, of course I'm pleased. It's just that – well, my cousin's a pilot and it could have been him up there. I couldn't help thinking—'

'Yes, well, you're a woman, ain't you, and a nurse, what's more. And that's why men fight wars and women kiss them better,' the torpedoman said. He turned back to the window. 'Looks like we seen 'em off for the time being, anyway. But they made a bit of a mess of Pompey, by the look of it.'

They all gazed out again. There was a huge black cloud, shot with orange flame, billowing from somewhere near the dockyard, and smaller clouds rising from all over the area. There was a tug on fire in the middle of the harbour. It looked as if the dockyard had been hit, but some of the explosions and fires seemed to be further into the city.

Elsie! Thursday thought with a stab of fear. Her family lived in Fratton. Was that one of the places hit? She stared doubtfully at the city across the water, not sure enough of its geography to know if the flames were burning in Fratton. She thought of Mr and Mrs Jackson, of Eddy, of Dave, and hoped they'd all managed to get to a shelter in time.

'When you've quite finished admiring the view,' Sister Burton's acid voice said behind her, 'there's a trolley full of dressings here that don't appear to have been changed. Were you thinking of doing any work today, I wonder?'

Thursday whipped round guiltily, her face reddening. 'I'm sorry, Sister. We were all watching – and I was thinking of Nurse Jackson's family, they live in Portsmouth. There'll be people hurt there – she must be terribly worried.'

'And your job is to nurse the patients we have here.' Sister Burton's face softened very slightly. 'I've already seen Jackson and told her she can have an extra two hours to go and see her family. But I won't be able to give her or anyone else such a concession every time there's a raid. We've work to do – and I'd be grateful, and so would the patients, I'm sure, if you'd just get on and do it!'

'Yes, Sister.' And as the all-clear sounded its more comforting wail, Thursday turned back to her trolley.

Sister was right. There were dressings still to be done, and a few bombs and aircraft shot down wouldn't be any excuse for not having got on with the allotted tasks.

Thursday consulted her list and then looked over at the burly sailor, a glimmer in her eye.

'Come on, Torpedoman Sellers. Let's have a look at that knee of yours. And now you've told me how used you all are to getting hurt, we won't have any of that yelling we had yesterday – *will* we?'

The raid had killed a number of people in Portsmouth and injured many more. The huge pall of smoke and flame had come from the gasholder at Rudmore, which had been struck by one of the first bombs. Another casualty had been a first-aid post, occupying a school in Drayton Road. It wasn't far from Elsie's home.

'Everyone's all right,' she reported when she got back from her hasty journey. She'd gone on her bike, knowing that the buses and trolleys would be disrupted, and arrived in the dormitory breathless and shaken. 'Dave and Eddy were already home and they all got down the shelter. Dad was on his way home from work and went into a street shelter – he got home just before me. Mum cried her eyes out when she saw him – she thought he was dead. But the damage is awful. Houses just smashed to bits, you wouldn't believe. Walls ripped out and roofs torn off, bricks and stuff all over the place, people's furniture all broken up and laying in the gutter. You can't get down some of the roads at all. And dust and smoke everywhere – the stink's horrible. And they don't know how many people have been killed. They're going through all the rubble, looking for people. They got a little girl out of a house just when I was going by, her mum was in hysterics.'

'I bet she was.' The girls listened in horror. They had been in different stages of preparation for bed – Patsy filing her nails, Thursday brushing her hair, Vera Hapgood lathering Pond's cold cream all over her face. Some of the others crowded round as well to hear Elsie's story, and they looked at each other in dismay.

'Are they going to keep on doing this?' one asked in a whisper. 'Are they going to keep on and on bombing us till we give in? Or till we're all dead?'

'We're not *going* to give in,' Patsy said stoutly. 'We're going to fight. We *are* fighting – we brought down some of those planes. We sent 'em back with a flea in their ear.'

Elsie sank down on her bed. Thursday looked at her and saw tears well up in her eyes. She moved across quickly and sat beside her, putting her arm round the other girl's shoulders.

'Elsie, you're shaking all over.'

'I know. I can't help it.' Elsie's voice trembled. 'I was all right till I got back here and – and started to talk about it.' She started to cry. 'Oh, Thurs, it was awful. All those bombed buildings, and the smoke and flames – a lot of them are on fire – and fire engines everywhere, and ambulances. And people just wandering about, crying or looking lost. I felt I ought to stop and help, but I only had those two hours Sister gave me, and I just had to get home and see that everyone was all right.' Her words became incoherent and she leant her head on Thursday's shoulders and gave way to huge, wrenching sobs. 'And then . . .' she went on with a gulp, 'then I saw this little baby, couldn't have been more than a year old, just *lying* there in the gutter, and I knew – I knew it was dead – it was all – all – oh – and then a fireman came along, and he pushed me out of the way and I told him I was a nurse, and he said there wasn't nothing we could do for the kiddy – I already *knew* that, but I couldn't leave it there in the gutter, could I, not a little *baby* – and he said he'd see to it and I ought to go and do something for the ones that was hurt. And I didn't. I *didn't*. I just got on me bike again and went the rest of the way home. I was so worried about Mum, you see, and Eddy and Dave. I just went home. And they were all right, so I *could've* stopped and helped. But then I had to get back here. I only had the two hours – and Navy time and all – I had to come back. And I know I'll *never* get that baby out of my head and I'll *always* be sorry I didn't stop and help.'

Thursday held her closely in her arms and rocked her to and fro, while the other girls sat round and gazed at them in dismay. Watching the raid from the windows of the hospital had been frightening, but also exciting as the RAF aircraft had swooped and dived in their efforts to drive the raiders away. The sight of flames rising from the city had been sobering, for they knew that there must have been people hurt and even killed. But Elsie's story gave them a different picture – a picture of what had been happening on the ground, in people's homes and the streets where they lived. They saw in their own minds the rubble-filled roads, the clouds of smoke and dust, the flames. They saw the dazed and injured people wandering amongst it all, searching for their families. They saw the baby, lying dead in a gutter.

'It had lovely fair hair,' Elsie said in a broken voice. 'And a little blue romper suit, all covered in blood.' And she began to cry all over again.

The girls were all in tears. The dead baby seemed to be a symbol of all that was most dreadful about this war. Until now, they'd thought of the conflict as being waged between adults – men, albeit some of them were not much more than boys, going off voluntarily to fight. Women staying at home to take on the work they had left behind, or to work in munitions factories to supply them with the equipment they needed to fight. Grown-up people with a choice, people who could listen to the news and read the papers, who understood – to some extent, anyway – what was going on.

None of them had ever thought of the war being waged against babies.

'We ought to have realised it,' Thursday said later to Patsy in the washroom. Elsie had been coaxed into bed and now lay fast asleep, exhausted. 'We've seen enough men hurt already. We knew there were going to be air raids. We ought to have realised there'd be kiddies killed. But what Elsie said – it made it so *real*. It sort of hit me, like it never has before. Not even when I heard about Mike and Steve being missing.'

'What I want to know is, why hadn't it been evacuated?' Patsy said, rubbing her toothbrush on her tin of Gibbs' toothpaste. 'I thought all mothers and babies had been sent to the country.'

'They didn't all go, though. Elsie said the woman next door to her mum wouldn't go because her hubby works in the dockyard and there'd be no one to give him a hot meal. And a lot of them have come back since Christmas, thinking nothing was going to happen.'

'Well, they know different now, don't they,' Patsy said grimly, and began to scrub her teeth.

Thursday looked at her reflection in the mirror above the washbasin. She saw a face that looked graver and older than it had done that morning. The raid had shaken them all, and none of them would sleep quite so easily at night now. Portsmouth had been attacked, and its streets lay in rubble.

The next time, it might be Gosport. It might be Haslar. It might be the hospital itself.

Chapter Twenty-One

The next time seemed a long time in coming. It wasn't for another month, and by that time other things had happened, too.

In Worcester, Denise was now certain that she was pregnant. She had missed two periods and if she didn't come on soon, that would be three. She'd never missed this many before. And she'd definitely been feeling a bit off in the mornings.

'It's not much,' she told Jenny as the two girls sat on Jenny's bed. 'But I do bring up some sort of yellowy stuff every morning. It tastes horrible – all bitter. What d'you suppose it is?'

'I think it's bile,' Jenny said doubtfully. 'I had it once, when I had a bilious attack. It's when your stomach's got nothing else in it. But hasn't your mum noticed, Dizzy?'

'I don't think so. I do it in the outside lav, and it really isn't much. Maybe it's something else. I've heard people feel bad all morning – it doesn't seem enough, d'you think?' Denise looked hopeful.

'I don't think it matters how much it is. You've missed nearly three times and you're sick in the mornings. It does look as if you're expecting, Diz.'

'Oh, flipping heck.' Denise flung herself back on the pillows. Tears welled from her eyes. 'What am I going to do, Jen, what the flipping heck am I going to *do*?'

'Well, you're going to have to tell them soon.' Jenny looked at her helplessly and thanked her lucky stars that she'd finished with Sam and wasn't in the same boat. 'It'll start to show in a month or two. What about Vic? What does he want to do?'

'He just wants to pretend it's not happening,' Denise said drearily. 'And I hardly see him anyway. He seems to get an awful lot of overtime, and he's got this auntie in Birmingham, she's poorly and he—'

'Dizzy! He's not trying to get out of it, is he?'

'No, of course not! He loves me, he says so every time we see each other. And it'll all come right, I know it will, he'll stand by me. I'll be sixteen in October and we can get married then, and—'

'Suppose your mum and dad won't let you? Have they met him yet?'

'No.' Denise leant up on one elbow and fiddled with the fringe along the edge of the bedspread. 'It's because of this auntie, he's been her favourite ever since he was little, and he says—'

'Dizzy, he's making excuses! Can't you see it? He's trying to get out of it. Pretending he's got overtime. Pretending he's got to go and see this auntie. It's weeks since Thursday said you ought to take him home to meet your mum and dad, and you still haven't managed to get him to go. One of these days, you're going to go in the post office and he won't be there any more – he'll have been called up. It's bound to happen soon anyway, and then he'll go off heaven knows where and you'll be left all on your own, holding the—' She stopped abruptly and bit her lip. 'Well, you *will*.'

'Jen – do you really think so?' Denise whispered, her face white.

'Well, yes, I do. I'm sorry, Diz, I don't want to upset you – but it seems so obvious. And now he knows how old you are, he must be scared stiff. It's not just a matter of having to get married, Diz. He could be in real trouble.'

'I didn't know. I didn't know that.'

'Well, nor did I. I mean, nobody's ever told us much about the facts of life, have they? We've had to learn them for ourselves. But that doesn't mean we've got any excuse. We're still the ones who'll get into trouble over it, and we're the ones who'll have to carry the can.' She looked soberly at her cousin. 'You're going to have a baby, Diz. It's not a doll that you can put in a cupboard when you're fed up with it. You're going to have to look after it, all day and every day, for years and years and years, and you can't do it all on your own. You've got to have a husband.'

'Vic. I want Vic.' Denise looked at her piteously. 'We really do love each other, Jenny. We *do*.'

Jenny reached over and took her hand. 'I know, Diz. I know.' Privately, she was sure that her cousin was in love – but she wasn't so sure about Vic. 'But you can't let him go on making excuses. He's got to face up to it – you both have. And you've got to tell your mum and dad.'

Denise nodded. She looked down at the bedspread and a large tear fell on the back of her hand. Jenny watched her with pity. It was the worst situation either of them had ever been in, she thought, the worst a girl *could* be in. Having a baby meant you'd been a 'bad girl', and everyone was going to know about it. Even if you got married, like Gladys Watson up the street who'd had a hasty wedding and then a 'seven-month baby'. The old gossips had had a field day with her. It would be even worse with Denise, who wasn't even sixteen.

'I'll tell Vic he's got to come and meet them,' Denise said at last. 'I'll tell him it's definite, there's no mistake and we can't hang about any longer. And – and I'll tell Mum first and ask her to tell Dad. I just – I just can't face them both together, Jen.'

Jenny nodded. It was what she and Steve and Thursday had always done, if they wanted something or had some small misdeed to confess. Get Mum on your side, and you had a better chance with Dad. And Mum nearly always *was* on your side.

I'm not so sure Auntie Flo's going to be on Dizzy's side

over this, though, she thought. But she's got to start somewhere. They've got to know.

'You make sure you get Vic round there soon after,' she said. 'You can't let him leave you in the lurch.'

'Oh, he wouldn't! He'd never do that.' But Dizzy's voice was uncertain, and more tears were falling. She looked up at Jenny and her eyes were wide and frightened. 'I don't know what I'd do if he left me, Jen. I just don't know what I'd do . . .'

As it happened, Percy was out that evening at a fishing club meeting. Denise and her mother sat knitting and listening to the wireless. It was the new Tommy Handley show, *ITMA*, and when it finished Flo turned off the wireless and looked at her daughter.

'You didn't seem to find much to laugh at, Denise.'

Denise bit her lip and concentrated on her knitting. Her heart was thumping. 'I didn't think it was as funny as usual.'

'That's funny, because the audience laughed as much as ever.' Flo waited a moment, then said, 'Put that knitting down a minute.'

'I'm just turning a heel—'

'It won't go bad. I want to talk to you. And I've got an idea you want to talk to me, don't you?'

Denise looked up, her eyes filled with tears. 'Oh, Mum . . .'

'I'm right, aren't I,' Flo said after a moment, her voice flat. 'You're in the family way.'

Denise burst out crying. 'Oh, Mum, I've been so frightened! I've been nearly frantic, wondering what to do. I didn't know what ought to happen, you see, and someone at work told me there was morning sickness and I *have* been a bit sick in the mornings – not much, and I still didn't know for certain – and I haven't come unwell for nearly three months now so I thought it must be, and I – I just don't know – I don't know what to do, and I didn't know how to tell you, and – and – oh, Mum, what am I going to *do*? Will you throw me out? Will you and Dad throw me out?'

Flo stared at her. She'd been prepared to be angry, she'd been afraid she might even hit her daughter when the fears that had been growing in her over the past few weeks were finally confirmed. She'd been dreading this moment ever since she knew Denise was knocking about with a boy so much older than herself. But now, seeing the girl's fear and distress, she couldn't be angry after all. It was just the same as when she'd fallen out of a tree and broken her arm, even though Flo had warned her it would happen, the same as when she'd broken her china doll through making that cradle to hang from the same tree, and anyone could have seen it wasn't strong enough. Denise had always been the same, rushing head first into trouble, but you couldn't be cross with her somehow. Not when she was your little girl and turning to you for comfort.

She crossed the little space between the chairs, and knelt in front of Denise to put her arms around her. Denise leant against her, sobbing.

'You silly girl. You silly, *silly* girl. I thought that's what it was. You being so quiet lately – and slipping down to the lav early every morning – and not using your pads. I wondered a few weeks ago when you missed, and thought, no, it couldn't be, she wouldn't be so daft. But the past few days – oh, Denise, you silly girl. You *naughty* girl.' The anger she'd expected to feel was beginning to come through, like the pain when your hands had been very cold and were now warming up. 'You bad, *naughty* girl!'

'I'm sorry, Mum. I really am. I didn't know – I thought it wouldn't happen, not to me—'

'And why should you be any different to anyone else?' her mother asked. 'Whatever did you want to go and do it for? Haven't we always tried to teach you right from wrong? Haven't I always said what'd happen if you brought trouble to the house? And here you are, not even sixteen. We can't even get you decently wed. And that Vic – whatever was he thinking of? He's old enough to know better. He shouldn't ever have been going out with you in the first place.'

'He didn't know,' Denise whispered. 'He didn't know I was only fifteen. He thought I was eighteen.'

'Well, I know that. You told him, didn't you? You made your face up to look older and spun him a line. You lied to him, as well as me and your dad.' Flo sighed. 'I'm sorry, Denise, but I'm ashamed of you, ashamed and disappointed. I never thought you'd let us down like this. And how we're going to break it to your father, I don't know.'

'I thought – would you tell him, Mum? I can't face him on my own.'

'Well, you're going to have to, aren't you? You're going to have to face a lot of people over this. And so'm I, more's the pity. Everyone will know, everyone in the road. I wouldn't be surprised if that Mrs Hawkins never speaks to me again.'

'Well, I don't see as that'd be much loss,' Denise said with a flicker of her old spirit. 'You don't like her anyway.'

'That's not the point! The point is, she's always tried to set herself up as better than me, and now she'll do it more than ever. *Her* daughter never got into trouble, they had that nice white wedding before the war started, and now she's got a baby grandson, born a decent year after.' Flo herself was crying now. '*You* won't be able to get married in white, even if you ever do get married. Not that anyone'll want you now. Soiled goods, that's what you'll be.'

'Mum! Don't say that! That's horrible – and anyway—'

'It's true, though,' Flo said drearily. She put her arms round her daughter again. 'It's what people'll say, see. And we've tried so hard, me and your dad, we've always given you a good home, seen that you went to Sunday school regular – you're even in the church choir with

Jenny.' A fresh thought struck her. 'What's the *vicar* going to say? You won't be able to go on going there, you'll have to leave.'

'Well, I would have done anyway,' Denise said. 'Because I'll be getting married – I'll be getting married to Vic. And *he* won't call me "soiled goods".'

Flo stared at her. 'Getting *married*? But you're only fifteen—'

'I'm not going to be fifteen for ever, am I? I'll be sixteen in a couple of months and we can get married then.'

'Your father'll have something to say about that.'

'No, he won't – because we won't be here!' Denise stared at her mother defiantly. 'We've talked about it, we've been talking about it for months. Before – before our Mike got – before Dunkirk. If you won't let us get married, we'll go to Scotland, they let you get married at sixteen there without anyone's permission. You won't be able to stop us.'

'Denise! Don't you dare talk like that! And don't be so silly. Of *course* you can't go to Scotland. And as for getting married or not, your dad and I will have to have a talk about that. We haven't even met this Vic yet. There's places girls like you can go, out in the country – places you can have the baby and give it up for adoption, and come back with no one any the wiser. That might be the best thing all round.'

'Give my baby up to *strangers*?'

'Yes. There's hundreds of people, *decently married* people, wanting a baby but can't have one. They'll take a baby like yours and give it a good home, better than what you could do, and you could start afresh. Nobody'd ever know.'

'I'd know. And you'd know, too. It's my *baby*, Mum. It's your *grandchild*. How can you even talk about giving it away? Would you have given *me* away? Or our Leslie? Or *Mike*?'

'Denise!' Flo put both hands to her mouth and tears

flooded down her cheeks. 'How can you *say* such things? Your brother—'

'I know. He's not coming back, he's never coming back.' Denise dropped to her knees and stared at her mother's distorted face. 'And you know how you feel about that. *I* know how you feel about that. Because that's what it would be like for *me* if I gave up *my* baby. Can't you *see*?'

Flo pulled a hanky from her sleeve and wiped her face. She looked at her daughter pleadingly. 'But your baby would be alive still. It would have a better life. Wouldn't you want that for it, Denise? Wouldn't that be best? We could say you'd gone away for work, or something, got a job in the country, or gone to stay with a relative – anything. And you could come back after a few months, when it was all over, and start again. You'd probably find yourself a decent young feller in time and get married, and then you could have your family in the proper way. And—'

'But I'm going to marry *Vic*,' Denise broke in. 'I've told you, Mum. And it's his baby, too – he ought to have some say. He might not want me to give it away. I don't know as I want to give it away myself. And there won't be any need to, anyway, not if we're getting married—'

'For goodness' sake, Denise!' Flo cried. 'Stop going on about getting married! I've told you, your dad and I will have to talk about that, we haven't even met him yet, and I very much doubt if we'll like him when we do – a chap his age, leading a young girl like you astray. And—'

'He didn't *know*!' Denise shouted. 'I told you, Mum, he didn't *know* I was under sixteen. It wasn't his fault! It was my fault, all of it – I *wanted* him to do it! And I want my baby! I'm not going to give it up – me and Vic are getting married. And that's it and all about it!'

She was on her feet, shouting at the top of her voice. Flo stared at her, appalled. And as Denise's voice finally died away, the door to the passageway opened and Percy himself stood there, his fishing things in his hand, staring from one to the other. Flo and Denise stared back, and Flo put her hand to her mouth and started to cry again.

'What in the name of all that's wonderful's going on here?' he asked at last. 'What the hell's all this shouting and yelling? I could hear you halfway up the street. And what's all this about getting married – and *babies*?'

Thursday was still nursing Heinz Schmidt. He had still never spoken, and she had never given way to any sudden impulses again, but a strange kind of rapport grew between them. His eyes looked relieved when she came in to take over from the night staff, and he gave her a cautious smile. Thursday smiled back and chatted as she changed his dressings or tidied his bed.

'I know you're German and supposed to be the enemy, but to me you're just a patient, see, and you get the same treatment as everyone else. And I talk to the others, so why not you – even though you don't understand a word I'm saying. And you can't have any breakfast this morning because you're having an op later on today, and Surgeon Commander Kirkpatrick says that'll be the last one, and your hands should be OK once everything's healed up. And then I suppose you'll be sent off to a prison camp for the rest of the war.' She straightened up and looked down at him. 'To tell you the truth, I'll be sorry. I'll miss you – and I suppose that's something else I shouldn't say, but you can't understand so what does it matter?'

The German gazed up at her. He was much stronger now, despite his operations, and although his face had lost its golden tan his eyes were still very blue. A strange expression came into them then, and his mouth widened in a broad grin.

'But I do understand,' he said clearly, with only the smallest trace of an accent. 'I've understood everything you've said to me.'

Thursday stared at him.

'You understand? You speak *English*?'

He tilted his head a little. 'As you can hear.'

'But – why didn't you do it before? Why didn't you *tell* me?' Thursday thought of all the things she'd said while she was attending to him and flushed scarlet. She'd talked freely, almost as if he'd been another VAD – grumbling about Sister, commenting about some of the other patients, letting off steam – things she would never have said if she'd known he could understand. And it wasn't just hospital gossip, she thought with sudden horror – had she said anything else? Anything she really shouldn't have said to the enemy?

She racked her brains. Not that she actually knew anything much, and not that he'd be likely to get the chance to pass it on to anyone while he was stuck here, but he was the enemy nonetheless. And he got letters from home and answered them, too, or someone did, writing at his dictation. Could he have passed on any information that way?

I don't think I've said anything, she thought, it's all been hospital gossip, but if I'd known he understood . . . And I definitely talked about the air raid.

A feeling of anger began to grow, pushing the embarrassment aside. Silly, girlish indiscretions didn't matter. Things that might help the enemy did.

'Why didn't you say before?' she demanded again. 'Are you a spy? Because if so, I think you've been really mean. I could have told you *anything*.'

He laughed. 'But that's what spies are – mean people! And you would expect one of your own men to behave in just the same way. We all have to fight for our own country, don't we, in whatever way comes possible to us.' He looked at her angry face and shook his head gently. 'No, *Donnerstag*, I'm not a spy. How could I be, lying here? And there is nothing you have said that I could pass on, anyway. You have been careful – and very, very illuminating.'

'*Illuminating?*'

'Yes. You've talked to me of your life, your days, your pleasures and your pains. You've made me laugh and you've made me want to cry.' His eyes were serious. 'You've made me understand that the English are just like the Germans – ordinary people, with ordinary hopes and fears, wanting nothing more than to live ordinary lives. If I were to pass on anything of what I have heard from you, that is what it would be.'

Thursday gazed at him doubtfully. 'But Hitler – the Nazis . . .'

'Not all Germans are Nazis,' he said. 'Many of us live in small villages in the country, sometimes high in the mountains. Politics are not important to us. We farm the land, we take cows to the pasture for the summer, we scarcely move from our homes. We are not all a part of Hitler's Youth Movement or his Nazi Party, and we don't all agree with what he has done to a people who have shared our lives for centuries yet retained their own race and customs. But I think we have been wrong in taking so little notice, for he has grown in power, and his party has grown with him, and now we can do nothing against him. We must join his army and fight his war . . .' he glanced ruefully at his bandaged hands '. . . whether we want to or not.'

'Did you live in a village?' she asked.

'Yes, in Bavaria. My father is a farmer. He thought I would work with him and take over the farm when he grew old, but my schoolmaster said I had a good brain and should go to a university. My father decided that I should have this chance and so I went to Berlin. I came to England, too.' He glanced at her, almost apologetically. 'I spent a year in Cambridge. It's a beautiful city and England is a beautiful country.'

'So that's why you speak English so well.'

'Partly. But I learned it when I was very young, from an Englishman who used to come and stay in my village, to walk and climb. He was a professor and he became friends with my schoolmaster. Perhaps, if he had not, I would never have left the village.'

'Would you rather that had happened?'

'How can I say? I have gained so much from all that I've learned. I've had wonderful opportunities. I've met wonderful, kind and loving people.' He sighed again and added, very quietly, 'And now I've been sent to kill them.'

'Couldn't you have refused? We have conscientious objectors—'

'In Germany,' he said, 'one cannot refuse. And besides – it is my country.'

Thursday was silent. She became aware that she had spent too long in this room and must go before Sister came in search of her. She saw the torment in the young face before her, and felt a wave of compassion.

'You're right,' she said. 'This war's being fought by ordinary people, who would rather be at home with their families, doing their ordinary jobs.' She hesitated. 'My cousin was killed at Dunkirk, and my brother's still missing. Neither of them ever set out to be soldiers, but when it came to it they were proud to go.'

'They died in a good cause,' he said. 'We all die in a good cause, if we are defending our country.'

'Even if it was our country that was wrong in the first place?' she challenged him. 'Even if it's done horrible, evil things?' And then she felt ashamed, as she saw his eyes cloud and his head droop. 'I'm sorry – but it's true, isn't it? The things they've done to the Jews – making them live in ghettos and wear yellow stars, and give up all their money – they're evil.'

'Let's not talk about it any more,' he said. 'We can't know it all. We can't decide.' He lifted his eyes again. 'That first morning, when you came to me – do you remember it?'

Thursday blushed, remembering the kiss she had given him. He smiled.

314

'It was the first tenderness I had known since I left home to join the Luftwaffe.'

'I shouldn't have done it,' Thursday said quickly. 'I don't know why I did. I just felt so sorry for you.'

'Do it again,' he said softly. 'Do it again, just once. I go for my operation this afternoon. It will be the last, and then I shall be moved to a camp. We may never see each other again. But I want to tell you how much you have meant to me, all these weeks – how your tenderness has helped me. Please, *Donnerstag* – do it again.'

'What was that you called me? *Donner*-something?'

He smiled. '*Donnerstag*. It's the German word for Thursday. You told me that first day that it was your name, and I've always thought of you so. *Donnerstag*,' he repated softly. 'A pretty name. A very pretty nurse.'

Thursday stared at him. She felt a lump in her throat and knew that tears were not far away. She could no longer deny that caring for him had meant something to her, too. His quiet face, his bright blue eyes, his smile of gratitude and welcome – all these had become part of her daily life, and she knew suddenly and unexpectedly that she was going to miss him.

'I must go,' she whispered. 'I've been here too long already.'

'A moment.' He lifted his hand towards her. 'One moment more. Please.'

Thursday looked at him and bit her lip. She could hear footsteps coming down the ward, the unmistakable clatter of a nurse's shoes. Sister Burton was on her way, and in a moment would be here, her eagle eyes missing nothing.

The footsteps were almost at the door. Swiftly, she bent and brushed her lips against his skin, then touched his cheek with her fingertips, and gathered up her things. She turned away, giving him one last glance, and walked out of the door, nodding brightly at the senior nurse.

'He's all ready for his pre-med, Sister. I've told him it's

his last – but, of course, he doesn't understand a word I say.'

Sister nodded and went on her way. Thursday made for the sluice and stood just inside the door, shaking a little, and felt the tears slip down her cheeks.

Poor boy, she thought, poor, poor boy. He could be our Steve, injured and alone in an enemy country.

Well, if Steve were, by some miracle, still alive and in a foreign hospital, she hoped that he had found a nurse who would care for him as she'd cared for Heinz Schmidt. A girl who would look on him as if he were indeed her brother. And she knew then just why she had felt that extra tenderness towards the young German, and why it was she was going to miss him.

Chapter Twenty-Two

It was only a few days after Heinz Schmidt had been taken away from Haslar that the Portsmouth area was bombed for the second time.

This time, they hit Gosport as well. Screaming out of a blue August sky, two dozen bombers swooped over the beaches and the sea walls to hurl hundreds of black sticks of death and destruction on the city and town which stood on either side of the harbour. To the wail of the sirens, people ran and dived for cover, and the hospital went rapidly through all the colours of the alert, ending up on double red.

Thursday wasn't in the hospital. She and Elsie had been over to visit Elsie's family, and were walking down the ferry slipway when the sirens went. They stared at each other in dismay.

'Where should we go?'

Dave had come with them, for the ride and to have a look at the harbour. He grabbed Thursday's arm. 'There's a shelter up the road – we'd better make for that.'

'I don't like those over-ground shelters,' Elsie said, hanging back. 'I can't see they're any better than anywhere else. Let's get on the pinnace, Thurs – we'll be back in five minutes and we can go down the cellars. You go to the shelter, Dave, we'll be all right.'

Dave was staring at the sky. 'Look at that! There must be a couple of dozen of them. Stukas, I reckon. Look at *that* one, shooting up all the barrage balloons! I always knew they'd never be any good.'

Thursday stared, too. The planes were coming in fast,

quick and lithe as silverfish in the sky, swooping and soaring between the lumbering balloons – and, yes, Dave was right, one of them was shooting the barrage down, clearing the way for the bombers to fly in low. One was coming right at them now – right at the nearby dockyard, right at the railway station.

'Get down!' she shrieked. 'He's going to bomb us – Dave, Elsie, get *down* somewhere.'

'The shelter—'

'There isn't time! Under the steps – up against the wall – anywhere!' It didn't make sense, she knew it dimly, for a wall or a building could fall on you and kill you, but somehow nobody wanted to be in the open. Instinctively, everyone dived for cover, however fragile. One woman even put up an umbrella.

A bomb fell somewhere in the dockyard and the ground shook. Almost immediately there were two separate explosions on the other side of the station, towards Old Portsmouth. Thursday, crouching against the station building, put both hands over her ears. She peered upwards and saw the bombers diving towards Gosport. Haslar, she thought, agonised, don't let them hit Haslar . . . Another explosion rocked the Hard, and she heard Elsie scream. She started to scramble up but Dave was beside her, gripping her arm and forcing her to stay down. She felt his breath, warm on her cheek, and then a blast of hotter air and a huge roar that seemed to knock her flying. Pain shot through her head, and she was conscious of a blur of sight and sound; of flashing lights, of thick black smoke and grey, choking dust; of screams and shouts and yells and shrieks; of the tearing crash of bricks and stone and plaster; and the thudding, pounding, thundering beat of her own blood as it surged in her ears.

She fought for breath, but it was as if the air had been sucked away and there was none left to breathe. Then, like a wave crashing on the shore, it roared back at her and it seemed there was then too much. Her lungs screamed and she gasped and heaved, until heart and lungs and pulses seemed to have won some kind of synchronisation once more, and then she opened her eyes and looked into Dave's anxious face.

'Was that a bomb?' she gasped, thinking with a strange, detached portion of her brain what a silly question that was. 'Have we been hit?'

'I don't know. It was pretty close, I know that.' The roar of the aircraft was diminishing, although explosions could still be heard over the city and harbour. 'I think they got the station with incendiaries.'

'I should just think they bloody did!' Elsie was crawling towards them, her face and shoulders covered with grey dust. 'It's on fire!'

'On *fire*?' Thursday turned her head and saw that Elsie was right. The station was already in flames and the fire engines were coming down the hard, their bells clanging through the din. A squad of ARP men were running from the pavement, shouting to everyone to get out of the way, while the Stukas were still roaring overhead and explosions could still be heard in different parts of the city.

'Get home!' Elsie said urgently to Dave. 'Get *home* and see if our Mum and Eddy's all right. Me and Thursday have got to get back to the hospital.'

'But how—'

'The pinnacc'll take us,' Thursday said, and threw her arms around him suddenly. 'Elsie's right, Dave, you ought to get home. We'll be OK.'

'I dunno. Oh, Thursday, I don't like leaving you here in all this—'

'We'll be all *right*. We *will*. You get back home.' She kissed him quickly and gave him a push. 'Go *on*.'

Without watching to see that he went, she turned away and gripped Elsie's arm. She felt it shake, and hardly knew whether it was Elsie shaking, or herself, or – more probably – both of them. For the first time, she realised that she, too, must be covered in dust. Her dress and sleeves were grey with it, and her eyes and nose felt gritty. 'D'you think we ought to stop and help?'

Elsie shook her head. Her face was white under the grime. 'They'll have plenty of first-aiders. Our job's to get back to Haslar while there's still some boats. The pinnace is there, I saw it, but it won't be hanging about, not in this lot. Come on, Thurs, we'll have to run for it . . .'

Hand in hand, they raced down the slipway to the pontoon. The Gosport ferry was there, rocking on the waves that had been driven in by a bomb that had dropped into the water, but there was nobody on board. The naval pinnace lay against the pontoon's other side, a matelot at the wheel and two anxious VADs and an officer crouching on the seats. The matelot saw Thursday and Elsie, and shouted at them to get a move on.

'I'm not hanging about here any longer. It's too bloody dangerous.'

'All right, you can go now,' Elsie panted, almost falling over the gunwale. 'The most important ones're here.'

'Slowest ones, you mean,' he grunted, spinning the wheel so that the boat moved away from the pontoon. 'Whatcher bin up to, then, loitering around talking to soldiers? Oughter know better.'

'We do,' Elsie said, with an attempt at a wink at Thursday. 'It's marines we're interested in.' She sank on to the seat and pulled Thursday down beside her. Despite her brave attempt at humour, there were tears making dirty runnels down her cheeks and she choked a little.

'Marines!' The pinnace surged away into the harbour. 'Blimey, I'der thought you'd have more taste. And who put that match to the poor old harbour station, eh? Tell me that.'

They looked back over their shoulders. The station was blazing now, smoke and flames billowing into the sky. As they drew further from the shore, they could see smoke rising from all over Portsmouth and Southsea, and when they looked ahead at Gosport they could see that there had been explosions there, too.

'Have they hit Haslar? Don't say they've hit Haslar.' Thursday felt her mouth begin to tremble. 'Oh Elsie . . .'

'It's all right, Thurs. It's all right. And they seem to be going away now.' The planes had disappeared, and only one or two RAF Spitfires were left, circling to make sure none were about to come streaking from the sun. 'Blimey, that was short and sweet, as they say.'

'Twenty minutes.' The officer moved over towards the girls and Thursday saw that it was the young surgeon who had spoken to her about Tony. His uniform was covered in the same dust that had laid itself over the entire harbour station and ferry pontoon; it had smothered itself over his curly light brown hair, making him look as if he had turned suddenly grey, and the gold braid on his cap and sleeves was dull and dingy. 'Are you all right?' he asked them.

Elsie nodded. 'We're OK, sir. We were up by the station when the siren went. I reckon they've done a bit of damage.'

He nodded ruefully and looked at the black, flame-spattered smoke rising from all around the harbour. 'There'll be a fair number of casualties, I should think. We'd better be prepared for some in the hospital.' He looked at Thursday, his blue eyes puzzled. 'I know you, don't I?'

'Tilford, sir. You talked to me about my friend SBA West. He – he died a few weeks ago. He was badly hurt at Dunkirk.'

'So he did. And you've been nursing the young German pilot, haven't you? He spoke very well of you.'

'Did he?' Thursday said in surprise. The pinnace lurched suddenly as the steersman gave the wheel a sharp twist to avoid some floating debris, and she reached out involuntarily and caught the surgeon's arm. 'Oh – I'm sorry, sir.'

'Yes, he did.' Commander Kirkpatrick smiled as she regained her balance. 'He told me you didn't realise he could speak English till that last day.'

'I don't know why he pretended he couldn't,' Thursday said. 'I must have driven him mad, nattering away about this and that all the time. I never said anything I shouldn't have, though,' she added hastily.

'I know. And he wasn't trying to catch you out. He told me that he thought if you'd known he could understand, you wouldn't have chatted to him as you did. He was enjoying it!'

'Blimey,' Elsie said ironically, 'must be the first time anyone's ever said that to you, Thurs.'

'Funny, ha-ha.' The 'raiders passed' signal began to sound over their heads and the matelot gave the engine an extra burst of throttle to celebrate. Thursday glanced at the commander. 'Did – did his last operation go all right, sir? He went to a different ward next day and I didn't see him again.'

'Yes, it went very well. He'll live to fly again – but not until the war's over!' Commander Kirkpatrick grinned and she saw again how boyish that made him appear. 'He's been sent to a POW camp in Derbyshire. Used to be a health and beauty centre – seems appropriate, in a funny kind of way.'

The pinnace was drawing alongside the Haslar jetty. Commander Kirkpatrick nodded at the girls and sprang up on to the jetty, setting off at a run towards the hospital. The girls climbed out, too, and walked quickly along the paved way where trolleys had once been run to take wounded men from the boats to the hospital wards. The slabs were smooth and polished under their feet. They paused for a moment and stared along the quarter-deck, with its avenue of trees, towards the little church of St Luke. They had stopped shaking now and were beginning to recover themselves. The talk with Commander Kirkpatrick had helped, too. He was nice, Thursday thought.

Strong and comforting, and friendly with it, the sort of man you could just talk to, without any side or rank getting in the way.

'I'm glad they didn't hit Haslar,' she said softly. 'It's awful to think of it being bombed and torn to pieces. It's so peaceful – so sort of healing.'

Elsie gave her a sideways glance. She had got over her shock quickly and was always at her most robust when Thursday went what she called 'all poetical'. She gave her friend's arm a punch.

'Well, that's what it's meant to be, isn't it? Healing. It's a bloody hospital, after all. And if you ask me, we'd better go in and sign our names in the book, or Madam'll be after us to know why we're late – and then it'll be *us* what needs healing! And I reckon your friend the Commander's right and all – we're likely to get a few more patients coming our way. Better be on the spot, ready for them.'

She set off quickly through the arcade, leaving Thursday no chance to ask what she'd meant by calling Surgeon Commander Kirkpatrick her 'friend'.

The raid had been a bad one – as well as the fire at the station, the church of St John at Portsea was completely destroyed and a lot of houses were too badly damaged to be occupied. The people who had been made homeless were sent to temporary accommodation, salvaging what possessions they could from their ruined homes. They did their best to sort themselves out, and then went back to work as usual. There was, they said, nothing else they could do.

At Lee, HMS *Daedalus* was bombed. Three hangars were destroyed and over forty aircraft lost. Miraculously, nobody was killed, but the devastation shocked everyone. No longer did the residents of Portsmouth and Gosport glance up casually and shrug when the air-raid warning went, assuming it was yet another false alarm – now, at the first rising wail, they grabbed what valuables they could and scurried into their shelters, either the sunken Andersons that had been built in most gardens, or the overground ones that stood on street corners.

It looked as though the 'fighting in the streets' was about to begin.

As the daylight raids continued, the VADs at Haslar swiftly got used to the yellow, purple and red alerts. If a double red was announced, everyone possible had to be taken down to the basements, and they quickly developed a routine of getting the stretcher cases into the big, creaking lifts. Once, as the hospital shook to bombs falling in the nearby town and thudding into the harbour, the lift got stuck.

'For God's sake,' panted the seaman orderly who had just got in with two beds and four up-patients. 'This is a bloody fine time to be stranded. Who's on maintenance this week?'

'Whoever it is, he's probably all snug and safe down in the basement,' one of the patients said bitterly. 'And mind your language – ladies present.' He nodded at Elsie, who had helped wheel in the beds.

'Oh, don't mind me, I learnt all the words at me mother's knee, and what I didn't know when I come here I've picked up since.' Elsie knelt by one of the beds. 'You OK, mate? It's all right, I reckon we're as safe here as anywhere. Bloody *hell*!' she added as an explosion rocked the big, metal cage. 'That was a bit close.'

'We're a sitting target here,' the patient said. 'That bleeding water tower, it's like a guide for the planes to know where they are.'

'Maybe they won't bomb it, then,' the orderly said, trying to cheer them up. 'Too useful, see. Anyway, they're more interested in the dockyard than a hospital, stands to reason.'

'Oh, yeah? And us right alongside *Dolphin* and all them subs? Use your head, mate, we're front line here and no mistake about it.' Another explosion shook the building.

'Flippin' heck, ain't no one going to try to get us out of here?'

'I'm bothered about my mate in the ward,' said the man on the other bed. He had both arms in slings and a heavy bandage round one thigh. 'Strapped up to one of them Balkan beams, he was, leg up in the air like a cancan dancer, and they just *left* him there. Three of 'em there are, strung up like that, left all on their tods, and what happens to *them* if the hospital gets hit? Tell me that.'

'We did leave a knife to cut them down, if they got to be rescued,' Elsie said. 'I mean, what else can we do? It'd be murder to unstrap them now, and their legs'd break all over again. They could even lose 'em altogether. It's like being between the devil and the deep blue sea.'

'Yeah. And I reckon that's where we are now,' the gloomy patient complained. 'Stuck in this bloody lift. I'm going to need a bottle soon, too. D'you reckon they'll ever get it going again?'

'Course they will,' Elsie said stoutly. 'Don't be such a misery. I can hear people outside now – they're trying to do something. They'll have us out in no time, soon as the raid stops, and then you can have your bottle. It won't be long.'

'That's one thing,' the orderly remarked, backing her up, 'they never seem to last long. Twenty minutes, half an hour, and it's all over. They got our boys chasing 'em by the tail.'

'What's left of our boys,' the misery grumbled. 'Shooting 'em down left, right and centre, they are. My cousin's in the RAF and he says some of the boys coming in now've had hardly any training, and only last a couple of days before they're blasted out of the sky. It's like the Great War over again, cannon fodder, that's what they were then, and sky fodder's what they are now. And I'll tell you another thing—'

'No, you won't,' Elsie interrupted. 'You won't tell us anything more at all. You've told us too much already.

We're supposed to be keeping our peckers up in this war, not spreading alarm and despondency. That's treason, that is. You just shut up, and be grateful you're here in a nice safe hospital with me and the others to look after you, even if we *are* stuck in a lift for the time being.'

'Now, you listen to me—'

'I've told you, I'm not listening to another word, and nor's anyone else.' Elsie looked round at the others, who were nodding agreement. 'I'll tell you what we're going to do, we're going to sing a few songs—'

'Songs! I've sung enough bleeding songs to be at Covent Garden.'

'You don't have to join in if you don't want to. But it'll let people know we're here and we're OK, and it's better than yelling for help. Now then, who's going to start?'

Thursday, struggling down the cellar stairs with a 'special watch' patient on a stretcher, heard the voices and grinned. Trust Elsie to get a party going! She tightened her grip on the handles of the stretcher as another explosion rocked the building above. They really were close today, she thought, nodding at the orderly on the other end to keep going, and she felt a pang of anxiety for the patients left behind. But it was the patient on the stretcher who mattered now. Once he was safely below, she would go back and at least be with those still strapped to their Balkan beams, helpless and alone.

The vast maze of cellars had been fitted out for occupation months before. There were benches all around the walls, space for stretchers and even some beds. A full operating theatre had been set up for emergencies, although there was talk of it being used full time if the raids continued. There were emergency food supplies and a small galley where mugs of tea and wads of cake or sandwiches could be given out.

'Home from home!' Thursday declared, setting the stretcher down. 'It'd take a bomb as big as the moon to get us here.'

She set off towards the stairs, intending to return to the patients left above, but as she slid through the big doors Miss Makepeace materialised from the shadows and put out her hand.

'And where do you think you're going, Tilford?'

Thursday stopped, startled. 'Oh – Madam! I – I was just going to make sure there was no one else who should be brought down.'

'There isn't. I checked that myself.' The bright brown eyes regarded her. 'There are only the trauma patients left. You wouldn't have been going up to stay with them, by any chance?'

Thursday gazed at her helplessly. 'It seems so awful just to leave them there on their own. With all these bombs dropping around them. It doesn't seem right. We're supposed to be looking after them.'

'I know.' The eyes were kind. 'It's a dilemma – which patient needs us most, which to choose when there's a decision to be made. It always will be. But our choice is made for us, Tilford. Our orders are to remain under cover. Remember, the men we treat here are all on active service – even when they're strapped to a Balkan beam.'

Thursday nodded reluctantly and then glanced at Madam again. They were standing just outside the first big pair of doors, in the space of the stairwell. The lift doors were to one side, and they could hear Elsie exhorting her fellow prisoners to pack up their troubles in their old kitbags and smile, smile, smile. Another explosion shuddered through the ground.

'You weren't thinking of going up yourself, were you, Madam?' Thursday asked innocently, and watched the older woman's face break into a smile.

'Thursday Tilford, you're too clever for your own good! Well, I suppose since you've caught me out, I might as well admit that I *was* just going to slip up to see that they were all safe. Only for a moment, mind – I don't intend to break any rules.' She caught Thursday's eye again and Thursday could have sworn she winked. 'Just bend them a little, perhaps. And now I suppose you'll tell the Surgeon Rear Admiral on me!'

'Not if you let me come, too,' Thursday said demurely, and the two of them ran swiftly up the stairs together and into the ward.

It was oddly peaceful up there, in the lull. Almost all the beds were empty, the up-patients' chairs scattered untidily where they had been left when the warning had sounded, and a curtain blew in at an open window. There were three beds still occupied, the men shackled by their ankles to the pulleys.

'Blimey, just when we was getting a bit of peace and quiet,' one of the men remarked when Madam and Thursday appeared. 'Thought we'd seen the back of you lot for a bit.'

Thursday gasped, expecting Madam to reprimand him, for the patients were as much in awe of her as the VADs, but instead Miss Makepeace shook her head and went to close the window, drawing the curtain in case of flying glass. She then went to each bed in turn, looking down at the men.

'You know we can't stay here, don't you?' Another bomb, landing somewhere in Gosport, thundered above her voice. 'We have to go below. But either I or Tilford here will come up every half-hour to see that you're all right. We haven't forgotten you.'

'You're angels, you are,' a skinny, monkey-faced mechanic told her. 'Ruddy angels. But we don't want none of you coming up here, risking your lives, see? What could you do if the roof fell in? Bugger – I mean, nothing. You're better off stopping down below and having a bit of a sing-song. We can hear one goin' on now, sounds lovely, too.'

'That's Elsie – Nurse Jackson,' Thursday said. 'They're stuck in the lift.'

'Stuck in the – well, I'm buggered!' The man forgot to moderate his language and laughed. 'Only happen to her, it could. Wonder who she's got in there with her, then?'

'I'm not sure, but I think I saw Writer Donkett going in.'

'Blimey, she's in for a jolly time, then. Don't say she's got *him* singing an' all!' The man called over to the patient opposite. 'Hear that, Knocker? Old Eeyore's stuck in the lift with Nurse Jackson, and she's got him singin' a roundelay! Wonders'll never cease.' The building shook again. 'Look, love, you'd better get cracking and go below. We'll be all right, and if we ain't we got these knives you so thoughtfully left to cut our throats with!'

Thursday scurried across the ward to where Madam was waiting impatiently, and they both descended the stairs. Elsie and her choir were now embarking on a medley of romantic songs – 'The bells are ringing, for me and my gal' and 'You made me love you', its effect rather spoilt by a raucous voice declaiming 'You woke me up to do it! Woke me up to do it!' at which the entire company in the lift apparently broke down in giggles. Thursday, biting her own lip, glanced sideways at Madam and saw her smile.

'She's a good girl, Nurse Jackson. Understands the importance of morale. And you're a good nurse, too, Tilford. I shan't forget today.'

Neither will I, Thursday thought as she went back to her stretcher patient and made sure he was comfortable before sitting down beside the others. Because today's the day I decided to go for proper training, the minute I can. I'm going to be a registered nurse – perhaps a QARNN – and make nursing my career.

How funny, she thought with amused surprise. Before the war, I never even thought of a career – I did my tailoring apprenticeship because that's what Mum wanted me to do, and so that I'd have a trade to follow if I needed to work when I was older. But I never thought of a *career*.

Girls didn't, did they. Not before the war started, anyway.

Chapter Twenty-Three

Once Percy had walked in on Flo and Denise in the midst of their argument, the whole story had had to be told again. As everyone had known he would be, he was furious and declared that he was going to go round and sort that young man out now, this very minute, no hanging about.

'You can't, Dad! You mustn't.' Denise was in floods of tears again. 'Anyway, you don't know where he lives.'

'I'll find out! I'll go to the post office, that's what I'll do. I'll see his boss and tell him what's been going on. I'll see him sacked from his job, just for a start, and then I'll give him the hiding of his life. He'll not get away with this!'

'It wasn't his fault—' Denise began, but he silenced her.

'Oh, made him do it, did you? I bet you hardly knew what it was all about. Me and your mum have made sure you never heard any filthy talk, pure as the driven snow you were till you started knocking about with that bloke. What was he thinking of, that's what I'd like to know, picking a girl hardly out of school? Aren't there enough girls his own age to go with?'

'He didn't—' Denise began, but this time it was her mother who interrupted.

'He thought she was eighteen, Perce.'

'Thought she was eighteen? Why would he think a thing like that? Couldn't he see for himself?'

'Perce, you know our Denise can make herself up to look older when she wants. She told him that's how old she was, that's why he thought it. You can't blame the chap entirely.'

'I can blame him for doing what he done, whatever age

he thought she was. It's not decent behaviour, Flo, and you know it. People should wait till they're married, same as we did.' He glared accusingly at his daughter.

'We *love* each other—'

'So did your mum and me love each other! But we never went together till your mum had my ring on her finger. I wouldn't have asked it.'

Denise said nothing, and Flo knew she was thinking that they couldn't have loved each other like she and Vic did. All young couples thought that. They all thought they'd invented it, that nobody else had ever felt this way. But telling her that wouldn't help matters.

'It's no good arguing about it now, anyway,' she said. 'What we've got to do is think what to do next.'

'I've told you what I'm going to do next,' Percy growled.

'No, you're not. Sit down, Perce, and let's talk this over like we always do. I'll make a cup of tea. I need one, and I'm sure you do too, and Denise is looking as white as a sheet. She's still got to be looked after, whatever she's done.'

She went out to the kitchen and filled the kettle, then stood trembling beside the stove. I've been expecting this, she thought, ever since Mary told me her Jen had let out that Denise and that feller were talking about secret engagements. I've known it might happen, but I've tried to tell myself I was being silly. I wasn't, though, and I ought to have done something about it before it got this far.

Denise came out and stood beside her. She was crying again.

'I'm sorry, Mum.'

Flo put her arm round her. 'I know, love. I know.'

'I never meant it to be like this.'

'I don't suppose you did,' Flo said with a little sound that was half laugh and half sob.

'It wasn't Vic's fault, honestly.'

'Well, you say that, but it takes two, you know. And he's a lot older than you. He could at least have been careful.'

'Well, he was,' Denise began, and then stopped, embarrassed. 'I mean, he always – he – well, he *said* it'd be all right. Safe. You know.'

'Well, now you know it isn't,' Flo told her. 'There's only one way to know you're safe, and that's to say no. And if you weren't going to do that, he should have been *more* careful. But you never ought to have done it in the first place.'

The kettle began to whistle and she turned to make the tea. Denise slipped past her and went outside to the lavatory. Flo fetched the milk from the meat safe outside the back door, and poured three cups of tea. She put them on a tin tray and carried them into the back room.

Percy was sitting in his chair, staring at the empty fireplace.

'This is a bad job, Flo,' he said as she set down the tray. 'Just as if we hadn't got enough to bear, with losing our Mike.'

'I know, love.' She handed him a cup of tea. 'Here, drink this. I've put extra sugar in.'

'Sugar! I thought we could only have saccharin in our tea now.'

'Saccharin's no good for shock. It's sugar we need.' Flo sat down in her own chair opposite and faced him. 'What are we going to do, Perce?'

'I dunno, I'm sure. It's her age that bothers me. I mean, are the police going to be getting involved? That's what I've been wondering.'

'Perce!' Flo's hand went to her mouth. 'You don't really think they would, do you? I mean, they don't put girls in prison for—'

'No, but they might put the bloke in, and our Denise would have to go to court and testify, and I expect they'd have to have a doctor's report and all that, and—'

'Oh, Perce, no! That'd be awful. We can't let our Denise go through all that.'

'We might not have any choice. Once a doctor sees her . . . Has she been to one yet, d'you know?'

'I don't think so. She'd only just told me about it when you walked in. D'you mean a doctor'd have to tell the police?'

'Well, I don't think he'd have any choice. I don't really know, Flo.' Percy rubbed his hand over his face. 'It's not the sort of thing you take much notice of in the ordinary way.'

The door opened and Denise came in. She looked uncertainly from one to the other and sat on one of the dining chairs that stood against the wall. Flo nodded towards the table.

'Cup of tea there for you, Denise. Drink it while it's hot.' She waited while Denise sipped and then said, 'Your dad and me've been talking about this.'

'Well, I didn't suppose you'd been discussing the weather,' Denise said in an attempt to lighten the atmosphere, and jumped as her father brought the flat of his hand down hard on the arm of his chair.

'And that's enough of that! I won't stand any cheek from you, my girl, we've got trouble enough without any of your funny jokes. There's a lot to think about, and it won't help if you take that attitude.'

'I wasn't—'

'Don't start arguing again, please,' Flo begged. 'Let's just try to sort it out.' She looked at the clock. 'It's getting late. We've missed the nine o'clock news and everything. Why don't we all go to bed now, and get some sleep, and talk about it properly tomorrow?'

'Sleep!' Percy said. 'I don't reckon I'll sleep a wink, and neither will you, Flo.'

'Well, our Denise ought to anyway. Whatever the rights and wrongs of it are, she *is* expecting and she's got to look after herself. You're looking worn out,' she said to her

334

daughter. 'You go on up now, and get some rest. Your dad and me'll think about it.'

Denise nodded. She finished her tea and stood up. Awkwardly, she bent and kissed her mother, then looked at her father and hesitated.

'Oh, come here, for goodness' sake!' he said, reaching up a big hand. 'I've never been that angry with you that I wouldn't give you a goodnight kiss, and I'm not now. You do as your mother says and get a good night's sleep, and me and your mum will think what's best to do. All right?'

Denise hesitated. 'Well . . .'

'Well what? What's biting you now?'

'Well – you won't go round and see Vic, will you, Dad? And you won't get him sacked, or put in prison? Please. Because if you do . . .' Her voice shook. 'If you do, I don't think I'd ever forgive you.'

Percy stared at her. Then he pulled her down and kissed her.

'Just you go to bed,' he ordered her. 'We'll talk about it tomorrow. I won't do anything till we've done that. But don't you try telling me what to do and what not to do, my girl. Just remember you're still under my jurisdiction, and so you will be for the next five years, and *I'll* be the one to decide what happens. All right.'

Denise stared at him. Then her lips trembled again and she turned and ran from the room. They heard her footsteps on the stairs and then her door slammed and they heard the sound of muffled sobbing.

'It's not going to be easy,' Flo said. 'Deciding what to do and making sure it's done – it's not going to be easy, Perce.'

'Nothing's easy these days, Flo,' he said heavily. 'Seems to me, nothing's ever going to be easy again.'

'I know,' she said. 'And while we've all been talking, something else has come into my mind, Perce.' She hesitated, then said, 'Things are so queer these days – with the war and all, none of us knows what's going to happen from one day to the next. And with our Mike going so sudden, and Leslie risking his life every day, and all the bombing – well, our Denise is all we've got, isn't she, in a way. I mean, she's the only one we've got at home. We *can't* turn her out, Perce, we just can't.'

'I know, love. I don't reckon I could have done anyway. Not really.'

'And there's another thing. This baby. It's not just Denise's baby. It's our *grandchild*, Perce. Our first grandchild.' Flo looked at him and tears slid from her eyes and rolled down her cheeks. 'It might even be the only grandchild we're ever going to have,' she whispered. 'We can't let it go to strangers.'

The raids continued throughout the autumn. Once they had started there seemed to be no stopping them. At first they were mostly during the day, but as the days grew shorter they started to take place after dark, and then late into the night. You never knew when they would come over, except that on clear nights people would look at the sky and say it was a 'bomber's moon' that night. No longer a harvest moon or a hunter's moon, Thursday thought sadly, but a bomber's moon. It didn't sound nearly so romantic.

The bright moonlit nights of the autumn were good for Allied bombers, though, as well as the enemy. You could hear them going over – the steady, determined note of the RAF Lancasters, heading off to wreak destruction on Germany. And then the whining, sonorous note of the Luftwaffe Stukas, bringing revenge. London was being especially badly hit, and the news every morning was of fresh destruction. It was as though the whole of Europe would be smashed and destroyed before the conflict was over.

You never knew, when you came out of the shelters after the 'raiders passed' signal, what you would find. A mountain of rubble at your own front door – you might be lucky just to find your front door. The house next door, gone as if it had never been, with nothing but a gaping crater in its place. A changed skyline – a church spire missing, a shop flattened, a fire blazing.

In Gosport, the Market House above the Dive Café was gutted and the electricity company's offices in the high street reduced to a splintered mass. Two houses in Forton Road were smashed to smithereens and every window for a hundred yards on either side blown out, yet a car in next door's front yard remained untouched. At Elson, eight houses were completely demolished and one Anderson shelter blown apart – yet the seven people inside were unhurt, and so were all those who had hidden in the dozen other shelters within a few yards of the wreckage. It just showed, people said when they came to look at it, that the shelters did work, and they gave thanks to Mr Anderson who had designed them.

In Worcester, it was still fairly quiet. The sirens sounded often enough, but it was generally planes going over, heading for Birmingham and the other industrial cities. Places like Worcester and Gloucester, with nothing much but a few local factories like the porcelain or such, wouldn't be of much interest to the Germans. Mind, there were the docks at Gloucester, but Worcester would be all right. Even so, quite a few people took to leaving their homes every evening and trekking down to the riverside and racecourse to sleep out under the stars. They thought that was safer, but it wouldn't be much fun when winter set in.

Vic had finally run out of excuses not to come and meet Denise's parents. Denise hadn't seen him for nearly ten days when she finally caught him, waiting outside the post office until he left work. He looked guilty and uncomfortable when he saw her, but kissed her and let her slip her arm through his and they walked away together, towards the river.

'I was beginning to think you didn't want me any more,' she said after a few moments.

'Don't be daft. Of course I still want you.'

Denise took a deep breath. 'Well, you might not when you've heard what I've got to tell you. Vic – you know what I said about thinking I might be – well, having a baby?' She looked at him. 'I am. It's definite. Next February, probably.'

Vic stopped dead. 'Oh, God. Oh, *God* . . . Denise, are you sure—?'

'I've just told you, haven't I?' Her voice rose shrilly and he glanced uneasily around him. 'Look, I wouldn't make a joke about it, would I? It's not funny. I'm having a *baby*, Vic, and it's *yours*. And we've got to decide what to do about it.'

Vic ran his hand nervously through his dark hair. 'Denise, I don't know, you can't just spring it on me like this—'

'I haven't. I told you weeks ago I thought I might be. You wanted to forget about it, and ever since then you've been either working overtime or going to visit your auntie in Birmingham.' Her glance sharpened. 'I suppose you *have* got an auntie in Birmingham?'

'Yes, of course I have. Auntie Aggie. She's my mum's aunt, actually, so she's really my great-aunt, but I always call her—'

'Vic, I don't care what you call her! What I care about is what you're going to do about me and our baby, and when you're going to come round and see my mum and dad about it.'

'See your mum and – God, Denise, they'll kill me! Your dad'll go up the flipping wall. Here, you haven't said anything to them, have you?'

'Well, of course I have. And Dad was all for going straight round and killing you straight off, only Mum persuaded him not to. And they've been on about it ever since, only I said we'd got to talk to you about it before – before I go to the doctor.'

'You haven't been to a doctor yet? So it's only your family that knows?'

'Mum and Dad know, and so does Auntie Mary, so I suppose Uncle Walter does, too. And Jenny, and—'

'And all the rest of bloody Worcester, by the sound of it,' he said bitterly. 'And all of them wanting my guts for garters. Well, thanks for finally getting round to telling *me*, Denise.'

She stared at him. 'Vic, don't be like that. What was I supposed to do? You're never around – either working late or off up to Birmingham. It seemed to me as if you were avoiding me.'

'Don't be daft.'

'I'm not being daft. Just remember, it was you kept on about secret engagements and said you loved me. But where have you been lately, eh? You knew I was worried, you knew there was a chance, but I've hardly seen you for the past few weeks. It seemed as if you were just trying to get rid of me. What else was I to think? And don't tell me not to be daft again,' she added as he opened his mouth. 'It doesn't matter now anyway. You'll have to make time for me, never mind all this overtime and going to see your auntie. *I'm* the one that needs you, not some old lady thirty miles away.'

Vic ran his hand through his hair again. He looked scared, she thought, and remembered what her parents and Thursday had said.

'They won't really put you in prison, will they, Vic?' she asked anxiously. 'I mean, they wouldn't do that, not if – if we were to get married.'

'*Married*?' he yelped. 'But we *can't* – you're not—'

'I *know* I'm not bloody old enough! D'you think everyone else hasn't told me that till I'm sick of hearing about it? But I will be in October – well before the baby's born. And I think – well, I've got an idea Mum and Dad

339

are coming round to the idea. Look, the police won't do anything to you if we're married, surely – what would be the point? You'd have a wife and baby to support, they couldn't be so cruel. Anyway, you'll probably be called up soon, it would be better to have you in the Army than in jail, I'd have thought.'

'Well, ta very much,' he muttered. 'That's *my* future mapped out – jail or dead. Blimey, not much of a prospect either way, is it.'

Denise was silent. They started to walk again and after a few minutes she said in a very small voice, 'Don't you want to marry me, Vic? Don't you love me any more?'

Vic stopped again and looked into her face. He sighed and put his arms around her and rested his cheek against her hair. She felt small and slight against his body and he felt a sweep of tenderness.

'Of course I love you, you daft ha'porth,' he said. 'Of course I do. And I want to marry you. It's just – well, it's come as a shock, that's all. And I didn't want it to be this way. I didn't really.'

Denise lifted her face and looked at him with shining eyes. He could see the relief in them, the relief and the certainty, and he felt ashamed, and bewildered, and trapped. I can't go back on my word now, he thought. I can't ever go back.

'I don't mind which way it is,' she whispered. 'Just so long as we're going to be together, I don't mind anything.'

Portsmouth fared even worse than Gosport in the raids. It was true that on some nights no one was killed and hardly anyone injured, but on others the casualties were heavy. The gasworks at Hilsea was hit, and nobody could cook anything for days. One of the churches in Copnor, not far from Elsie's home, was destroyed. Pickford's Furniture Store was set ablaze, and so was Government House. An unexploded bomb in the mud of the harbour, where once little boys had begged for pennies to be thrown, stopped the Gosport ferry for nearly a week.

In the middle of November, twenty high-explosive bombs were dropped around the Copnor and North End districts, and one of them fell on Elsie's home.

'They were down the shelter, Mum and Dad and Eddy,' she told Thursday through her tears. 'They were safe. But our Dave – he'd gone up to the house to make a jug of cocoa. It was a quiet spell – they'd almost thought of going back in, the lot of 'em. But Dad said no, and Dave said he'd go and make a hot drink. Mum had a cold or she'd have gone, and then it would have been her. But it was *Dave* – our Dave.'

'Oh, *Elsie.*' Thursday was crying, too. She had been to the house so often, cycling up from the ferry through Portsmouth and North End. Now it was in ruins, all of it. The railway had been hit, Copnor Road was closed, and so was Milton Road. You couldn't get up nor down, Elsie said. 'Oh, Elsie, your Dave – oh, it isn't *fair!*'

They all knew it wasn't fair, and they all knew it was no use complaining about it. But when it was a young chap like Dave, already crippled by illness yet bravely carrying on and living his life, when it was boys like Steve and Mike and Leslie – and even Heinz Schmidt – well, it *didn't* seem fair, and you couldn't help saying so.

'I don't seem to be able to take it in,' Elsie said, shaking her head. 'Our Dave, gone, just like that. We oughter be getting used to it, but – I can't believe it's true, Thurs, I really can't.'

'You've got to go and see for yourself,' Thursday told her. 'That's the only way you'll be able to believe it. And you must want to go and see your mum and dad anyway. D'you want me to come with you?'

'Oh, Thurs, would you? I'd be ever so grateful, and so would they. I've asked Madam if I can have an extra couple of hours tomorrow, and she said I could ask you or

Patsy, too. I don't know what I can do, but I just want to *see* them – you know.'

'I know. Like I wanted to see my family when we heard about Mike. I'll come, Else, whenever you like.' She hesitated. 'There – there'll be the funeral too, I suppose.'

'I suppose so. I hadn't even *thought* about that. Next week some time, probably.' Elsie blew her nose and rubbed her face with her hanky. 'I don't even know where they're going to live. Or how much they've managed to save. It might all be gone – all our clothes and stuff, the wireless Dave made out of crystals, all his Glenn Miller and Ambrose records, and my Frank Sinatras – and Mum's glass ornaments and things what we brought back from the Sunday school charabanc outings – and our Eddy's collection of train numbers – it'll all be gone, Thurs, all of it!'

'I know, I know.' Thursday stroked Elsie's yellow hair. 'It doesn't bear thinking of. We'll go tomorrow and see them. D'you know where they'll be?'

'The lady I spoke to on the phone told me to go to the church hall,' Elsie said dully. 'They're all stopping there, apparently, all them that's been bombed out, while they sorts out places for them to go. I hope they don't get sent too far off, Thurs. Mum's never left Fratton in her life, she just wouldn't settle down anywhere else.'

'She'll be all right.' She'll be too upset about Dave to worry about where she was living, Thursday thought. She went back to the ward, her heart heavy, thinking of the fun she and Dave and Elsie had had together. The bike rides over the hill, to Southwick and Hambledon and up the Meon Valley. The day they'd stopped for a drink at the White Horse at Droxford, and Dave had persuaded Thursday to try a local beer. I'd hardly been able to ride straight the rest of the way home, she thought, half smiling and half weeping at the memory. And there were the summer afternoons at Hilsea Lido, where Dave proved that having one leg shorter than the other didn't have to stop you being a good swimmer and diver. He was like a fish, she thought, remembering how he would disappear beneath the surface and how you wouldn't know where he was till you felt his hand on your ankle . . . Oh, Dave – Dave . . .

She went with Elsie the next day, and found her parents and young Eddy sitting on camp beds in the church hall, their faces grey with misery. It seemed as if everything had been taken away from them – everything but their remaining two children. Mrs Jackson leapt up when she saw Elsie and flung her arms around her, bursting into tears on her shoulder. Elsie, crying too, held her tightly, both patting each other's shoulders as if to give comfort as well as to receive it, while Mr Jackson hovered nearby, anxious for his turn, and young Eddy sat on the flimsy folding bed, staring dully into space, barely seeming to know that they were there.

Thursday dropped on her knees beside him. 'Hello, Eddy.'

He didn't answer. She took the hand that lay limply on one knee and held it to her cheek. It was like ice.

'Eddy, it's me, Thursday. You know me, don't you?'

He shrugged a little but still didn't answer. Thursday gazed at him and then touched his colourless cheek. It was as cold as his hand. His body was shivering.

She pulled a blanket from the next bed, and wrapped it round his shoulders, holding him against her. He turned his head and his eyes searched her face. He seemed totally bewildered, like a baby thrust into a strange environment. She stared at him, feeling pity well up within her, and then drew him close again.

'Oh, Eddy. Poor, poor Eddy. What have they done to you, then?'

He didn't answer; he couldn't answer. Nor did Thursday expect him to answer. She knew that he was in deep shock, that it would take time, and warmth, and comforting words for him to come slowly out of it. But what

343

comfort could you give to a boy who had sat night after night in an underground shelter, listening while bombs pounded the streets where he lived? What comfort could you give to a boy who had come out of the shelter one morning to find his home smashed to rubble and his brother killed?

Thursday held him against her. She rocked him gently to and fro, feeling the ice of his body freezing her own heart, when all she wanted to do was give him some of her warmth; when all she longed to do was give him comfort, although she knew that there was only one thing that would comfort him. And that was the return of the world to the way it had been yesterday.

Chapter Twenty-Four

Things could never be as they had been yesterday. 'Yesterday' meant so much – a day before, a week, a year, a century. Whatever it meant, things could never be the same again. The world changed a little each day, and some days it changed a lot.

Elsie's parents and brother were allotted a house to live in, a small terraced house whose tenants had been evacuated. Mr Jackson tried to persuade his wife to be evacuated too, but she wouldn't hear of leaving him. Who would give him a hot meal when he came home from work, she asked, and who would wash his clothes? But she agreed to Eddy being sent away to the country.

'Mum never liked the idea of Ed going to live with strangers,' Elsie told Thursday as they measured out pills one morning. 'But she says she can't stick the idea of losing another boy, so he's got to go. Tell the truth, I don't think he's all that keen to stop in Pompey anyway. He ain't bin the same boy since the raid, jumps at his own shadow now, he does.'

'It's a shame.' Thursday thought of the bright, cheeky little boy who used to rush to meet her and was now so pale and subdued. 'People don't realise what it's like for kiddies. Some of them are scared stiff.'

'Not all of 'em, though. Most of the nippers in our street think it's some sort of glorified firework display, and they're out after every raid, looking for souvenirs. Boy next door's got half a ton of shrapnel under his bed! I don't reckon it's the bombs that've upset Eddy, it's what happened to our Dave. Thought the world of Dave, Eddy did.'

'I know.' Thursday worked in silence for a while, then said, 'What d'you think of the moves, Elsie? I'm looking forward to going into Theatre.'

Elsie chuckled. 'Fancy your name up in lights, then? You sound like a star-struck actress!'

Thursday made a face. 'Don't think I'm going to get a chance to be a star, down in the basement. Surgeon Commander Kirkpatrick does all his ops there now.'

'You going to be working with him?' Elsie rolled her eyes enviously. 'Coo, some people are jammy!'

'Not at all,' Thursday said defensively, aware of a warmth in her cheeks. 'I don't expect him to take the slightest notice of me. Anyway, I should think he's already spoken for.'

'Yeah, I heard one of the QARNN sisters had got her eye on him. That one with the long ginger hair.'

'She wouldn't like to hear you say that – she thinks it's auburn,' Thursday said. 'Anyway, how d'you know it's long? I've never seen her with her cap off.'

'Yes, you have, she was at that dance at Lee Tower. Here, are we going to the dance at Grange next week? There's invites for anyone that wants to go.'

'I don't know . . .'

'Come on, Thurs,' Elsie said persuasively. 'You haven't been out for weeks. We can't sit indoors and mope for ever, you know.'

'I know.' Thursday washed her hands, staring at the scrap of pink Lifebuoy soap in her hands. Elsie was being braver than she was, she thought. She had cried bitterly over Dave and then just got on with things. Thursday didn't seem able to do that. Maybe there'd been too many young men gone already: Mike dead; Steve still missing and almost certainly dead, too, one of those whose bodies would never be found and whose fate never known; Tony, so horribly wounded, going through operation after operation only to die at the end of them; and now Dave, who had ignored his limp and gone cycling and swimming, always with a joke on his lips and a smile in his eyes.

It wasn't just that. Thursday was worried about her mother. With the weeks and months going by with no news about Steve, Mary Tilford was growing more and more depressed. Her letters were short and, although Thursday could see she was trying hard to be cheerful, there was a thread of sadness through them. It was as if she was losing hope, not just about Steve but about everything. The war's getting her down, she thought. It seemed awful to think it, but it wouldn't be so bad if they knew for certain that Steve was dead. It was this not knowing, the constant wondering, that ate away at your heart.

And then there was her cousin Denise, who was getting married next week. Her mother had written to tell her about it. There wasn't going to be any white dress or cake, and hardly any guests, just the family, and it wasn't even going to be on a Saturday, which was the proper day for weddings – instead, it was going to be a hole-and-corner ceremony on a Friday morning. No one seemed to be looking forward to it   Auntie Flo and Uncle Perce hardly talked about it at all. Denise had brought Vic round to meet Thursday's parents one day and they'd liked him all right, and thought Flo and Percy would too, in time, but it was all the wrong way round, and not the way Flo had wanted it at all.

'Come on, Thursday,' Elsie urged, watching her. 'It'll do us both good. After all, you're luckier than I am. *I'm* not going to be the one down in Theatre with the gorgeous Commander Kirkpatrick. *I'm* going to be in Zymotics, with all the nasty infectious diseases!'

Thursday laughed. 'It doesn't sound so romantic, I agree.'

'It's not. Madam's slipped me the wink that I'm starting on VDs. Nasty little bugs that the boys have picked up on shore leave. You know the Rear Admiral made a stink about VADs working with them, but Madam, bless her cotton socks, put up a fight and said we were as good as any QARNN and ought to be allowed to work anywhere.' She grinned. 'She must have thought she was doing us a favour, I suppose! Truth is, he didn't even like the QARNNs nursing VD cases, said it wasn't right for women to have to do it, but he had to give in since any blokes that are still left are likely to be drafted at any time. Can't leave 'em to fester all on their own, can we!'

'Well, you just watch you don't catch anything,' Thursday warned, and Elsie hooted.

'Only one way to pick that up, didn't you know? It don't come off a lavvy seat, you know. Not like crabs, anyway.' She giggled. 'Someone wrote on the wall in the men's the other day, "Do not sit upon the seat, The crabs in this place jump six feet!" I cleaned it off right away, of course, but I had to laugh.'

Thursday laughed, too, and thought that a year or two ago she wouldn't have even known what the joke was. I've learned a lot since I became a VAD, she thought, and not all of it to do with nursing!

'That's better,' Elsie said, watching her face. 'So you'll come?'

Thursday nodded. 'Oh, OK, Elsie – I'll come.'

Fort Grange stood at the entrance to the local aerodrome and dances were often held there, in one of the empty hangars. A lorry was going from Haslar and the girls scrambled over the tailgate, laughing and looking forward to their evening's fun. Thursday, who had almost backed out at the last moment, had been dragged out by Elsie and Patsy. She climbed aboard quietly and huddled in one corner.

'I'm getting worried about her,' Elsie murmured to Patsy. 'I thought she was cheering up a bit when we talked about coming, but she seems to have slipped right back.

It's as if she just starts to feel better and then it all comes over her again. It's almost like she feels she didn't *ought* to be happy any more.'

'Well, we'll just have to do our best to put some life back into her. Maybe she'll find some nice chap here tonight. That's what she needs, you know. There's been nobody since Tony went.'

'I don't think she was all that serious about him, really,' Elsie observed. 'It was only that he came back in such a mess, and then popped it. Flipping shame, but she can't live like a blooming nun because of it.'

The lorry arrived at Grange and they all piled out and trooped into the hangar. The band was playing Victor Sylvester tunes and the floor was crowded with dancers. The big space had been decorated for the occasion with flags and bunting, and looked very festive. Elsie nodded with approval.

'That's the kind of thing we need. A bit of patriotism to remind us what it's all about. King and country! Land of Hope and Glory! Kick old Hitler up the—'

'All right, Elsie, we know what you mean!' Patsy giggled and gave her friend a push. 'Madam's just over there, look, with Commander Kirkpatrick – you don't want her hearing you, do you?'

'Why not? What's wrong with a bit of patriotism? And I was only going to say "backside". I don't know what sort of a girl you think I am, Patsy Martin.'

'A smasher, that's what *I* think,' said a new voice, and they turned to see a sailor standing close behind them. He was an electrician and had been checking the wiring in Elsie's ward, so they'd already exchanged a bit of banter. He grinned and held out his hand. 'Want to dance?'

'That's what I'm here for,' she responded, and they swung away into a foxtrot. Another sailor pulled Patsy into the throng and Thursday was left alone.

She stood hesitating for a moment, then slipped along the wall to an empty chair and sat down. She felt lonely and out of place. I shouldn't have come, she thought. I'm not in the mood for dancing. I don't seem to be in the mood for anything just lately.

Someone came and stood in front of her, and she looked up. It was Commander Kirkpatrick, and he was smiling down at her.

'Will you give me the pleasure of this dance?'

'Oh . . .' Thursday scrambled to her feet. 'It – it's very kind of you, but I'm really quite all right – I mean, my friends will be back soon and—'

'I'm not taking pity on you,' he said with amusement. 'I'm asking you to dance because I'd like it.'

Thursday felt her blush rise. Thank goodness the lights were dim! She went into his arms and they moved off into the fast, intricate steps.

Thursday loved dancing, and Commander Kirkpatrick was good at it. He led her firmly into manoeuvres she had never attempted before, but because his guidance was so sure, she found them easy and fun. She liked the way he held her, too – lightly but confidently, with none of the clumsiness of some of the partners she'd had at other dances. She smiled at him as he took her back to her seat, and thanked him.

'That was lovely.'

'I enjoyed it, too. I hope you'll give me another dance before the evening's over.'

Patsy and Elsie were already there. They gazed at her, and Thursday coloured.

'There's no need to look like that. He was just being kind.'

'Looked as if he was enjoying it, all the same. And what lovely manners! "Hope you'll give me another dance before the evening's over." Not like my bloke, he just said "Ta, see you later" and sloped off.'

'Well, some of us attract a better class of partner,' Thursday said innocently, and Elsie hooted.

'That's one in the eye for you, Pats! Anyway, he seems

350

to have bucked our Thursday up a bit, so it's all to the good. Listen, that's a quickstep. Look lively, or we won't get asked.'

There was no question of not being asked to dance. The hangar was crowded with sailors and local boys who were all eager to hold a girl in their arms for a few minutes. The girls found themselves besieged, and by the interval they were all breathless and ready for a rest.

'It's a smashing dance.' Elsie declared. 'Just what we needed to take us out of ourselves a bit. I saw you dancing with Kirky again, Thurs.'

'Only once. It was another foxtrot. He's a good dancer, I'll say that.'

'Maybe you could take a turn or two round the theatre in a quiet moment,' Patsy suggested. 'You're moving down there on Monday, aren't you?'

'Yes, and I don't suppose he'll even recognise me, so you can take that look off your face, Patsy Martin! *And* you, Elsie Jackson. You notice I'm not making a lot of remarks about your partners.'

'Well, they're not as interesting as yours. Except for that tiffy I did the square tango with, he was a bit of all right. Radio ops, he is, from *Collingwood*. I wouldn't mind doing a bit more with him.'

'Well, I expect you'll get the chance, there's another two hours to go.' The band was striking up again and Thursday looked up as Commander Kirkpatrick approached and held out his hand. The other two girls watched as the couple moved away, Thursday almost floating in the commander's arms.

'I don't care what she says,' Patsy remarked, 'I bet he *will* notice her in the theatre. Three times in one evening – and two hours still to go! Don't tell me he's just being kind.'

The dance was a waltz, and there was more time for partners to talk to each other. Thursday, feeling suddenly

351

shy, said nothing but after a moment or two the commander spoke in her ear.

'You're a very good dancer, Nurse Tilford.'

'Thank you,' she said. 'I love it – always have. I wanted to be a ballet dancer when I was little, but I dare say most little girls want that.'

'I don't know. My sister always wanted to be a circus rider!'

They laughed. Then he said, 'D'you have any sisters? Or brothers?'

'Yes.' Thursday paused for a moment. 'A younger sister, Jenny. And – and a brother. But he was reported missing at Dunkirk and we haven't heard any more about him.'

He looked at her. 'You mean you don't know if he's alive or not?'

'He was "missing, believed killed". And now it's five months and we still haven't heard, so . . .' She shrugged. 'It'd be better in a way if we knew for certain that – that he was dead. It's not knowing that's the awful part.'

'Of course it is. I'm really sorry.' They danced in silence for a few moments, then he said quietly, 'I had a brother at Dunkirk, too. He was on one of the ships that was sunk. So we're in much the same position over that.'

'Oh that's awful. I'm sorry, too. Was he a doctor as well?'

'Yes. Runs in the family – our father was a surgeon captain when he retired. He went into general practice in Devon then, and lives in a village on the edge of Dartmoor. Pillar of the local community and all that – he's very involved in local defence, Home Guard and so on. And my mother's a leading light in the local WVS, so they're both doing quite a lot in the way of war work. It's a good thing – takes their minds off Stephen.'

'Stephen? Was that your brother? My brother was called Stephen, too, only we always shortened it to Steve.'

'Well,' he said, 'that's a coincidence, isn't it? We seem to have quite a bit in common.'

Thursday didn't think that their both happening to have a brother with the same name exactly counted as having a lot in common, even if both had been lost – or missing – at Dunkirk, but she smiled anyway, and they went on dancing. After a few moments, just before the dance came to an end, he spoke again.

'You're coming into theatre next week, I believe.'

'Yes, sir.'

He glanced at her. 'Why the "sir" all of a sudden?'

'Well – I didn't realise you knew me, before. I was just a dancing partner. But now you know who I am, and you know I'll be working for you, so it's different.'

'Not while we're off duty and dancing together,' he said. 'And that reminds me, I don't like calling you "Nurse Tilford". You must have another name.'

'Well, yes,' she said reluctantly, and then, as he looked at her expectantly, 'It's Thursday, actually.'

'*Thursday?*'

'Yes. I was born on Armistice Day, you see, in 1918, so my parents thought they ought to give me a special name. My first name's Rosemary for Remembrance but they've never used it, and I've always been Thursday.'

'So it's your birthday the day after tomorrow – and you'll never be able to hide your age!' He grinned at her, and she laughed. 'Thursday,' he repeated, as if tasting the word. 'It's a nice name. And it's certainly unusual.' The music came to an end and they stood for a moment looking at each other. Then he smiled.

'And my name's Connor. So now we're equal, all right? When we're dancing, anyway.'

'Yes,' Thursday said uncertainly, wondering if he really meant her to call him by his name, and he smiled again and led her back to her seat. But this time he didn't leave her there. He stayed with her and asked her for the next dance as well, and the one after that.

Towards the end of the evening, he gave her a rueful smile and said, 'I'll have to go and do my duty again, I'm afraid, Thursday. But I've really enjoyed dancing with you. We fit very well together.'

Thursday coloured and smiled. 'I've enjoyed it, too. Thank you . . .' She hesitated.

'Don't you dare,' he said, reading her mind. 'Don't you dare say "sir". I've told you my name. You haven't used it at all, but you might do it now. Just to say goodnight.'

Thursday bit her lip, feeling the colour rage into her cheeks. She took a deep breath. They might have been dancing all evening, but it still took a bit of daring to use an officer's first name.

'Goodnight, Thursday,' he said, smiling, and held out his hand. 'And I hope you have a happy birthday.'

She took it, feeling suddenly shy, and felt the warm strength of his fingers. It was oddly comforting and her shyness fled.

'Goodnight, Connor,' she said, and smiled back into his eyes. 'It's been a lovely evening.'

He nodded and took her back to her seat, and this time he left her there and a few minutes later she saw him dancing with the QARNN sister with the long, auburn hair.

Connor Kirkpatrick, she thought. It was a nice name. Different. Classy. But, then, he *was* a commander – way out of her class. And on Monday he would be her boss, and there would be no question of first names or special smiles. They would be there to do a job, and he wouldn't take the slightest bit of notice of her.

She wouldn't even expect him to.

There hadn't been a raid over Gosport or Portsmouth for nearly two weeks, and even over London the raids didn't seem to be quite so bad. People began to think that perhaps the Germans were slowly giving up, or maybe even running out of ammunition. Or perhaps, as Elsie said, just getting ready for the real invasion – the one that would come by sea.

'And all that barbed wire they've put up along the beach won't stop 'em,' she said as they collected their lunch in the mess. 'Few pairs of wire cutters'll soon sort that lot out.'

'Oh, yeah, and we're going to stand by and let 'em, aren't we!' Patsy argued. 'What about the gun emplacements? What about the Army and the Marines? And the RAF? They won't get within an inch of Stokes Bay, nor anywhere else round the coast.'

Thursday listened in a dream. She was still thinking of the dance at Grange the night before, still whirling round the floor in the arms of Connor Kirkpatrick – *Commander* Kirkpatrick, she reminded herself sharply. From tomorrow, he was going to be her boss and she'd better put paid to any other dreams she might have had. It was a dance, nothing else, and he wouldn't even know her in her mask and gown.

'Coming for a bike ride this afternoon?' Elsie asked. 'We could go round Stubbington and Titchfield, maybe call in on Gran for a cuppa. It's a nice afternoon, hardly cold at all.'

Thursday nodded. The trees had turned a glorious golden brown but the leaves would soon be gone and winter beginning. She loved autumn – it was her time, after all – and a day like today, with the sun lighting up the mellow colours and a soft blue sky fading into an early dusk, was far too good to stay indoors.

She ate her lunch absently, thinking of all that had happened during the past year. It was her birthday next day – she would be twenty-two. It seemed far more than a year since the party at home, when Dad had given her that huge key and everyone had sung over the cake Auntie Flo had iced. She had never dreamed then that she would be a nurse, here in Haslar Hospital, or that her brother Steve would be missing somewhere in France, her cousin Leslie flying Spitfires, Mike dead and Denise getting married.

Mum'll be feeling it even more tomorrow, with me away as well, she thought. I ought to have tried to get home this weekend. I ought to have told Madam it was my birthday and that things are difficult there. I ought to have done something about it . . .

The wail of the air-raid warning split the air. The girls looked at each other and hesitated. Was this going to be red, a double red or just a yellow? But almost before the sound had died away, the signal came for a double red, and they leapt to their feet and made for the wards.

On duty or not, everyone turned to for a double red. There were patients to be got out of their beds, on to stretchers if they couldn't walk, and down into the cellars. Meals were left on the table, books and newspapers flung down to be retrieved later, and the entire hospital thrown into orderly turmoil. Almost before the first planes came over, everyone who could be got down below was there, safe from the bombs that would soon begin to fall.

'Sunday bloody dinnertime,' a patient grumbled as a friend helped him down the stairs. 'Don't we never get no peace?'

'Not flaming likely in wartime, mate!' his pal said caustically. 'That's what it's all about, innit? And our lads are givin' as good we get, you can depend on that. I bet there's Germans havin' to leave their Sunday dinners an' all.'

Thursday, still in the ward with some of the trauma patients, looked out of the window. She could see planes coming in fast over the Island, a black cloud of them. Fascinated, she stared as they came nearer, so low that she ducked instinctively as they passed almost directly over-head. She dropped to the floor and froze, waiting for the explosion. Surely they wouldn't pass a complex like Haslar without bombing it. But the planes roared overhead, so close that she thought they must brush the roofs with their undercarriages. And then they were gone and, almost immediately, the expected explosion rocked the building.

'Blimey,' said a nearby sailor with his leg strapped up. 'That was bloody close.'

'It was.' Cautiously, Thursday raised her head. The planes were coming round again and she flattened herself once more. What were they aiming at?

'*Thursday*!' The voice jerked her head up again. 'What the hell are you doing here? Why aren't you down in the cellars?'

'Connor!' She remembered where she was, in a ward if not officially on duty, and hastily amended it. 'Sir! I was just—'

'You were just being a bloody heroine!' he said angrily, and then dropped to the floor beside her as another explosion rattled the windows. 'Makepeace told me about you, slipping back up here during the raids. What good's it going to do the patients if you're killed? You ought to be down below, with the others.'

'I was going to. They came so quickly.' She looked into his face. It was oddly intimate, lying here beside him on the floor. 'Where are they bombing, sir? It sounds ever so close.'

'Grange,' he said briefly. 'That's what it looks like, anyway. You could see them from the other side of the hospital, making their run in along Cambridge Road. They're after the aerodrome.'

'But there's a big ammunition dump there too,' she gasped. 'If that goes up—'

'I know. And if people are hurt, they'll be brought here. They're going to need nurses – live ones. So for God's sake, get down below. *Now*.'

'They'll need doctors, too,' she said boldly, and gave him a challenging look. 'Are you coming as well?'

'For crying out loud,' said a voice above them, 'either go or shut up about it. It's Sunday afternoon, for Gawd's sake – can't a bloke have his blooming siesta?'

Thursday and Connor looked at each other in surprise. They'd almost forgotten there were other people around them. Connor's lips twitched and Thursday began to giggle.

Commander Kirkpatrick stood up and regarded the sailor. 'I could put you on a charge for talking to an officer like that,' he said severely. 'But I'll let it go – just this once. Provided you can persuade this recalcitrant VAD to be sensible and go down below. Because *I* don't seem to have any influence with her.'

The sailor grinned back at him. 'With all due respect, sir, I'd say you had. And I'd say she was right, too – you ought to be below as well.' Another violent crash shook the ground. 'Bloody hell, it *hurts* when they do that!'

Connor grabbed Thursday's wrist. She shook herself free angrily. 'I can't, sir! Not when the patients are suffering.'

He grabbed her again. 'You can't do anything to help them. You can't stop the bombs shaking the place about. What use are you going to be if you end up in a hospital bed yourself – or worse?' Another bomb fell. 'Tilford, if you don't come down below this minute, I'll put *you* on a charge! And never mind what your Miss Makepeace says. And it'll be insubordination, and nothing less.'

Thursday stared at him. Their eyes locked. She felt fury blaze up from her breast, flaming brightness into her cheeks and eyes. She wanted to defy him, to jerk her wrist from his grip, but his fingers were tight and strong and she knew she was beaten. He had rank, power and sheer brute strength on his side. She turned and gave the patients an apologetic look. The one in the nearest bed grinned and gave her a thumbs-up.

'You go on, love,' another one called out. 'Get down below, where it's safe. And give the rest of the buggers our love while you're there.'

'I'll be back the minute it stops,' she promised, but Connor gave her arm a fierce jerk.

'Come *on*, Tilford.' He hauled her out of the ward and along the corridor to the landing. They ran down the wide stairs to the cellars, and he paused and looked at her. 'I hope to God you're going to be a bit more disciplined when you're on theatre duties,' he said harshly. 'I can't work with nurses who won't do as they're told.'

Thursday stared at him. It was as if their encounter on the dance floor had never happened. The man who had held her in his arms and talked softly in her ear and seemed to understand about Steve and Mike had disappeared, leaving a coldly efficient surgeon who was prepared to cut out anything that didn't work – including his theatre nurses. Including her.

Her eyes filled with tears and her lips trembled. Connor sighed and put his hand on her arm.

'Don't look like that, Thursday. It has to be this way, don't you understand? We're here to do a job, and we've got to look after ourselves so that we can go on doing it. Not for selfish reasons but because we're pieces of *equipment*, if you like. *And you must obey when an officer gives you an order* – whatever it is. Yours is not to reason why – haven't you heard that?'

'Yes, sir,' Thursday said, staring at the floor. 'Ours is but to do or die.'

'Exactly. Except that I don't want you to die. I really don't.' He put one finger under her chin and lifted her face so that she was forced to meet his eyes. 'That isn't in my plan at all,' he said quietly.

Another bomb rocked the floor. Thursday jumped and Connor's hand slipped down to her shoulder and gripped her tightly. They stared at each other and then he said, 'Get below. And this time, *stay there*.'

359

Chapter Twenty-Five

Getting the patients back to the wards when the 'Raiders passed' signal sounded was even worse than getting them out. Everyone was tired after the ordeal of getting them down to the cellars, the sense of urgency was gone and the men were fractious and upset. For some of them, any movement meant pain of some degree, and to think that there had been no need for it, as they arrived back in wards that looked just the same as when they'd left them, seemed to be an added insult.

Even worse was the fact that those who had been left strapped to their beams had the laugh on them. 'Here they come, out of their burrows . . . Been nice and peaceful up here without you lot . . . Had a nice afternoon down in the mines, have you? Brought us up a shovelful of coal for the stove?'

But the news that Grange had been bombed and that there was a hangar ablaze beside the moat that separated it from Fort Rowner subdued everyone. 'We were there only last night,' Elsie whispered to Thursday. 'A few hours earlier and we could've been in that hangar.'

'You mean it was the one they had the dance in?'

'So they say.' Elsie shivered. 'I dunno, Thurs, what with this and the raid over the station, we seem to be getting nearer and nearer to these bombs. About as near as I want to get, too. I hope we don't get a double red tonight. I couldn't face hauling them all down below all over again.'

However, Elsie was to be disappointed. Just as she and Thursday got into bed a few hours later, the scream of the siren rose yet again. Everyone groaned and waited for the alert – yellow, purple or red – and then stared at each other as the sound of bells took over from the dying wail.

'That's church bells!' Thursday whispered. 'It must be Alverstoke – they've got bells there, haven't they?'

'St Mary's, yes.' Elsie nodded. 'You know what this means!'

'*Invasion* . . .'

The whisper ran round the dormitory, and then the whole room exploded into life. The girls leapt from their beds, grabbed shoes and coats, ran for the doors. Clad in an assortment of pyjamas and nighties, they scurried along the corridors and downstairs, out of D Block and across the quarter-deck to the main hospital. No matter that they were off duty – the patients came first. No matter that the Germans might even now be landing on the sea wall and Stokes Bay beach – the sick and injured must be made safe. No matter that the girls themselves might be at terrible risk – the men who had put their own lives at risk, weeks or months before, must be cared for and protected.

They arrived to find people already thronging the stairs – up-patients, doctors, VADs and QARNNs, all working to carry the stretcher cases to safety. Thursday caught sight of Miss Makepeace and the Surgeon Rear Admiral struggling with a huge stoker on a stretcher that looked as if it had been stretched just as far as it could go. Connor passed without seeing her, an injured man's arm looped over his shoulders. Patsy was guiding a sailor whose eyes were bandaged, and Helen Stanway was helping Sister Burton to manoeuvre a trolley into the lift. But there was no more time to notice who was passing. Swinging into a routine that was becoming all too familiar, Thursday and Elsie went into the ward and began getting men out of bed again, men who had already been hauled out once that day and were now becoming bitterly resigned to being dragged up and down the stairs and in and out of the lifts at the behest of a screaming, banshee siren.

At last they were all safely below. The men rested on their trolleys and stretchers, the doctors and nurses found spaces to sit where they could. And then they waited.

They didn't know whether they were waiting for the signal that the skies were clear and it was safe to emerge again, or whether they were waiting for the invaders that were expected to storm the beaches. They didn't know whether they were waiting for life, or for death.

There was nothing else to do but wait.

There had been no invasion. Nobody ever really knew who had given the signal for the bells to be rung, but St Mary's was not the only church to have sounded its warning. And the rumours next day told of hundreds of German soldiers, drowned and washed up on Stokes Bay beach. Or down in the New Forest. Or perhaps it was Brighton.

Or perhaps all three. Or none of them at all. Whatever the truth, the rumour persisted, yet strangely the fear of invasion receded. It was as if everyone felt that the invaders had indeed been beaten off, and a small feeling of victory lifted Gosport hearts. People told stories of having gone out with guns, to fight as Churchill had said, on the beaches and in the streets. The Pioneer Corps and Home Guard, pitifully unarmed, had marched up Clayhall with broomsticks and garden tools. You could do a lot of damage with a spade or fork or hoe in hand-to-hand combat, one elderly allotment-holder remarked cheerfully. ''Specially if you'd been in the last lot, and trained with a bayonet . . .'

Those children still at home came out into the street, too, with scraps of red, white and blue ribbon fastened to sticks; one or two even had real Union Jacks. They marched the streets singing 'Rule Britannia' and 'Land of Hope and Glory', and 'Run, Rabbit, Run'. They shouted 'God Save the King' and stood to attention, their grubby hands held to their foreheads in salute. They got as near as they could to the gun emplacements and begged to be allowed to climb on the guns, and have a go at firing them.

None of the soldiers had the heart to tell them to go away. Everyone was too well aware of what might have become of these same children if the invasion had really happened.

Thursday, reporting for her first duty in the operating theatre down in the cellar, felt both elated and subdued. It's as though we've actually won, in some queer way, she thought. Yet we haven't won at all, really. We're in as much danger as ever we were. In other ways, it feels as if we've hardly started.

By the end of the week, she knew just how true that thought was. For on Friday, 15 November, the day of Denise's wedding, the city of Coventry was razed to the ground and its great cathedral left nothing but a shell.

'I had an auntie and uncle in Coventry,' Patsy said, her face white. 'I don't know what'll have happened to them. You say it's all gone, Thurs?'

'So the papers say. Look at these awful pictures — street after street, just knocked to bits, and people picking their way through the rubble like refugees. Well, I suppose that's what they are, really. They say there's thousands just walking out of the city, with nothing but a few bags or a pram or barrow with their things in, looking for somewhere to stop. They've got nothing left, nothing. It's terrible.'

'My Uncle Tom would never be able to do that,' Patsy said. 'He's got arthritis in both knees, he can hardly walk. And they can't afford a wheelchair. They don't even go down the shelter . . . What's he going to do, Thurs? Whatever's he going to do?'

Thursday didn't know. She couldn't begin to imagine what the citizens of Coventry were going to do, with their homes torn away from them, their great church smashed to pieces, their city nothing more than rubble. And it didn't help to know that people in Germany were being bombed in the same way. That there were families trudging the ruined streets in Berlin and other cities, their homes destroyed, all that they loved gone for ever. Furniture they'd scrimped and saved for. Best teasets. Sheets and blankets, tables and chairs. Photos. Pets. All blasted away to nothing – and for what?

Because of one man's greed for power. And because none of the men and women who were supposed to lead the world had been able to stop his onslaught.

There ought to be another way, she thought. There *must* be another way.

'I don't know, Patsy,' she said sadly. 'I don't know what your uncle's going to do. But there'll be people to help him and your auntie. They won't be left to stay out in the streets.'

A few days later, Patsy heard that her uncle had survived the bombing, crouched beneath the stairs of his little two-up, two-down house, and had managed to stagger down the ruined street in search of help for his wife, trapped beneath a beam. But by the time they got back, she had died, and now Patsy's heartbroken uncle had been taken to stay with Patsy's parents in Evesham. 'Where they ought to have gone in the first place,' Patsy said through her tears. 'Mum asked them often enough, she begged them to go, but the obstinate old man wouldn't have it that Coventry was in any danger, no German was going to make him run away, he said. And now poor Auntie May's dead.'

There were tears in plenty as November dragged on. Only a few days after Coventry's destruction, Haslar found itself on red alert again as planes snarled overhead and dropped more bombs on the town. Shops and offices in the high street were ruined, and a house in Alverstoke village reduced to rubble. And a Wrens' billet in Lee-on-the-Solent was destroyed, killing eight young Wrens sleeping inside and injuring others.

They were brought to Haslar, and Thursday found herself assisting at operations on several. She looked at the young faces with sorrow. As Madam had said when they first began their training, the VADs would learn to get used to seeing people in pain, but this was different. Until now, their patients had been mostly serving men, wounded in action. These were girls, some of them no more than seventeen or eighteen, and their injuries seemed all the more cruel.

'Will you be going to the funerals?' Commander Kirkpatrick asked her as they watched the last young patient being wheeled out of the theatre. 'The ones who died – they're being buried in our cemetery, you know.'

'Yes. They've asked us all to go, if we can. I want to – but I'm afraid it will make me cry.' She gave him a wavering smile. 'I just hope no one looks at me.'

They had had no conversation since Thursday had begun work in the theatre – there had been no time. After his words during the raid, Thursday had been determined to prove her worth as a nurse, and had striven to remain cool and efficient, waiting for the theatre sister's orders and carrying them out swiftly. Although they were in the same room, her work with the autoclave kept her away from the operating table and she had barely encountered Connor himself unless they had passed in the doorway or stood together at the basin as Connor scrubbed up. And although she knew that at those times he was remote from everyone, concentrating on what he had to do, she couldn't help feeling hurt by his lack of attention and had begun to believe that the warmth she had felt in him on the dance floor had been no more than a dream.

Now, suddenly, she sensed that warmth again.

'I think it will make a lot of us cry,' he said quietly. 'Young girls like that, thinking they were safe to sleep . . . it seems so unfair.'

'It *is* unfair,' she said passionately. 'All these people being killed – nearly all of them are young, too. My brother, my cousin, these Wrens – and hundreds of others. Thousands, probably.' She looked up at him with angry eyes. 'What do they do, count them and see who's got most left – if there are any left at all? And who's supposed to build the brave new world they talk about, when all the young people have gone? It'll be just old men and children. Where's the *sense* in it?'

'Shh,' he said, touching her arm. 'Don't let yourself get upset, Thursday. You're tired. And we all wonder these things, but there's nothing we can do about them. We just have to grit our teeth and carry on. Eventually, they'll sit down and talk, and it'll be all sorted out. Eventually.'

'Yes,' she said, 'that's what they did last time. On the day I was born. And what happened on my birthday this year? Grange was bombed, just a few hours before, and we spent the night in the cellars, waiting for an invasion. And that's how well they sorted it out the *last* time!'

Connor sighed. 'Well, let's hope they do better when they finally sit down to sort this lot out.' He looked at her. 'And did you manage to celebrate your birthday at all?'

'She shook her head. 'I forgot all about it, till the end of the week. When Coventry was bombed, I looked at the date, and realised . . . So much had happened . . . I just didn't have any heart for it. What does a birthday matter, when people are being killed?'

'I know,' he said, 'but you ought to celebrate it, all the same. Birthdays do still matter. Why not come out and have some tea with me?'

Thursday looked at him, startled. 'But – I couldn't do that, sir! I mean, you're a surgeon and a – an officer, and I'm just a VAD. And I'm one of your theatre nurses.'

'I don't think that need matter. What about tomorrow afternoon – after the funerals? I have a feeling you're going to need a little cheering up.'

Thursday bit her lip and looked down. Tears crept into her eyes. She had seen funerals already, in the cemetery close to the hospital grounds, and she had even attended some, when the person had been a patient she had nursed, but the funeral of eight young women, even though they were unknown to her, was something she knew would be hard to bear.

'I don't know if I'll want to go out,' she said in a small voice. 'I think I might just want to go – go to bed or something.'

'And cry,' he said. 'And brood. No, Thursday, it'll be better if you come out with me. Just for a little while, just to be somewhere different, between different walls. It'll do you good.' He paused, and then added, 'I could make it an order if you like. And so I will, if you insist on calling me "sir" when we're off duty!'

Thursday smiled. She looked up at him and nodded.

'All right. I'll come out with you.' She paused, then added with a straight face, 'Sir.'

Their eyes met. He inclined his head and smiled back, and the warmth was there in his eyes once again.

Thursday looked at the trees, standing with bare branches around the graveyard as the funerals of the eight young Wrens was conducted by the Haslar chaplain. The leaves had fallen without her even noticing them. It was almost as if the trees had wept them away during that terrible fortnight.

Grange. Coventry. The Wrens. And countless other casualties, too. Portsmouth, Southampton, Bristol, Birmingham, Liverpool – all the major cities had been bombarded. And poor London – you wondered how the people there were managing, with the city being blown to pieces night after night, never knowing where the bombs would fall or the fires blaze. Thursday had heard that everyone just went to their shelters as a matter of course every night now, and since many of them didn't have shelters they went to the Underground stations instead and slept on the platforms. Bunks, they'd got down there, she'd heard, and tea-urns and even little libraries so you could get a book to read if you couldn't sleep . . .

She heard the chaplain's voice saying the grace and came back with a start to the cemetery. The coffins had been lowered into their graves, and the earth scattered over them. A few flowers had been tumbled in last, and as the mellow voice faded, there was silence.

A woman sobbed somewhere, and a blackbird burst into unexpected song. Someone whispered that it was the girls' souls being received into heaven, and then everyone began to move. Thursday, her eyes full of tears, turned away from the graveside and found herself face to face with Surgeon Commander Kirkpatrick.

'Oh – sir, I'm sorry, I didn't know you were there.'

'It's all right.' He touched her arm. 'Are you all right, Thursday?'

'Yes.' She brushed away her tears. 'Just – you know.'

'I know. It seems so cruel – eight young women, killed as they slept. I went in to see the others this afternoon – the ones we've been operating on, and another couple who are still in bed. They're being very brave, but it's hit them hard. They just want to get back to service as soon as possible.'

'You'd think they'd be frightened,' Thursday said, but he shook his head.

'It doesn't seem to work that way in wartime. Seeing your mates killed . . . just makes you all the more determined. And now, what about that cup of tea?'

Thursday drew back a little, aware of the other people moving around them. Patsy and Elsie were there some-where, and the other VADs and QARNNs. And there were officers, too, who must be wondering why Commander Kirkpatrick was so interested in a little VAD. She started to shake her head.

'I don't know. Perhaps it would be better not—'

'Now, don't start having second thoughts. Remember, I said I'd make it an order if I had to! Come on, it's a pleasant enough afternoon, we'll walk out to Lee. You've got time, haven't you? We can catch a bus back.'

'Yes, sir – I mean . . .' She floundered into silence and he smiled.

'All right, I'll let you off that one. While we're on the premises. But as soon as we're safely out of earshot, I expect you to stick by our agreement yesterday. It's Connor, all right?'

They walked down Clayhall Road to Anglesey and then along to Lee. Thursday thought of the day she and the other girls had cycled out here for the first time, and met Tony and Roy and Doug. That had been the first of many teas in the little café opposite the Tower. She remembered the time she'd lost her temper with Doug about some silly joke, and had flounced out, and wondered how she could ever have thought such a thing important enough to lose her rag over. Now Tony was dead, and Roy somewhere in the Mediterranean, and Doug – she'd lost touch completely with Doug, had no idea where he was.

'Penny for them?' Connor asked, and she jumped and came back to the present.

'Sorry. I seem to keep drifting off this afternoon. I was just thinking how much has happened in the past year. I volunteered straight after my birthday – they only take you once you're twenty-one, so I couldn't before – and then I had to do extra training before I was posted here. And since then . . .' She shook her head. 'Sometimes, I just can't believe it all – can't seem to take it in, somehow.'

'I know. It was all so quiet to begin with – the war was being fought mostly at sea, and the threat of invasion and the bombing just didn't seem to happen. But now they've started, it's even worse than we thought. And there's more to come, I'm afraid.'

She looked at him. 'D'you think we're going to be invaded? Last week – did it really happen? Were there really hundreds of bodies washed up on the beaches? I don't see how—'

'I think it was just rumours. How could it be hidden – *why* should it be hidden? If there really had been so many, something would have had to be done about them, and it's something we'd want the Germans to know about. A victory for us.' He shook his head. 'But there's no doubt that the bombing happened. We've seen that for ourselves.'

Thursday thought of the eight young Wrens who had just been buried, and nodded soberly. No older than she was – some even younger. It was so tragic. So cruel. And we're doing the same over there, she thought. Somewhere in Germany, there are people walking away from the funeral of other young men or women, and wondering just what was the point of it all.

'How long is it going to last?' she asked. 'How long can we go on like this, being bombed day after day – night after night? I don't see how people can stand it.'

'I don't think we have much choice,' he said. 'And that's the point of it, isn't it? Go on hammering us until we can't take any more. What we've got to show the world is that we *can* take it.' He looked down at her. 'I had to go to London a few days ago – you remember, when Commander Peters took over my duties. The damage there is just incredible, yet all over the bombed and boarded buildings people have painted signs. Slogans like "Go Home, Hitler" and "Britain Can Take It", or jokes like "No Milk Today". They're cocking a snook at him, you see. They're determined not to be beaten – absolutely determined.'

'But how many people are going to die before it's all over?'

'I don't know,' he said quietly. 'I just don't know.'

They walked in silence for a while. The gorsy heath of Browndown rolled away to their right, the sea lay to their left, beyond the strung-out huts of the military establishment. There's barbed wire everywhere, Thursday thought, barbed wire and War Ministry notices. Yet in a strange way this must be just what Gosport was used to. It had always been a garrison as well as a naval town. Look at all those forts, those so-called 'follies' that had been laughed at because Napoleon didn't invade after all – but which were proving so useful now.

'How are you enjoying working in theatre?' he asked suddenly.

Thursday turned to him, relieved to have something different to talk about. 'Oh, it's great! It's so interesting. Seeing all the different injuries being put right – it's almost like magic. Actually . . .' she laughed a little '. . . it's not so very different in a way from what I did before the war started. I was a dressmaker – sewing's what I was trained to do!'

'Really? We'll have to ask you to demonstrate a bit of fine stitching some time.' They discussed some of the operations that had been done that week, and then went on to talk about what they'd done before the war. Connor had already been a naval surgeon, of course, and had served in the Far East and Malta. He told Thursday stories of Singapore and Hong Kong, and she listened in fascination.

'I'd love to go to places like that.'

'Well, maybe you will, some time. I wouldn't be surprised if some of you VADs didn't get posted abroad. They did in the last war, after all.'

'It's the only chance I'd ever get to go to those sort of places,' she said wistfully. 'People like me don't travel much.'

'Why not? What stops you?'

'Well, we just don't. My dad's never been anywhere, except France in the last war, and that wasn't exactly a holiday. He and my mum would never think of going abroad. The furthest we've ever been is Tenby!'

'Well, that's practically abroad,' he said teasingly. 'Wales – they speak a different language after all, don't they.'

She laughed. 'Yes, but you don't have to go overseas to get there. That's what makes the difference. And we didn't need passports.'

Connor looked at her. He said, 'You'd like the Far East, Thursday. It's so different from here. The weather, the people, the buildings, the whole way of life – everything's different. I'd like to see you there, enjoying it all.'

Thursday laughed. 'Well, you'll have to put in for a draft for me. Maybe they'll take VADs in the hospitals there.'

'Oh, they will,' he said. 'Perhaps we'll meet there. I'll take you for tea in a real teahouse. Just like this afternoon. We'll pretend that's what we're doing, shall we?'

Thursday laughed. 'There's some difference between a cup of tea in Lee-on-Solent and a trip to the Far East!'

'Well, maybe,' he said with a grin, 'but it's only a difference of distance. If Singapore was just over the harbour instead of Pompey, you wouldn't bat an eyelid.'

'Well, it's not,' she said firmly, 'so stop talking nonsense. We're going to Lee, not the Far East, and we're going to have a cup of tea, not – not . . .'

'A cup of tea?' he supplied helpfully. 'It really is what they drink there, too, you know – China tea. Or did you think they drank some exotic brew flavoured with foreign spices and poppy-seeds? Actually, they do that as well – maybe we could try those. D'you think the café at Lee will have any on the menu today, or will it be "off" this afternoon?'

'Oh, stop it! You're just an idiot!' She heard her words with amazement. I can't be talking to him – a commander – like this, she thought, as if he were no more than an ordinary seaman or an artificer. Someone of equal or lesser rank to herself. But it seemed as if rank had disappeared somehow. They were just two people, a man and a woman, out together for a walk, and exchanging the sort of banter that helped you get over those first awkward moments.

Not that there seemed to be any awkwardness between her and Connor Kirkpatrick. It was as if they had known each other for years.

She was aware of a glow spreading through her body. He likes me, she thought. And I like him. I've liked him, from that very first moment, even though I was so upset over Tony.

She smiled up into his face.

'Let's go and have that cup of tea,' she said. 'But not in Singapore. We'll just go to Lee – it's nearer!'

Chapter Twenty-Six

After their wedding, Denise and Vic went back to live with Flo and Percy. There didn't seem to be much point in getting rooms anywhere else, since Vic was sure to be called up soon and the boys' room was empty now. The two beds were put together and Denise moved her things into their cupboards. Her room would now be Leslie's – if Leslie ever came home again.

Flo had decided to make the best of things and make Vic welcome, but Percy found it more difficult. He couldn't look at Vic without thinking of what the young man had done to his daughter, and the sight of Denise's swelling body brought it home even more harshly. It was even worse that Vic started work early in the morning, and the two men were falling over each other as they tried to get ready, both wanting to shave at the same time or both heading for the lavatory door. As for sitting down to breakfast with him, Percy just couldn't stomach it.

'I'll have to take a bite to eat when I get there,' he said to Flo. 'A sandwich or something. I tell you, I just can't sit across the table from him eating cornflakes like a – a married couple! It can't be expected.'

'Well, if anyone's going to take a bite to eat on the way, it ought to be him,' Flo said. 'But can't you try a bit harder, Perce? He's our son-in-law now, for better or worse, and we've got to make the best of a bad job.'

'Better or worse is right,' her husband growled. 'And it's the worse we're getting now. I'm still not sure we've done the right thing, Flo. That girl's much too young. Sixteen! It's a daft age to get married. And seeing them go off to that bedroom together every night – well, it's embarrassing, that's what it is.'

'So you'd rather we had a by-blow in the family? I've told you, Perce, I won't countenance her giving it away—'

'No, love, I know that. And I dare say it'll be different once the kiddy's born, and once they've got a place of their own. Or once that feller's called up. At least we won't be tiptoeing round each other of a morning.'

It was no easier for the newly-weds. The whole of their wedding day had been clouded by the news of Coventry's bombing. They'd had no honeymoon, just the brief wedding in a chilly, badly lit church and then a stilted, uncomfortable meal at home, with Mary and Walter and Vic's mum and dad. Mrs Pearce had been as upset by it all as Flo, although not too upset to give the house a thorough going-over with her sharp eyes, and Mr Pearce, who was a tax officer, looked as if he suspected them all of smuggling. They'd picked critically at the shepherd's pie Flo had made, using a whole week's meat ration, and refused second helpings of stewed apple, even though there were a few of Flo's precious bottled blackberries in it. They'd left at the soonest possible moment, and after Denise had helped her mother to wash up nobody knew quite what to do next.

'We mustn't stop too long,' Mary said after they'd had a cup of tea. 'It's so dark these nights, with the blackout and everything.'

'Oh, don't go yet!' Flo was dreading the long evening ahead before they could decently go to bed. The thought of Denise and Vic going to bed together, even though it was now quite legitimate, was so embarrassing she hardly knew how they would all face it. 'It won't be any darker at nine o'clock than it is now. Stop and have a game of cards, and we'll have some supper before you go. I've got some sardines, we can put them on a bit of toast.'

'I don't know,' Walter said. 'I think we ought to be getting back. There was that raid last night . . . we don't know where they might choose next. I think we ought to get home. It could be us next time.'

'You could come in our shelter,' Flo urged. 'Anyway, I don't suppose our boys will let them come this way again.' She thought of Leslie, one of 'our boys', and the fear that was always present clutched a little more tightly at her heart. 'Stop for a while, do,' she pleaded. 'We need to do something to make the day a bit special.'

A game of cards, making a wedding day special! Mary thought pityingly, and nodded. 'We'll stop till after the nine o'clock news,' she said firmly. 'Flo's right, we're as safe here as we are at home, and anyway they won't bother with Worcester. What have we got to interest them here? A porcelain factory! They're not going to bother about smashing a few cups and saucers.'

They all knew that Worcester and its porcelain factory had more than cups and saucers to interest the enemy – not least, the army barracks just outside the city – but nobody pointed it out. The day had been a strange one and would be a complete anticlimax if it was just allowed to dwindle into nothing more than an evening listening to the wireless. At least a game of cards usually produced a few laughs.

The game did ease the tensions a little, but nobody could forget the poor people of Coventry, trudging away from their ruined city with their possessions piled into prams and barrows and carts. It was like something you heard about in other countries. Refugees, fleeing from an oppressor. Where would they go? What would they do?

'Some of 'em have come to Worcester,' Walter said. 'People that have got relatives in other places are all right. The rest – well, I dunno. There must be hundreds – *thousands* – got no homes now. And the state Coventry's in, I don't reckon they ever will have. There's nothing left. No gas, no electricity, no water – it's all been smashed to bits. There's no telephones, no buses running – nothing. It'll never be rebuilt, not like it was.'

'But what are people going to *do*?' Flo asked. 'What about their jobs – what about all their papers, their insurances and bank books and things?'

'Well, anyone with any sense takes all that down the shelter with them, same as we do. But the banks are bombed as well.' Percy shrugged hopelessly. 'I dunno. It's a bad job.'

Denise looked around the table. The cards had been stacked in the middle of the table after the last round, and nobody had bothered to pick them up. She shoved them suddenly, so that they scattered over the table.

'Come on,' she said shrilly, 'whose turn is it to deal? It must be someone's. We're playing a game, if you remember. It's my *wedding* day, if you remember. If this is the only celebration I'm going to get, you might at least try to make it a decent one, and not all sit there with chins down to your knees. I know it's awful – I know people have got killed – I know there's lots of people having a horrible time because of it – but can't you just think about *me* for once? Just for one evening?'

The family stared at her. Vic put his hand on her knee. Flo's eyes filled with tears and Mary gave her an anxious glance. The two older men looked at each other, and Walter cleared his throat uncomfortably.

'Think about you?' Percy said. 'Think about *you*? Isn't that what we've been doing all day? Haven't we had to think about you for the past three months, wondering whether the police were going to press charges against this – this young chap what ought to have known better – and wondering if you were going to have to go to court and have your shame dragged up in the papers for everyone to know about? Haven't we had to think about whether it was best to let you get married only a month after your sixteenth birthday, to keep you out of all that and give the baby a name? Blimey, I don't think I've done anything *but* think about you, all that time! And I won't say it's a relief to think about Coventry and the poor buggers there – I'm sorry, Flo, but I can't help it, she's been getting my goat for weeks, I've got to say what I think – I won't say it's a *relief* to think about them – but at least it makes a change! And it'd make a change if you thought about someone else for a bit, too. You've got a selfish streak in you, our Denise, and always have had.'

Denise stared at him. Her face reddened and her mouth turned down. Tears sprang to her eyes and she jumped up, tried to say something and then ran from the room and up the stairs. Vic gave them an uncomfortable glance and stood up awkwardly.

'I'd better . . .' He followed her, and they heard the bedroom door close and then muffled sobbing, interspersed with Vic's low voice.

Percy looked defiant. 'I'm sorry, but it had to be said. It's been boiling up inside me for weeks.'

'Well, it's a pity you couldn't have just let it simmer a bit longer, instead of letting it boil over tonight of all nights. She'll never forget this, Perce, never, none of us will.' Flo drew in a deep breath. 'Well, there's no use going on about it, we can't call the words back. Why don't you take Walter down the shed and show him what you've been making?' She gave Mary a crooked smile as the two men went out, then reached out and scooped the cards together.

'Well, that's the end of *that* game, I suppose. I'll make a cup of tea, Mary. I don't know about supper. I don't feel hungry somehow.'

'Nor do I.' Mary touched her sister-in-law's arm. 'I'm sorry the evening had to end like that, Flo.'

'Well, it had to come. And I dare say it won't be the last time either. But it's mostly talk, you know. Perce thinks the world of Denise, always has. He's upset that this happened and even more upset that it happened so quick, but he'll get over it, same as she will. Walter'll tell you.'

'Walter? Why?' Mary looked at the other woman's face. 'What *is* it Percy's making down in the shed, Flo?'

Flo smiled. 'Only a cradle, for the baby! You see? It's all talk, really.'

By Christmas, the family was beginning to settle down. Denise's pregnancy was obvious now, although everyone knew about it from the hastiness of the marriage. But Denise had always been a favourite in the street as well as the family, and Vic had a pleasant, open face that endeared him to most of the women. And things were different in wartime, you had to be a bit more open-minded. They'd been silly, but Vic had stood by the girl and everything would come out all right in the end.

Thursday managed to get home for two days just before Christmas, and Mary and Walter decided to bring Christmas forward to give her a proper family celebration. They had one of Percy's cockerels, specially fattened, and a Christmas pudding that was more black treacle and grated carrot than anything else, and they gave out Christmas presents just as if it were Christmas Day itself.

Most of Thursday's presents were light and easy to carry back to the hospital: a warm scarf in bright red, knitted by Flo; a new pair of stockings from Denise and Vic; a pair of mittens knitted by Jenny; and a writing case in dark blue mock leather from Mary and Walter. Inside were a brand-new pad of Basildon Bond, a packet of envelopes, a new fountain pen and six twopenny stamps. Thursday looked at them and grinned.

'Is this to remind me to write to you more regularly?'

'Don't be silly, you're a good girl for keeping in touch. Not like Mrs Jeffers's girl that's gone in the Wrens – they're lucky to hear once a month from her.' Mary was busy unwrapping Thursday's present to her and Walter.

'Oh, look, Walter, it's a record. Ambrose and his Orchestra, playing "Stardust". That's my favourite song!'

All Thursday's gifts were records – she had slipped into the shop in Worcester as soon as she'd got off the train and done her Christmas shopping all at once. For her sister, she had bought Dinah Shore singing 'Maybe'; for Vic and Denise, Count Basie's 'Louisiana'; for her uncle and aunt, a recording of Winston Churchill's speech 'This Was Their Finest Hour'. She watched anxiously as they unwrapped it, half-afraid that she had done the wrong thing, and her heart sank as she saw Flo's eyes fill with tears.

'Oh, Percy, look. The speech he made after Dunkirk. Oh, what a lovely thing to have. It's like a memorial to our Mike. Oh, thank you, Thursday, love, it's a lovely present.'

'I nearly didn't buy it,' Thursday confessed, with a sigh of relief. 'I didn't know if it might upset you . . . I'm glad you like it, Auntie.'

'We won't play it now,' Flo said as Walter began to wind up the gramophone. 'We'll wait till we get home. Let's just have the music now. But we really are pleased with it, aren't we, Perce?'

Percy cleared his throat and nodded. Walter looked at the little pile of records as if deciding which one to play first, but before he could speak Thursday produced another parcel wrapped, like the others, in brown paper with holly leaves and berries drawn on it in green and red crayon.

'I brought a present for Steve, too,' she said, meeting her mother's eyes. 'I know we might never find out what's happened to him – but there's still a chance he's alive somewhere. And if – if he doesn't ever come home again, I want you to have it, Mum. In his memory, like Auntie Flo's record is in memory of Mike.'

Mary reached out slowly and took the thin, square

package. It was obviously another record. Her eyes questioned her daughter.

'It's Hutch,' Thursday said. 'You know he always liked Hutch. It's a song called "There'll Come Another Day". And I think there will, too. There'll come another day for all of us – Steve as well. He'll be back, Mum, you just see if he isn't.'

'Oh, Thursday,' Mary said softly, and took the parcel. 'Thanks, love. I'll put it with the others.' She smiled. 'We've bought him presents, too, all of us. He's going to have a real pile to open when he comes home!'

With the gramophone cranked, they began to play the records, old ones as well as the new ones Thursday had brought, and Walter produced an old favourite which they played every year – a noisy, sing-song party called 'Jolly Old Christmas', with Billy Cotton's Band and Tommy Handley. At last Denise said she was tired and wanted to go home.

'You don't have to come,' she said to her parents. 'Vic and me can go on our own.' She looked at Thursday. 'Don't suppose we'll see you again if you've got to go back tomorrow. I dare say I'll be a mum when you get home again.'

'I suppose you will. It's due in February, isn't it?' Thursday looked at her cousin's blossoming figure. 'What do you want?'

'I don't care what it is, so long as it gets born,' Denise said. 'I just want to get it over with. Not that I think about that more than I can help,' she added. 'It scares me too much!'

'Well, we've been through it and survived,' her mother said a little tartly, and Thursday knew she had only just stopped herself from adding that Denise hadn't been forced into it. Quickly, she thought of another question to ask.

'Got any names yet? I was thinking of some on the train yesterday.'

'Vic's mum wants us to call it John if it's a boy, but I think that's a boring name. I'd rather have something a bit different – Robin, or Mervyn, something like that. Or Jacqueline if it's a girl. I saw a new baby in the paper the other day called Jacqueline, I think it's a lovely name.'

'It'll get shortened,' her mother said disapprovingly. 'You want something that can't get shortened, and nothing too unusual.'

'Why? Why shouldn't it be shortened? Jenny's name's shortened and nobody complains about that. And look at *Thursday* – you couldn't get anything much more different than that.'

'Well, it's for you to decide, of course, but if you ask me—'

'We're not asking you!'

There was an awkward silence. Flo looked upset and Denise ready to burst into tears. Vic, who had been quiet all through the evening, put his arm round her shoulders.

'Come on, sweetheart. Let's get you home. You're tired out.' He fetched her coat and helped her into it, talking soothingly all the time. 'There's plenty of time to think about names. We don't have to decide anything now. And we don't have to call it anything we don't want to. Now, where are your things?' He gathered together their bits and pieces, including the Count Basie record. 'Thanks, Thursday.' He bent and, to her surprise, kissed her lightly on the cheek. 'It's been smashing, seeing you and having a bit of Christmas with you. And thank you, Auntie Mary and Uncle Walter, we've had a really good time. Will we see you on Boxing Day?'

Mary nodded, knowing that he and Denise had promised to go to Vic's parents for Christmas Day itself. The family waited until the young couple had gone, shutting the front door quickly behind them so that no light escaped, and then turned to each other.

'Well!' Flo said. 'Now you see what I mean, Mary, about our Denise. Flies off the handle at the slightest thing. And those names she's on about. Robin – I ask you! And Mervyn – what sort of a name's that?'

'It's an old Cornish name, she told Jen. She's been looking it up.'

'Well, this isn't Cornwall. And *Jacqueline* – well, I know it's quite popular just now, but think what the kiddy'll get called. Jack, just like a boy! I don't think she's given it any thought at all.'

'Well, it is her baby, Flo,' Mary said. 'For all she's no more than a kiddy herself, she does have her rights. And anyone gets a bit aeriated when they're expecting, you know that. Is she very frightened?'

'She doesn't say much about it, not to me anyway. I don't know what she tells him. I suppose I come second now, being only her mother.'

Thursday looked at her aunt's aggrieved face and felt sorry for her. It had all happened too quickly and too soon.

'He seems a nice chap, though,' she said. 'He looks after her, and he didn't forget to say thank you to us all. I should have thought she could have done a lot worse.'

'Oh, I'm not saying that. I've got to admit he's all right – so far. It's just the way it's all happened.' Flo sighed. 'Well, we don't want to spoil your Christmas with it all, Thursday. It's been a nice day, and it's been good to see you again, and looking so well too. I dare say you're being kept busy in that hospital.'

Thursday nodded, thinking of the constant air raids, the victims of the bombing, the Wrens who had been killed. Like everyone else at Haslar, she seemed to be permanently on duty these days, and permanently exhausted. It was as if rest and sleep had been postponed somehow. Rest, and sleep, and time off – except for the hasty visit to the Swiss Café, or the Dive – were little more than memories. And since that day after the Wrens' funeral, when she and Connor Kirkpatrick had walked to Lee together, she had seen him only in the theatre, when they had once again become 'Nurse Tilford' and 'sir'.

She yawned and then smiled apologetically. 'I'm sorry – just thinking about it reminded me how tired I am! I'll have to go to bed soon, I'm afraid, or I'll fall asleep on the floor.' As Flo and Percy stood up and began to say their own goodbyes, she got up too and kissed them both. 'Thanks for coming. It's been a lovely Christmas. And just think, we've still got the real one to come! Let's hope it's a happy one for everyone, and we don't have to eat our dinners in an air-raid shelter!'

'I know what'd make it a happy one for me,' Mary said wistfully, and she looked at the packet that Thursday had given her to keep for Steve. 'Just one little brown envelope, telling me my boy's all right. That's all I want now.'

Chapter Twenty-Seven

It seemed as if there was to be an undeclared truce for Christmas. No German bombs fell anywhere in Britain either on Christmas Day or Boxing Day. The sirens were mercifully silent and nobody had to eat their Christmas dinner in an air-raid shelter. Presents were opened in peace, games were played and carols sung, and people went to church to give thanks and to pray for an end to the war.

Thursday went to the little church at the end of the quarter-deck. St Luke's was full of nurses, doctors and patients, and the chaplain led the service and gave a short but moving sermon about the men who were at sea, and the families who waited. They came out to bright, cold sunshine, and Thursday found Connor Kirkpatrick walking beside her.

'Did you have a good trip home?' he asked her. Thursday had had to ask his permission to go. 'Family all well?'

'Yes. Mum's still looking for the telegram boy every day, but I think she's slowly coming to accept that Steve must be dead. He must be, mustn't he?' she added, turning her head to look at him with troubled eyes. 'I mean, what else could have happened to him? We'd have heard by now if he was a POW. He must be just one of those thousands who were killed and never found.'

'I'm afraid it does seem most likely. But strange things do happen. It must be a help to your mother to think that there's some hope.'

'I don't know if it is or not,' Thursday said. 'I think it's sort of holding her back. She's going to have to admit it some time, and the longer it goes on the harder it's going to be for her.'

They had come to the end of the quarter-deck. Thursday made to turn left, but Connor reached out and touched her arm. 'Don't go yet, Thursday. I haven't wished you a happy Christmas.'

'Happy Christmas,' she said, smiling. 'But I've got to go, I'm helping on the ward.'

'I'll probably see you then. I'll be doing the Christmas rounds with the rest of the doctors. Armed with a pair of garden shears to demonstrate my calling! But look here . . .' He reached out a hand as if to detain her. 'Can't we make some arrangement to see each other on our own? It's a long time since we walked out to Lee that day.'

'Well, only three weeks,' she said, thinking that it seemed much longer. 'Not all that long, really.'

'A long time,' he repeated firmly. 'What are you doing the rest of the day? We've got no operations.'

'We've got a special tea for the VADs. Madam's gone to a lot of trouble – I couldn't miss it.'

'Tomorrow? Boxing Day?'

'Well, Elsie's asked me and Patsy to go round to her gran's. She lives in Gosport. Her mum and dad are going to be there, too. And I'm on the ward in the morning, so that another girl can go home. I don't know when—'

'Thursday,' he said as sailors and nurses streamed past them, 'there must be a minute in these two days that you can spare for me. Can't you leave early? Go a little late? Well, what about after this special tea? That's not going to go on all evening, is it? You can slip out for half an hour.'

'But – won't you be having your own – I mean, isn't there a dinner in the wardroom?'

'Yes,' he said, 'and nobody's going to miss me if I nip out before it starts. Say about seven.'

'But it'll be dark.'

'Well, that's all right,' he said. 'I'll have you to look after me.'

Thursday stared at him and burst out laughing. She looked into his dark blue eyes, thinking what a different man he was outside the operating theatre. At work, he was self-contained, stern, concentrating on what he was doing. There was no time for the odd smile or moment of communication. The only eye contact was made when an instrument or dressing was required, and it was required instantly. Commander Kirkpatrick could be very sharp with any nurse who didn't immediately provide him with what he needed.

Thursday's job was to look after the autoclave, where instruments, dressings and everything else needed for the operations were sterilised. She wasn't involved in the operations themselves, though she hoped that one day she would be. The thought of standing beside Connor – or any other surgeon – and handing him the instruments directly, taking swabs and even being allowed to do the stitches when they were particularly busy, was a thrilling one. Back to sewing, she'd thought with a giggle when she'd first realised how fascinating theatre work was. But more interesting sewing than ever it could be making frocks or suits.

'Well?' Connor repeated with a touch of urgency. 'Can you slip out for a while tonight? *Will* you?'

'Yes,' she said, smiling into those dark blue eyes. 'Yes, I will.'

'Coo,' Elsie said as they went into the ward to help serve the Christmas dinners. 'You've made a bit of a hit with the gorgeous Kirkpatrick. I saw you, holding hands after church.'

'We weren't holding hands! We were just discussing an – an—'

'Don't tell me you were discussing an operation, 'cause I won't believe you! Even a surgeon commander doesn't discuss operations on Christmas Day, not with that look in his eye, anyway. He fancies you, Thurs.'

'Don't be daft!' Thursday retorted, feeling the heat in her cheeks.

'And you fancy him,' Elsie said, observing Thursday's blush. 'You'd better be careful, my girl.'

'I don't know what you're talking about,' Thursday said with dignity, and Elsie hooted.

'Well, I've a feeling you're about to find out! When are you seeing him?'

'Oh, for goodness' sake!' Thursday caught Elsie's eye and grinned. 'Well – this evening, actually. After tea. But it won't be for long – he's got a wardroom dinner to go to. Anyway, it'll be dark and there's nowhere to go on Christmas Day.'

'Oh, you'll find somewhere. Some secluded little corner. I must say, I'm surprised at him, a commander and all, leading an innocent young nurse astray—'

'Shut up, Elsie,' Thursday ordered. 'It's time to go to the ward. And you needn't go spreading gossip all over the hospital either. He's my boss. He probably wants to talk about bandages or something.'

'Oh, yeah,' Elsie said, rolling her eyes, 'and Mr Churchill's coming to tea at my gran's tomorrow. Pull the other one, Thurs.' She smiled and nudged Thursday's arm. 'It's all right, kid. I'm not going to go blabbing. You go and have a nice little cuddle somewhere. You deserve it. I just wish it was me, that's all – he's a real smasher!'

Connor was waiting at the corner of D Block when Thursday slipped out, her cape thrown hastily round her shoulders. It was a cold, clear night and the stars gave a faint, silvery light, just enough to see their way. They walked together through the avenue of trees along the quarter-deck, decorously apart at first until Connor took Thursday's hand and slipped it through his arm, where he held it closely against his side. She trembled and then relaxed. His arm felt warm and strong, and her own fitted against his side as if it was meant to be there.

'What a lovely night,' she said after a moment. 'It's so quiet. You can't imagine bombers coming over, can you?'

' "*Silent night, holy night*," ' Connor quoted from the carol they had sung that morning. 'There really is something special about the stillness you get on Christmas Day. I suppose it's because there isn't any traffic on the roads, no trains or ferries running, the ships in the harbour are all tied up and, best of all, no aircraft! And in homes all over the country, people are enjoying their Christmas with the family. In homes all over Europe, I suppose.' He was silent for a moment, then added sombrely, 'But not enough of them. There are too many homes that have been torn apart by this war, Thursday.'

'I know.'

He glanced down at her and she saw the shine of his eyes. 'I'm really very sorry about your brother, Thursday.'

'Yes. It's all the worse because Mike – my cousin – must have been near him, they were in the same regiment. And then there's Leslie, my other cousin, Mike's brother – he's a pilot in the RAF. He's on bombers now.'

'But he's all right, isn't he? Last time you mentioned him—'

'Oh, yes,' Thursday said, 'he's all right. So far.'

Connor said nothing. They both knew that the odds were stacked high against the young pilots. Leslie himself, managing to get home for a couple of days' leave just before Thursday, had told his parents that there were none left in the squadron who had joined with him. He had already won several medals, but brushed them aside, saying that there were so many to go round that you couldn't help getting the odd one or two. Flo turned them over in her hands, marvelling that her son could have become a hero in such a short time, but Percy, although just as proud, shook his head over them. The boy was flying on borrowed time, he said gloomily, but Leslie just laughed and said that he was like a cat, had nine lives and every one of them charmed.

Mary, telling Thursday about this, had said that his laughter didn't ring true. It sounded like fragile glass being broken. She said that Leslie was living on his nerves, and Flo lived in daily terror of another telegram.

'Thursday,' Connor said suddenly, 'I've got something to tell you. I've got a draft.'

'Oh!' She stopped and turned to him, trying to see his face in the darkness. 'A ship, you mean?'

'Yes. That's why I wanted you to come out tonight. One of the reasons, anyway. I didn't want you to hear it on the grapevine.'

Thursday didn't know what to say. They'd had so little conversation really – the time when Tony had died, the short trip across the harbour in the pinnace during an air raid, the dance at Grange and the walk to Lee after the Wrens' funerals. It was true that they had seen each other every day in the operating theatre, but that was different. They hardly knew each other – and yet, she felt again that they had always known each other. And at the thought of him going away, it seemed as if cold fingers touched her heart.

'I can't tell you where we're going,' he said, 'but I can tell you that we may be gone a long time. I've got another three or four weeks. I want to be able to see you during that time – so that we can get to know each other a bit better. Can we do that?'

But we already know each other, Thursday wanted to say. Instead, she nodded and said, 'Yes. Yes, we can do that.'

'Provided we don't get too many more raids,' he added with a wry grin. 'If we do, we'll probably be in the theatre all the time, which isn't quite what I mean.'

He's going away, she thought desolately. He's going away for months – maybe longer than that. He may never come back. The realisation of what it meant to her shook her heart. She reached up and laid her hands on his lapels.

'I'm right, aren't I?' he said quietly. 'We do want to get to know one another. Both of us.'

She nodded, then realised he couldn't see her, and whispered. 'Yes. Please.'

His arms wrapped themselves suddenly around her and he drew her close against him. The doeskin of his jacket was soft against her cheek. She felt his face against her hair, and lifted her head. Their lips met and clung.

'Thursday,' he whispered. 'Thursday . . .'

It was like no other kiss she had ever received. His lips were gentle, barely touching hers at first, yet there was something, almost an electricity, that transmitted itself between them and she could not have broken away. It was like the tender brightness of a candle flame, trembling in the darkness yet shining a soft, true light into her heart. She closed her eyes, losing herself in the leaping delight of a wild, sweet emotion such as she had never known, and when she felt his lips break away softly and his fingertips touch her cheek she sighed and opened her eyes to look up at his face, dark against the frosty stars.

'Connor,' she whispered.

'Thursday.' He looked down at her and then kissed her again, and this time the kiss deepened and he caught her fiercely against him. She clung to him, feeling as if they were sweeping together into the starry skies, wheeling far above the cold earth and riding the high, soaring wind of the night. She felt his body against hers, hard and urgent, and let herself melt against him. 'Connor. *Connor* . . .'

They broke apart at last, breathing quickly. He held her close and she laid her head against his chest, wanting nothing more for the moment. This is what I've been waiting for, she thought. This is what I wanted all the time . . .

'What was the other reason you said you wanted to see me?' she asked at last. 'You said there was something else.'

'Good heavens, I almost forgot!' He let go of her with one hand and felt in his pocket. 'Here. It's nothing much,' he added quickly as she stared at the little box. 'Just a little Christmas present. You'll have to open it when you get back – you won't be able to see it now. But I hope you'll like it.'

Thursday looked at him, and opened the box anyway. She could barely see its contents, but her fingers traced the shape of a crown. A naval brooch, such as sailors gave their sweethearts. She looked up at him again, doubtfully.

'It's just a token,' he said quietly. 'Something to remind you of me while I'm away.'

'It's lovely. I can tell it's lovely. But—'

He took her in his arms again, silencing her with a kiss, and they stood for a moment, close in each other's arms, before he drew away. 'I've got to go in soon. The dinner – we have to be on time, curse it. Can I see you tomorrow?'

'I'm going to Elsie's gran's . . .'

'All day?'

'I'm helping on the wards first. We're covering for other girls. But we're not going to Elsie's gran till about three o'clock. After lunch—?'

'Before lunch,' he said firmly. 'Listen, I can have the loan of a car for the afternoon. I've managed to scrounge some petrol. We'll go out the minute you come off duty, get away from this place for a couple of hours. I'll have you back here in time to go to Elsie's gran, never fear. And we'll take a picnic with us – of sorts, anyway. I can get a few sandwiches from the wardroom, or some sausages from breakfast – something, anyway. You won't starve!'

Thursday stared up at him, her heart beating quickly. Go out in a car? She'd only ever been in one once before. And with Connor – away from Haslar, away from sharp eyes, from wagging tongues. She felt a little dizzy. 'But . . .'

'But what?'

'But – why *me*? There must be lots of other girls –

better-looking girls, girls of – of your own sort. I don't understand . . .'

'Girls of my own sort? What on earth to do you mean?'

'You know what I mean! I know a lot of VADs are quite posh, but I'm just an ordinary girl, from an ordinary family. My dad's a foreman in a factory. I was apprenticed to a tailor's shop. I'm not like Helen Stanway, been to a smart boarding school and all that. I'm just *ordinary*.'

Connor put one finger beneath her chin and tilted her face up to his. She could just see his expression and the glimmer of his eyes. 'Now, let's just get a few things straight,' he said. 'For one thing, Thursday Tilford, there's nothing ordinary about you. How could there be, with a name like yours? And your family can't be ordinary either, or they wouldn't have had the nerve to give you such a name. Or the imagination. And for another, you're talking rubbish and you know it. You know very well why I want to see you again. Don't you?'

Thursday caught her breath. She swallowed a little and then whispered, 'Yes.'

'Yes. I should think so! So we'll have no more nonsense about *why me*, all right?' He looked down at her gravely. 'I'm not asking you to make any promises, Thursday. I'm not asking you to hand your life over. I just want this time with you, just to see if I'm right about what I think – what I think about us. D'you understand that?'

'Yes,' she whispered again. 'Yes, I do.'

He laid his lips on her forehead and then trailed them down her cheek to her mouth. 'Then we both understand,' he murmured, 'and for the time being, that's enough. That's all we need.'

He took her out through Fareham and over to Boarhunt before swinging up the road which led along the top of Portsdown Hill. Thursday sat at his side in the rattling Austin Seven, remembering bike rides with Dave. The tears came to her eyes as she thought of him, limping up

393

to the house to make cocoa during a lull in the air raid. And then hearing another plane come snarling over – the bomb falling . . . Only they said you didn't hear the one that hit you, didn't they? So what had he heard? What had it been like for him? Sudden unbearable pain as his body was torn apart – or just nothing? Just, suddenly, nothing. No more Dave. No more anything. And was that it, just nothing left, for ever and ever? Or was he truly somewhere else now, perhaps even able to see her, to know what she was doing, to know what everyone was doing . . . ?

'Thursday!' Connor said in alarm. 'Thursday, what on earth's the matter? You're crying your heart out. What is it? Is it your brother – have you had bad news?'

He drew the car into the side of the road and stopped. He took her in his arms and Thursday leant her head against his chest and sobbed. He held her close, his hand moving on her hair, cradling her head against him, waiting until the storm began to diminish. He produced a large white handkerchief and when Thursday looked at it helplessly, he mopped her face and then held it over her nose.

'Blow.'

'Connor, I—'

'*Blow.* It's all right, I've got another one. One to show and one to blow, as they say. Come on. Now, tell me what it is. What's happened to make you cry like this?'

She shook her head and gulped. 'It's nothing – nothing that's only just happened, I mean. It's Dave – Elsie's brother. We – we used to come for bike rides together up here. We used to go to Southwick and Hambledon, and the Meon Valley – all over the place. And then – and then he was killed. In an air raid, only a few weeks ago.' She blew her nose again. 'I haven't been up here since, and it all just reminded me.'

'I see.' Connor watched her for a moment. She was

wearing his brooch, a small, naval crown worked in silver and gold. 'And this Dave – was he special to you?'

'I don't know. We hardly had time – it was like Tony – there's never time. But, yes – he was special. You see, he'd had infantile paralysis and one of his legs was shorter than the other. He couldn't serve in the Forces, but he could swim and cycle, and he'd just joined the LDV. He was going to ride a motorbike, be a dispatch rider. And then there was a raid one night and they were in the shelter, him and Elsie's mum and dad and Eddy – he's the youngest – and Dave went up to the house to make a cup of cocoa for everyone and – and a bomb hit it. There was nothing left.' She drew in a great, shuddering breath. 'They – they never found him, properly. Just – just—'

'All right, Thursday,' he said quietly. 'You don't have to go on.' He glanced ruefully at the slope of the hill, the harbour lying spread beneath them. 'And I thought this would be such a good place to bring you.'

'It would have been,' she whispered. 'It's just that it brought everything back. Poor Dave – he was so thrilled to be in the LDV. He wanted to do something. And instead – it was such a *waste*.'

She began to cry again and Connor held her, one arm around her shoulders, the other stroking her hair. His face was grim and after a while he said, 'I think we'd better go back. You're in no fit state to enjoy a picnic.'

'I'm sorry,' she said miserably.

'No need.' He started the engine again and turned the car. 'Maybe we'll try again some time.'

Thursday stared at him. His face was closed and his jaw tight. He didn't look at her as they cruised along the top of the hill.

'Connor—'

'There's no need to explain. I got the wrong idea, that's all.'

'*Connor*—'

'Please,' he said, 'don't say any more. I'm sorry. I've

been rather a fool. I just thought . . .' He glanced swiftly sideways at the brooch. 'I did tell you it was just a token, didn't I?'

Bewildered, she touched it. 'Yes, but – Connor, are you angry with me?'

'Angry with *you*? No, of course not! With myself, for being such a blundering fool, but never with you.' He drove fast, the little car almost leaping along the road. 'I'm only sorry that you've had so much to put up with. One boyfriend dying before your eyes – another blown up in an air raid. And then a fool of a doctor making himself a nuisance—'

'Connor, *no*, you're *not* a nuisance.'

'Well, it's good of you to say so, but—'

'Connor, stop it! What's the matter with you all of a sudden? You're not jealous, surely – not of Dave?' She looked at him in sudden anger. 'If I can't cry for a friend . . .'

She saw him bite his lip, and then once again he pulled the car in to the side of the road. He turned and looked at her gravely.

'I'm sorry, Thursday. I'm behaving abominably. And I'm ashamed to say that yes, I think I am jealous. Of Dave – of young Tony West – of anyone else who's special to you. And I know that when you've lost so many people you love – well, it takes time to recover. You can't let anyone else be special, perhaps for a long time. So I'm sorry I—'

'Connor, I don't know what you're talking about,' she broke in. 'Dave was special because he was, well, because he was so brave and so willing, and just when he'd got the chance to help it was snatched away from him. And Tony was special because he was the first boy I'd ever felt anything for at all.' She thought of Sidney, who had been her boyfriend for so long and for whom she'd felt hardly anything. He'd been at Dunkirk, too, her mother had told her, and had come home safely, ready to go again. 'But neither of them was special in the way that you are. That's quite different.'

He stared at her. She saw his eyes darken, and her heart leapt. He put out one hand and touched her cheek. She turned her head and laid her lips against his palm.

'Thursday—'

'We haven't got much time,' she said quietly. She lifted one hand and touched the brooch he had given her. 'I know you said it was just a token. But when I got back to D Block last night and looked at it – I knew it was more than that. It is, isn't it?'

'It's whatever you want it to be,' he said.

'And what do *you* want it to be?'

He kept his eyes on hers and laid his fingers over hers so that their hands both covered the little brooch. She felt the pulse beating in his fingertips.

'I would have liked it to be a ring,' he said.

Chapter Twenty-Eight

The respite was brief. On the day after Boxing Day, a raid on London left six hundred people dead or injured. And just two days later, on the Sunday evening, the worst attack yet left London almost entirely in flames.

'Look at this picture of St Paul's on the front page of the *Daily Mail*,' Elsie said at breakfast. 'Standing there amongst all those fires. "The War's Greatest Picture", they're calling it. It's like the whole city's on fire.'

'How will people manage?' Patsy wondered. 'I mean, how can they get to work? Even supposing there's any work to get to. It doesn't look as if there's going to be much left of London.'

'Oh, I don't know. It's a big place,' Thursday said. 'I went once with Mum and Jenny, and we went to the Tower and Buckingham Palace and the Houses of Parliament, and it was miles between them all. We went to St Paul's as well,' she added, looking at the picture of the great dome standing amidst the smoke and the flames. 'It's a lovely church. You can go right up high in the dome and look down at the people down below, just like tiny little dolls they are, and there's a whispering gallery and all sorts. It'd be terrible if that was ruined.'

'Well, it's not.' Elsie poured milk on her bowl of Force. 'And it's not going to be. There's some things even the Germans can't smash.'

In the next few days, it seemed as if the enemy had heard Elsie's words and were determined to disprove them. It wasn't only London that was under attack. Cities such as Cardiff and Bristol were being relentlessly bombed, and although the weather on New Year's Eve prevented any planes from reaching England there was little time to celebrate. The streets were full of rubble, fires were still smouldering and, as Patsy had said, just getting to work was difficult. The damage was almost unbelievable, with the papers full of pictures of devastation. And you never knew where the enemy would strike next.

It was Portsmouth's turn ten days later.

Connor, with only days to go before joining his ship, had been working at full stretch and his theatre staff had worked with him. It sometimes seemed to Thursday that this would be the pattern of their relationship for ever – clad in green or white gowns, only their eyes visible as she passed the instruments from the autoclave to the nurse who would, in turn, pass them to the surgeon. Will we ever get a chance to be together again? she wondered. Will we ever get more than just a few moments, snatched between duties?

'We've got to get away for an hour or two,' Connor said as they met at what had become their 'special' corner. 'I've only got a few more days. Look, neither of us is in theatre this evening. Let's go out. I can borrow Freddy's car.'

Driving at night wasn't easy, with the streets blacked out and only a sliver of light allowed to shine through the covered headlights. Cautiously, Connor drove on to the slope of Portsdown Hill, as far as you were allowed to go, and pulled on to the verge. They sat looking down over the darkened city. Somewhere above them were the anti-aircraft gun emplacements and the searchlights. As yet, they were switched off and there was no sign of a light anywhere. If you hadn't been up there in the daytime, Thursday said, you wouldn't believe that there were buildings and streets and thousands of people down below.

'You can see why they're so keen for people not to show a light. It really would show up.'

'Yes, but wait till the moon comes out. It's like daylight then, and not a darned thing we can do about it.'

The moon had been behind a cloud. The edges showed silver against the blackened sky and then the cloud drifted past and the moon shone down, throwing the harbour and coastline into sharp relief. Portsmouth, Gosport and the Isle of Wight lay below like a relief map in black and silver, ready and waiting for any enemy bomber that chose to pass over.

'Gosh, look at that,' Thursday said in dismay. 'They might as well turn on the streetlights and have done with it!'

Connor looked down soberly. Then he turned to Thursday and put his arms around her.

'Listen, darling. We haven't got long. I'm going on Monday. That's only two days, and we may be busy.' He kissed her. 'We haven't had as long as I wanted to get to know each other.'

'I know,' she whispered.

'And yet – it doesn't seem to matter somehow. I feel that I *do* know you, Thursday. I know all the important things about you.' He paused and laid his lips against her ear. 'I know that I love you.'

Thursday felt a shock run through her body. I wanted him to say this, she thought, I knew he would say it, yet it still comes as a strange kind of surprise. Like something I've dreamed about but never really thought would happen. Something I knew, yet didn't know.

'Oh, Connor,' she breathed. 'I love you, too.'

She felt him relax against her, as if he had been tense and anxious. But he must have known, she thought, he must have known I'd say it. Perhaps it was the same for him as it was for me – we both knew, yet didn't dare believe it.

'Thursday, I want to say so much. I want to plan – I want to talk about the future, our future, together. But I'm going away on Monday and God knows when I'll be back.

There might not *be* any future, for us.' He was kissing her as he spoke, small, passionate kisses that covered her face. 'Oh, my darling – if only we had more time. If only we *knew* . . .'

'We *will* have time,' she said. 'You *will* come back, Connor, and we'll have all the time in the world. The war *will* be over one day. We do have a future.'

'I believe it. We have to believe it. But . . .'

'What?' she said, disturbed by his change in tone.

'I wanted to give you a ring. I wanted to give you an engagement ring.' He laughed suddenly. 'No, what I really want to give you is a *wedding* ring. But we haven't had time for any of it, and I'm not sure it's right to ask you to wait.' He looked down at her soberly and she could see his face, pale in the moonlight. 'I'm not asking you to wait for me, Thursday. I could be gone for a long time. I'm not tying you down.'

'And what if I want to be tied down?' she asked with spirit.

His teeth glimmered as he smiled. 'I can't stop you tying yourself down, can I! But I don't want you to sit in the mess, moping and knitting, while the other girls go out and have fun. I don't want you living like a nun. I want you to be the Thursday I know and love – the one that's always got a smile and a laugh, who goes out on her bike and has tea at the Swiss Café or a cup of coffee in the Dive – yes, I know all your haunts! – and goes dancing. All we've got, these days, is *today*. So I want you to make the most of every today, you understand? And then write and tell me all about it!'

'I'll write to you every day.'

'And I'll write back,' he said, 'but you may not get a letter every day.'

They sat quietly for a while, their arms about each other, their cheeks close. And then a different sound broke into the silence. The distant snarl of German aircraft.

'A raid,' Thursday whispered, and as she spoke the

sirens began their wail and the searchlights sprang into life. Their long, bright swords lanced into the sky, criss-crossing it with a latticework of light. A plane was caught in the brightness and there was an instant rattle of ack-ack fire. The city below seemed bathed in light. It was so bright that Thursday and Connor could see the aircraft; they could see the bombs, falling away.

'They're bombing *Portsmouth*!'

'*Christ*!' Connor said, but anything further was drowned by the blast that followed. In that moment, it was as if the entire city were exploding. Searing white light, shot orange and black with flame and smoke, erupted somewhere in the centre. Splashes of brilliance flashed, like the graphic pictures in a comic strip. Fires began to burn, searchlights fanned the heavens and the gun emplacements all over the area spattered shots like spots of brightness into the darkness. A plane fell in a ball of flame, another trailed a plume of fire at its tail as it streaked, comet-like, across the sky. The drone of aircraft, the thunder of the explosions, the violent rattle of the guns were almost visible in the flares of scorching light. And then, in the centre of it all, in the city itself, the flames began to burn, blazing orange and white-hot heat into the darkness. The city and the waters that surrounded it were lit by an unearthly, pulsating glow, as if some devilish beast had been woken from a long sleep and was breathing a deadly fire.

'They can see every bloody ship in the harbour,' Connor whispered. 'Every shed in the dockyard. Every last street and every smallest house . . . It's all laid open to them, Thursday.'

'The whole city's going up in flames,' she said in a small voice. 'Oh, *Connor* . . .'

'We should get back.' He started the engine. 'We shouldn't be here anyway, on the hill. There'll be casualties . . .' He turned the car and began to drive down towards Fareham. 'The whole place is likely to catch this. It's going to be as bad as London.'

As bad as London. Or Bristol, Manchester, Cardiff. As bad as Coventry ... Thursday remembered the photographs she had seen in the newspapers – of Coventry Cathedral left no more than a burnt-out shell, of the miles of devastated buildings in London – and felt sick. Was there going to be any city left unravaged? What of Worcester, her own home town? Was it, even now, being bombed as Portsmouth was being bombed? Was this happening everywhere tonight?

There was no need to drive cautiously now. The whole area was lit by the burnished glow. You could have read a newspaper by its light, Thursday thought as they came down into Fareham and turned down the Gosport road. Bombs had fallen all over the surrounding area and there were damaged and destroyed buildings at almost every turn. The fire engines were out and ambulances, many converted from vans, raced along, demanding right of way. As Connor, avoiding a street which was blocked by fire engines, drove down a side street, a man rushed out of a flaming building and yelled at him to stop.

'We'll have to help,' Connor said. 'We can't just go by.'

'But Haslar – they'll be needing us.'

'I know, but we're here now and there are people who need us here as well.' He was out of the car and running with the man. Thursday leapt out and followed them.

'Connor, don't go in—'

'It's all right, I'm not going to. There's a child here.' He bent, and Thursday saw the figure of a small girl lying on the pavement. Her body was twisted and her clothes in shreds. Blood matted her hair and covered her face with ugly splashes so that it was impossible to tell where it came from. Her eyes were closed and her mouth twisted in a grimace of pain.

'Oh, the poor little mite!' Thursday was on her knees

403

immediately, brushing the blood-soaked hair back with tender fingers. 'Connor, we must help her.'

'Of course we must.' His fingers were moving swiftly over her body. 'She's badly hurt, I'm afraid. Is she your child?' he asked the man, and added, 'I'm a doctor.'

'A doctor? Oh, thank God. She ain't mine, no, she's my sister's kiddy. Our Meg – she was in the house when the bomb hit, getting the youngsters out of bed. Her other little 'un's been poorly, see, and she didn't want to take her down the shelter if it was a false alarm.' He drew in a long, shuddering breath and wiped his sleeve across his face. 'They were in the house – I tried to get 'em out, but . . .' His face crumpled. 'Oh, God. Oh, *God*. Our Meg. And young Rosie – they're both gone. I couldn't get near 'em, see. I tried. I *tried*.' He gazed at Connor as if expecting to be blamed. 'I managed to drag young Susie out, but when I tried to get back in . . . She ain't dead, too, is she? You can help her?'

'I'll do my best.' Connor turned to Thursday. 'We've got to get her away from this building – it could topple on to us at any minute. But we'll have to be careful – she's got broken bones, and there may be internal injuries as well.' He looked back at the man, who was staring down at the child, lying like a rag doll amongst the debris on the pavement. 'Can you find something – a door, perhaps – that we can use to carry her away?'

'A door . . .' Susie's uncle looked helplessly about, then darted away. He came back a moment or two later, staggering under the weight of a door that had been blown from its hinges. It was torn and splintered at one end, but it was still large enough to carry a child. He laid it down and, very carefully, Thursday and Connor lifted the broken figure on to it.

'God knows what harm we're doing,' Connor muttered. 'But what choice do we have? Well done, Thursday. Now, let's get her away from here and find an ambulance.'

But there were no ambulances to be had. The streets

were filled with people needing help, and as many as possible had already been carried away. Thursday looked at him.

'We can use your car.'

He frowned. 'It's hardly big enough. We'd never get this door in, and I don't want to do her any more damage. And I want to get her out of the street – there could be more bombs.'

'There's a street shelter round the corner,' Susie's uncle said. 'We could get her in there.'

'Right. You help me carry the stretcher. Keep it as level as possible. Thursday, my emergency bag's on the back seat, fetch it out and bring it along. I'll do whatever I can once we're there.' The two men set off, carrying their fragile burden, and Thursday ran for the bag. By the time she caught them up, they were manoeuvring the makeshift stretcher through the narrow door of the street shelter, and the people inside were pressing back to make room.

'Hurt kiddy, is it? Poor little mite. Here, ain't that Meg Jones's little Susan? Where's her mum, then? And where's young Rosie?'

'Gone,' the man said brokenly. 'Direct hit. I managed to get Susie out, but the other two . . . The flames was just too much. I tried. I *tried*.'

'Lay her down there,' Connor ordered, and then looked round for Thursday. 'Oh, good girl. Now then, let's have a look. Can someone get some light over here, please?'

A hurricane lamp was brought and held over the child, and Connor began a more thorough examination. Thursday crouched beside him, holding his bag open. She watched as he gently lifted away the torn and scorched clothing – a little red kilt, it looked like, and a red jumper with a yellow teddy-bear knitted into the front. Her mum probably knitted that, she thought, and felt a lump come into her throat.

'We've got to get this stuff off her,' Connor muttered.

'Can you help me, Thursday? Very gently, now – it's going to hurt . . .'

The child had been unconscious, and as far as Thursday could tell was still unconscious, yet even through the depths of her numbed mind the pain was still enough to penetrate. Her cries brought a collective sigh from the others in the shelter, a whisper of sympathy and a sob or two from those who knew her. Somewhere behind Thursday, the little girl's uncle was telling his story, and she heard his own sobs and the soothing murmurs of the neighbours as they tried to comfort him. But all he could say was, 'I tried. I *tried*,' over and over again, as if his failure would haunt him for ever.

'How is she?' she asked Connor in a low voice, and he shook his head.

'Not good. It's not just the burns. They're fairly superficial, as far as I can tell, though they're more extensive than I like. But it's this leg – see? It's a bad compound fracture, and the bone's splintered and piercing a deep vein. She's losing too much blood, and there's nothing I can do to stop it. If something isn't done quickly, she won't survive.'

'Oh, Connor . . .'

'It's an amputation,' he said quietly. 'And it needs to be done as soon as possible.'

'But we'll never get her to the hospital! The War Memorial's the nearest, and they must have hundreds of patients coming in . . . Can we take her to Haslar?'

'It'll be the same there,' he said, 'and it's further away. We just don't have the time, Thursday.' He was fumbling in his bag as he spoke and she realised with horror what he intended to do. 'Clear a space. I don't want spectators.'

'*Connor—*'

'You'll have to help me,' he said. 'You've seen amputations before. It's a straightforward enough procedure. But you've got to be able to give me what I need without delay.' He didn't ask if she felt capable of it. He started to make up an injection while Thursday quickly pushed back the crowd. As they understood what was about to happen, most of them dropped back quickly, while two or three pressed forward, offering help. One said she was a member of the Red Cross and had done first aid, another said he'd nursed his old mother through her last illness and didn't mind the sight of blood, and a third had been a stretcher-bearer in the Great War of 1914. Thursday stationed them beside her and around Connor, and asked a couple of the other men to keep the rest back.

'She's got to have enough air. We can't have everyone breathing all over the poor little thing.'

'Choke her with carbon dioxide, that would,' the first-aider said knowledgeably. 'It's oxygen she needs.'

Thursday spread a piece of clean cloth on the ground and laid out Connor's instruments. She looked at the saw and felt faintly sick, then reminded herself that she was a nurse, and just because this wasn't a proper theatre it didn't give her any excuse to be squeamish. She looked at Connor, and their eyes met for a moment.

'All right?' he asked, and she nodded, knowing that he wouldn't see her as herself again until the operation was over. From this moment, she was a nurse – as much a piece of equipment as his scalpel.

A sudden thundering explosion shook the ground and reminded her that there was an air raid going on outside. She thought briefly of the fires she had seen, of the devastation of Portsmouth and its surroundings, and wondered what would be left when morning came and the raiders were driven away. And then she forgot everything in the concentration of the moment. There was nothing in the world now but the three of them – herself, Connor and a little girl called Susie, who was about to lose her leg. There wasn't even time to feel sad. From this moment it was a job of work, which must be properly done.

It took a surprisingly short time. There was a silence in the shelter, a lull in the bombing and in the roar of aircraft. The only sounds were those of Connor's steady breathing, the whimpers of the child, now deeply unconscious, and other sounds, the inevitable sounds of the operation, that grated in her ears. The pain of the child seemed to trickle through the entire shelter, to be shared by everyone present. The uncle was quiet now, numbed by his own pain. He crouched just within Thursday's sight, his head cradled on his knees, and whimpered softly like a hurt animal.

'That's it,' Connor said quietly at last, and straightened his shoulders.

Thursday looked down at the child and felt the tears come at last. The stump of the little leg was bandaged just above the knee – or where the knee had been until just a few minutes ago. The stretcher-bearer reached forward and lifted the remainder in his arms and carried it to the door of the shelter.

'We'll get her to the hospital as quickly as we can,' Connor said quietly to the little girl's uncle. 'You'd better come, too. Are there any other relatives? What about her father?'

'In the Army,' the man said tonelessly. 'I was stopping along with our Meg, see, they won't have me on account of me eyesight. There was only her and the two kiddies. Now there's just me and Susie. And how'm I going to look after her when I've got to go to work in the dockyard every day? I dunno what we'll do, I don't straight.'

'Hasn't she any grandparents?'

'Our dad's dead, got flu after the last lot, and Jack's mum and dad are up north. Manchester. I dunno what we'll do.' He started to cry again. 'I tried to get 'em out, I did, I tried. But it was the flames, see, the flames, they was just . . .' He shook his head blindly. 'I couldn't get past 'em, I couldn't, and our Meg, she was *in* there, her and young Rosie, and I just couldn't get to them.' He stared at them piteously. 'I *tried*.'

'I know.' Connor touched his shoulder. 'Look, we

should get this little girl to the hospital as soon as possible. I'm a doctor at Haslar, and if my car's still all right out in the street I'll take her there straight away. Will you come as well?'

'Haslar?' the man said doubtfully. 'But that's a naval hospital.'

'That doesn't matter. We'll take her there. She's my case now, and if necessary we'll enrol her as a Wren!' He nodded at Thursday. 'You'll sit in the back with her, so go and get in, and I'll get this useful chap here—' he glanced at the stretcher-bearer '—to help me carry her out. And you can sit in the front and direct me,' he said to the uncle. 'We may not be able to go by a straight route.'

They couldn't. They had to go round through Stubbington and back along the seafront at Lee and through the village of Alverstoke. Everywhere there was damage – houses on fire, incendiaries flaming in the middle of the road, shrapnel flying through the air. Connor twisted the wheel this way and that to avoid hoses and rubble, and finally they were driving down Clayhall Road, past the long, high wall of the hospital and in through the gate.

Connor leapt out and ran into the hospital, calling for help, and two QARNNs came running out. They looked into the back and lifted the child carefully away from Thursday's lap. The uncle got out and stood uncertainly for a moment before following them in, and then Thursday got out, too, her legs shaking. She also stood still for a moment or two before going inside.

The sky was lit with the glow of the fires burning in Portsmouth. The raddled light flickered on the walls of the buildings and lit the straight narrow road of the quarter-deck as if it ran with blood. The roar of the aircraft was dying away, slowly vanishing into the distance as the planes, their deadly loads disposed of, returned home. She thought very briefly of her cousin Leslie, wondering if he had been up there, trying to fight them off in the darkness, and then she turned and followed Connor and the QARNNs into the hospital.

It had not occurred to her once that she and Connor could themselves have been injured during those hours as they'd driven through the burning streets and crouched over the injured child in the street shelter. It had not once entered her mind that she could be in any danger. Now, suddenly, the realisation hit her, and she reeled and put out a hand to steady herself.

'It's all right,' Connor's voice said in her ear, and she felt his arms wrap themselves around her. 'It's all right, Thursday. You're safe. And little Susie is going to be all right.' He held her close and rocked her gently in his arms. 'It's all over, sweetheart, all over now. You're safe. You're safe with me.'

Thursday turned her face into his coat and felt the tears seep from her eyes. Her body shook, and he tightened his hold on her. For a few moments they stood quite still, aware only of each other, while around them the light of the flames flickered bright and crimson on the walls, and the scarlet colour of blood lay flung like a discarded cloak upon the ground.

Chapter Twenty-Nine

Thursday and Connor had returned to Haslar to find the place in as near chaos as the Navy would ever allow. Because the raid was so huge, all military and naval personnel had been called out to help, and inevitably there were countless injured, many of them ferried straight across to Haslar despite the bombs that rained down on the harbour as well as the city. Everyone was on duty; those not in the underground shelters with their patients were at the jetty, bringing in new ones. There was a constant coming and going along the paved way into the hospital.

"Take Susie down below,' Connor said to Thursday. 'Make sure she gets immediate attention – that amputation's got to be watched. And you stay with her   I want you safe.'

I want you, safe too, Thursday thought, but what use would it be to tell you that? She caught a passing QARNN and together they manoeuvred the makeshift stretcher down the stairs. Swiftly, she explained what had happened.

'Poor little soul,' the QARNN said. 'But she seems to be all right. We'll take her over there – there's a couple of Wrens who've been brought in, they're not too badly knocked about. She'll be best if she can just sleep now. I'll keep an eye on her, if you've got others to see to.'

Thursday nodded and dashed back up the stairs before anyone could stop her. There were plenty of people down here, looking after the patients from the wards, and she had no intention of obeying Connor's orders to stay safe.

Not while he was up there, amongst the bombs, and not at all safe.

She found him on the jetty, examining the injured as they were brought ashore. The whole of the harbour was lit by the fires that raged all through the city only half a mile away, and new ones broke out with every fresh explosion. From Portsdown Hill came a constant, deafening roar as the huge guns there fired at the planes that circled the city. More firing came from the other emplacements all around the area, and a massive barrage from the *Corbet*, the French battleship impounded at Hardway. You could only hear what someone shouted at you if they put their mouth to your ear, yet people were yelling anyway, gesturing to make themselves understood. For the first time, Thursday fully understood the effects of the strict naval discipline. You just knew, from intensive training, what the slightest movement of hand or head meant and you knew almost from instinct what to do. All the apparently petty and irritating rules came into their own when emergency demanded action.

Connor straightened up and saw her beside him. He shouted at her, his mouth forming the words 'What the hell are you doing here?', but Thursday shook her head impatiently and there was no time for argument. Together, they slipped into their routine, surgeon and nurse, and as the planes and the bombs and the guns all roared about their ears, they worked together as if in an oasis of their own calm, receiving their patients, examining them, giving them immediate treatment or handing them on to an SBA or QARNN.

The bombs were not confined to Portsmouth. Many of the planes flew low over Gosport, and every now and then there was an explosion close by. At some point, one came so low that Thursday ducked and Connor flung his arm across her shoulders. They staggered together and fell, and as they lay on the paved slabs they felt the rocking thud of an explosion nearby. Connor swore in Thursday's ear and she felt him cover her body with his own. Debris rained around them; she heard a cry as someone was hit, and prayed that it wasn't Connor. Not now, she begged, not now . . . And then the shuddering of the earth slowly ceased and, cautiously, she lifted her head.

Connor rolled off her. He looked back at the hospital buildings.

'Haslar's been hit.'

'Oh, no. The patients. *Susie* . . .' Thursday was on her feet. She could see flames, people running.

'It's not the wards. And she'll be all right, down in the basement.' He screwed up his eyes against the burning light. 'Looks like the stores to me. Or the museum.'

'The museum!' It was full of medical specimens and oddities. A skeleton, used for anatomy lessons. Jars of organs, preserved in formaldehyde. A duck with four legs. But there was no time to worry about that now. Another pinnace had arrived, bringing more casualties, and Thursday turned back with Connor and the other doctors and nurses to bring them ashore and race them into the safety of the cellars.

The raid lasted for seven hours. It was four in the morning before Thursday finally crawled into her bed, sent there by Miss Makepeace who had caught her swaying beside a patient and immediately ordered her away. 'You'll become a danger to yourself and others if you don't get some sleep. Haven't you been on duty since early this morning – yesterday morning, I mean?'

'Yes, Madam.' Thursday didn't mention the drive up Portsdown Hill, or the amputation in the air-raid shelter. 'But really, I'm quite all right—'

'*Bed*,' Madam repeated forcefully, and Thursday, more thankfully than she would have admitted, obeyed her.

She slept until ten, then got up and went back on duty. There was plenty to do, but her first thought was for Susie. Eventually she tracked down the QARNN who had taken her over, and was told that she'd been transferred to the War Memorial Hospital in Gosport.

'She'll be all right there. There was a man asking for her—'

'Her uncle. I think he's almost all she's got left.'

The QARNN nodded. 'He's gone to see her. He seems very fond of her. Poor little mite, losing her leg.' She sighed and then looked at Thursday again. 'You helped with the operation, I hear. You did a good job.' Her hand rested a moment on Thursday's shoulder. 'You should think about training properly once all this is over.'

Thursday went down to the basement, thinking sadly of the child who would go through life with only one leg. At least she had survived, but how was she going to adapt, not only to her physical problems but to the loss of her mother and sister as well? Poor little Susie, Thursday thought, and made up her mind to go and see the little girl as soon as she possibly could.

The operating theatre was already in full swing. Thursday reported to the theatre sister and waited until she was called.

'Hullo,' said Ellen Bridges, spotting her as she wrapped herself in her green overall. 'Bit of a night last night, wasn't it? Heard about the duck?'

'The *duck*?' Thursday stared at her uncomprehendingly. 'What duck?'

'The one in the museum. *You* know – the one with four legs. Apparently it got lost when the museum was hit, and they want everyone to go and look for it.' Ellen's voice rose with a touch of hysteria. 'Just as if we hadn't got enough to do, we've got to go and pick through the rubble for a bloody duck with four webbed feet! You can't help laughing.'

There wasn't a lot to laugh at, however. The raid had been the worst yet known in the whole area – a blitz every bit as bad as those on London. Gosport and Alverstoke had both been badly hit, with incendiary bombs close to

Haslar itself, damaging houses in Clayhall Road, Foster Road, Bury Crescent and the bridge, and many others falling in Stokes Bay and on the allotments. Fires had broken out almost simultaneously all over the town, and over eighty fire engines, with almost five hundred men, had been sent to deal with them. The raddled glare could be seen for miles.

Portsmouth itself had been devastated. The first stick had fallen on the electricity station, plunging the entire city into darkness. The fires that Thursday and Connor had seen had started in Palmerston Road, one of the main shopping centres, and it wasn't long before Commercial Road and King's Road were also alight. The next planes to come over attacked the Guildhall (which was still on fire days later) and so many other public buildings that it was almost impossible to count them. Six churches had gone, the Eye and Ear Hospital, part of the Royal Hospital, Clarence Pier – its blackened ruin visible from Haslar – three cinemas and the Hippodrome theatre, a hotel and drill hall, the Royal Sailors' Rest and the Salvation Army citadel. Amongst these were countless small ships and businesses, together with over three thousand private homes, an underground shelter with nearly fifty people inside, which had received a direct hit, and most of the gas and water mains. There were nearly two and a half thousand fires.

And they want us to look for a four-footed duck that's been dead for years anyway, Thursday thought with an echo of Ellen's hysterical laughter as she tied her green theatre gown and answered the sister's call. All this, and they're worried about a flaming *duck*!

Connor left two days later. He went at first light, catching the early pinnace across the harbour to board his new ship, which was at the Southern Railway jetty. She was due to sail on Friday, and he would not be able to come ashore again.

Thursday came down to the jetty to see him off. She stood, shivering a little in her scarlet cape, her throat aching but her eyes dry. They stood together, gazing into each other's eyes, unable to think of the right words. Perhaps there were no right words.

'I've got something for you,' Thursday whispered at last, and felt in her pocket. She handed him a small package. 'You can open it now, if you like.'

Connor unwrapped the little packet and took out the small cloth badge that lay inside. He stared at it for a moment, and then his eyes went to Thursday's sleeve, where her VAD badge should be proudly displayed. The sleeve was bare, with only a few small needle-holes to show where it had been.

He looked at the badge again. It was black, with a golden, jewelled crown above a circle of gold. Within the circle was the word 'Mobile' and in the centre was another gold circle, with the letters 'VAD' in gold on a red background. It was the badge that all mobile VADs wore, the badge they wore with pride.

'Won't you get into trouble?' he asked with a smile, and Thursday grinned.

'I'll just have to pay for a new one and sew it on. It was all I could think of to give you.'

'It's all I want,' he said quietly, and slipped it into his breast pocket. I'll keep it with me always.'

'Take care, won't you?' she begged with sudden desperation. 'Come back to me. I love you, Connor.'

'I love you, Thursday,' he said gravely and then, regardless of the sailors in the waiting pinnace, bent his head and kissed her. 'And you take care, too. No freewheeling down Pneumonia Bridge on that old rattle-trap of yours!'

'As if I would,' she said, and laughed, but her laughter was dangerously close to a sob. She gave him a little push. 'One last kiss and then go, Connor. Please.' They clung together for a moment and she tried to believe the unbelievable, that he was here in her arms now, his lips on hers, and that in a few moments he would be gone, out of her reach. She would see him step down into the pinnace and she wouldn't be able to call him back, she wouldn't touch or kiss or even see him until – until when?

Nobody could tell her that. Nobody knew. It could be a year. It could be years.

She stood on the jetty, where so many sailors had in the past been brought from their foundering ships, and watched the pinnace draw away. It turned into the waves and began its short, choppy journey across the harbour to the still smoking city. Connor stood in the prow, his cap off, his hair ruffled by the wind. He lifted his hand, and Thursday lifted hers in farewell.

When she could no longer see him clearly, she turned and made her way back to the block. She would be on duty in half an hour, and before then she must wash away her tears. She could not go on duty without a smile.

The bombing went on. Sustained raids, lasting for hours, and lightning strikes with the planes making a swift dash across the Channel to hurl their bombs into the cities below, and swooping away like lightning itself, ready to reload and return next night – and the next – and the next.

In Worcester, the raids were mostly 'hit and run', a few bombs dropped as the planes flew over on their way to Birmingham or Liverpool. It was still enough to force people to take shelter, or trek into the countryside or down to the open ground around the racecourse and on the riverbank.

Vic and Denise were settling into a more stable but still uneasy relationship with Flo and Percy. The problems of two men trying to get ready for work in the mornings had been sorted out by Flo, who had pinned up a rota for the lavatory and the washbasin. Percy had glowered at this, muttering that he didn't see why he couldn't use either just whenever he liked in his own home, but Flo had been sharp with him and pointed out that she was sick and tired of his grumbling, and it wasn't good for Denise. The girl was expecting, and needed a peaceful home.

'You don't have to tell *me* she's expecting,' Percy growled. 'That's just why we're having to put up with having this bloke in the house. Calling us Mum and Dad, and all.'

'Well, he has to, doesn't he, he's our son-in-law now for better or worse.' She went on quickly, biting off Percy's inevitable retort. 'Look, Vic's not so bad. He's a decent lad, and if you gave him the chance you'd see it for yourself.'

'So decent he gets a fifteen-year-old girl in the family way,' Percy said. 'You and me must have different ideas about "decent", Flo.'

'I know they did wrong, but they've put it right now, and she could have done a lot worse for herself. And it was her fault as much as his, telling him lies about her age. Not that it would have been any excuse if she really had been eighteen,' Flo added fairly. 'I must say, I'm disappointed in her, same as you. But it's happened now and we've got to make the best of it. So it's your turn in the lav first, and don't sit in there for half an hour, keeping the boy waiting. He's got to be down the post office at six, for the sorting.'

It was easier in the afternoons, when Vic came home first. He was often home before Denise, who had managed to get a cleaning job at the school for the last couple of months of her pregnancy, and it was on one of these afternoons that he came in to find Flo sitting at the table, staring at a scrap of paper, her face like a stone.

'Mum! What's the matter? You're as white as a sheet.' He saw the piece of paper. 'What's that?'

'It's a telegram,' she said tonelessly. 'It's what I've been waiting for. I knew it was going to come, some time. I knew he couldn't go on and on like that, flying night after night, and since he's been on bombers, going all that way to Berlin and places, I knew it was going to happen. I knew it. He was the only one left out of all those boys, the only one. He couldn't go on much longer.'

'It's not Leslie!' Vic said. He picked up the telegram and read the few words. 'Oh, *Mum*. When did this come? How long have you been sitting here like this, all on your own?'

'I dunno. About half past two, I think. I dunno what time it is now, I dunno how long it's been—'

'It's a quarter to five. Haven't you moved in the last two hours?'

Flo shook her head wearily, as if to ask why it should matter. 'He's *dead*,' she said, breaking into tears at last. 'My *Leslie*, shot down and killed. That's both of them now, both my boys gone, and what for? It hasn't stopped the Germans coming, it hasn't stopped us getting bombed and killed and blown out of our own homes. What's it all for? What good has it done? Oh, Leslie, my *Leslie* . . .'

She raised both hands to her face and began to rock to and fro, great choking sobs forcing their way up from her breast and breaking, like waves on the shore, in a storm of tears. Vic put both his arms around her and held her. He didn't know what to do. He only knew Leslie slightly, and hadn't had a chance to make friends with him, but he had taken it for granted that Denise's brother was a likeable young man and they would be friends once the war was over. Now he would never have the opportunity.

'I'm sorry,' he said, thinking how useless and inadequate the words were. 'I'm really sorry.'

'He always wanted to fly an aeroplane,' Flo wept. 'We used to tell him not to be so daft, people like us don't fly planes. You've got to have money and education . . . Even when he joined up, we never thought he'd be able to be a pilot, but he was so set on it, he did all the classes and exams and everything and next thing we knew he had those wings on his shoulder . . . He was so pleased with himself, and we were so proud of him. And he got all those medals that he showed us last time he came home

. . . And now he's dead. He's dead. *My Leslie's dead.*' Her voice rose in a little scream, and Vic began to wonder what he would do if she got really hysterical and couldn't stop, started throwing herself about and banging her head on the wall like he'd heard about. He didn't want to have to slap her face, not his own mother-in-law . . . He held her tightly and murmured things in her ear, silly things that meant nothing. 'There, there . . . it's all right, everything's all right . . .' Stupid things, he thought savagely. Everything was *not* all right.

'I'll make you a cup of tea,' he said. 'You haven't had anything all afternoon, have you? You've just been sitting here.' He let go of her cautiously, as if she might start to thrash about, but Flo sat still, her head on her arms, sobbing. 'You have a good cry, and I'll make some tea.'

When he came back with the pot and a bottle of milk and two cups on a tray, she was sitting up a bit and mopping her face with a sodden handkerchief. Vic set down the tray and went back to the scullery. He found a clean teacloth and gently wiped her face. Then he poured the tea and put in three teaspoonfuls of sugar.

'I've been having saccharin,' Flo objected weakly. 'And I never have that much anyway.'

'Sugar's better for you when you've had a shock. It can come out of my ration. Sweet tea's what you need.' He put the cup into her hands and she bent her head to it, as if she didn't have the strength to lift it. Vic poured a cup for himself, adding no sugar, and then pulled a chair round the table and sat down beside her. He put his arm around her shoulders and she leant against him.

'I've been sitting here all afternoon,' she said, between hiccuping sobs. 'Waiting for someone to come. I didn't know what else to do. I couldn't take it in, somehow.'

'Of course you couldn't. It was a terrible shock for you, here all on your own.'

'If our Denise hadn't got that job round at the school—'

'I know. But you know what she's like, she won't sit about, and we do need the money for the baby.'

'She's never been one to sit about,' Flo agreed. 'And she's so self-willed anyway, we couldn't have stopped her. You couldn't ever stop our Denise doing something she'd set her mind on.'

Vic said nothing. He held her firmly, comfortingly, and poured another cup of tea.

'Don't put all that sugar in,' Flo said. 'I'm all right now.'

'You still need it. Shock doesn't wear off that soon.' But he only put in two this time. 'Denise won't be long now.'

'Oh, I'm all right now you're here.' She gave him a shaky, watery smile. 'You're a good boy, Vic. Good as a – a . . .' Her voice broke and she began to cry again. His own face twisting with sorrow, he held her close. 'Oh, Leslie, Leslie! And Mike – both of them gone. Both my boys, that used to be together all the time, both gone. My boys, my lovely, lovely boys.' She looked at him with reddened, streaming eyes. 'I used to be so proud of them when they was little. They had little red knitted suits, I made them myself from a pattern in *Woman's Weekly*, little round hats and everything, and we'd take them out for a walk on a Sunday afternoon and they'd run on ahead, looking so smart and lovely. People used to admire them. I was so proud. And now they've gone, and I'll never see them again. Neither of them. Oh, *Vic*!'

'Shh,' he whispered, both his arms holding her close as she wept against his chest. 'Shh, shh.'

He knew she wouldn't stop crying. He knew she couldn't. But the soft, hushing sound seemed to offer some small comfort, if only to reassure her that there was someone here, someone who would share her grief and listen to her words, and wipe away her tears.

It was all he could do. It was all anyone could do.

Chapter Thirty

Denise's baby was born two days after the telegram about Leslie had come. The doctor said the shock could have brought it on, but Denise had never been too sure of her dates anyway, and when the baby was born he didn't look more than a couple of weeks early. Because they thought it was more than that, Denise had been taken into hospital and stayed there for two weeks. She came home in the middle of February, on St Valentine's Day.

Thursday had managed to get leave again, four days this time. Miss Makepeace always tried to let the girls go home if there had been a loss in the family, and with a new baby arriving as well, she made no objection to the request. As before, Jenny met her at the station and they hugged, tears coming at the thought of Leslie, and then walked along the platform together.

'How are Denise and the baby? Does he look like her or Vic?'

'He looks like Winston Churchill at the moment,' Jenny said. 'Mum says she can see a likeness, she thinks he's like Mike when he was a baby, but Dad . . .' she shrugged. 'You know what Dad's like. He couldn't tell one baby from another if he was paid for it.'

'How are Mum and Dad? The news about Leslie must have upset them.'

'Yes, it did. Set them off thinking about Steve again. But Mum writes to you, doesn't she?'

'Yes, but you can't always tell from letters, can you. She tries to be so cheerful . . . I'm sure she's not, really.'

Jenny was silent for a moment, then she said, 'No, she's

not all that cheerful, not all the time. Tell you the truth, Thurs, I think Dad's worried about her, and I am, too. She seems to have sort of gone back into herself. I can't explain it, but it's as if she's not really *there*. D'you know what I mean? She goes all quiet and you can see her trying not to cry.'

'She's bound to be still worrying about Steve,' Thursday said. 'It's not surprising, 'specially now. If we could just *know* what happened.'

'I know. I think about him, too. I say my prayers for him, Thurs, do you?'

'Yes, I do.' If I don't fall asleep first, she thought ruefully. But God would know that she meant to.

'Anyway, I've done what you said and joined the Red Cross, and I've applied for a job at the Infirmary as an orderly I've put in for nursing training as well, but there's a waiting list. You wouldn't believe that, would you. You'd think they'd be taking all the girls they can get. But a lot of older women have come back into nursing to let the younger ones join up.' Jenny sighed. 'I've thought of applying to the QARNNS or the Army nurses. At this rate, the war'll be over before I get a chance to do anything.'

'Well, I hope it is. I don't want it to go on a minute longer than it's got to.' Thursday's hand went to the little naval crown she wore on her lapel, and Jenny looked at it.

'Oh, that's pretty! Where d'you get it, Thurs? Special boyfriend?' She saw Thursday's colour rise and gave a crow of delight. 'It is, isn't it! You dark horse, you! You've never breathed a word. Who is he, what's his name? Is he in the Navy? Is he one of your patients?'

'We're not allowed to fraternise with the patients,' Thurs said austerely, not mentioning the fact that, to her own knowledge, at least three VADs had regular assignations with some of the up-patients, in the sluices or the little galleys where late-night cocoa was prepared. 'And I don't know that I'd call Connor a boyfriend. We've only been out together a few times, for a walk or a drive.'

'Connor! That's an Irish name, isn't it? Is he Irish?'

'I think his family is, but he was born in England. He's a doctor. A surgeon.'

'A *surgeon*? So he must be an officer!'

'Yes, he's a commander,' Thursday admitted, feeling embarrassed.

'A *commander*? Whew!' Jenny rolled her eyes. 'Bit out of our class, isn't he?'

Thursday said nothing. This aspect was one which had bothered her the most, yet when she was with Connor the difference in their backgrounds didn't seem to matter in the least. They shared so much in their work, and when they were off duty they fell into an easy, comfortable companionship that was shot with passion when they touched. She ached to be with him again, yearning for his kisses and dreaming of a future together. It didn't matter that they had grown up in different kinds of houses, with different people. They had the Navy, the war and the hospital in common, and that was their true background.

'Well, good luck to you,' Jenny said after a moment. 'I think it's smashing. And it's time we had a bit of good news in this family. When are we going to meet him? Have you got a photo?'

'I've got one photo,' Thursday said. 'It's one he had taken for his mother before the war started, so it's two or three years old. He got her to send him a copy for me. And I don't know when you can meet him, Jen. I don't even know when I'm going to see him again myself. He's on a ship and I think they're going to the Far East.'

'Oh. Oh, so he'll be gone a long time, then.' Jenny squeezed her sister's arm. 'I'm sorry, Thurs. You must miss him ever so much.'

'Yes,' Thursday said, 'I do.'

They had walked the length of the main street and were now crossing the bridge over the River Severn. Thursday paused to set down her kitbag for a few moments and to watch its steady flow, and looked downstream to the soaring tower of the cathedral.

'I'm glad they haven't bombed it. It's awful to think of churches being smashed to pieces. We've had a horrible time around Portsmouth.'

'It's been bad here a few times,' Jenny said. 'Mostly, it's planes on their way to Birmingham. They drop their leftovers on the way back. People have been going down to the racecourse to sleep.'

'What, out in the open? They must be freezing.'

'Well, they take blankets and things, but I suppose they think it's better than being bombed.' Jenny tugged at her sister's sleeve. 'Come on, Thurs. Dizzy's waiting to show you the baby.'

Thursday hefted her kitbag again and they trudged on. The February sunshine was pale and weak, glimmering on the river, and a few early almond trees were showing their delicate blossom. Spring was coming again, the second spring since the war had begun.

'Have they chosen a name for the baby yet?'

'You'll have to ask her that yourself. When she heard you were coming, she said she'd wait till you were here before she told anyone. We're all going round to Auntie Flo's this evening to see them.'

'How do they feel about it now? Auntie Flo, and Uncle Percy?'

Jenny shrugged. 'Dunno. They don't say much. Uncle Percy doesn't anyway. Auntie Flo cries whenever she looks at the baby and it's as if Uncle Percy can't bear to see the poor little kiddy. I mean, it's not *his* fault, is it? He didn't ask to be born.'

'But that's awful,' Thursday said. 'I mean, I know they must be ever so upset about Leslie but, like you say, it's not the baby's fault. I don't suppose they think it is, not really. They can't do.'

By the time they reached home her arms were aching

and Jenny carried the kitbag the last few hundred yards. Mary was sitting at the window, looking out for them, and as they approached the front door it flew open and she rushed out, her arms held wide. Patch raced out, too, leaping with delight at sight of his mistress.

'Thursday! Oh, Thursday, I'm so glad to see you!'

'It's not all that long since I was home,' Thursday protested, laughing as she hugged her mother and bent to pat the dog. 'It was only just before Christmas.'

'I know, but it seems ages. So much has happened since then.' Mary held her away and inspected her anxiously. 'You're all right, are you? You look a bit washed out.'

'We've been working hard. There's been a lot of bombing around Pompey. We've had hundreds of new patients in.'

'I was worried stiff about you in all that blitz and everything. I mean, they might just as easily drop bombs on the hospital. It's right on the harbour, isn't it – no distance at all from the city. You must have been able to see it all.'

'We're down in the cellars during the raids. We don't really see much at all.' Thursday hadn't told the family about her night with Connor during the worst of the blitz, when they'd amputated little Susie's leg. The child was out of hospital now and had gone to stay in the country, but she still wrote to Thursday every week, short letters with big, scrawled capitals and rows of kisses. 'One bomb did drop on the hospital, though – just a small one. It hit the museum and we lost our four-footed duck.'

'You lost *what*? You're having us on!'

'No, honestly, they had this duck with four legs, and we all had to look for it next day. I think someone found one foot, but that was all.' They were indoors by now and Thursday unwrapped her big coat and dropped thankfully into her father's armchair. 'Oh, it's lovely to be here!' Patch leapt up on to her lap and she hugged him close against her as he licked her face.

'It's lovely to have you here.' Mary was bright-eyed and animated, with no sign of the depression she'd been suffering. She bustled about, making tea and getting out a packet of custard creams she'd been saving specially. She came in with the tray. 'Did Jenny tell you, we're all going round to Flo's after tea to see the baby?'

Thursday nodded, but before she could speak, Jenny butted in excitedly. 'Thursday's got some news, too, Mum. Haven't you, Thurs?'

Thursday gave her an exasperated look. 'You don't have to go blurting that out the minute I get through the door.'

'What's that, then? What news? You're not going away, are you? They're not sending you overseas?'

'No, nothing like that – in fact, it's nothing at all, it's not news—'

'Oh, yes, it is.' Jenny was determined to have her say. 'She's got a boyfriend, Mum, a serious one. He's given her this lovely brooch, see?' She held up Thursday's coat. 'He's an officer and he's a doctor – a *surgeon*. What d'you think of that, then?'

Mary sat down and looked at Thursday. 'Is this true?'

Thursday sighed. 'Well, yes, I suppose so. Only we're not engaged or anything. We haven't known each other long enough. But we've met a few times, and we've been working together, and – well, we like each other, that's all.'

'It's not all,' Jenny said. 'You must like each other a lot for him to have given you this lovely brooch.'

'Well, maybe we do, but it hasn't gone any further than that.' Thursday gave her mother a reassuring look, knowing what was going through her mind. 'And it won't, because he's gone to sea now and I don't—' she felt a sudden, unexpected ache in her throat '—I don't know when we'll see each other again.' Her mouth trembled.

'Oh, Thursday. Oh, you poor girl.' Mary got up and gave her a hug. 'It's all right, lovey, we know how y

427

feel.' Her face grew grave. 'It's how all of us feel these days – all of us who've got men away.'

There was a little silence. Then Thursday said, 'Is Auntie Flo taking it very badly? About Les?'

'Well, she's better than she might be, considering. She told me Vic was ever so good to her, he was the first one home when she had the telegram and he looked after her really well, made her a cup of tea and let her cry, and was a proper help. She says it's really made her see what a good chap he is. And I think the baby's helping. He might have come at the wrong time, but he's here now and you can't help loving a baby, can you. Denise has only been home a day or two, of course, so it's early days, and Percy'll take a bit of bringing round, but what can you do? You've got to put up with things the way they are, haven't you. It's no good wishing for what you can't have.'

There was an odd note in her voice and Thursday looked at her. Mary met her eyes and nodded.

'I've taken it in at last,' she said quietly. 'I've decided I've got to accept it. Our Steve's dead – he must be. We'd have heard by now if he wasn't. The Army should have let us know, but I suppose it just got overlooked, what with everything . . . But I'm going to ask your father to write to them and get it sorted out. There's a bit of paper we ought to have – a certificate . . .' Her voice broke and now it was Thursday who went to her. 'That's three, just from this one family,' she said, the words muffled by Thursday's shoulder. 'Mike, Steve, and now poor young Leslie. That's why I don't want you to go away, Thursday – not overseas. Don't let them send you away, will you? Please don't let them.'

'I won't, Mum,' Thursday promised, holding her and stroking her hair. 'I won't.'

By the time Walter came home, the tears and the teacups had been cleared away. The table was laid with a clean ᵇecked cloth, the fire was lit and an appetising smell was

wafting from
Thursday.

'Well, you're a si
wondered if you'd get
doolally. And what's that I ca
the fatted calf, has she?'

'She'd have a job,' Mary remarked
'They haven't even had any thin calves rou
lately, let alone fat ones. It's curried corned be
potato jane, with carrots.'

'Potato *who*?'

'Jane. I got the recipe off the wireless. One of Gert and
Daisy's. It's layers of sliced potato and cheese and leeks,
with some breadcrumbs, only since we're having corned
beef I left out the cheese. Well, I did just put a spoonful
in, for the taste,' she added a little guiltily.

'Well, it smells good, whoever it is. And what's for
pudding, apple betty?'

Mary poked her head round the door and made a face at
him. 'It's bread pudding. I made a big one so it'll see us
through the week.'

'As the little boy said when he went to the butcher's for
a sheep's head. Leave the eyes in, so it'll see us through
the week.' Walter winked at Thursday and she grinned
back. She knew his old jokes off by heart, but it was good
to hear them again, and good to hear her mother
responding. Perhaps it was a good thing that she'd finally
made up her mind that Steve was dead, even though it did
seem sad, almost a betrayal in a way. She'd hoped against
hope for too long.

Do I think he's dead? Thursday asked herself, and
didn't know the answer. It was too difficult. How could
she know, how could anyone know, if nobody had told
them – made it official? I don't know if I'll ever believe it,
she thought sadly, and wondered if her mother did even
now, in her heart of hearts.

The meal was warming and substantial. When it was

_____ Flo's and Percy's. Flo would _____ a cup of tea, Mary said, so there was _____ having one first, and besides, Denise would probably be tired and wanting to go to bed early.

'She won't be having good nights yet, what with having to feed the baby every four hours. It's that two o'clock one that's the worst, breaks the night in half, it does.'

'Does the baby sleep all right apart from that?'

'Far as I know. Course, they've only been home a couple of days, you can't really tell. I didn't like to ask too much when Flo was round here yesterday. She's still all at sixes and sevens over Leslie.'

It was queer, Thursday thought, going to see an aunt and uncle who had lost their one remaining son and acquired a new grandson, all in the space of a couple of days. What were you supposed to do first, offer condolences or congratulations? And how was Dizzy feeling, having lost her brother? And Vic, who had hardly known him? It must be even more awkward that they were all having to live together, with all their different feelings.

They came to Flo's door and Mary lifted the knocker. Percy answered it. He looked grey and drawn, and somehow his clothes looked too big on him, as if he had shrunk. He nodded at them all, put his hand on Thursday's shoulder for a moment, then led the way indoors.

Denise was sitting in her mother's armchair. The baby was in her arms, wrapped in a white shawl that Thursday thought she remembered from when Jenny was a baby. Vic was beside her, and Flo came in from the kitchen, where she had gone to put on the kettle.

'Thursday, love! It's good to see you.'

'Oh, Auntie Flo,' Thursday said, her awkwardness vanishing as she kissed her aunt. 'I'm so sorry about Leslie. I was ever so upset when I heard.'

'I know, love. But we're getting over it now, a bit. At _____st I don't have to worry about him any more.' Her mouth twisted a little, but she went on determinedly, 'And have you seen our new little boy? He's a real smasher, he is.'

'Let's have a look.' Thursday grinned at her cousin and crouched down beside her. 'My, isn't he lovely! Look at those curls already. What did he weigh?'

'Seven pounds six ounces,' Denise said proudly. She looked different, Thursday thought. Plumper, which was inevitable really, since she was nursing, but different in herself. Grown-up, that was what it was. She looked more grown-up.

'He's gorgeous,' Thursday said. The baby's eyelids fluttered open and the milky blue eyes gazed at her. 'Look, he knows me already. It's your Auntie Thursday,' she crooned, and then laughed at herself. 'No, it isn't! I'm his cousin, aren't I? Second cousin – or is it first cousin once removed? I can never––'

'It'll be *removed* all right, if you don't stop talking nonsense,' her father told her, pushing her gently aside. 'Come on, Denise, love, let the dog see the rabbit.'

'Well, that's nice, I must say! Calling my son a rabbit.'

Walter took no notice. He touched the baby's cheek with the tip of one finger and then glanced round at Percy. 'Fine lad, isn't he, Perce? What d'you think of your grandson, then?'

Percy grunted something and Thursday saw Denise's eyes go to him. There was a pleading look on her face, but her father didn't return the glance. He was busying himself with his bootlaces and didn't look up. *Wouldn't* look up, she thought with sudden anger.

'Where's the proud father, then?' Walter went on, apparently determined to make his brother-in-law acknowledge the baby's presence. 'Thursday was hoping he'd be here.'

Percy flushed a dull red, but before he could speak Denise said, 'He'll be in soon. He had to do some overtime. We're hoping to get a place of our own,' she s to Thursday, although the words were obviously meant for her father. 'Somewhere we feel a bit more welcome.'

Percy dropped the boot he was holding. His face was red and his eyes angry. 'Now, look here, my girl—'

'*No!*' Flo darted in from the kitchen, where she and Mary had gone to make tea. She put her hands on her hips and faced her husband. 'No, *you* look here! We're just about fed up with this, all of us. What good's it going to do, treating our Denise like something the cat brought in? Eh? Tell me that. Isn't it enough we've lost both our boys? Isn't it enough that she's the only one we've got left, and this might be the only grandchild we ever have? I've told you and *told* you, Perce, we've got to look on the little mite as a gift from God. And I thought you agreed with me, yet ever since she came back from hospital you've been acting like a bear with a sore head. Why? *Why?*'

Percy's glance shifted sideways. He stared down at his feet in their thick socks, and muttered something. Mary and Walter looked at each other in embarrassment and Thursday knelt down again beside Denise.

Flo sighed and put her hands on her husband's arms. 'Come on, Perce,' she said more gently. 'It's not like you to take it out on an innocent little baby. What is it, now?'

'Well, what do you *think* it is?' he said miserably. 'It's everything. This war – the bombs – our Mike, and now our Les. Steve, not heard of since last June. Everything's upside down. And on top of it all, I've got to come to terms with – well, you know. The whole street whispering behind their hands. Blokes at work sniggering. And we were lucky to get away without a court case, you know. It was touch and go, that was.'

'I know, but we did get away without that, and thank heaven for it. And thank heaven for this little chap as well.' Flo moved over to her daughter and laid a tender hand on the white shawl. 'I know it's not happened as any f us wanted it, Perce, but the little boy's here now and 've got to forget all that. He's our flesh and blood. And

432

Vic's as good a boy as you'd wish to meet. What's more, he'll be gone himself before long, so why don't we all try to make this a happy home for him and Denise in whatever time they've got left.'

Thursday stared at her cousin. 'Has Vic got his papers, then?'

Denise nodded and bit her lips. 'He got them yesterday. They let him defer it till the baby was born, but he's got to go in a fortnight.' She looked at her father. 'Please, Dad. Do what Mum says -- let bygones be bygones. We're sorry for what we did, but I can't say I'm sorry to have my baby. And I'm not sorry me and Vic had to get married neither. At least when he goes away, I'll know he's mine, and I'll have a bit of him left to look after.'

Percy stood irresolute for a moment, then he came over to her, bent and kissed her awkwardly.

'All right, love. I can't say I've enjoyed feeling like I have. And Vic's done his best, I'll give him that. But about you finding a place of your own . . .' He shrugged and looked at his wife. 'I don't see as how we can allow that, do you, Flo? 'Specially if Vic's going away. We've got to have a bit of life about the place.'

Flo gave a sigh of relief. 'Well, that's settled, then, and thank heaven for it. I was beginning to think you'd never see sense. Mary, did you put the whistle on the kettle? It must be boiling itself dry out there.'

They hurried out to the kitchen again and Thursday sat on the chair beside Denise and held her arms out for the baby. She looked down into the tiny face and thought she'd never held such a small one before. Jenny sat beside her, playing with the baby's tiny fingers. Percy went to have a wash, and Walter sat down and picked up the evening paper. Mr Churchill was going to broadcast again tomorrow, it said, and there would be one of J.B. Priestley's 'Postscripts'. He liked them, the man was down to earth and didn't mince his words.

Vic came in just as Flo brought the tea through.

came straight over to kiss Denise, and then gave Thursday a quick peck before bending to his son.

'Well, what d'you think? Isn't he a smasher? Look at those legs, he's going to be a footballer for certain.'

'He's lovely,' Thursday said. 'But what we all want to know is what you're going to call him. Nobody seems to have any idea.'

Vic grinned. 'Dizzy wanted to wait till you were here and we were all together before telling anyone. But I reckon we can now, eh, Diz? I must say, I can't wait much longer myself!'

Denise smiled. She held out her arms for her baby and Thursday laid him carefully back on her lap. Vic sat on the arm of her chair and they both looked at the expectant faces around them.

'I hope you'll be pleased with what we've decided,' Denise said. There were tears in her voice. 'It's partly because of – of when he was born, and partly because we just wanted to keep their names alive.' She looked at her parents and added quickly, 'But we won't do it if you don't like the idea. We don't want anyone to feel upset about it.'

'Upset about what?' Flo began, but Thursday had already guessed what Denise was going to say. She laid her hand swiftly over her aunt's and waited.

'We want to call him Leslie Michael,' Denise said, and then she looked at Mary and added, 'Leslie Michael Stephen. After all three of our boys. That's what he's going to be, because he's like that man said on the wireless the other day – he's our hope for the future.'

There was a silence. Flo drew in a long, shuddering breath and put her apron to her eyes. Mary patted her arm, heedless of her own flowing tears, and Thursday squeezed her hand. Percy, across the room, cleared his throat.

'Well, I think that's a very nice thing to do, our Denise. very nice thing to do. And I think we all ought to have a drink to mark the occasion and celebrate. Flo, where's that bottle of sherry we had at Christmas?'

Half crying, half laughing, Flo hurried to the sideboard to get it out. Jenny produced glasses and when they all had one, Percy cleared his throat again and called for silence.

'I want to propose a toast,' he said, and held his glass towards Vic and Denise. 'To Denise, Vic and little Leslie. May they always be a happy family. And to all the rest of us as well.' He looked at his glass and added quietly, 'To families everywhere.'

'To families everywhere,' they echoed softly, and clinked glasses.

Percy set down his glass and moved across the room to his daughter. He held out his arms.

'Well,' he said, a little gruffly, 'what about it, our Denise? Aren't you going to let me hold my grandson?'

Chapter Thirty-One

Every major city seemed to be on the Germans' list. As spring advanced, so did the Luftwaffe. City after city found itself devastated by raids which left thousands dead or homeless. London, the main target, was hit night after night, with even Buckingham Palace struck by two bombs.

Portsmouth had its second blitz exactly two months after the first. Thousands of bombs were aimed at the naval dockyard and its ships, the shore establishments and the marine barracks at Eastney. Once again, Haslar found itself besieged with wounded sailors and marines, and the QARNNs and VADs were run off their feet looking after them. Thursday was too busy to worry very much about Connor. She scribbled a page or two to him every night when she went to bed, and sometimes managed more, and she lay for a few minutes every night longing for him and praying that he would be safe, but sleep overcame her so quickly that she felt almost cheated when she woke next morning. I want longer to think about him, she thought, I want more time. But time was another luxury that the war had taken away.

In April, they heard that Portsmouth's sister naval port, Plymouth, had been almost flattened. There was nothing left of the centre but rubble, with a lone clock tower standing in its midst and services still being determinedly held in the shell of the city church. Coventry was attacked again, and in May it was the turn of Liverpool, with over a week of bombing that left nearly four thousand people dead and seventy thousand homeless. The brilliance of another 'bomber's moon' brought more devastation to the North-East and then London's worst raid yet.

'I don't see as they *can* get any worse,' Elsie said, staring at the pictures in the newspaper. 'Look at it. Just look at it. The only comfort's that we're giving as good as we get. They reckon we've done just as much damage to some of them German cities – Kiel and Berlin and everywhere. If they knock us flat, we'll do worse to them and no mistake!'

'So there are people being bombed out of their homes there, just the same as here,' Thursday said. 'People losing their families and everything they've got, little children being killed, people looking for somewhere to live . . . It can't be right, Elsie. There ought to be another way.'

But it seemed that there was no other way. The fighting continued, spreading across the world. Russia, Yugoslavia, Hungary, Greece, Italy, Africa – all were being drawn into the conflict. Only the Far East and America still stood apart, and even Japan had begun to wage its own war with China.

A few days later came the first good news. Italy, after less than a year allied to Germany, had surrendered. That made one less country to fight – even if it also brought thousands of prisoners to be fed and looked after. And at least they could be made to work . . . But almost before this had sunk in, the country was stunned again by the news of the sinking of HMS *Hood*, the world's largest battle cruiser. It had gone down in only four minutes, with only three out of the fourteen hundred men aboard surviving.

At Haslar, any naval loss was keenly felt. The patients were depressed and gloomy, and the nurses were hard put to it to stay cheerful. In fact, as Patsy said, it seemed wrong, in a way, even to try. Nobody should be ashamed of being upset about that lovely ship and all those brave men.

'They say Mr Churchill's told them to go all out to sin the *Bismarck*,' Elsie said. 'He's taken it personally – s he'd go and fire the guns himself, if he could.' And indeed it was only three days before the German ship went the same way, chased across the Atlantic by over a hundred ships. She finally sank a few hundred miles from the coast of Brittany, losing over two thousand men.

It seemed a fitting revenge. But Thursday couldn't help adding the two crews together. Nearly four thousand men lost altogether, all sailors, all brave and mostly young. Four thousand families left to grieve. Four thousand wives and sweethearts, and heaven knew how many children, parents, brothers, sisters, friends. What was happening to the world?

'It's no good thinking like that,' Elsie told her. 'You'll drive yourself mad with it, Thurs. You've just got to close your mind to it.'

Thursday knew she was right. But it seemed so wrong, almost wicked somehow, to close your mind to all that suffering. Yet what good would it do to anyone if you didn't, if you tried to take all the suffering into yourself and, as Elsie had warned, drove yourself mad doing it? You wouldn't be able to do anything. You wouldn't be able to nurse the men who needed you. You'd need a nurse yourself, and what help would that be?

Why, it was practically treason.

'We need something to cheer us up,' Elsie decided, and on their next half-day they cycled over the patched-up Pneumonia Bridge and went to the Swiss Café for tea. They debated going 'over the water', as Elsie's gran called it, to Portsmouth, but the thought of the devastation there put them off. It was bad enough in Gosport, with bombsites like missing teeth along the high street, and the market hall no more than a shell.

They had tea and penny buns, and then left their bikes propped against the wall and strolled down to the esplanade. The harbour was as active as always, with the ferryboats bustling to and fro and ships moored up in the dockyard. The girls leaned on the railings and gazed at the busy scene.

'It's a wonder there's so much left,' Patsy remarked. 'The Semaphore Tower's still there, and HMS *Victory*, and the cathedral, *and* the station, even though it was on fire that time. You'd have thought with all that bombing there'd be nothing left standing at all.'

'There isn't much in the middle,' Elsie said. 'Commercial Road and all around there are just nothing. McIlroys was all burnt out, you know, and the Landport Drapery Bazaar. I dunno how they're ever going to build it all up again.' She sighed.

Thursday put her arm around her. 'How are your mum and dad, and Eddy?'

'Oh, much as you'd expect. Getting on with it. Mum's managed to get a few bits of furniture together – lucky she'd got all the savings certificates and things down the shelter with her – and the house they've got's not bad. There's no electric, though, and not even any gas upstairs, they have to use candles . . . And Eddy seems to have settled all right, out near Winchester he is with the school, so he's got his mates around him. As Mum says, you mustn't grumble.'

Patsy was staring down at the pontoon where one of the ferryboats was just pulling away, allowing the next to take its place. 'Look, isn't that the one that went to Dunkirk?'

'So it is,' Thursday said. 'The *Ferry King*. Let's give her a cheer – she deserves it.' They waved and cheered at the little boat and the skipper, standing on his bridge, waved back. The little exchange lifted their spirits and as they turned away Patsy said, with a sudden, shy little smile, 'I've got some news for you.'

'What?' The other two stopped and stared at her. 'What news? What haven't you been telling us, Pats?'

'You've got a funny look on your face,' Thursday said. 'Come on, out with it. What have you been up to?'

Patsy's twitching mouth broke into a broad grin and sh

laughed. 'Can't you guess? It's me and Roy – we're getting married!'

'Getting *married*? But you're not even engaged.'

'Yes, we are,' Patsy said, smiling.

'Since when?' Elsie demanded. 'You've been holding out on us, Patsy Martin, and us supposed to be your best friends.'

'Since last week. I never said anything because of all the *Hood* and *Bismarck* business – there just didn't seem to be a good moment. But the ship's going to be in Plymouth next week for repairs and they're all getting a bit of leave. He says we can get a special licence and get married at the weekend, and then we can have a honeymoon. I've seen Madam, and she says I can go. I can have a whole week! A whole *week*.' She sighed blissfully. 'I can't believe it's true.'

'Nor can I,' Elsie said. 'I can't believe you've gone and got all this fixed up and never said a word about it. Didn't we have breakfast together yesterday? Haven't we just had tea in the Swiss Café? Don't we sleep in the same dormitory every night? What d'you mean, never been a good moment?'

'Well, I wanted to tell the two of you when we were out of the hospital, not when there were lots of other people waggling their ears. And I never got a chance in the Swiss Café, you were going on about that tiffy you met at the dance last Saturday.' Patsy giggled. 'Anyway, guess who's going to be best man.'

The other two stared at her. 'Not Doug Brighton!' Thursday said at last.

'That's right. You know Roy and him have always been good mates, and Doug's been on the same ship this last twelvemonth. He asks after you now and again,' she said slyly to Thursday.

'Oh, yeah? Pull the other one,' Thursday said scornfully. Even after Tony had told her about Doug's heroism, she'd never been able to take to him and although they'd accepted one another on the jaunts the six of them had had together, they'd never become real friends. 'More likely to be Elsie he asks after.'

'No, it was never more than a bit of fun between us,' Elsie said. There had been a number of young men since for her to have fun with, mostly matelots, but she'd not found anyone to be serious about. 'Trouble is, there's never time for anything more than that. You just start getting interested and it's off to sea again, like the song says. And you know it's probably true, a wife in every port. Sweetheart, anyway. Well, you can't blame 'em, can you, after weeks at sea.'

They strolled back up the high street and collected their bikes. Cycling back up Stoke Road to the White Hart, and then along Avenue Road to Alverstoke, Thursday thought longingly of Connor. He was in Singapore now and there was no knowing when he'd be back. He was keeping her VAD badge like a talisman, he told her in his letters, always close to his heart, to keep him safe. She hoped it would – but how could a cloth badge, even if it bore the King's crown, keep a man safe in these perilous times?

Already there was anxious talk of the Japanese threat to Singapore, and Mr Churchill was known to have asked America for help, but so far the United States was unwilling to become involved. Like Switzerland, it seemed, it would stay neutral unless threatened itself. And Singapore was British, not American. Suppose the Japanese invaded? Suppose Connor's ship was lost, as the *Hood* had been lost . . .

Her thoughts refused to take her any further and she came back with a start to the present.

'When is this wedding, then?' Elsie asked. 'And where's it going to be? You're not going to go to Plymouth and leave us in the lurch, are you?'

'No, Roy and Doug can get warrants to come to Pompey, so it makes more sense to do it here.' She looked up at the little grey church they were passing. 'I'd like it to be here at Alverstoke, but if the rector can't do it, we'll have to make it the registry office in Gosport. There's so many weddings now, with men going overseas, that the churches are all booked up. We don't mind too much, the main thing is to get married. We're hoping it'll be next Friday,' she added. 'Sixth of June.'

'Next *Friday*? We'll never be ready in time! I suppose we are asked, aren't we?' Thursday added.

'Of course you're asked. I want everyone to be there. Mum and Dad can't make it, so I want all my mates. Anyway, you two're going to be my bridesmaids.'

'Oh, are we? Thanks for telling us! What are we supposed to wear?'

'Oh, anything,' Patsy said carelessly. 'Something pretty. A frock'll do.'

'Well, I wasn't going to wear slacks and a jumper,' Elsie retorted. 'Honestly, Pats, I do think you could've told us before. And where's this honeymoon going to be, then? Lee?'

'Not on your life! We're going to Cornwall. See,' she explained as they coasted along Clayhall Road, 'Roy's warrant will be a return, and I can get one to go down there, and that'll be a return too, so the fares as far as Plymouth and mine back here won't cost us anything. We can get a train to Cornwall – Penzance or somewhere – and find a room there for a few nights.' She stretched out her arms, cycling no-handed for a few yards. 'It'll be lovely.'

'Even lovelier if you've got both arms in plaster!' Thursday said. 'What about a wedding dress?'

'Shan't bother. I'm just going to get a couple of new summer frocks that I can wear any time. Well, one really nice one and a more ordinary one, I expect. I thought I'd go over to Pompey and do some shopping next Monday. We could all go, we're not on duty in the afternoons.'

'I am,' Thursday said. 'You know how busy we are in theatre.'

'Oh, yes, I forgot. Well, you don't need to buy anything anyway, you can make yourself a frock. Go down that shop in Stoke Road, they've got some nice materials in there, even with the shortages.'

'And when am I supposed to do all this sewing?' Thursday enquired. 'In between passing the boss his scalpels and things?'

They swept in through the gates, waving cheekily to the sailor on guard, and then dismounted to walk down the quarter-deck. Thursday had once been seen cycling along its length, when she was late back from a trip into town, and had been severely reprimanded by Miss Makepeace. Next time, she'd been told, it would be gates for a week. They didn't dare take that risk, with Patsy's wedding so close.

Next morning, she slipped in early, taking Elsie's advice to go to the haberdasher's and buy some material for a new frock. She had just enough money, and chose a fine, pale blue cotton. The woman measured it out for her and told her she was lucky to have it. 'We've got hardly anything left now. It's a wonder they haven't put clothes on ration, like everything else. I don't know what we're supposed to live on, now there's almost nothing to sell.'

Thursday pedalled back with her parcel. Even on Saturdays, operations were still carried out and she was to be on duty at nine. A year ago, she thought, men were being brought back from Dunkirk. A year ago, we were just hearing about Mike, and Steve. And we still haven't heard anything about Steve. He must be dead. He must be.

Tears came to her eyes as she pushed her bike up the steep slope of the bridge. She paused at the top and gazed over Haslar Lake towards the church tower and the big blue gasholder. The little boats were there, the flotilla of yachts and sailing dinghies that had set off so bravely to cross the Channel a year ago. A few of them hadn't returned, but the rest lay beneath her, rocking very gently on the calm waters. Hundreds, perhaps thousands of men had been saved by those little boats. Mike could have been brought back in one. So could Steve. Instead, both had been left behind to die.

Oh, Steve, she thought sadly. Oh, Steve, I miss you so much . . .

It was lucky that Thursday had bought her material on Saturday, because on Monday it was suddenly announced that clothes would be rationed. Patsy and Elsie stared at each other in dismay, and Thursday tried not to feel smug. Her frock was already half-made, and she was pleased with it. Her pleasure was spoilt when she saw that Patsy was near to tears.

'Can't we buy anything new at all?'

Elsie was studying the *Daily Express*. 'It says we've got to use our margarine coupons till they can issue special ration cards. We'll get sixty-six coupons, to last us a year.'

'So what does that mean? What does a coupon buy?' Patsy demanded. A fresh thought struck her. 'We don't even *have* our own ration books, the hospital's got them! They're not going to hand over our marge coupons, are they – stands to reason.'

'There's a list here. Examples. A man's overcoat needs sixteen coupons—'

'Never mind men's overcoats!' Patsy broke in. 'What about a frock?'

'Well, a woollen dress will be eleven—'

'It's the middle of flaming June, you twerp!'

Thursday giggled and Patsy turned on her. 'It's all right for you, sitting there all pleased with yourself because you've got yours. How am I going to get anything now? I'll have to get married in my uniform, that's what! And spend my honeymoon in it, too, more than likely.'

'Oh, come on, Pats, you've got some civvy clothes, haven't you? What about that red skirt you wore to Kimballs?'

'If you remember,' Patsy said coldly, 'I wore a black blouse with it and it got torn when the wardrobe door stuck. I am *not* getting married in a red skirt and a black blouse with a tear in one sleeve.'

'If it's not wool, you can get a frock for seven coupons,' Elsie said on a note of triumph. 'There, that's better, isn't it? And you can get a new blouse for five, and a pair of stockings for two, and a couple of nice hankies to wipe away your tears for just one. So you can be fitted out for fifteen coupons and still have enough marge for Christmas!'

Patsy gave her a withering look and turned to Thursday, who was giggling helplessly. 'You're useless, the pair of you. I might as well forget about getting married at all. Roy's not going to want to walk up the aisle with a nurse, he'll feel like a flipping invalid. Oh, why did this have to happen now? Why couldn't they have given us some warning?'

'Because everyone would have rushed out and bought up every scrap of clothing in the shops, like they did when food was put on ration,' Thursday said. 'Look, Patsy, it's not the end of the world. You can have my frock.'

Patsy stared at her. 'What frock? I thought you didn't have anything decent either.'

'The one I'm making, goof! We're much the same size, I can easily do any alterations to fit you. And it's a really pretty blue. What do you say?'

'But it's for you. You chose the material and the pattern and everything. I can't take it off you.'

'You're not going to. I'm lending it to you – not giving it. You can wear it for your wedding and you can take it away for your honeymoon, and then I want it back, all right? Look, it's the ideal answer – something borrowed, something blue!' Thursday jumped up. 'Anyway, I haven't got time to argue about it – I'm due in the theatre. It's settled.' She grinned at Elsie. 'Don't think I can find anything to fit you as well, but if you've got anything we can alter I could have a go.'

Elsie didn't have anything, but when the other VADs heard what was happening they sorted through their few civilian clothes and produced an assortment of garments which they spread out on the beds. When Thursday came off duty she and Elsie inspected them thoughtfully.

'Blimey, it looks like a blooming jumble sale in here,' Elsie commented. 'Whose is that enormous grey thing? I'd look like a barrage balloon in that!'

'I don't know, I've never seen anyone wearing it. What about this pink? No, perhaps not,' Thursday added hastily. Pink was definitely not Elsie's colour. 'Tell you what, suppose we all wear blue, all three of us? Patsy'll be in my new frock, and I could wear my blue check skirt and this white peasant blouse of Annie Gardner's, and you could – you could . . .'

'Yeah? I could what?'

Thursday shrugged helplessly. 'There doesn't seem to be anything else blue here.' The real trouble was that Elsie was the fattest girl in the dormitory, and even if there had been something blue, it was hardly likely it would have fitted her. 'Hang on a mo – what's this?'

'It's a nightie,' Elsie said scornfully, looking at the flowing garment Thursday was holding up. 'I am *not* wearing a blooming *nightie*.'

'I don't see why not. It's perfectly respectable. And it's quite pretty, too – look at these little flowers embroidered all round the neckline.' Thursday held it against Elsie. 'I bet it'd fit you, too, it looks nice and loose. Look, we could make a belt with that blue wool Jeanie got to make a baby coat with – she could knit that up in no time – and if we both wear little caps made of flowers, we'd look all sort of countrified. And Vera Hapgood's got a waistcoat you could borrow, just to set it off. You don't need to do it up. You'll look a real stunner, Else!'

'Vera Hapgood won't ever lend me her waistcoat,' Elsie

446

said, grudgingly allowing Thursday to drape the night-dress around her body. 'She wouldn't lend her own mother tuppence.'

'Yes, she will, we'll make her.' Thursday wasn't going to take no for an answer. 'Look, Elsie, it's either this or your VAD uniform, and *I* think it'll look very nice, so what about it?'

'Oh – all right. Maybe it won't look so bad. At least it'll be comfy.' Elsie giggled suddenly. 'And if I get too tired, I'll be ready for bed, won't I!'

Thursday sighed with relief. She was going to have enough to do, she reckoned, finishing the blue dress and altering the peasant blouse so that it wouldn't slip too far off her shoulders. The last thing she wanted to do was to have to dismantle something with enough turn in the seams – even if you could find such a thing – to fit Elsie.

'That's settled, then,' she said. 'Now let's get to work . . .'

Everyone was on tenterhooks that nothing would happen to prevent the wedding. To Patsy's delight, she had managed to book the church for half past four on Friday afternoon. Saturday was all booked up, the rector said, but he would be very happy to marry her and Roy on Friday.

'We'll just have to hope the train from Plymouth isn't held up. Roy and Doug are leaving at eight o'clock, so they ought to make it.'

All the VADs and even some of the QARNNs who were able to get off duty were going to attend. Miss Makepeace would be there, and so would at least two of the doctors. Patsy rolled her eyes when she heard this. She hadn't thought they'd even known she existed, she said. VADs were invisible, weren't they?

'Unless something goes wrong,' Elsie said. 'Then they can see us plain enough.'

'Mind you,' Patsy said with a wink at Thursday, '*some*

of 'em know we exist. How *is* the Commander these days, Thursday?'

'Shut up,' Thursday said, laughing. 'As a matter of fact, he's very well, thank you. I had a letter this morning.' She touched her breast pocket, where the letter crackled beneath Auntie Maudie's watch. It had come with the first post that morning and she'd slipped away through the gate to the sea wall to read it alone, looking out over the crinkled blue waters of the Solent.

My Darling Thursday,

It's so different here in the Far East, and yet I seem to feel you with me with every step I take. Perhaps one day, when all this is over, we'll come here together and I can show you this strange land, with the narrow, bustling streets filled with rickshaws and Chinese pedlars, and the rivers crammed with sampans and Chinese junks. The sun is hot by day and the moon is a soft, saffron gold by night, and I miss you every moment, more than I can say, more than I can ever show you — but oh, how I long to show you and to love you, and when this is over I swear we'll never be parted again, never. I love you, my darling, and I shall always be yours, your very own, your deeply loving Connor.

Thursday had sat for as long as she dared, holding the letter in her hands, reading the words over and over again until she knew them by heart. She stared at the hard blue of the sea and thought of a softer light, a mellow saffron moon that threw a golden carpet down upon the gently moving waters of the river, and she gazed at the great grey warship that was steaming out of the harbour and thought of the sampans and junks of a more ancient world.

Connor had said nothing about the Japanese threat to Singapore, perhaps because he didn't want to worry her, perhaps because it had no place in his words of love. Most of his letters were more prosaic, telling her as much as he could about their work, although all spoke also of his love. But this was the first he had ever written that was so poetic, and through Thursday's tender love there wove a cold, narrow thread of fear. It was almost as if he were saying goodbye . . .

Suddenly she remembered where she was. The other girls were looking at her with sympathy, and Patsy's bantering tone changed to a more compassionate one. 'You must miss him ever so much.'

'Yes, I do. But I'm not the only one, am I? And your Roy will be going away again soon, so we'll be back in the same boat. Again. We've just got to put up with it.'

'That's right. And it's the same for naval wives even when there isn't a war on, when you come to think about it. They're always being left on their own.' Patsy made a humorous face. 'Maybe we should think again while we've got the chance – find some nice young motor mechanic who works in the local garage to marry!'

Friday was bright and sunny. The girls were on duty most of the day and came off at three, with just time to have a quick bath – 'no more than five inches, mind, even if it is your wedding day!' Elsie said with a grin – and get changed. By ten past four they were arrayed in their finery, and Patsy was in a blind panic.

'How do I look? Suppose he takes one look and changes his mind. We haven't seen each other for nearly a year! What if we're making a mistake? Thursday, I feel sick—'

'No, you don't. It's just butterflies. All you've got to do is get them flying in formation. And you look smashing.' Ruefully, Thursday surveyed the dress she had intended to wear herself. It suited Patsy, with its slim waist and flared skirt and the pretty, sweetheart neckline. Someone had produced a blue necklace that went just right with it, and Miss Makepeace had given Patsy a bunch of blue and white flowers from the hospital garden. Thursday had woven circular headdresses from some raffia, with more blue flowers poked into them, and she, Patsy and Elsie set these on their heads.

'You look the bee's knees,' Elsie agreed, adding wryly, 'Dunno so much about me in this nightie!'

'Don't be daft, you look lovely, and nobody would ever know it was a nightie. It looks more like a ball gown – really posh.' Patsy gave one last look in the mirror. 'Well, come on, we'd better go. It'll take us a good ten minutes to walk there.'

Thursday gave herself a last, hasty glance in the mirror and then, as an afterthought, snatched up the little silver watch Auntie Maudie had given her. She pinned it on to her dress, her fingers shaking a little. It's been lucky for me so far, she thought. It'd be a shame to leave it off today.

All the VADs and nurses who were able to come were waiting outside, and they cheered as Patsy and her bridesmaids emerged. They were all in uniform, and they made a protective group around the three for the walk through Clayhall to Alverstoke. Laughing and excited, they made their way towards the gate.

The sailors on guard saluted smartly, and then one of them held up his hand for attention. They all fell silent.

'I hope you're not going to make a speech,' Patsy said. 'No funny jokes, mind.'

'I'm not going to say anything,' the matelot said. 'There's a phone message for someone. A telegram. VAD Tilford, it says here. Isn't that the girl they call Thursday?'

'Yes!' Thursday stepped forward, her heart thudding. 'A telegram for me? A phone call?'

'Well, I can't make out which it is, but you've to go back to D Block straight away and see the Red Cross Commandant.' He looked at her. 'It sounded pretty urgent.'

'Oh, no!' She looked frantically round for Patsy. 'Pats, did you hear that? I've got to go—'

'It's all right. We – we'll wait for you.' Patsy stared at her fearfully. 'Roy won't mind.'

Thursday shook her head. 'You can't do that. It could be anything. Mum – Dad – our Jen – I might have to go home. Madam wouldn't have sent a message down to the gate if it hadn't been serious. Anyway, she's supposed to be coming to the wedding, too.' She put a hand to her face. 'It might be Connor . . .' She turned away.

'I'll come with you,' Elsie said, but Thursday pushed her away.

'No. *No.* You go with Patsy. I – I'll come if I can.' Her voice made it plain that she didn't expect to be able to. 'Oh, Pats, I'm sorry. I'll have to go—' She was off, running back along the road, heading for D Block.

The others gazed after her.

'Poor Thursday,' Patsy said. 'I wonder what it's about.'

'Whatever it is,' Elsie said, 'there's nothing we can do to help her now. Madam's with her, she'll see to it all. You've got a wedding to go to.'

'I know,' Patsy said, turning to go through the gate. 'But it won't seem the same, somehow, without Thursday there.'

Thursday arrived panting at the top of the stairs. Miss Makepeace's office door was open and she was inside, pacing anxiously to and fro. She turned as Thursday skidded to a halt at the door, and gave her a warm smile.

'Tilford, child, you'll have an accident if you race about like that. There's been a telephone call for you.'

'Yes, Madam. Is it a telegram?'

'Not exactly, but I gather there's *been* a telegram. It was your mother. She's ringing again in five minutes, from a telephone kiosk, I gather.'

'Yes, Madam. That'll be at the top of the street. We don't have a telephone at home.'

'No, I understand. Well, she said she would ring back to see if we'd managed to catch you.' The phone on her desk rang and she picked it up quickly, listened for a moment and then handed it over to Thursday.

Her hand shaking, Thursday held the receiver to her ear. She heard her mother's voice, made small and unfamiliar. Almost without thinking, she lifted her other hand to touch the watch at her breast.

'Thursday? Is that you?'

'Yes, Mum, it's me. What's happened? Is it Dad? Or our Jen? It's not the baby, is it?'

'No, no, none of them. It's all right, Thursday.' For the first time she realised that the strange tone in her mother's voice wasn't grief, but excitement. 'Thursday, it's our *Steve*! He's *alive*! He's a prisoner of war somewhere in Germany, but he's *alive* and we've had a telegram to say so, and we'll be getting a letter soon. Thursday, did you hear me? It's our Steve! He's *alive*, he really is, he's not dead after all, he's *alive*! Our Steve!' Her voice went on, repeating the words over and over again, while Thursday stood, holding the receiver tightly against her ear, unable to speak, her other hand fastened tightly over the watch. Slowly, her eyes filled with tears. She looked at Miss Makepeace and realised that she already knew, that she'd wanted Thursday to hear it from her own mother, and she gave her a trembling, tearful smile. At last, Mary Tilford's voice faded into silence, and Thursday took a deep, wavering breath and managed to speak.

'Oh, Mum. That's wonderful. It's *wonderful*.' There must be other words, but she couldn't think of them. 'Oh, Mum, you must be so pleased. But where's he been all this time?'

'We don't know yet. The letter will tell us. Oh, Thursday, I can't tell you – can't think straight – I just had to ring up.' Thursday heard a little sob, then her mother seemed to take a deep breath and went on more steadily. 'Here, aren't you supposed to be at a wedding?'

'Yes. You just caught us, we were on our way out of the gate. It's in ten minutes!'

'Well, you'd better go, then, hadn't you.' Mary's voice sounded suddenly brisk, though there was still a betraying tremor in it. 'Go on, Thursday. I'll write as soon as I get some news. You go on now, and enjoy yourself – I want to go round to Flo's. And there's your gran too, I must go and see her. And—'

The phone suddenly cut off. Mary's money had run out. Thursday handed the receiver back to Miss Makepeace and felt a huge smile break out over her face, even though tears were pouring down her cheeks.

'Oh, Madam. It's my brother. We thought he was lost at Dunkirk, and he's turned up as a POW. Isn't it wonderful?'

'It is indeed.' Miss Makepeace came round her desk and gave Thursday a kiss. 'I'm so pleased, my dear. And now we'd better get our skates on or we're going to be late for this wedding. Come along.'

Thursday glanced at the clock on the wall, above the big world map that showed where the war was being waged and where VADs were already being sent. 'We're going to be late anyway. It's in ten minutes' time – we'll never get there now, even if we run.'

'There's no need for that.' Madam led her briskly out of the office and down the stairs. 'Sister Burton has organised a taxi for us. It should be waiting now.'

'A taxi!' Thursday caught her breath as she saw the car waiting at the gate. Together with Madam and the sister, she scrambled in and the car swept down Clayhall Road, to arrive at Alverstoke Church just as the organist was beginning to play 'Here Comes The Bride'.

Patsy and Elsie stared as Thursday arrived, breathless, beside them.

'What was it? What's happened?'

She shook her head, smiling. 'Tell you afterwards. Look, Roy's there, he's waiting for you. Let's get you married off, Pats. Let's make this the happiest day of your life!'

It already was, for her, she thought as she and Elsie followed their friend up the aisle. Maybe there would be others as happy, even happier, in the future, but she couldn't remember any that soared higher than this. Her brother, thought dead in the sea and the bullets and bombs of Dunkirk, was alive. After a year – a whole year – of waiting, and just as they had finally given up their last shreds of hope, he had been returned to them. He wasn't coming home, he wouldn't be coming home until the war was over – whenever that might be – but he was safe. They could write to him, send him comforts. They could get letters from him, letters that he had written on paper that he had touched.

He was alive.

Thursday stood beside Elsie and watched as their friend stood beside her groom and made her marriage vows. Will this be me one day, she thought, me and Connor? Will it all come right in the end after all?

She didn't know, nobody knew, how long this war would last. Already, it had been nearly two years. It might be another two, perhaps even longer. But there could still be moments like this – this moment of soaring joy that her brother was alive after all, that people like Patsy and Roy could still find happiness for even a little while, that the sun could shine and a church be full of friends who wished each other well. She glanced round and saw their faces – Jeanie, Ellen and Louisa, all of them. Even Vera Hapgood who had, after all, agreed to lend Elsie her waistcoat.

They're lovely people, Thursday thought. They're all good friends, and together we're doing a good job, a worthwhile job. And we'll go on doing it, as long as the war goes on.

She sent a thought to Steve, and another to Connor, and to all the men who were still serving or who, like her brother, had finished their war and had to wait. Not all of them would survive, she knew – there would be many more deaths before it was all over. But here in this little church, on a sunny June day, seeing the radiance on Patsy's face and the joy of all her friends, she could not doubt that the war would be won in the end.

However long it took, the struggle would one day be over. The world would, once again, walk free.

available from

THE ORION PUBLISHING GROUP

☐ **Goodbye Sweetheart** £6.99
LILLIAN HARRY
978-1-8579-7812-4

☐ **The Girls They Left Behind** £6.99
LILLIAN HARRY
978-0-7528-0333-3

☐ **Keep Smiling Through** £6.99
LILLIAN HARRY
978-0-7528-1564-0

☐ **Moonlight & Lovesongs** £6.99
LILLIAN HARRY
978-0-7528-1564-0

☐ **Love & Laughter** £6.99
LILLIAN HARRY
978-0-7528-2605-9

☐ **Wives & Sweethearts** £6.99
LILLIAN HARRY
978-0-7528-3396-5

☐ **Corner House Girls** £6.99
LILLIAN HARRY
978-0-7528-4296-7

☐ **Kiss the Girls Goodbye** £6.99
LILLIAN HARRY
978-0-7528-4448-0

☐ **PS I Love You** £6.99
LILLIAN HARRY
978-0-7528-4820-4

☐ **A Girl Called Thursday** £6.99
LILLIAN HARRY
978-0-7528-4950-8

☐ **Tuppence to Spend** £6.99
LILLIAN HARRY
978-0-7528-5889-0

☐ **A Promise to Keep** £6.99
LILLIAN HARRY
978-0-7528-5889-0

☐ **Under the Apple Tree** £6.99
LILLIAN HARRY
978-0-7528-5929-3

☐ **Dance Little Lady** £6.99
LILLIAN HARRY
978-0-7528-6420-4

☐ **A Farthing Will Do** £6.99
LILLIAN HARRY
978-0-7528-6492-1

☐ **Three Little Ships** £6.99
LILLIAN HARRY
978-0-7528-7707-5

☐ **The Bells of Burracombe** £6.99
LILLIAN HARRY
978-0-7528-7804-1

All Orion/Phoenix titles are available at your local bookshop or from the following address:

Mail Order Department
Littlehampton Book Services
FREEPOST BR535
Worthing, West Sussex, BN13 3BR
telephone 01903 828503, *facsimile* 01903 828802
e-mail MailOrders@lbsltd.co.uk
(Please ensure that you include full postal address details)

Payment can be made either by credit/debit card (Visa, Mastercard, Access and Switch accepted) or by sending a £ Sterling cheque or postal order made payable to *Littlehampton Book Services*.
DO NOT SEND CASH OR CURRENCY.

Please add the following to cover postage and packing

UK and BFPO:
£1.50 for the first book, and 50p for each additional book to a maximum of £3.50

Overseas and Eire:
£2.50 for the first book plus £1.00 for the second book and 50p for each additional book ordered

---

BLOCK CAPITALS PLEASE

name of cardholder ....   *delivery address*
....   *(if different from cardholder)*
address of cardholder ....
....
....
....

postcode ....   *postcode* ....

☐ I enclose my remittance for £..

☐ please debit my Mastercard/Visa/Access/Switch (delete as appropriate)

card number ☐☐☐☐☐☐☐☐☐☐☐☐☐☐☐☐

expiry date ☐☐☐☐   Switch issue no. ☐☐

signature ....

prices and availability are subject to change without notice